P9-CQJ-575

The Night Journal

ALSO BY ELIZABETH CROOK

The Raven's Bride

Promised Lands

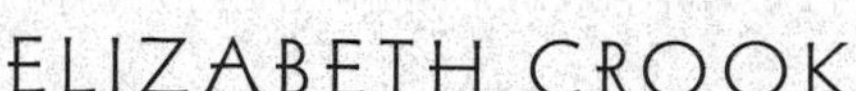

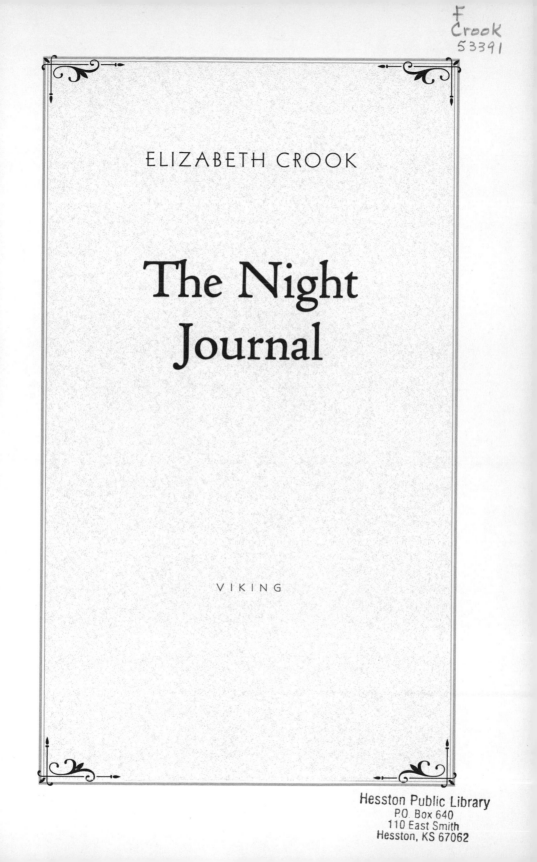

ELIZABETH CROOK

The Night Journal

VIKING

VIKING
Published by the Penguin Group
Penguin Group (USA) Inc., 375 Hudson Street,
New York, New York 10014, U.S.A.
Penguin Group (Canada), 90 Eglinton Avenue East, Suite 700, Toronto,
Ontario, Canada M4P 2Y3 (a division of Pearson Penguin Canada Inc.)
Penguin Books Ltd., 80 Strand, London WC2R 0RL, England
Penguin Ireland, 25 St. Stephen's Green, Dublin 2, Ireland
(a division of Penguin Books Ltd)
Penguin Books Australia Ltd, 250 Camberwell Road, Camberwell,
Victoria 3124, Australia (a division of Pearson Australia Group Pty Ltd)
Penguin Books India Pvt Ltd, 11 Community Centre,
Panchsheel Park, New Delhi – 110 017, India
Penguin Group (NZ), Cnr Airborne and Rosedale Roads, Albany,
Auckland 1310, New Zealand (a division of Pearson New Zealand Ltd)
Penguin Books (South Africa) (Pty) Ltd, 24 Sturdee Avenue,
Rosebank, Johannesburg 2196, South Africa

Penguin Books Ltd, Registered Offices: 80 Strand, London WC2R 0RL, England

First published in 2006 by Viking Penguin, a member of Penguin Group (USA) Inc.

1 3 5 7 9 10 8 6 4 2

Publisher's Note: This is a work of fiction. Names, characters, places, and incidents either are the product of the author's imagination or are used fictitiously, and any resemblance to actual persons, living or dead, business establishments, events, or locales is entirely coincidental.

LIBRARY OF CONGRESS CATALOGING IN PUBLICATION DATA
Crook, Elizabeth, date.
The night journal / Elizabeth Crook
p. cm.
ISBN 0-670-03477-0
1. Young women—Fiction. 2. Diaries—Authorship—Fiction. 3. Women pioneers—Fiction. 4. Waitresses—Fiction. 5. New Mexico—Fiction. I. Title.
PS3553.R545N54 2006
813'.54—dc22 2005042401

Printed in the United States of America Set in Electra, Cloister, and Loire
Designed by Francesca Belanger

For Joseph Rainfield Lewis

and

Elizabeth Holdsworth Lewis

The Night Journal

February 12, 1902
Las Vegas, New Mexico

The noise of her own breathing is beginning to trouble her. She wants clarity, and the sound distracts her. The codeine has made her weary, morphia seizes thoughts from her mind and sends them flying off like stringy clouds borne this way and that.

She struggles to draw them in.

She is too cold.

She wishes a log would fall on the fire and erase the terrible crackling of her breathing.

I will hold on, she thinks, *a little longer.*

It is the doctor's voice in the hall. He is talking to one of the Sisters. "She is—" he says—but the rest of it is lost.

She is—what is she—dying?

I am a gone case now, she thinks. *I'm finally there.* All she cares about now is Claudia.

I want my child.

She opens her eyes. Vicente is seated beside the bed. He has tethered his gaze to her face. Flakes of snow are melting on his coat. *He is too young to look old.*

What will Claudia do without me? How will she live?

I have lost this battle.

She would find the strength to turn over and roll onto her side if not for the bag of ice on her chest. She wishes Vicente would take it away—the smell of its rubber is sickening. But she is unable to ask him. Her voice has gone extinct, her throat is sore. Her lungs have turned to sponge. She smells the rubber and oily iodine and tastes the blood.

Vicente takes hold of her arms and tries to warm them with his hands. She lifts her hand and moves the fingers as if to wrap them around a pen, and Vicente stands and takes a pen from the table, and also a book, which he spreads to an empty page. He gives her the pen and places the book beside her on the bed. When he begins to lift her onto the pillow, she motions him away. Dragging the bag of ice from her chest and dropping it to the floor with a sloshing sound, she takes the book. Turns onto her side, away from Vicente. She views the rocking chair, the lamp, the shimmering fire, the Persian rug. The arched window filled with the blue of evening.

She turns the pen in her fingers, but lacks the strength to lift herself onto her elbow. "I am—" she writes; her hands are cold, the writing is unsteady. The ink is stuttering out. She attempts to shake the pen. *I want to go home.*

Closing her eyes, she allows the pen to feel its way across the page.

I am
becoming tired of the taste of blood.

If it leaves the ink, or not, it doesn't matter.

"Hannah," she hears Vicente saying, and feels him leaning over her. His voice breaks— "My friend—" and falls to a whisper against her face, "—Fly away."

Her heart is fluttering nearly as fast as the wings of a hummingbird. Her eyes are closed yet she perceives a movement. She sees the sudden flight of a bird outside her window, back at her home in the valley below the ruins—was it long ago? Her eyes are startled open toward the window, and she is aware of the inexplicable smell of junipers and sage. *Did she drink the milk? Claudia? Claudia!*

"She has not kept down a single glass," she hears the Sister saying in the hall.

I hope there is no afterlife, she thinks. *I hope it is over.*

She wishes to govern the moment. *Someone should govern the moment.* At least she has ceased to cough.

Her breath is louder now. Her teeth have begun to clatter. She watches the darkening window, and feels Vicente's warmth against her back. Bless him. He is on the bed with her. For a moment she allows herself to think it is the warmth of Elliott pressed solidly against her, and closes her eyes.

Elliott is on the bed beside me.

But no, he is walking away. She sees him on a moonlit road, casting a strong shadow, his overcoat thrown open by the wind.

Fly away.

No.

She cannot remember Claudia's voice. She can see her on the hill with the two dogs, in the snow. Her black curls. But everything is silent. Like a moving picture, she sees her, turning and leaning for something and making her way with the dogs, among the boulders on the hill. And yet there is not a sound except for the rattling noise of her own breathing. It is the rales crackling in her lungs. She draws her knees up to her chest, and in the yellow lamplight looks at the blackened window framed by the flowered wall.

Is that my Claudia on the hill? Is that my daughter? I can't see her anymore. The snow is making everything too bright.

Or is it sunlight?

Something is giving way. The rocky ground.

Fly?

On her knees, she tries to crawl.

ONE

Claudia Bass's house stood on the high part of a sloping acre under a large oak tree that had cast its shadows long before the house was built beneath it. It was a 1920s white frame bungalow with layers of old paint snaking off the exterior, and the only maintenance in recent years had been Claudia Bass stomping through the yard whacking weeds with her black cane. The place had an unkempt look, pebbled and weedy, and was starkly shadowed on this bright October afternoon.

Meg Mabry drove up in her pickup truck, parked at the weedy curb, pulled the keys from the ignition and stared at the house. Seizing a package of office paper from the seat beside her, she slung her purse strap over her shoulder, slammed the door as she got out, and stalked up the cracked walkway with the package under her arm, noting her grandmother's rusty Pontiac parked in the center of the uphill drive, the wheels at a different slant from what they had been yesterday. She climbed the porch steps, pounded on the screen door, then peered in through the window to see her grandmother, whom she had always known by the ill-fitting name of Bassie, at the rolltop desk, talking on the telephone in a puddle of sallow lamplight, her shoulders jutting as sharply as wings under her nylon robe and her skull showing in patches where the hairpins tacked her braid down flat. Bassie did not turn to look at Meg, though Meg was certain she had heard the knock. The coils of a space heater glowed a lurid red against Bassie's mule-toed slippers, emitting a buzzing sound loud enough for Meg to hear clearly through the windowpanes.

Meg rummaged through her purse, found a key, and let herself in, as Bassie swiveled in her chair to glare at her, still pressing the phone receiver to her ear. Bassie had fought harder, in Meg's opinion, against old age than she should have done: her hair was dyed a harsh, unnatural black, her lipstick was a gaudy red, her parted lips revealed the gleam of over-whitened dentures. Her glasses magnified her eyes so they looked as if they floated in a fishbowl, the black rims casting errant shadows on her sagging cheeks. Nothing flickered in the eyes themselves, however. The stiff hairs of her eyebrows were painted into dome-like arches, though the brow itself was fiercely level. She had not accommodated age; she had painted a new face on the old one. She clenched her lacquered lips with intimidating fixedness and growled into the telephone, "Well, Jim, I like dead ones. I don't give a rat's ass what Phil Barker says; this isn't just about the dogs. It's about the hill. I don't have many memories of my mother, but I remember her digging those dog graves on that hill. If Phil is going to build on that hill, he can give me the bones. I'll bury them somewhere else."

Meg dropped the package of office paper on the sofa in the center of the room. The sofa was an ugly 1970s orange plastic affair, hovering low to the floor on short chrome legs, ridiculously at odds with the Victorian furniture around it. It had belonged to Meg in college; she had bought it at a thrift shop and later tried to sell it, but Bassie disapproved of getting rid of things and made a point of laying claim to it. Since then it had remained here, squatting in the center of the overfurnished room, like a garish monument to every bad choice Meg had ever made. She could remember mornings from her college years when she awakened on this sofa, in her efficiency apartment, her face sticking to the plastic.

"You've been driving," she told Bassie. "Mrs. Chen just called me."

Bassie waved her off, turning in her swivel chair to face the desk, and continued snapping her demands at the person on the phone.

Meg made her way down the hallway between stacks of papers and moldy books piled along the baseboards, passing a room filled with boxes and the same assortment of old file cabinets that had been there since her childhood. She had lived in the house with Bassie from the age of nine until eighteen, and this room had been her bedroom, called the file room even then; she had slept here stored away at night with the other detritus of Bassie's life. The bed was now reduced to a dusty mattress on box springs. The blinds were closed; the room smelled like stale paper. It was no wonder, Meg thought, passing the room—it was no wonder she had wanted to empty her life to such an extent that now this clutter shocked her every time she came here, annoying her at some deep inner level.

At the end of the hall she went into the bathroom and began searching for a rubber band to secure her hair. She looked under the sink in an old revolving caddy filled with hairpins and cosmetics but found nothing resembling a rubber band. The lead soldering of the water pipes under the sink bothered her, not for the first time, with the thought of how much lead she inevitably had consumed from these pipes when she had lived here.

Closing the cabinets, she tugged at the handle of a drawer beside them. The drawer stuck, then gave way suddenly, plopping out onto the warped floor and revealing, bunched inside like a nest of spiders, an expanding, grotesque mound of Bassie's black hair which she had been storing away in case someday she should lose her hair and need to have a wig made. Synthetic wigs, Bassie always said, were absurd.

Meg irritably wrestled the drawer back into its slot, stuffing the hair down in it, and then returned to the living room. "You tell Phil he'll regret it," Bassie was snarling into the phone. "I'll come out there. I'll tell the press I've come to get the bones. And isn't that going to look pathetic to the public. An old woman collecting little tibias and fibulas of her mother's dogs." She sucked volubly on her dentures, listening to the reply, her computer screen glowing with a large-print section of text on the extinct language of a Pueblo Indian tribe. The rolltop desk predated by a century the equipment on its writing space—the computer and printer and fax machine, with electrical cords festooned from the top and knotted in a tangle of extension cords that trailed down near the window. "I don't give a ripe fig about that, Jim," Bassie snapped. "I don't care if Phil ends up with every Native American in the entire state demanding ancestral bones. Either he can call off the project, or you can figure out where the graves are, and let me have what's left of my mother's dogs. . . . No, I don't know the exact location of the graves; how would I remember that? They're on the hill. You can find them. I was three years old, for crying out loud. And don't you cite that museum law to me. I wrote that law. Now, I'll be out there tomorrow unless I hear from Phil. I'll call you from the airport. Here. Talk to my granddaughter. She can make the arrangements."

Bassie shoved the phone at Meg and began to sift through papers on her desk. Meg put her hand over the receiver. "Who is this?" she asked Bassie.

"Jim Layton," Bassie said. "At Pecos. Work things out. Call him back if you have to."

"What am I supposed to work out?"

"Just talk to him."

"I don't want to."

"Talk to him."

"Hi. This is Meg," she said reluctantly into the phone.

"Hello, Meg. Jim Layton. Did she tell you the situation?"

"No."

Bassie was taking hold of her walking cane, jamming it into the floor and dragging her bony weight up against it. She began making her way to the kitchen. Her nylon robe clung to her underwear with static and was cinched with a patent leather belt. She apparently had lost the sash.

"We've been given money to add a room onto the visitors' center," Jim Layton said. "And the only logical place to build is on the hill beside the center. Which is where your great-grandmother buried her dogs. So Bassie wants us to find the graves and excavate them."

"How hard would that be?" Meg asked, attempting to keep the impatience out of her voice.

"It's just two graves, and I have ideas where to look, so I can probably find them. But getting our superintendent to let her have the bones is going to be a problem. This is federal property, so the bones would legally belong to the government. Not that the government wants them. But Phil's prickly about this sort of thing. You know Bassie's going to want you to come with her."

"That's not going to happen."

"I've met you once," he said.

"Sorry. I don't remember."

"There's no reason why you would. I don't think you were even in high school yet. I was lecturing at U.T. and stayed at Bassie's house."

"Oh. She probably gave you my bed. That's what she usually did when somebody came."

"She tried to," he said, with an undercurrent of amusement. "I want you to know I didn't take it."

Meg actually thought she remembered the incident now. She vaguely recalled an unremarkable-looking young man stoically resisting Bassie's mandate that he take over Meg's bed, and insisting he would sleep in the living room.

"So you owe me one," he was saying. "I need you to come out with her and run interference."

"Can't," she told him.

"Is she there listening?"

"No. But she'll be back in a minute."

"Then hear me out. She's got a reason to be upset. She has some strong memories associated with that hill, and we're basically going to have to dynamite and flatten it so we can build the room. She's going to need you out here. More to the point, I'm going to need you out here."

"She hasn't invited me."

"Offer."

Bassie was returning from the kitchen, a ballpoint pen stuck behind her ear and a yellow pad under her arm. "I'll see what I can do," Meg said.

But she had no intention of going to New Mexico with Bassie. As she hung up the phone, she looked at her, standing at the desk rifling through a stack of papers. "You've been driving," she said. "Mrs. Chen called and told me."

Bassie snapped her dentures with her tongue. "Yes, I have been driving. I'm not surprised I got found out. The only time that slanty-eyed spy ever speaks is to tell on me. She lived over there for fifteen years before I knew that she could talk. And now she reports everything I do. Perfectly mute, until this urge to tattle."

"She's always talked, Bassie. Just not to you. You terrify her."

"Not enough, I don't. Now don't bother me about any of that." She continued her search through the pages.

"I brought the paper you needed," Meg said, retrieving the package of office paper from the sofa and tossing it onto Bassie's desk.

"I told you I needed it this morning."

"No, you told me this morning that you needed it," Meg said.

"I needed it when I called."

"So I take it that you went and got some for yourself? You're going to kill somebody with that Pontiac."

"Don't threaten me. Did you get the pineapple I wanted?"

"Not yet."

"Aren't you even curious about the hill? Did Jim tell you what they're doing? They're digging up the last of my memories, that's what. The last of my past. Blowing up the hill and flattening it, to put a room on it. That pea-head Phil Barker would dynamite the *camposanto* to put in extra toilets if he thought they'd be a tourist draw."

Meg lifted her eyes to the lacquered wide-mouthed bass that was gaping at her from its place of honor over the mantel. It was affixed to a plaque emblazoned with the words BASS'S HOUSE. She sat down on the sofa and crossed her legs, trying to appear comfortable, though she had never, once, been comfortable on the sofa since the day that Bassie had planted it in the living room. "I'm not that interested in the hill, frankly," she said. "But we have to solve the driving problem. You can't be driving."

"You would know about the hill," Bassie said, "if you had read the journals."

Meg stopped herself from glancing involuntarily in the direction of the famous journals standing solidly in their permanent place on the shelves of the far wall.

"You're refusing to face your heritage just because it happens also to be mine," Bassie said.

"I've done all right without it."

"Not so anyone would notice. You have very little to show for yourself."

"I have two thousand people depending on me. That isn't very little."

"Oh, and any woman in her right mind would want two thousand dialysis patients dependent on her engineering skills. The biggest obstacle at Pecos now," she said, "is the superintendent. Phil Barker. Phil the Pill. Phil the bitter pill. Now get me that book over there on the table."

"It must be ninety-five degrees in here with that heater on," Meg observed.

Bassie looked at the rattling space heater as if she had never seen it before. "Get me the book," she repeated, lowering herself into the chair at her desk.

"All right, but then I have to go. I have a meeting." Meg got up and retrieved the book, titled *Seven Centuries of Pecos,* and moved aside some papers to make a place for it on Bassie's desk. It was a large book of photographs. Bassie flopped it open and turned through several pages.

"Look. There," Bassie told her, smoothing her fingers across a full-page aerial view of a rocky mesa with a valley below it. A stone wall encircled the edge of the mesa, and within the wall, across the top of the mesa, mounds of earth overgrown with vegetation obscured the pueblo ruins so that they resembled low hills more than anything that had once been inhabitable. There were two rings of stones with holes in the center of them and ladders protruding out of the holes, descending into underground chambers. The ladders threw spidery shadows over the rocky ground. By far the most prominent feature in the photograph was a roofless old adobe church perched on an edge of the mesa, orange sunlight tinting the adobe and stretching long shadows from the weathered walls. Below the church was a contemporary building with a parking lot, which appeared to be a visitors' center.

"This," Bassie said, pointing to the sloping ground between the church and the visitors' center, "is Dog Hill. Where Mother buried our dogs. Milton was a one-eyed, pug-nosed little tramp. Argus was aggressive. And large. I never liked him."

The hill was, at best, a rugged area rising from the valley floor up to the church ruins. It was covered with wiry grass and what looked like cactus and small cedar bushes, and on one side had a length of about forty yards of cliff bordered by a line of jagged rocks and scrub trees.

Bassie moved her finger to the adjoining valley, not far from the visitors' center, saying "Our home was here," and then slid her finger back up to Dog Hill, pointing out a scruffy slope covered with boulders. "The graves are in this area. Now, take this back."

She closed the book, shoving it toward Meg. Meg returned it to the table. She was starting to perspire from the heat.

"You would think," Bassie said loudly, "that the Indians would put a stop to this. They've got twelve tribes out there that have to be consulted before there's digging. And they've approved the plan. They apparently like the idea that their former camping grounds are about to be converted into square footage. Jim says the Hispanos are all gung-ho too. You would think he would have told me sooner what was going on."

"You would think he wouldn't have told you at all," Meg said.

"You're going with me," Bassie retorted.

"To New Mexico? I don't think so."

"You're going with me, yes, you are. Tomorrow."

"I'm not going, Bassie. I'm not going. I have a Q.A. meeting at St. David's Hospital."

"I can't imagine what a Q.A. meeting is. You can cancel it."

"It's a quality assurance meeting, and I have to be there."

"I thought you had employees to do those things."

"Not conduct the Q.A. meetings. I have to be there myself."

"Then we'll leave afterwards," Bassie said.

"Look, I can't just pick up and leave."

"Well, that's gratitude. After everything I've done for you."

Meg retrieved her purse from the sofa.

"Now listen here," Bassie said, the lamplight furrowing shadows into the folds of her face and illuminating the dark hairs of her chin. "You've heard the aeronautic term 'on the bubble'? It refers to an astronaut who's ready to launch. Well, I'm on the bubble. I'm old. I want two things from you before I go. Are you listening? I want you to read the journals. And I want you to go to Pecos with me. I raised you, didn't I? I taught you manners. Now I'm calling in the chips. I would hate to die," she said, her voice descending, "thinking that the blood I left behind got watered down. And I'm not talking about your mother. I'm talking about you. There's something the matter with you. You have six volumes of heritage staring you in the face, and have managed not to look at them, in what—thirty years?"

"Thirty-seven. It isn't like I need to find my roots, Bassie. If anything, I need to get untangled."

"Well, isn't that poetic," Bassie said, and with a pressure of her foot in the mule-toed slipper, swung the chair around to face the window.

Looking past the porch toward the gnarled branches of the oak tree, she said, "It has the wilt," as if she had been speaking of the oak tree all along. "I need that pineapple from the store. Not canned. And I want my blood pressure medication refilled. The Dyazide. The bottle's in the kitchen."

Meg went into the kitchen, yanking open the cabinet where Bassie kept her medications, and started reading labels on the bottles. "Why does she need a pineapple if she's leaving town?" she was asking herself, aloud, when the phone on the wall beside her rang suddenly.

TWO

"Answer it," Bassie called.

"You answer it," Meg grumbled under her breath as she picked up the receiver. "Hello?"

It was her assistant, Carolyn Stott, calling to tell her that the manager of C-TECH, one of Meg's clients, had called with an emergency. He was running out of purified water for the X-ray machines. C-TECH made turbines for jet engines, and used X-ray to examine for cracks and defects.

Meg scribbled his phone number onto an Austin Light and Power bill that was lying on the counter, and returned the call.

The manager, Tom Steiner, answered. "Boy, am I relieved to hear your voice," he said. "I can't figure out the problem. We've only got about two hours of capacity. Can you get here?"

The company was in Round Rock, thirty minutes north on Interstate 35, and Meg was tempted just to walk Tom through the diagnostics over the telephone and have him systematically override the safety shutdowns until the water system activated. Instead she told him to expect her at the service door in forty minutes, and called her accountant to reschedule her meeting with him, in which she was to scrutinize purchase and resale numbers for an income tax audit defense.

"What are you doing?" Bassie called from the other room. "Who was on the phone?"

"It was for me," Meg shouted back.

She found the prescription bottle and returned to the living room. Bassie was typing at the computer. "I've got to go," Meg said. "I'll make your airline reservations, and I can get you to the airport. If I can't take you, I'll have a cab pick you up."

Bassie didn't respond.

"I'll bring you the prescription. And the pineapple. Is there anything else?"

"Nothing," Bassie said, continuing to type. "I am in need of nothing but a granddaughter who shows some respect and gratitude."

Meg cleared security at C-TECH and pulled up at the service door, where Tom Steiner was waiting to let her in. They went together to the water treatment room, and Meg performed the diagnostics on the equipment, discovering that the problem involved a failure in a low-pressure shutdown contact. She corrected the situation temporarily by mechanically overriding the contact, which brought the system back on-line.

"You look tired," Tom observed as they started down the corridor toward the service exit.

"It's the hair," she said.

"No. It's you. You need a break. You need to enter some kind of a different realm for a while."

"And let your water run out?"

"Put somebody else on duty. You've got people."

"Mind your own business, Tom."

But he was right. She was tired. She was irritable. She was beginning to act like Bassie.

She started back to Austin listening to a physician on talk radio comment on genital herpes and pinkeye, followed by a right-wing pundit discussing Manuel Noriega's indictment in the United States for drug trafficking and China's imposition of martial law in Tibet, and praising George Bush's first year in office. She was surprised that Bush had been in office for a year—she still thought of Ronald Reagan as the president. Her political opinions, she knew, when she had them, were usually based on nothing more substantial than an emotional reaction against Bassie's opinions. Bassie claimed to be a Democrat, but was scornful of quotas for minorities and women, and of any policy that made life easier on anyone.

Meg rolled her window down to feel the breath of fall and found herself wondering if Bassie was right that there was something pathological about the fact that she had never read the journals Bassie's mother had written. Several million other people certainly had read them. They were as famous as Carlos Castaneda's Don Juan narratives and the memoirs of Madame du Barri, and had won so many awards that even Bassie at times could not recall which volumes had garnered which prizes, among them the prestigious Bancroft Prize for the best book about the history of the Americas and the Francis Parkman Prize from the Society of American Historians. And now Bassie had made a last request that Meg read the journals and go to New Mexico, where the events recorded in them had taken place. Of course, this was more of a demand than a request. And it would not turn out to be her last. Still, Bassie was going to need an ally in New Mexico.

Meg stopped at a Sonic drive-in and ate a fried-chicken sandwich with the windows down, watching grackles fighting over french fries in the parking lot, then drove to her office. It was nothing but a warehouse in a warehouse district of north Austin, but it was new, and had room enough for her equipment.

Carolyn Stott was out, so Meg had the office to herself. She returned some phone calls, then called her mother, Nina Witte—Bassie's only offspring—who was working in Los Angeles as a sales representative for Texaco. Nina was the opposite of Bassie in most ways, but she had the same capacity, in Meg's opinion, of immediately sucking the air out of every room she entered. She was a recovering alcoholic who had been in therapy of one form or another for nearly twenty years. The latest was a type of psychodrama in which she acted out her dreams.

A message recorder answered the phone—Nina's voice saying she was out to lunch. Her lunches often lasted hours and involved male clients whom she had a special talent for seducing.

"Hey, Mom," Meg said to the recorder. "Bassie wants me to go to the pueblo at Pecos with her. There are some things going on there. Call me if you get the chance."

• • • • •

Three hours later, her mother had not called. Meg scheduled Bassie's flight, filled her prescription and purchased a pineapple. When she stopped at Bassie's house, Bassie was working at the computer and did not speak to her. "Southwest has curbside check-in," Meg told her as she left. "I've arranged a taxi. The driver will come here to the door at eleven-fifteen and help you with your suitcase."

Bassie continued typing.

An architect from San Antonio whom Meg was dating, named Paul Boyd, was in Austin for a conference with the city planners about a downtown building he was bidding to restore, and intended to stay the night with Meg. His visits were never as companionable as Meg hoped they would be, but nevertheless she was looking forward to having him around. It was nice to have a man in her apartment. It suggested some potential for the future. Though not much.

They went out to dinner at a restaurant on the east side in a quaint old plank-floored house, but Meg declined the offer of wine. She felt tired and sedated, deprived of oxygen, a sensation that she often suffered before a migraine started.

"Bassie's going to New Mexico tomorrow," she told Paul after they had placed their orders. "She wants me to go with her, and I can't decide. I think I probably shouldn't, actually. It would be complicated. Her mother buried some dogs on a hill near some pueblo ruins, and now somebody has given some money to add on to the visitors' center out there, and the addition is supposed to be built where the graves are. Bassie doesn't know the exact location of the graves; she wants the archaeologist to find them. And then she wants to have the bones. Have you ever been to New Mexico?"

"No."

"Neither have I."

He was studying his menu, though he had already selected his dinner. "What would she do with dog bones?" he asked.

"I think she wants to bring them home and bury them."

He looked at her. "That's crazy. Where would she bury them? In her backyard?"

"I don't know if it's crazy. They were her mother's dogs."

"What's she going to do, pack them in her suitcase? It's a crazy woman's thinking, Meg. To even want the bones."

"It isn't about the bones, Paul. It's about her past. It's about the fact that they're going to dig up one of the few memories she has of her mother."

"You're defending her."

"I should defend her. She's done a lot for me."

"But you don't owe her this. You don't have to go to New Mexico with her to bring home dog remains."

"I didn't say I was going. I said I probably wasn't."

Paul took a sip of wine. "I wouldn't go," he said.

She could feel the headache swelling. She disliked the way Paul sipped his wine; she disliked his attitude, his removed manner, his air of entitlement, the ease with which he seemed to know what was required of him and what was not—what, in other words, others had a right to ask of him. She didn't want that kind of certainty extended to herself.

"How come you're always complaining about her, but if I agree with you, you get defensive?" he asked.

"I'm defensive because she's my grandmother. I've got a right to complain about her. You don't."

When the food arrived, Paul said, "Let's start over for tonight. Cheers." He offered his wineglass, and she clinked her water glass against it.

But it was too late for starting over. The migraine was taking hold. Sounds were assuming the muted, dull quality that preceded a headache, and Meg felt irritable and tense. She survived the meal without revealing how miserable she was, but when she and Paul arrived back at her apartment she admitted ruefully that she did not feel very good. The nausea then crept in, and she spent the next two hours in the bathroom. Between bouts of vomiting and diarrhea and dry heaves, she lay on the bathroom floor, resting one side of her head and then the other against the cool tiles.

Paul was helpful enough to hand her Cokes and ice packs through the bathroom door, but at one point his judgment abandoned him and he knocked on the door and called in, "By the way, I have a headache too." She was crouching on the floor with her arms around the toilet seat. Staring into the bowl for a minute before answering, she finally said, creating an echo in the bowl, "A bad one?"

"No."

"Have you taken anything?"

"Some aspirin."

"Do you need to lie down?"

"No. It may be sinuses or something. I think molds were high today."

"Paul?" she asked, too sick to lift her head. "Would you go home?"

"What, you want me to leave?"

"If you don't mind."

"Am I being banished? Did I do something wrong?"

"I just think I'd do this better by myself."

It was one o'clock in the morning. "All right," Paul said. "I'll call you tomorrow. I hope you feel better."

After he had gone, she ventured out and managed to keep down a cocktail of painkillers by lying motionless on the bed.

THREE

At three o'clock in the morning she was awakened by the sound of sirens down below, heading south on Lamar Boulevard. She lay awake for a while, fretting about Bassie and other problems. She loathed the frequent migraines and the toll they had been taking on her schedule; she had tried every plausible cure. She had even suffered through a demoralizing session with an acupuncturist during which she had become so bored and agitated during the half hour on the table that she'd managed, in spite of the needles, to sit up and make notes in the margins of an article on pseudomonous bacteria. The acupuncturist had returned and found her at work, and accused her of "heat-pernicious influence," "yin deficiency," and "excess of yang." He told her she had set herself adrift from her life, and if she wanted to cure her headaches she would have to step into the stream of life again.

The episode had depressed her. She remembered it now in detail, lying in bed, and recollecting it somehow caused her to think of Pecos Pueblo: the adobe of the roofless church a deep orange in the sunlight, the mounds of pueblo ruins overgrown with vegetation, and Bassie's crooked finger moving down the page to indicate the slope of Dog Hill where the dogs were buried—Milton the pug-nosed tramp, as Bassie had described him, and large, aggressive Argus. She thought of what Tom Steiner out at C-TECH had suggested—that she take a break from her work, and enter a different realm for a while.

Perhaps, she thought, she should go with Bassie to New Mexico. She could attend the Q.A. meeting at St. David's Hospital and make the flight with Bassie after that. She would have to alert her clients, and notify her technician and service manager, placing them in charge in case of emergencies. But these things could be done.

Of course, going would mean that Bassie had won.

Meg began to think of Bassie asleep in her house on Bouldin Street just a few miles south off Lamar Boulevard, and to wonder what the chances were that the sirens she had heard on awakening were on their way to rescue Bassie from some medical mishap. It was always possible that Bassie had fallen during one of her numerous nightly trips to the toilet. She had fallen once before and broken her hip, and while that hip had been replaced with a steel ball and socket, there was still the one remaining.

Meg got up and turned the light on, feeling the dull-headed sensation of a hangover caused by the last of the migraine and the blend of medications. She made herself a cup of coffee for its vasoconstrictive properties and sat on the couch in the living room, telling herself that Bassie was not in need of her at the moment. The apartment around her, lit by a glow from the city, was spare and contemporary, clean and underfurnished, the opposite of Bassie's house. There was nothing hanging on the walls. Meg had come a long way from the dense overbearing crowdedness of Bassie's rooms. Yet she had not come far enough. Here she was, just a seven-minute drive away.

She turned to look out of the plate-glass windows down Twelfth Street to the state capitol building, the familiar dome lit starkly against the dark sky. Traffic lights were blinking yellow in these early-morning hours. She watched them blink, and watched a few cars make their way down Twelfth. Then she got up and turned the television on to see which of the *Bonanza* episodes was playing. It was one that she had seen before, so she turned the set off. Her gaze was drawn to the bookshelves and the collection of Hannah's journals which Bassie had given her through the years, volume by volume, as they were published, the first two in white jackets from the University of New Mexico Press, the others in brown jackets with the Random House imprint. She walked over to them and pulled one out to look at it. Hannah stared at her from the cover, posed in a full-length studio photograph, young and fresh-looking, wearing a large, feathered hat. She was standing behind what appeared to be an ice-cream parlor chair, waves of brown hair spread over a shoulder, her hands resting on the back of the chair, the front legs of which she had tipped slightly off the ground, probably at the photographer's suggestion. Her dress was dark and fitted tightly to the waist, with buttons from the collar down. Draped over her shoulders was a shawl with an elaborate embroidery of peacock feathers reaching around her arms. Her gaze was slightly averted. She stood looking out from under the brim of the ridiculous hat as if it were not up there at all, as if there was nothing over her head but open sky. The painted backdrop of stone pillars and plant fronds seemed superfluous to her image.

Meg realized that she had never liked the photograph. Hannah seemed too distant and otherworldly. The very thought of her, and of her journals, bothered Meg. The original, unedited notebooks from which these volumes had been compiled had been stored, during Meg's adolescence, in a fireproof safe that occupied half the closet at Bassie's house where Meg had hung her clothes. Bassie had built her life around them, and founded her career on them as a professor of southwestern history, transforming them into these six published volumes that had become, through the years, a kind of cult literature for lovers of the American West and the Victorian era. Bassie worshiped her mother and the journals. But for Meg they were a source of embarrassment, documenting the story of an ancestor whose life had been more dramatic and interesting than Meg could ever hope that hers would be.

She opened the cover, and turned a page to look at the photograph of Hannah's husband—Bassie's father, Elliott Bass. He was standing in the sunlight in a rumpled suit in front of a large black steam engine, his arms crossed over his chest. His coat was opened to a buttoned vest, and dusty. He was holding his hat; his hair was brown; he had a mustache, and he looked small in front of the massive engine, with its intricate matrix of valves and pipes. He was not squinting, though the sun was in his eyes.

On the page opposite this photograph of Elliott was one of Vicente Morales with a caption describing him as Elliott's closest friend and Hannah's confidant. The photograph was poor quality and Vicente was not the only person featured in it; he was posed with about a dozen other men in front of a wooden fence, their names printed at the base of the photograph. Several of the men were kneeling in the foreground and the others were standing behind them, most of them Hispanic, all having removed their hats. Vicente was kneeling; he had cocked up one knee and perched his hat on it, and was supporting the edge of a large placard bearing the words SHEEP SANITARY BOARD, NEW MEXICO. His black hair glistened in the brilliant sunlight. He was wearing spectacles, and like Elliott, had a mustache. He was looking at the placard and therefore appeared in partial profile, making his features unclear.

Meg turned the page to the only other photograph in the book. It was of a house where Bassie had lived with her parents at Pecos in the shallow valley spread below the ruins. The image was pale, either faded or overexposed, and so appeared to be seen through a fog. It revealed the frame structure viewed from the front, with a picket fence around it and the slope of what Meg recognized as Dog Hill rising behind it. Higher still, looking up over Dog Hill, was the mesa, on the edge of which could be seen the ruins of the adobe church. Dog Hill was dotted with scrubby evergreens, the mesa above encircled by the low stone wall.

Opposite this photograph Bassie's introduction to the journals ran on for a few pages, which Meg skipped over until her attention was seized by several lines in the middle of Hannah's first entry, dated in June of 1891.

The lanterns had remained lit, and by their ghastly light I saw that the seats at the back were crushed into pieces resembling a pile of driftwood. From under this, the hand of a child was reaching. Lifeless, I could see. It occurred to me that it was severed from the body. It was the mother wailing. She and the father at once began to drag at the splintered wood to reach the child. There was a flame beside me and I saw that one of the lamps had spilled its oil. The car began to fill with smoke . . .

Abruptly Meg closed the book and returned it to the shelf. She was tempted, for a moment, to pull it back out and finish reading the entry. Instead, she returned to the bedroom, peeled her pajama pants off and pulled on blue jeans and a sweater over her T-shirt. She put on tennis shoes, and went down the flight of stairs to her front door and out into the parking lot where the autumn air was breezy. Getting into her truck, she drove down to Lamar and turned south, crossing the river bridge and going left on Riverside, and right on Bouldin, into Bassie's neighborhood. She stopped at the curb in front of the house. There was no ambulance here, of course. Everything was quiet. The house was dark. Meg sat in her truck with the radio off and the motor running, looking at the old house. It was ominously still, sadly familiar, strangely aversive to her. Bassie, she knew, had decreed in a will that Meg would inherit the house. The thought of that burden weighed heavily, and the thought of Bassie dying filled Meg with an escalating dread as she sat alone in the truck cab with the heater blowing hot air onto her face. Bassie's death would liberate her from the dictatorial demands, but to what purpose? What would she do with her time then? Fill it with more work?

She studied her face in the rearview mirror, the darkness deepening shadows under her eyes. She could hardly blame Bassie or anyone else for the fact that she was lonely. Bassie was the one who had given her a home. Of course, in doing so she had deprived Meg of a normal adolescence, with sleepovers and friends. Bassie had even refused to own a television back in those days. She had scared Meg's friends away with her confrontational, autocratic nature, and run off boys with her sarcasm. She had driven off the boys in the same way that she had driven off Meg's father.

Bassie and Meg together had pretty well made a mess of Meg's life, in Meg's opinion now, and someday Bassie was going to die and leave her, alone, to deal with it.

Perhaps the acupuncturist was right, and Meg had cut herself off from life. If that was true, she wished she could reconnect. New Mexico offered itself to her thoughts again. She would like to see the mountains. And she could meet Jim Layton; she had liked his voice. Perhaps he wasn't married.

But New Mexico was Bassie's place. It could be a mistake to go creeping onto the edges of Bassie's turf at this point in her own life. She should find her own place in the world.

FOUR

Daylight found Meg moving around her apartment in a cheap synthetic bathrobe that years ago had partly melted in the dryer; the heat had stiffened the seams. She wondered briefly, scratching her neck where the seams were prickling her skin, why she had not thrown the robe away. But she was not very interested in all the ways that Bassie's oddness had been passed on to her—what strand of DNA might cause her to continue wearing such an uncomfortable garment.

The telephone rang at seven-thirty. "It's Jim Layton. Did I wake you?"

"No. I've been up."

"I just talked with Bassie. She gave me your number. She told me you're coming."

"No. I never said that."

"Well, then she just assumes it," he said. "She seems to think you're coming. Look, I hope you will. She's apprehensive about all this, and I'm not going to be able to look after her out here."

He left an opportunity for Meg to respond, and when she didn't, he said, "We've started on the test trench. We have to excavate several places before we start construction, to make sure we're not destroying any sensitive areas or jeopardizing artifacts. I can figure out the places that look suspicious, but I can't tell which ones might be the dog graves. I'm going to start doing some exploratory digging this morning because I have a feeling that the more I can get done before she gets here, the better off we'll be. But I hope you'll come. Or maybe talk your mother into coming, though I know that's problematic."

"Mother would be a disaster."

"Well."

"And I think it's just as likely that I'd get on Bassie's nerves as anything else."

"Why don't you let her be the judge of that? She asked you to come, didn't she?"

"It's a sick codependency," Meg said, only half joking.

After she was off the phone, it rang again, with Paul calling from San Antonio to see if she was feeling better. She made a point of not asking him if he was. "I've decided to go to New Mexico," she said.

"How come?" he asked her. "It's a bad decision."

"To correct my yin deficiency," she said. "I have excess of yang. I have heat-pernicious influence."

"What are you talking about?"

"I have to get in touch with my roots."

He didn't care enough to figure out what she was saying, or discern her real motives. "I was planning to come stay with you again tomorrow night," he said. "I have another meeting in Austin."

Meg recalled how on their first date Paul had told her every detail of a long and tedious dream that he claimed exemplified the strain he was feeling in his relationship with his father. She had found the dream uninteresting, but had been flattered by the confidence. Then later he had related the dream again, in the same words, and with no apparent memory at all of having described it to her once before. She realized she was not the first to have heard it.

Basically, she thought, holding the phone receiver and scratching at the hardened seams of the bathrobe, she was looking for a man who wouldn't dare confide his hopes and dreams, not on the first date anyway. "You can stay here at my apartment if you want to," she offered. "I can leave you a key."

He agreed to this. She drew a black mark on the back of her hand to remind herself about the key.

It was not a good sign, she told herself, to have to draw dots on her hand in order to remember the man she was sleeping with.

She telephoned Bassie to tell her she would meet her at the airport.

The flight was at twelve-forty; she would leave directly from the Q.A. meeting.

"So this means you considered things last night," Bassie observed about Meg's change of heart.

"No, I was busy vomiting," Meg told her.

FIVE

During the forty-minute layover in El Paso, Meg watched the weather forecast on an airport television. Rain was predicted in central Texas. She called her office from a pay phone and talked to Carolyn Stott, advising her to have a technician on call in case of a problem. Rain often caused difficulties for dialysis clinics. Runoff in the hill country drained into the Llano and the Colorado rivers, and stirred up organic material, forcing municipalities to augment water treatment protocol. To control bacteria, treatment plants increased their dosages of chlorine, which was toxic for Meg's patients. If her machines did not work properly, patients could die on dialysis.

She called home for her messages and listened to a lengthy, lilting monologue that her mother had left on the recorder. "Hi, dear. I just can't imagine, sweetie, why you would think of going to New Mexico with Mother. She will run your life, you know, if you allow it. I learned the hard way with Mother. Anyway, New Mexico would be the worst place you could go with her. She's like a queen out there. And she will do everything possible to compare you to the image of her mother, and you will not measure up, I can assure you. At least I certainly didn't. Divorce yourself, sweet thing. It's the only way to keep your sanity. You know how awful she was to me when she decided that I didn't need that antidepressant that the doctor . . ."

Meg hung up on the rest of the message. She knew the gist of it. She had even known the gist of it before she called her mother in the first place: Nina was a broken record when it came to Bassie. But the truth of it was—and they all three knew the truth of it—Nina could only afford to neglect Bassie because Meg never would. If not for Meg, Bassie would be left with no one, which would suit her daughter fine, except that Nina, in spite of her faults, did possess a conscience. None of her fleeting philosophies had ever quieted her doubts about herself as a mother or a daughter.

On the flight from El Paso to Albuquerque Bassie antagonized Meg, dragging forth an old grudge against her for not marrying an Austin movie critic named Brent Biggs whom Meg had briefly been engaged to more than a decade ago. The name Brent Biggs itself, Meg had always thought, communicated a fairly accurate sense of the man: he was incredibly charming for an ass. On their first date, he had taken her to a birthday party for a colleague; Meg was twenty-two years old at the time, just graduated from the University of Texas with a degree in biomedical engineering. She was ill at ease with the verbal jocularity at this gathering of wordsmiths, and had attached herself to Brent like a lugubrious shadow, perfectly mute. He hadn't seemed to notice either the attachment or the muteness. His natural buoyancy had carried the evening, and had subsequently managed to keep both him and Meg afloat during the months of their engagement. But after that, Meg had started to resent him. He had the same unreachable quality that Bassie had—a busy, impatient, holier-than-thou attitude that made Meg feel childish and spiteful. At best, he was paternalistic, being ten years older than Meg. At worst he was Pygmalion-like and patronizing. She found herself defending her taste in movies as well as everything else—clothes, furniture, books. She began to realize that people confident enough to make a living by their opinions had opinions about almost everything, and Meg's protests against this were often burdened with sentiments that she knew sounded utterly naïve. "You always think you're smarter," she would say, knowing that when she finally got her footing and a job she liked, she would prove to be smarter than he, and more capable, and stronger at the core. Her resentment toward him had been more complicated and more valid than she could articulate, and eventually she had withdrawn into a hostile silence. Then finally Brent, in a torrent of anger, and in the face of her stoic calm, had laid out to her in facile language how the problems in their relationship were all due to her, to her pent-up anger toward her parents and toward Bassie. He said her father's abandonment of the family had caused her to be hostile toward men.

A resolve had settled over Meg while she withstood this blast, as if she had submerged herself in the murky waters of a quiet lagoon and was watching Brent above the silver membrane of the surface, flailing his arms and shouting something not at all discernible to her. Before he finished shouting, she had formed a plan. He was right, most likely, about her pent-up anger, but she did not care.

By noon of the next day she had broken off the engagement and moved herself out of his house.

Bassie had not forgiven her. Bassie and Brent had allied themselves during the engagement, odd accomplices, their relationship based mostly on impressing one another. They liked each other's cleverness.

Brent had called on Bassie when Meg left him. He had dissolved into tears, having suddenly realized—he said—how much in love with Meg he was. Bassie had taken him in, and their friendship intensified over a pot of coffee and a discussion of Meg's heinous act of sudden desertion. Being self-centered, articulate people, they convinced each other beyond a doubt of what they both believed already, that Meg had made a terrible mistake for herself as well as for Brent.

For her part, Meg had hurled her fiercest energies and almost spiteful efforts into proving them wrong. Within a week she had acquired the job of biomedical technical director at St. David's Hospital, launching a career that left her breathless with new urgency and passion.

Even now, years later, Brent and Bassie still kept in touch with one another. Brent was married, and had two children.

"I wonder," Bassie said reflectively, gazing out of the airplane window, a quiet meanness in her voice, "if you left him because of your mother." She extracted a plastic bag of floppy green onions from her huge old leather purse, fumbled the bag open, took an onion out, and began to eat it.

Meg ignored the speculation, flipping through an in-flight magazine. She settled on a story about fish hatcheries, but even with an empty seat separating her from Bassie, Bassie's presence was overbearing and distracting, the smell of onions being the least of it.

"I just wonder about it," Bassie said, pulling from her bag the galley proof of a book on Pueblo pottery that the University of Chicago had sent to her for a promotional blurb.

"Mother had nothing to do with it," Meg said. "She hardly knew Brent."

"She set the example," Bassie observed, opening the proofs, "for instability with men."

Meg tossed the magazine onto the seat between them. "I don't know why you have to be so critical of Mother," she said. "She's been sober for years. She likes her job. She looks great."

"She was a lovely-looking flower child, but that doesn't mean she had any substance to her," Bassie said.

Meg stood up and dragged her briefcase down from the overhead compartment, pulling out a stack of notes she had composed for a paper on high flux as opposed to high efficiency dialysis, which she was to present at an FDA seminar.

"Brent was nice," Bassie said.

"I never said he wasn't nice. I said he was a snob. It's been fourteen years, Bassie. Can't you let it go?"

"I bet you were with Paul last night. He always makes you cranky. I hope you're not sleeping with him. He's spineless. He's a human slug."

Meg settled down into her seat and started leafing through her notes while Bassie, the dark hairs on her jaw visible in Meg's peripheral vision against the light of the window, chewed her floppy onions.

After a while, Meg's thoughts began to settle on New Mexico. The last time she had seen the mountains was years ago when she attended a medical conference in Denver. She wondered if there might be snow.

"What exactly do you remember about Dog Hill?" she asked.

Bassie fished another onion from the bag. "I remember my mother digging a dog grave. In the moonlight. Vicente Morales was with her. There was snow on the ground. It was Argus they were burying; he was shot by poachers. I heard the gunshots from my bed. I got out of bed, and saw them digging. I watched them from the back porch. They had a shovel and a pickax. The memory was the end of my life as I knew it. My mother died soon afterwards." Bassie closed the bag of onions and tucked it back into her purse, turning to the window. "That, and one other, are my only memories of Mother. I remember, very clearly, a knock on the bedroom door. Vicente came in, and Mother cried in his arms. I don't know what she was crying about."

After reflecting on these revelations for a moment, Meg said, “Do you have any memories of your father?”

“He wasn’t home enough to be remembered.”

“Did you resent that he wasn’t home?”

“Don’t be stupid. I was a very small child. I had no concept of what I was entitled to resent. You’re talking about yourself now, aren’t you?”

“No.” But perhaps she was.

Soon the voice of the pilot came over the loudspeaker, announcing the beginning of the descent into the Albuquerque airport. Meg arranged the notes in her lap, leaned her head back and closed her eyes. She tried to think about anything but the obscurity of the past into which she now seemed blindly, and against her better judgment, to be slowly descending.

Just before they landed, Bassie’s voice came to her. “I have always had a bad feeling about that hill.”

SIX

Pecos was an hour and a half northeast from the Albuquerque airport; they made the drive in a red rental car, passing the outskirts of Santa Fe late in the afternoon under a damp overcast. Meg perceived the landscape of New Mexico to be fantastic and unsettling. She felt as if she were skimming along the surface of some vast foreign land rather than merely driving an interstate highway. There was nothing to crowd her vision, except, at times, the hills, and these seemed only to funnel her through to larger vistas. She felt herself transported by something less earthbound than the red rental car, as if she were entering—as Tom Steiner had recommended—some kind of a different realm. When finally the old ruined church of Pecos Pueblo appeared on the top of a mesa alongside the interstate, roofless and forlorn under the heavy sky, Meg was almost unnerved by the solid composure of the enormous structure. From such a distance, and elevated against the sky, the place looked isolated, standing above the rest of the world on an island of rock.

Bassie instructed Meg where to turn, and they parked at the visitors' center below the ruins. It was a flat-roofed structure built of adobe, with ornate entry doors carved from massive slabs of wood.

"You go in and find Jim," Bassie told Meg. "And don't go up to the ruins. Now I mean that. We don't have time today."

She had created a tight schedule, having determined to show Meg, before dark, the old Montezuma resort hotel where Hannah had worked when she arrived in New Mexico nearly a century before. It was uninhabitable now, about an hour's drive farther down the interstate from

Pecos. A modern college campus had been built around the Montezuma, and Bassie had arranged with the college president to admit them to the old hotel. It was on the verge of being condemned, and electricity had been shut off some months before.

Meg went into the visitors' center and inquired of a female park ranger at the front desk where she might find Jim Layton. "He's doing some work on the hill," the woman said. "Just go out the back doors there. Don't take the main trail up to the ruins; turn left on the path that goes between some boulders. It'll take you up the hill."

On her way to the back door, Meg passed racks of history books about Pecos and other pueblos, an exhibition room to her left and a doorway to a small theater. She exited the back door into the chilly weather again. Starting on the uphill path through a cleft in a row of boulders, inhaling the air, she felt exhilarated by the fresh smell of the evergreens, and autumn, and was surprised not to have more resistance to the feeling. Pecos, after all, was where Hannah had composed the largest portion of the journals. But Meg's grudge against it all these years, she realized now, was pointless; Pecos wasn't Hannah's place, or even Bassie's. They had both been relative latecomers like herself.

She could not, as she ascended the short path up the side of Dog Hill, catch sight of the adobe church above her, but she was aware of its presence. The trees on the slope she was climbing blocked the church from sight, but if she reached the top of the hill, she surmised, she would be just under it.

The hill was even less of an entity than it had seemed in the aerial photograph in the book on Bassie's table, being little more than a slope leading up the side of the mesa.

Moving aside the pungent branches of an evergreen intruding on the path, Meg almost stumbled into a shallow trench, about two feet wide, where the ground had recently been excavated. Stepping over it, she noticed two men seated on a rocky ledge beside some bushes a few yards farther up the hill. They were studying a large set of plans spread on the ground between them, the corners weighted down with stones. One of the men was wearing a park uniform and a Smokey the Bear hat.

"I'm looking for Jim Layton," she called up to them.

The one in the hat stood up and stepped down from the ledge. "That would be me," he said. He was average height or taller, clean-shaven and nice looking enough, in spite of the hat. She noticed he was wearing a wedding ring. Birds pecking at the berries in a bush beside him took flight as he came forward. "You decided to come," he said. "You kept me in suspense." He turned and introduced her to his companion, who had continued his examination of the prints and acknowledged her only briefly.

"So where is Bassie?" Jim asked.

"In the car," she told him. "She wants us to go look at the Montezuma before dark, and has arranged for somebody to let us in. She wants to know if you'll come with us."

"Now?"

Meg consulted her watch. "It's five 'til five," she said. "Apparently the Montezuma doesn't have electricity."

He lifted his hat and ran his hand over the top of his head. "Sure. I'll come."

She waved her hand at the prints. "So you're pretty far along."

"We've finished the test trench," he said, and turned and called up the hill in the direction of a stand of scrubby trees, "Tony? Are you there?"

A man's voice answered in Spanish. Meg couldn't see the man from where she stood, as trees blocked the uphill view. By contrast, the downhill vista was open and showed the roof of the visitors' center below, as well as the flat valley of yellow grass where the house Bassie lived in as a child had once stood, and rows of snowcapped mountain peaks in the distance.

Jim was calling up the hill in Spanish in a fairly bad accent, and presently the person named Tony came down through the brush carrying what appeared to be a slab of dirty wood about eight inches long, which he presented to Jim.

Jim introduced him to Meg as Tony Flores. He was in his seventies at least, she guessed, and missing several teeth. "Tony has known your grandmother even longer than I have," Jim told her, and then studied the piece of wood, running his hands over it and turning it over. "Bassie's going to like this."

"What is it?"

"A tray. About four hundred years old. Tony found it in a test pit."

"Señora is here?" Tony inquired.

"She's in the car," Meg told him.

Jim continued to talk with Tony in a mixture of Spanish and English, the topic, as well as Meg could tell, being the soil composition of the test pit from which the tray had been extracted. When they had finished examining the tray, Tony started down the hill to show it to Bassie.

"He worked with Bassie out here a long time ago, excavating the convent and the area around the church," Jim explained.

"He likes her?"

"Quite a bit."

Meg had always been puzzled by people who liked Bassie. There was a generous side to Bassie: she had tutored at least a dozen unlikely students through college free of charge, often paying their tuition. But once some poor soul had won Bassie's confidence he or she was never allowed to shake it; she prodded these people through life as if they were cattle. While some of them resented her for it, most, Meg had come to realize, were grateful to her.

The man who was still seated on the rocky ledge looking at the prints said suddenly, "I got it, Jim. I think I got it."

Jim stepped back onto the ledge and squatted down to look.

"We extend this for two more feet, over here," the man said, "and take three feet off here, which butts us up against this rock but gives us plenty of room. We'll only lose this little bit of storage space."

"But you would see the corner of this wall from the church wall," Jim remarked, pointing out a place on the prints. "We don't want to see any of the building from the ruins."

"We won't," the man insisted. "Not if we do it like I'm talking about."

"Go up there and look down," Jim told him.

"But look here at this slant," the man insisted, indicating something on the plans. "Do the math."

"I don't have to do the math," Jim said. "I know what you see from the church wall. You see this boulder right here." He planted his finger on the prints. "And if you see this boulder, you would see a wall."

The man studied the paper spread before him. "I guess that's right," he said reluctantly.

Jim stood up again. He said to Meg, "We can go, if Tony will agree to take the tray to the post office for me."

The man on the ledge said, "Look, I don't see why, if we butt this right up here"—he tapped at the prints—"and it's only a nine-foot wall—"

"Go up there, Sam, and just stand on the church wall. And look down at that boulder."

"All right. All right. I believe you. But Phil said it doesn't matter if we can see a section of a wall or a corner of the roof from up there, as long as it's not from the main trail."

"Phil said that? Well, Phil's not footing the bill. It's been stipulated from the beginning that we're not going to interfere with the view."

Meg said, "I'm going to go tell Bassie you're coming," and started down the hill.

Jim caught up with her in a moment, carrying an empty water bottle and a white chipboard box. "Let me ask you something," he said, and she stopped and waited for him. "Have you ever happened to see the original journals?"

"I shared a closet with them."

"What do they look like?" Jim asked.

There were a lot of them, she explained—an assortment—different colors, different sizes. Most of the covers had illustrations, though some were plain red or black, like old ledger books. She recalled several identical ones with etchings of Buffalo Bill Cody on horseback chasing a herd of buffalo with a lasso. One had a picture of a small girl standing on a stool. There was also a Grecian goddess, a woman at a spinning wheel, a scholar in robes. She guessed there were about twenty notebooks in all. "But Bassie thinks there must have been at least one more, that was lost, from the last year of Hannah's life."

"Do you remember if any of the ones you saw were leather?"

"A couple, I think. The ones without illustrations might have been leather."

A breeze was lifting the edges of Jim's hair under his hat brim, and the damp overcast hung so low it seemed to be sitting on his shoulders.

"I found this in one of the pits I started this morning," he said, opening the cardboard box he was holding.

Meg peered inside at a dirty, frayed leather cover of a notebook.

"Did they look like this?" he asked.

"I think so. Does it have any pages?"

"No. Just these." He carefully lifted the front of the cover, revealing the soiled endpapers adhered, inside, to the leather. The page affixed to the back cover had several lines of writing in faded pencil.

"What does it say?" Meg asked.

"I can't tell about most of it," he said. "It's too faded. But this part here, in Spanish, seems to be a record of a purchase from a fruit company in Juárez—Smith and Everts . . . or Smith and Evans. Something like that. See here, that's Spanish for canned peaches and . . . it looks like '*cuatro canastas grandes de manzanas.*' " He paused. "That's a lot of apples."

She looked at the lines he was indicating. They were bolder than the other scribblings on the page, and in a different handwriting, clearly done by someone else.

"Do you think Bassie would make anything of this?" Jim asked.

"I think the fewer things you show her, the better off we'll be," she answered. "Are you going to be looking any more in the area where you found this?"

"Yes."

"Then I'd wait and see what else turns up. This could have been anyone's notebook, right?"

"Anyone from about that time period." He placed the lid back on the box. "See?" he said. "I told you we needed you."

They started down the path again. "How is she?" he asked.

"Mad at Phil Barker. Mad at you. Otherwise, all right. When was the last time you saw her?"

"Three years ago. Maybe four."

"She's had her cataracts removed since then. From both eyes. Her glasses now are pretty indescribable. She had a hip replaced. For a while she used a walker, but now she's got a cane. How long have you known her?"

"I guess it's been almost thirty years," he answered, seeming surprised at the calculation. "She was a consultant here when I took this job. We used to camp out on the ruins together and drink gin and smoke cigarettes. We'd get up at dawn and start working before any of the rest of the crew got here. Watch that limb."

Meg had been glancing over her shoulder at Jim as he spoke, and now turned to see a needled branch in front of her face. She pushed it aside and held it back for Jim to pass. "We were excavating the convent and the interior of the church," he said, in front of her now. He had removed his Smokey the Bear hat; his hair was flattened to his head.

When they reached the bottom of the path, they turned together toward the back door of the visitors' center. "Bassie was kind of a mother to me for a while," Jim offered. "Have you ever been out here before?"

"No."

"Why not? If I'm not being too intrusive."

"I guess I've always thought of this as Bassie's turf," Meg said.

He laughed. "Try getting a shovel in it. So, what's your impression so far?"

Her impression, so far, was that the place moved her. The landscape seemed to have greater expanse and more dimensions to it than what she was accustomed to, and a more dramatic relief, even against a gray sky and without shadows. The air, even heavy with moisture, was invigorating. "I haven't got my bearings yet," she answered. "What's your impression?"

He had got his bearings, he said.

He ushered her into the visitors' center and exchanged a few words with the park ranger at the desk about when Phil Barker might return from Santa Fe. Then he placed the cardboard box with the remains of the notebook onto a high shelf behind the desk. As he and Meg went out through the front doors into the parking lot, they saw Tony Flores still holding the slab of aged wood and talking animatedly into the window of the rental car.

"Churned up any friars yet?" Bassie snapped at Jim as he approached.

Tony stepped aside as Jim leaned and reached into the window, taking hold of Bassie's hand. "Not a one," Jim said.

"No bones at all?" she demanded.

"Not even dogs'."

"How are your potholes coming?"

"The test pits are coming just fine."

"Found anything besides the tray?"

"A lithic scatter. A few sherds of Glaze Six. We're hitting bedrock in some places at half a meter."

"Tony says your crew is incompetent."

"They're a little green," he admitted. "You'll meet them. They'll be back in the morning."

"Students?"

"Yes."

"Archaeology?"

"Philosophy."

"Puh. How did you get hold of those?"

"I hired them as a favor to their teacher."

"What about the volunteer? Tony has been telling me that she's a menace with a trowel."

"Tony never lies."

"But you allow her to work?"

"I do."

"And how did you find her?"

"She used to baby-sit Meredith and Billy. I like her."

"The hiring standards are a little loose, don't you think?"

"Her parents were looking for something that might encourage her to go to college," Jim said. "This is what I had to offer. It's good to see you, Bassie."

"You're coming to the Montezuma?"

"Meg said I'm invited."

"We have to be there before dark."

"I'm ready," he said. "I've got to be home at eight-thirty to help Billy with something." He turned to Tony Flores. "Is there any way that you can package up that tray and send it overnight to the place in Tucson that does tree-ring dating? You'd have to get it to the post office by five-thirty. That's twenty-five minutes."

Tony shrugged. "*No problema,*" he said.

"I have a *problema*," Bassie interrupted. "Where is Phil Barker? Has he fled the grounds?"

"Not exactly," Jim said. "He's in Santa Fe; his mother had her toe amputated yesterday. She has diabetes."

"Well, that should make me easier on him."

"It should. However, I doubt it will, Bassie."

"You relayed my message to him? That I'm against the project?"

"Of course."

"You told him I was coming to get the bones?"

"I did."

"And he said?"

"He said we'll see."

"He said over his dead body, didn't he?"

"I believe those were his exact words."

"Well. Then. We'll see. We'll see what he has to say when I get the press out here. You're on my side, I hope."

"No, Bassie, unfortunately I'm in the middle, as always when you come out here to see us."

"Well. It's good to know who my friends are not. Are you following or leading to the Montezuma?"

"I'll lead, so you won't have to direct Meg." He turned to Meg. "Do you want a map? In case we get separated? That way you're free of Bassie."

"Meg will never be free of me," Bassie remarked.

SEVEN

Meg followed Jim over to a dirty Mazda pickup and watched him sift through the items in the glove compartment. The interior of the truck was littered with debris; papers were strewn across the seat. There was a dilapidated box of what appeared to be a collection of artifacts wrapped in bubble plastic, an open box of vanilla wafers, and a pair of mud boots on the floor beside the stick shift. The damp air had turned misty; droplets sprinkled down as Jim found the map and unfolded it. He pointed out to Meg their present location at Pecos Pueblo, a couple of miles off Highway 25. The town of Las Vegas, he showed her, was farther on, along the same highway, and the Montezuma was just ten miles up in the mountains from there.

Meg took the map and got into the rental car with Bassie, who was speaking with Tony in Spanish through the window as they pulled away. Leaving the parking lot, Meg looked in the rearview mirror at Jim behind her in the Mazda pickup, eating from the box of wafers. She waved her hand out the window, indicating for him to pass her, and he took the lead. "I like him," she told Bassie.

"He was overqualified even thirty years ago when he came to work here," Bassie said scornfully. "He'd got his wife pregnant. She wasn't his wife then. I told him not to marry her, but he's one of those men who does right by everyone but himself."

"I've never met one of those men," Meg remarked.

"It is not a trait that breeds success, I'll tell you that," Bassie said. "He declined a position at Stanford to stay here so his wife could finish her degree. I have never liked her. Don't you need the wipers on?"

Meg turned them on.

"And he's been here ever since."

"Maybe he likes it here," Meg suggested.

"He's obstinate. He's here because of stubbornness, not devotion. Turn the heat up, would you? It's cold in here."

Meg shoved the heat on high and directed the vents toward Bassie.

"He's got plenty of ambition. What he lacks is nerve," Bassie said.

"I take it he's not from New Mexico," Meg said.

"Kentucky," Bassie answered. She said nothing for a moment, and then said, "His parents died in a car wreck when he was six years old. The same age my father was when his parents were killed. That's why Jim feels so bonded to him."

"To Elliott?"

"Yes. He idolizes him. And wants to be like him. But he's nothing like him; he's too cautious. You've met him before, you know."

"You offered him my bed, but he slept in the living room."

With Jim still rattling along in front of them in his pickup, they eventually turned off the interstate and followed his taillights for a few miles farther up into the hills, passing dingy, scattered houses and industrial buildings. The vehicles parked alongside homes were mostly old pickups. At last they rounded a curve in the road and Bassie said, "There it is."

Through the droplets on the window, the spires of what appeared to be a castle rose from the hills off to the right, a hulking, dark, gigantic structure. Contemporary buildings clustered on the hills below it were innocuous and brightly lit, and the contrast made the Montezuma, which had clearly been magnificent in its day, seem dismal and unsettling.

"I didn't know it was so big," Meg observed.

"You're going to miss the turn," Bassie warned her. "Jim's turning."

She slowed and followed the pickup over a narrow river crossing. The fact that a modern campus surrounded the ominous-looking Montezuma was almost a relief.

Several parking places designated for the use of visitors bordered the soccer field, just off a street winding its way up through the center of the college. Meg pulled the car into a place beside Jim's truck. She could see the towers of the Montezuma emerging from the trees on the hill beside them, many of the windows broken out.

Jim got out of the truck and came around the car to help Bassie. A path edged by tall trees ascended the slope, and the three of them made their way up, Bassie setting the slow pace and lecturing Meg over her shoulder about the origins of the red sandstone on the exterior of the Montezuma. She seemed to have expanded when emerging from the car, as if to fill the empty spaces left by the shortage of oxygen at these higher altitudes. Her old fur coat, which she had owned for decades, hung to the middle of her calves, speckled by the drizzle, and her ankles appeared extraordinarily thin in tan stockings with the cloddish black shoes on her large feet.

When the path broke free of the trees, the Montezuma appeared suddenly before them, surrounded by a long, rotting veranda and a flat, bare area of ground. A stout, pleasant-faced man stood below the veranda holding an umbrella that he had not yet unfurled. He came forward to greet them, opening the umbrella for Bassie and extending his hand.

"Dr. Bass?" he said, "Frank Lopez. Welcome to United World College. It's such a pleasure finally to meet you."

"Thank you," Bassie answered flatly. "And thank you for not splitting your infinitive. I understand you know Jim Layton?"

He sheltered her with the umbrella. "Of course I do; everybody knows Jim Layton," he told Bassie, shaking Jim's hand.

"This is my granddaughter, Meg Mabry," Bassie said. "She's never seen the Montezuma."

Frank Lopez ushered them around the corner of the building to a large, empty graveled parking lot closed off by orange construction cones. "I apologize that you had to park on the hill," he said. "If I had thought about it when you called, I would have had you come around the back way and park up here. We don't usually allow it, because of liability, but of course you would be an exception."

"This area," Bassie said to Meg, moving her cane in an arc, "was a circular driveway. Bellmen greeted the guests here. Hannah used the service entrance at the back."

"We had to close all the entrances except for this one, to keep the students out," Frank Lopez said. "We quit offering tours to the public a couple of years ago."

The front doors opened to a large reception lobby. Faded daylight, already darkened by the overcast, was further screened in here by the dirty windowpanes. Bassie's cane thumped loudly on the floor, and Frank Lopez's voice was magnified inelegantly by the empty spaces.

"I'm sure I could find a chair around here somewhere, Dr. Bass, if you would like to sit down," he said.

But she had not come to sit. She made her way into the cold expanses of the room and stood looking around her at the pillars and the dusty, ornate paneling. Her mouth puckered in disgust. She looked toward an elevator shaft that had been roped off, and toward the main stairwell, sealed off on the first landing with a Sheetrock wall. "I take it," she said, "that your restoration plans did not fly."

"I haven't given up on them yet," Frank assured her. "The problem is, we want to do it right, and even just replacing the dining room chandelier, for instance, would cost nearly twenty thousand dollars. It's recorded somewhere that the original cost fifteen hundred dollars and that was around 1890."

"It's recorded in my mother's journals," Bassie informed him.

"Is it? I wish I knew what happened to that original chandelier," he remarked.

"The Jesuits took it," Bassie said, adding pointedly, "If you wish to know, then ask."

While Bassie and Frank Lopez talked, Meg walked over to look at the fireplace, which was made of terra-cotta tiles with floral designs and spanned fifteen feet along the wall opposite a large structure that had been the registration desk.

Jim came over to join her, and she remarked on how impressive the place must have been a hundred years ago. But instead of responding to the comment, Jim inquired about her work.

"I service water treatment systems for businesses and hospitals," she said. "Mostly dialysis machines."

The statement was usually met with a blank stare and a change of subject matter, but Jim's response was different. He was interested. "I wrote a research paper once in college on dry-rot problems in New Orleans," he said. "How the surface drainage and runoff system in the old district was drying out the subsoil and dry-rotting the buildings on cypress piers."

Meg knew about the situation in New Orleans. She had once been called in to consult on the problem. "How did you get into that?" she asked. "That's not archaeology."

"It was before I picked a major," he said. "I started out in anthropology and then went into environmental history and then archaeology. I'm curious, what does Bassie think about your job?"

"I did a science fair experiment with pond water in the seventh grade, and I think that's how she still sees me," Meg said, "carrying around baby-food jars of pond water. That's probably about as far as her thoughts on it go. Actually, she finds the concept of pure water elitist. She won't even change out her old lead pipes."

They spoke for a moment about the job. Most water treatment companies had stayed away from anything that had to do with life support, Meg explained—the liability was too high. But the problems were unique, and she had liked that. She was often summoned to investigate life-threatening problems of rare bacteria that confounded even the large, publicly held water companies.

"Elliott was an engineer," Jim said. "Maybe it's in your blood."

Bassie called across the room to them, saying that Frank Lopez was leaving.

"She's driven him off," Meg said to Jim.

"He's giving us the keys," Bassie called.

"Be careful if you go upstairs or into any closed-off areas," Frank warned them. "The floors are rotted out in some places, and there's a lot of broken glass lying around."

When Frank had gone, Jim unlocked the doors into the dining room, and Bassie led the way in. It was a long, rectangular room with a high ceiling and tall windows down either side. A row of industrial metal pillars had been placed down the center to shore up the ceiling, causing visible structural distress and pushing one of the walls out by several inches.

"Jesuits," Bassie said disgustedly, pointing out the damage with her cane. "The YMCA nearly destroyed the building by 1912. And then the Baptists got hold of it. The Jesuits were hot on their heels. And when the Jesuits gave up the roost, a gang of radical Chicanos moved in and used it for a hideout. Did you see *The Evil*? It was filmed here."

Jim invited Meg to see the room that had been Hannah's when she was employed at the Montezuma, and went outside to get a flashlight from his truck. When he returned, Bassie was inspecting the dining room windows to ascertain which of them still retained its original glass. Leading Meg back into the lobby and down a hall to a narrow stairwell, Jim switched his flashlight on before starting up the stairs. The old wallpaper was in shreds here, the floors littered with garbage and rat droppings. The stair railing was broken off. "Vandals burned the banisters and a lot of the paneling for firewood," Jim explained.

On the third floor, the stench of bat guano became suddenly overpowering and Jim suggested that they go out onto the balcony for air. Meg followed him up another, even narrower stairwell, through a small door and out onto a large circular balcony that resembled a turret.

The air was blowing in from the canyon, damp and cold. The view extended almost 180 degrees. Jim turned off the flashlight. Meg walked to the railing and stood looking out over the lighted soccer field of the campus and across the river toward an abandoned power plant, which Jim explained had been in operation back in Hannah's time. "A spur rail came up here from the depot in Las Vegas," he explained. "It stopped down there on the other side of the river, and then the people were transported in buggies over a bridge and up here to the Montezuma." Indicating the soccer field bordered by the blue tin roofs of the dormitory buildings, he said, "Down in that area were gardens and tennis courts and a croquet course. Then there was the archery range and a petting zoo. The hills over there, and back all the way around this way"—he explained, waving his hand toward the surrounding hills covered with dark evergreens—"were pretty well denuded then, because the railroad used the trees for fuel." He paused. "So it would appear, from what Bassie said, that you've never read the journals. How come?"

"I might, sometime," she answered. "It's Bassie's dying request. Of course, she isn't dying."

After a moment, Jim turned his flashlight on again and lighted the way for Meg to precede him down the stairs. She reached the third-floor level and turned to watch him pull the warped door shut and make his way down. He ushered her past the stairwell that they had ascended from the first and second floors, and along the dark, musty hallway; they held their breath as much as possible against the stench of guano, until reaching a wing of the building where the air was clearer.

"So how did Bassie break her hip?" he asked.

"It appears to have just snapped," Meg said. "She was in her kitchen, and just fell. I'd been trying to get her to wear one of those emergency call buttons, since she wouldn't let anybody stay with her in the house. I'd tried having someone live there with her, but it didn't work. I tried several people."

"You hired and she fired," Jim said.

"Three times, actually," Meg told him. "And she wouldn't even talk about the button. She was lying on the kitchen floor for nearly three hours before she got the phone down off the hook. She threw a box of Ajax at it from under the sink, then dragged herself over and called 911."

"And used the episode to prove she didn't need an emergency button," Jim said.

"Precisely."

The area where they were now, on the third floor over the kitchen wing, was dilapidated to the point of being hazardous. There were holes in the Sheetrock walls, and the floorboards were loose. Jim ushered Meg into a room at the end of the hallway. It was cramped and narrow, with a sharp-pitched, vaulted ceiling where the eave of the roof descended overhead. Meg's impression in the near darkness, with only the flashlight and the faded light through the window for illumination, was of something even less than empty. The room contained a single dismal shade of gray. One of the panes from the window was missing, and the pungent smell of autumn overcast crept in through the open frame, along with throaty murmurings of the pigeons.

Meg crossed the room to a window, which overlooked a small, irregularly shaped courtyard paved with flagstones. Weeds and sprigs of grass grew profusely between the stones, and scrubby junipers had sprouted along the walls. The reddish sandstone of the first two stories enclosed the courtyard, topped by the gray slate of the third story and a rusted tin roof with a matrix of drainpipes and rotten window frames, where pigeons were settling for the night.

"The first time I ever came here was with Bassie about twenty-five years ago," Jim said, "—and it looked just about the same."

Meg stood looking out the window. "This may sound like a stupid question," she said, "but what exactly did Hannah do at the Montezuma?"

"You really don't know?"

"I know she was a Harvey Girl. And they were basically waitresses."

"They were women who worked in Fred Harvey's resorts and restaurants," he said. "A lot of them just wanted to come west, and if they could get a job with Fred Harvey that gave them a way to do it without losing their reputations. Working for Fred Harvey was considered a respectable job."

"Is that why Hannah came?"

"She came for the salary. But she also wanted to write about the West. It's hard to believe you lived with Bassie all those years and never read the journals. How did you pull that off?"

"I guess I just didn't do it," she said, and then added, "At one point she even tried to use them to educate me about sex."

"You've got to be kidding," Jim said.

"When I was thirteen she gave me the first couple of volumes and said I had to read them, that they would teach me about sex. This was in lieu of actually telling me about sex. I remember, as if it were yesterday. She came into my bedroom wearing a pink muumuu and dropped the journals on the bed. Apparently they have a lot of sex?"

"Not a lot, no. But what they have is pretty interesting. I would contend it's one of the reasons the journals have sold so well." He paused. "Of course, Hannah intended to publish the journals herself and take some of that out. But then the editing was left to Bassie."

"Who didn't take it out."

"Not a word of it, as far as I know."

"I wonder why Hannah put any of that in the journals in the first place."

"She was thorough. And it was part of her life."

"Yes. But why did she think her life would be of interest to the ages? Or was she basically just writing for herself?"

"Not for herself," he said. "She made that very clear. She was writing as a chronicler of her times. She wanted to leave a record of what it was like to be a woman in that era, and thought she would live to the next century and record the world's progress. Which is part of what makes it so tragic that she died when she did. So tell me, at thirteen years old, how did you resist reading the journals, if you knew they had sex in them? That wasn't an enticement?"

He had lowered the flashlight beam to the floor. "I guess I was more interested in pond water," Meg answered.

"I was in my twenties when I read them," he said. "And I wasn't more interested in pond water."

"You were interested in Elliott. Bassie told me."

"When I read the journals," he said, "it was the first time I ever felt a personal and direct connection to an individual in history."

"I have the impression that Elliott wasn't a great husband. That he was gone a lot," Meg said.

"He was gone a lot. He was restless and driven about his work. But he was in love with Hannah. Why don't you read the journals?"

"That's hard to say. I once dropped a history course at U.T. because they were required reading."

"You're pretty hard on Bassie," Jim observed. "I've seen pictures of her at your age. You look like her, you know. Mostly in the eyes."

"So I've been told. I hope I age better."

"I meant it as a compliment."

She knew he did. She had inherited Bassie's impressive height and statuesque figure and had a similar, downward slant to the outer corners of her eyes, which people seemed to find exotic. But her hair was rougher than Bassie's; and reddish like her mother's. Her skin was lighter, and prone to flushing.

"Subtract about two inches, and add a heart," she said. "I'd be the spitting image." He didn't respond to this, and she added, "Actually I don't mind the resemblance. I just don't like the idea that she's rubbed off on me."

"She's rubbed off on you, all right." He studied her. "So how has it been for you? Being with Bassie."

"She was fine on the plane. It was a little hard getting her around the airport."

"I meant in general. Growing up."

"It was okay."

"I doubt 'okay' quite captures it. What is your mother like? I've never met her."

"As different from Bassie as you can get. Do you always ask this many questions?"

"Almost never. So you lived with Bassie all through junior high and high school?"

"Except when she did field work. Then she'd send me back to Mom."

The flashlight beam was fading, and Jim shut it off. The room sank into darkness but for the last vestige of light from the window behind Meg.

"My mother's a recovering alcoholic," Meg said. "She hasn't had a drink in ten years. She's been married and divorced three times. My father was her second husband. She stole him from his first wife. Then Bassie ran him off. I was two years old when she ran him off. He died of cancer a couple of years ago. Technically, I haven't lived with Mom since I was nine." She stopped, then said, "Bassie pretty well demolished her, I guess. She was always more interested in editing than in being a mother. Mom could never compete with the journals. About the time she was supposed to be blossoming, so was Bassie's career. So she rebelled, and got married, and had me, and then became something like a flower child, and later did a lot of drugs. I think the last straw in her relationship with Bassie was when Bassie missed the rehearsal dinner for Mom's third wedding because she was on a promotional tour for some volume of the journals. Bassie didn't like the person Mom was marrying, but that wasn't the point. The point was the journals came first. Always. Someday I'm going to write a book about our family and call it 'Bassie Bass and Who She Ate.' Or 'Whom She Ate,' I guess it would be. Chapter one will be about my mother. My father probably fits in at about chapter six."

"And where do you fit in?" Jim asked.

"I don't. I'm not eaten yet." She turned to the window again, the air from outside so wet she felt the weight of it. Drizzle glistened on the tin roofs jutting out from the second story below them, and Meg could see the dark shapes of the pigeons strutting over the eaves, nestling in around the water flues and stone windowsills. The quiet was unsettling, broken only by the doleful cooing; Meg could hear no sound at all to indicate the campus and dormitories filled with students beyond the confines of the old courtyard.

"So this is the windowsill where Hannah must have put the red geraniums," Meg said.

"Excuse me?" he asked.

"I said this is where she must have put those red geraniums. I heard Bassie talk about them once." She turned briefly to look at him. "Do you remember? Hannah? And the red geraniums?"

"Oh," he said, seeming to relax and shake free of something. "Of course I remember the geraniums." He came to stand beside her, and tapped his finger on a windowpane, pointing to a stone bench in the weedy garden at the center of the courtyard. She could barely make it out; it looked forlorn in the drizzle and the near darkness. "Do you see that bench down there?" he asked. "That's where Hannah and Elliott had their first conversation."

EIGHT

Bassie was irritable with hunger by the time they drove the few miles down through the mountains to the old town square of Las Vegas and the Plaza Hotel. The town square looked to Meg like something out of an Old West movie, with the Plaza, a three-story red brick building, the most prominent structure. It was nearly seven o'clock in the evening when they pulled up in front, the drizzle turning to rain. A bellman came out to carry their suitcases in, and Martin Estes, who owned and managed the Plaza, appeared at the curb with umbrellas, saying he would take Bassie inside and send the bellman back out to park the car for Meg.

When Meg entered she was wet and uncomfortably cold, but found herself cheered instantly by the warmth of the lobby. The ceilings were high, a wide old staircase ascended around the corner at the far end, and chandeliers sprinkled light over the walls, in contrast to the depressing atmosphere and darkness of the deserted Montezuma. Meg glanced into the dining room on one side of the lobby and the bar on the other; the place had an air of grandeur that was slightly decayed but all the more authentic for it. Area rugs spanned the hardwood floors, and lace curtains were drawn open at the windows, revealing a view of the glistening street. A teenage boy wearing tennis shoes and an orange windbreaker, with earphones on his head, sat on the old-fashioned chaise longue bobbing his head to music, while a woman who appeared to be his mother searched the postcard stand beside the front desk.

The woman working at the desk told Meg that Martin Estes had taken Bassie up to a room on the second floor. She gave Meg a key to the room across the hall from Bassie's.

Meg climbed the staircase instead of waiting for the elevator to descend, then made her way down the hall and located Bassie's room. The door was open and Martin Estes was there with Bassie, telling her about a new chef he had hired for the restaurant. Martin Estes was a large, nearly bald man with a fleshy face; he paused from speaking with Bassie and introduced himself to Meg more formally than he had done in the rain outside.

"I like your hotel," Meg told him.

"I wouldn't own it if not for your grandmother," he said. "I wouldn't even be in New Mexico if not for her."

Nor would I, Meg thought.

"Martin is an honors graduate of U.T.," Bassie said, in her usual habit of praising other people to Meg. "A stock market analyst."

"And before that I was a college dropout," he said, "until Bassie got hold of me. I had run off with a girl and wasted all my savings. My parents weren't going to pay my tuition after that, so Bassie very generously offered to lend me the money. She was my history professor."

"He paid back every penny," Bassie said.

"What do you do for a living, Meg?" Martin asked her.

"Water consulting," she said.

Bassie interrupted the exchange to tell Martin that she would like to have dinner brought to the room, and Meg offered to go downstairs and give the woman at the desk a credit card imprint, as they had not officially checked in.

"I've checked you in," Martin said, moving to the windows to pull the draperies closed, shutting out sight of the town square in the rain below. "Now, what can I order for you two? We'll fix whatever you want." He went over to the phone and dialed room service.

"I want a hamburger and fries," Bassie said. "The meat well cooked."

"Juan?" he said into the phone. "We need a well-done hamburger and fries up here." He covered the receiver. "Anything to drink?"

"Hot coffee," she said. "Hot."

"Hamburger, fries, and regular coffee, very hot," he said. "Meg?"

She shook her head. "I'll get something in the restaurant later."

"Put the coffee in a Thermos," Martin said into the receiver. "Did

Silvia make flan today? Tell her we need a serving of flan, on the house. Can you do this in fifteen minutes?"

When he hung up the phone, he said to Meg, "Your room doesn't have a view like this one. But it's got new carpet. And my wife selected the wallpaper. We have a policy of decorating every room differently."

He stayed for a moment to visit, recommending that Meg try a southwestern chicken dish that was offered on the restaurant menu, then left to see that the food would be coming on time. Meg assisted Bassie in removing her shoes and peeling the snagged stockings from her legs, then helped her glide her feet into the mule-toed slippers and brought her a nightgown from the suitcase. When Bassie had got the gown on and was in bed, Meg set the suitcase on a stand in the closet and began unpacking it, hanging up the clothes. Bassie sat propped up in the bed, her looming eyes behind the fishbowl lenses of the glasses seeming disembodied from the sockets. "Do you need anything after I get you unpacked?" Meg asked.

"Just dinner. And sleep. I've got Phil the Pill to deal with tomorrow. At least Jim's on our side."

"I had the impression he was neutral," Meg observed. "In fact he told you he was."

"That's a cover. Jim doesn't disappoint me. He only disappoints himself."

Meg arranged the few items left inside the suitcase—underwear and an extra pair of stockings. "He doesn't seem disappointed," she observed.

"He is. Because he compares himself to Elliott."

Meg took Bassie's fur coat from the chair and hung it in the closet.

"His parents were killed in a car accident," Bassie said.

"You told me."

"He was with them when it happened. Six years old. He was in the backseat. His grandparents raised him after that. These are parallels."

"With Elliott, I presume."

"Elliott was six when his parents were killed. He saw them die. The same happened to Jim. He sees Elliott as a role model for how to deal with that. A father image."

"That is psychobabble, Bassie."

"It certainly is not. He was lost when I met him. I became a mother to him."

Meg let out a snort of laughter.

"He could have done worse," Bassie said.

"You think so?"

"I do fine for a mother, in a pinch," Bassie said. "As you well know. I may not be nurturing, but I tell the truth, and that's better than the wheedling and bargaining most mothers get themselves into. And while I will not drag forth your mother as Exhibit A, or you either, for that matter, I will say you are both functional people, thanks to me. You hold down jobs. You don't have much besides your jobs, but that's your own fault, not mine. Now. I have to say. The parallels between Jim and Elliott stop at the age of six. They certainly did not carry into adolescence. Elliott ran off to fight Confederates when he was fourteen, while Jim wormed his way out of Vietnam. Elliott lived; he moved around. And Jim, bless his stubborn soul, found a rock and squatted on it. He built his career on a mesa the size of a football field. And he's married to Julie. Or Judith. I can never remember that woman's name. Elliott had Hannah. Quite a difference there."

"I would hate to hear what you'd say about me behind my back," Meg said. "Jim's your friend. Isn't there anyone that you're loyal to?"

"Don't end on prepositions. And yes, there are people to whom I am loyal. You happen to be among them, though that may surprise you. I tell the truth, Meg, to your back, to your face. That's loyalty."

"Funny," Meg said, arranging Bassie's medications on the table in the corner, "I would define it differently."

"Oh, now you're mad," Bassie said accusingly.

"I am not mad."

"Then go downstairs and enjoy the restaurant. Remember that your great-grandparents used to dine there on occasion. Eat the chicken dish that Martin recommended."

"Don't tell me what to eat."

She left Bassie sitting up in the bed, awaiting her hamburger. Across the hall in her own room, Meg found her suitcase inside the door, and the lights on. The room was furnished with antiques and period pieces, the walls covered in flowered wallpaper. A reproduction gaslight fixture hung from the center of the ceiling. The ceiling was high, the bathroom small. The windows faced an alley and a brick wall.

Meg unpacked her suitcase and pulled off the damp, bulky lime-green sweater—a hand-me-down from a former boyfriend. She draped it over the shower rod in the bathroom and put on a cotton sweater instead. The room was overheated, so she found the thermostat and turned it off. Plunking herself onto the bed, she reached for the phone receiver and called Carolyn to see if any problems had occurred in the office. Carolyn assured her that Steven, the technician, had taken care of the calls. He had been to C-TECH and completed the repair work Meg had wanted him to do. Meg gave her the phone number of the Plaza, then hung up and went downstairs, feeling uncomfortably displaced.

Martin Estes was standing in the center of the lobby discussing the local football team with several men who were dressed as cowboys but who were not, in Meg's opinion, even close to the real thing. They were all hat and no cattle, as Texans would say. She had met a few cowboys over the years who were all cattle and no hat—she had even slept with one of them, at the age of eighteen, when her college roommate had invited her to visit a dude ranch outside a little town called Comfort, Texas. One of the ranch hands had been about Meg's age; he was shy and moderately good-looking, and had taught Meg how to saddle a horse and ride. They had made love on a boat dock—a rickety canoe dock, actually—one night after Meg drank too much beer. The boy was named Ben Milam after a Texas hero that Meg had never heard of. He was sweetly, and sincerely, smitten with Meg, while Meg, to her discredit, was only intoxicated on the beer and flattered by the fact that Ben appeared to like her. She was uneasy with boys because of her awkward tallness, but her insecurity had seemed to vanish for an hour under Ben's caresses, which she had to admit to herself even now had been as nurturing as the warm night air.

It was, ridiculously enough, now that she thought back on the scene, his imperfect grammar that had spoiled the evening. Meg had been unable to complete the lovemaking because of something Ben had said, some ungrammatical something that dragged her to her senses and jolted her into a train of thought involving Bassie and what Bassie would say if Meg should ever show up on her doorstep with Ben Milam in tow.

How long ago, Meg thought as she stood talking with Martin Estes and the faux cowboys in the lobby of the Plaza, how *long* ago that was. It was before she had paraded a succession of unlikely candidates in front of Bassie's critical eye in the hope of attaining her approval of one of them, and before she had paraded them for the satisfaction of attaining Bassie's disapproval. It was before she had become engaged to the egocentric Brent Biggs, or had shored up savvy enough to leave Bassie out of the mansearch altogether. And it was long before she had developed a condemning and critical eye herself.

Meg could almost wish for those old days now. In those days, she had fallen in love with almost anyone who fell in love with her. There had been a lot of heartache, but there had also been a lot of hope. Any of those men, possibly, could have turned out to be the prince. Of course, none of them had. Meg had gone through a long period of thinking the fault was in her judgment, then a period of thinking it wasn't, which had led her to the present period of not thinking much at all about it, but instead discerning very early the untenable aspects of every relationship she dipped her toe into, and consequently bailing herself out. The genesis of the problem, she suspected, had something to do with her father and his abandonment of her, but she could see no reason to go searching into those obscure crevices of childhood. She had enough to deal with in adulthood without dragging forth the buried hurts and old resentments.

Martin Estes asked if Bassie was now settled comfortably into her room, and Meg assured him that she was. He told Meg he was going to have dinner with these gentlemen—indicating the cowboys—and invited her to join them. She declined. The cowboys were flirting with her, and she was relieved when none of them followed her into the bar.

The bartender was giving out doubles, and a local bearded character with a guitar was strumming country-western songs. Meg sat by the tall windows that looked out across the street at the old town plaza. The bar was just inside the hotel entry doors, and drafts of cold air blew in whenever someone entered the hotel or left it. The place looked like an old saloon. The walls were decorated with pen drawings of adobe houses and old photographs of local people. A 1920s photograph of students from a local college, and one of Charles Lindbergh standing in front of a small airplane somewhere with mountains behind him, hung on the wall beside the window near her table. The Lindbergh photograph was signed by him, in ink that was now faded, with the inscription, "To the Plaza in Las Vegas, for its gracious hospitality."

The bar itself was long and lacquered with polish, the backer extending almost to the ceiling with bottles and glassware. Customers appeared to be a mix of hotel guests and local residents. Meg ordered a glass of Riesling. She had a theory that Riesling triggered headaches less often. The waitress was young and talkative. She disclosed to Meg that this was only her first week on the job; she was a student at the state university in town. "That picture over there on the wall is of Highlands U. in the twenties," she said. "That's my dorm room on the right."

Meg inquired if the Plaza bar was usually so crowded.

"Oh, yes," the girl told her. "There's not really anyplace else in town to go. It's really interesting here when there's ice storms. The electricity goes out in town and no one has TV, so they all come here and play guitars and sing."

The guitarist of the moment favored old Hank Williams songs, which he punctuated with a round of the Beatles' "Yellow Submarine," half the people in the bar joining in: "We all live in a yellow submarine, yellow submarine, yellow submarine . . ."

Outside, the rain was bouncing on the sidewalk and the street, illuminated by old-fashioned streetlights. There was no traffic, and Meg decided that the square probably looked very much as it had looked a hundred years ago. The gazebo in the center was empty, and Meg sat watching the rain dancing through it and thinking about Jim Layton. During the discussion in Hannah's empty bedroom at the Montezuma she had told him more about herself than she typically revealed, and now wondered why she had done so. Probably because he had asked, she decided. Not many people asked. She envied his relationship with Bassie. It had a presumption of equality.

When she had finished her wine, she went across the lobby to the restaurant and sat by the windows looking out on the same scene. The restaurant was small and had only a dozen tables, but the tall windows gave an impression of space. Martin Estes and his cowboys were seated closer to the kitchen, and Martin came over to extend another invitation to Meg to join them. She declined again, saying she intended to go to bed early, that Bassie would have her up at dawn.

After studying the menu, she ordered the southwestern chicken dish Martin had recommended, and when it arrived found it remarkably good. She listened to the two men seated at the table next to hers, discussing the weather. They had flown into Albuquerque from Los Angeles and driven to Las Vegas to photograph the campus of United World for a new brochure, but been thwarted by the weather, which they were concerned would detain them.

"Cold out there, isn't it?" one of them remarked to Meg.

"I like it," she said flatly, cutting the conversation off.

After dinner, Meg stopped briefly at the front desk to leaf through a brochure on the history of the hotel. The outlaws Doc Holliday, Billy the Kid and Big Nose Kate had stayed here, the brochure said, and "the famous diarist, Hannah Troy Bass, and her husband Elliott Bass, a noted survey engineer for the Santa Fe Railroad, spent their honeymoon night at the Plaza."

Meg was placing the brochure back on the desk when she noticed some books for sale on a low shelf partly obscured by a revolving rack of postcards. Among them, she saw, were three boxed paperback sets of Hannah's journals. Recalling the scene she had read last night in her apartment—the image of a child's hand under a pile of debris—impulsively she took one of the sets and paid the bellman, who had been left in charge of the desk. She carried her purchase upstairs. Bassie's light, she saw, was on, and the dinner tray was in the hall.

Meg went into her own room and showered and got in bed. Rain was falling in the alley outside of the window; the curtains were open, revealing a view of the brick wall opposite. Unwrapping the box from its protective shrink-wrap, she withdrew the first volume and sat looking at Hannah on the cover in her feathered hat. Then she opened the book and turned to Bassie's introduction.

These are the journals of Hannah Troy Bass, who in 1891, at the age of twenty-one, traveled from Chicago to New Mexico to earn her living. For the next ten years she depicted her life in a series of journals. Her honesty and pragmatism relieve these writings of the circumspection often found in Victorian chronicles and elevate them as a commentary on the times. Scholars of the Victorian era will find . . .

Meg grumbled to herself. The journals were a shrine. The introduction was the entry to the shrine. She dreaded entering. Flipping a few pages, she read random lines. Bassie's footnotes, clustered in small print at the bottom of each page, seemed intrusively thorough. Appended to Hannah's description of Las Vegas were several dense paragraphs of facts on the town's history, listing the businesses and mills that existed in Las Vegas when Hannah had arrived in 1891, the "wool-scouring establishments" (whatever those were, Meg thought), and "manufactories" that carbonated mineral water or made wagons and carriages. Hannah had written vaguely that "a number" of houses were for sale in Las Vegas, and Bassie had supplied the exact number, explaining that there were more houses for sale in Las Vegas in that year of 1891 than anywhere else in the territory at the time—more lawns, parks, trees, retail establishments, and factories. Hannah had observed obliquely that the industry was based on sheep, and Bassie had expounded, saying that Las Vegas at the time exceeded every other New Mexican town in the shipment of sheep, cattle, wheat, oats, hay, lumber, and pelts—everything but fruits and ore. Hannah had mentioned that the town was half "Mexican" and half "American," and Bassie had explained the origins of the terms "Neomexicano," "Anglo," "Nativo," and "Extranjero." She had dissected the population into facets of racial percentages, including two Chinese men who owned a "notions" shop. In all, what Hannah had observed, Bassie had documented. What Hannah had mentioned, Bassie had burdened with facts.

Meg thumbed through the pages, to the end of the volume, where she discovered several appendices. There were family trees for both Hannah and Elliott, showing their ancestry, and a timeline of Hannah's life from her birth in Chicago through her ten years in New Mexico, which included her employment at the Montezuma, her marriage to

Elliott, the birth of Bassie, the date of Hannah's final journal entry in November of 1900, and her death of tuberculosis, just over a year later, at the age of thirty-one. Following this was a timeline of Elliott's life, designating the places he had lived and the jobs he had held as well as the major events, including the murder of his family in the notorious Mountain Meadows Massacre when he was six years old and his marriage to Hannah in Las Vegas at the age of forty-three.

There was also a calendar of occurrences in New Mexico during the years 1891 through 1900 and biographical information on the prominent Morales family of Las Vegas, featuring several paragraphs on Vicente, who had moved to Mexico not long after Hannah's death and never returned to Las Vegas. The book ended with a map of Santa Fe Railroad trackage in 1900.

Grudgingly, Meg settled back against the pillows, returned to the introduction, and read the end of it, which concerned Elliott's ultimate, mysterious disappearance while laying track in Mexico, and Hannah's death.

> In 1900 Elliott Bass failed to return to New Mexico from a survey expedition for the Mexican Central Railroad in northern Mexico. Officials of the Mexican Central claimed he had boarded a train in Mexico City bound for Las Vegas, New Mexico, and his home at Pecos, New Mexico, but an investigation did not confirm this. No evidence of him or his belongings was ever uncovered. There was no indication he had ever boarded the train. The last people to have seen him, according to inquiries conducted by the Santa Fe and Mexican Central railroads as well as Mexican officials, were members of his survey team, who said he had started alone from camp for Mexico City two days ahead of them. It was concluded he was killed en route before reaching Mexico City, presumably by bandits. Hannah's last known journal entry was written at her home at Pecos Pueblo, where she and her daughter, Claudia, then three years old, were awaiting Elliott's return. Shortly after this entry, Hannah developed symptoms of tuberculosis and died within the year. It is probable that she continued the journal during the last year of her life, at Saint Anthony's Sanatorium for Tuberculars, but if this was the case, the writings have not been discovered.

This concluded the introduction. Meg laid the book across her knees. How typical of Bassie, she thought, to dismiss the reader so abruptly. She had demanded the reader's attention and then closed him out without so much as a sign-off.

Turning to the first of Hannah's entries, Meg found it dated July 22, 1891, when Hannah was twenty-one years old.

A smoky old oil lamp casts the shadow of my head on the page. We have electric on this train, but they have turned it off.

A smoky old oil lamp, Meg thought. What a long time ago that was. Hannah seemed as distant as Queen Victoria.

I must lean my head aside to see my writing or scribble in the shadow of my head. I have no vision of my destination but will record everything and some day will publish the account, so it will be of use. I am going to a new place and eventually a new century and I am going to write about it, and about the people. Brother would insist I am only here and owe my occupation to the fact I was not chewing on gum in the interview at the Harvey office, as was the applicant before me, but it is not so. I have more purpose than that. Brother never had a thought he doubted. At any rate, here I am, on a train that bores a tunnel through the dark, and I can only guess what is out there to the left and right of me. Not to mention out beyond ahead. We have not passed a single light in miles. It is pouring rain outside. The reason they have turned off the electric is to prevent shorting in the rain. The dark is pitch. The world seems to be closing but I know it is opening. We are still in Colorado and will travel at a stiff grade up a steep mountain and through a famous tunnel before we descend into the territory of New Mexico and arrive at our destination of Las Vegas in a few hours. The industry there is sheep. There are two other girls on this train hired to work for Mr. Harvey, but they are going to a place called Lamy, not the Montezuma. They are in the car ahead of mine, and have teamed up to go west looking as brave as Nellie Bly, wearing large plumed hats in which I know they are discomfited in these cramped conditions.

I am sleepless, restless, my feelings are uncomfortably caged. My nerves are strained, to sit so long with strangers. I should relate to them, but am impatient with their habits. One man has been spitting on the floor, I hope he is not consumptive. A woman two rows behind has a laugh three octaves amplified from normal, but she is fortunately gone to sleep. The porter is only a boy; he and almost all of the passengers are sleeping, sitting up or propped against windows, the children with their heads in their mothers' laps. The woman beside me has her head drooping nearly on my shoulder. I am seated by the window and have viewed more territory than I had thought was out here. The antelopes are graceful but not shy. They raced so close to the train this morning before the rain started, I could have touched one from the window.

We are cramped in here together and it is overly hot with the windows closed because of the rain. It is mostly women and children in here, as some of the men are still in the smoker. My pass was promised to secure a berth in one of the sleepers, but there was a confusion in the seating. This chair car is not so bad however. It is not vestibuled to keep out soot from the outrageous smokestack, but neither does it hold too much of the bad air in. Some of the travelers are packing rancid food along. I believe there are in excess of one hundred and fifty passengers on the entire train.

I see one other person in this car awake now—an old man reading a *Scribner's*. Earlier the air was agitating him by wrestling with his pages, so I suppose he is happy now that the windows are closed.

The constant sway and churning of the wheels reminds me I am moving farther off. My contract guarantees a return trip to Chicago in six months if I should wish to visit Brother. I have in my lap a copy of the second volume of *Villette* and brass plates for my luggage, and am glad for the weightiness of the plates, because they represent all I own.

The walls in here are black with soot, so I am loath to lean against the window. I can see my image in the window and can only hope I do not look as bad as I appear. A distortion in the glass elongates me into the wrong proportions, pulling my forehead too high. The oil lamp overhead illuminates my hair. Light settles on my nose. I am in need of a bath, but have brought extra cuffs and a new collar for arrival.

Closing her eyes, Meg recalled what Jim Layton had said earlier about the journals giving him his first real sense of a personal connection to someone in history. She did not feel this affinity with Hannah. The pathways into history seemed closed off. Hannah was the woman who had ruled Bassie's life, and therefore, through the tricks of time, in thousands of irritating ways, had come to rule Meg's. She was taking a train in this direction nearly a hundred years ago, and the events would file down through the linear path of time until they came to this very moment.

Meg glanced at Bassie's footnotes. She found them exasperating. They listed the Santa Fe's acquisitions of other railroads up to the date of the entry, explained that in 1891 the company had recently undergone a name change and was now called the Atchison, Topeka and Santa Fe, and told how the company had grown from an upstart fledgling and become so aggressive in buying smaller lines that stockholders were becoming nervous. One note explained the history of electricity in Santa Fe cars, another related facts about Pullman sleepers, and another described wildlife on the plains.

For a moment Meg wrestled with her grudge against Bassie. She would rather not be here, about to plunge into events that would involve a gruesome train wreck.

Nevertheless, here she was.

Stuffing her pillows down again, she settled in to read.

NINE

I have just been brought to the Montezuma, my hands continue to shake, my clothes are wet, I have been brought to a room, a parlor. I am unable to settle the images into anything I can bear to remember. The train was wrecked in a freakish accident on a flooded culvert. I have been offered tea here. A woman has come to talk to me but she is gone now. I can hear her voice in the lobby, she is telling someone what to do for me. To take me to my room, that I have no bags. To bring dry clothes. I believe she is the woman in charge of employees.

I had fallen asleep upright and was awakened by someone passing down the aisle and setting his hand on my shoulder, instructing me to brace myself for a stop. "Brace yourselves, take hold of your children," I believe is what he was saying to everyone. I recall my reflection on the window—that I could not see outside—but perceived that we were traveling downhill. I remember the screeching sound of brakes and a scatter of sparks from the rails, like fireflies. I heard the man in the aisle telling some people in the seats at the back of the car to move their children up to the center, and then he shouted for everyone to get on the floor and we did so. I could feel the wheels rolling over the joints in the track very swiftly but could not see anything. The woman beside me held on to my arm so tightly that I thought I could not get up if it were necessary. I recall her reciting a psalm against my shoulder. In a moment a rumbling noise like thunder began to roll toward us, and we were shaken and felt ourselves to be descending at a steep angle. My teeth clattered together before I managed to clench them firmly enough. The car was rocking side to side and the woman holding on to me fell into the aisle and would have dragged me with her, had I not held on to the metal bar where the seat was anchored to the floor. There was a chicken bone and some bread on the floor. We tipped from one side to another, and I thought we would go over. When I looked up I saw a travel case falling from the rack; it appeared to come down slowly. I wanted to shout a warning but could not force the sound out, or if I did, I don't remember. The case struck a man on the back of his head and knocked him down in the aisle. Immediately there was a terrible jolt that knocked my head against the wall, and a noise like an explosion. Broken glass tumbled down on us. I felt unable to breathe. The sole of a man's shoe was in front of my eyes. When the shoe was dragged out of my line of vision I could see the disarray. People began to rise up and look about them; for a brief moment, I believe, no one spoke. And then someone began to wail horribly. I was helped to my feet and my eyes were drawn in the direction of the sound, and I saw at the rear of the car a vision that will haunt me forever. The sleeper had entered the back of our car, plunging its nose through the wood as if it were parchment. The lanterns had remained lit, and by their ghastly light I saw that the seats at the back were crushed into pieces resembling a pile of driftwood. From under this, the hand of a child was reaching. Lifeless, I could see. It occurred to me that it was severed from the body. It was the mother wailing. She and the father at once began to drag at the splintered wood to reach the child. There was a flame beside me and I saw that one of the lamps had spilled its oil. The car began to fill with smoke. Smoke came in from the outside also, through the broken windows. It was black, with a strong odor. Several people were screaming that there was fire; I had to remind myself to be calm. The windows presented the only exit. Rain was coming in through windows shattered in the concussion. There was a great rush for the windows. A girl of about fifteen climbed up and took hold of the baggage rack and knocked the shards out of a broken window with the heel of her boot, then climbed out, cutting her knees and tearing her skirt. She vanished into the dark outside. In a moment I heard her calling to her mother to hand the other children out. I am not certain, but I think it was then that I noted water seeping in. It was coming through the floorboards. I realized that the girl who had gone out the window must be standing in water. The mother of this girl was frantic to get her children out but she was holding a screaming baby, so I took the baby and she got the children out. One of them was in a state of terror, and clung fiercely to her, and was difficult to disengage. A man—I believe the same who had awakened and warned us—pried the child's hands from the woman's skirts and forcibly put him out the window kicking and screaming into someone's arms. The man then went about opening windows and helping people out. The fire caught the linoleum of the ceiling and spread, causing a great panic. I saw a woman lift her skirts and remove the muslin skirt beneath it before climbing out. There was a large man who had to break the window frame with an ax that he removed from the wall before he could fit himself through the opening. I remember a woman shoving a hatbox from a window. Also a man tucking his wife's skirts around her body for modesty as she climbed out. The smoke intensified when the windows were open, and I could hear the horrible hissing of steam. I could see through the smoke and the broken shards the locomotive on its side in muddy current and surrounded by black smoke and white steam. The mother whose baby I was holding took the baby and handed her out, after which the man who had been assisting everyone showed me a window from which to make my exit. "Get out through that window," he said. "The children are all out."

And yet not the girl still buried under the nose of the sleeper. I saw her father still tearing the boards away. Her face was revealed, her eyes open, something trailing from her mouth. The man who had instructed me to exit had gone to assist the father. The mother of the dead girl had got out with her other children. I dropped to my waist in water and powerful current. My hands were cut but it was after my exit that I was aware of discomfort. The flesh was sliced in places, so that the current seemed to pull it away from the bone. When I was out of the car I could see that the other chair car was worse off than ours. It lay on its side in the water, the occupants escaping through windows on what now was the top, as if they emerged from the roof. I remember a woman with a baby running the length of it and someone shouting at her to give them the baby but she would not. The only light, I recall, was the flame light from the car that I had exited and a feverish glow from the firebox of the locomotive. Some men had come with buckets and were dousing the flames from our car. I attempted to get myself to shore but was trailing the weight of my skirts which caught on debris and nearly dragged me under water, toward the locomotive. The water was hot around the locomotive, the smoke dense. The rain was hitting my face and at times I did not know which direction to go. I could not find anything solid to get hold of, it all gave way. People were shouting above the noise of the rain. I got to the land and had to grope my way from rock to rock up to the sleepers. People were crowded at the water's edge and others were crowding into the sleepers. Many unharmed passengers attempted to stay in the sleepers for shelter. The arm of a child's nightdress was given to me at the sleeper to wrap my left hand in. My right hand was cut but did not need wrapping and so I was not useless. A doctor had taken control of the sleeper and was assisted by some women. Discovered among the cargo in the front car was a shipment of house shutters and these were employed as litters on which to carry the wounded to the sleepers. The doctor had no supplies, and I was sent with the porter to retrieve a medical bag from the baggage car that was in the water. The porter was a frightened boy, he brought along a taper and some matches so that we could search the car. The rain was still pouring on us. We were walking into the heaviest smoke, I could hear shouting from the water around the locomotive and could see a glow of fire from the firebox. The flames from our car were doused by this time, from buckets of water thrown on them, and the rain. We waded into the water and saw a sight so cruel I wonder now if I did see it. Illuminated as if for a stage by a smoky glow emitted from the door of the firebox, in a grotesque tableau, a man was trapped by the tender, which had rammed into the back of the engine cab and struck his legs, pushing him against the hot firebox and I believe nearly severing his legs. I suppose he was the fireman or the engineer. I could see him through the smoke, twisting and trying to free the lower section of his body. I cannot describe the suffering apparent in his motions, or the terrible desperation of his screams. The boy with me vomited into the water, as I suppose he knew the man. He started sloshing toward the locomotive but some other men were there trying to rescue the man by dislodging the tender, and they shouted at the boy to keep a distance because the boiler might explode. I believe I recall even the suffering man shouting to the boy to stay away. The boy was crying. I thought it horrible that the only light available to us was the source of such agony for the man—I wanted the rain to extinguish the fire and leave us in darkness, even forever, and would in that moment have chosen this could it have stopped his agony, so horribly displayed for all to see. I tried to comfort the boy but he would not have it and pushed me away, and when he had got control of himself we made our way through the current without speaking, though he was sobbing aloud, and to the baggage car that rested in flowing water higher than the boy's waist. The water level was above the bottom of the door, and we got in mostly by swimming. When we were in, the water was up to my thighs and hot, as we were downstream from the locomotive. Now and then the current shifted and brought in cooler water that gave us some relief. Most of the matches were wet but after some effort we lighted the taper. We could still hear screaming from the man, but we did not remark on this but went about our business, though the boy was crying as we did so and I found myself so sick at heart that I could hardly breathe. The water was hot enough to steam. The door was facing the current so that the water made swirling eddies over and around the luggage, some of which was completely submerged, and some which stood above the surface. Occasionally we sat on a trunk to draw our legs out of the water, but most of the time we waded about in search of the doctor's bag, also the bag of a woman named Mildred Turner. It was said to have her name on the plate and to contain sewing supplies. Some of the items from the chair car that had overturned had washed in—I remember a woman's shawl floating just under the water. The water was muddy. We had only the one taper. The doctor had described his bag for us, but there were many of that size. I believe we took half an hour to find it. We did not find the bag with a plate for Mildred Turner though we read all that we could see, perhaps a hundred plates, some on bags we hoisted up from the water and held to the taper, which was constantly in danger of going out, and often did, causing us to have to light it in the dark. My skirts floated around me and impeded movement. When we had got the bag we dragged it out of the car together so that it would not be washed away. The man who had been trapped against the firebox had ceased to scream and I believe that he was dead; I looked in that direction only once. We made our way through the current, and the boy lingered at the water's edge, and I do not know what became of him after that. I took the bag to the sleeper. I believe it was less than an hour before a dismal morning light revealed the sight of the littered banks and the train in the water. The people were sitting about helpless on the banks in the rain. For several hours we existed in the rain. The people from a nearby town brought us food, and tarps to hold over our heads. A woman gave me a biscuit. The mother of the dead child lay in a heap under a tree beside the body, and would not respond to any living person, not even her husband, whom I saw attempt to take her away. Her other children cried for her to comfort them, but she did not even look at them. Her heart and soul were with the dead.

A search continued for two people swept off in the water.

Three men were captured and cuffed to a tree for picking pockets of the wounded.

A small boy with no instinctive humanity went about collecting items spilled from the baggage car along the banks, being nearly swept away but managing to hide some valuables behind a tree while his father sat in a sleeper complaining of a backache.

At some time before noon, a rescue train came.

These are my memories, set down on paper.

Would that I could leave them here.

July 26. I have been here some days now. I am trying to set my thoughts forward but they return to that place. All the talk here is about the accident. It was the fireman who died against the firebox. From what I have since heard, it seems that the engineer had died already by the time I went to the baggage car. He was trapped in his cab, which was crushed and formed a cage from which there was no escape; it filled with water that nearly boiled from the heat of the locomotive. The brakemen and some other men chopped a hole in the exposed side of the cab but the engineer died as he was pulled forth, either from drowning or heat, as he was badly scalded by the water and by steam spewing into the area of the cab not occupied by water. The steam was from a rupture of the crown sheet of the boiler, the rupture threatened to explode the locomotive—this is the reason why the men attempting to rescue the fireman had warned the boy in my company away from the wreckage.

The railroad is said not to be at fault, though an investigation is under way. The fault appears to lie with heavy rains dragging debris against a culvert. The culvert was sound and above water flow and would have been navigable had the boards, wire, and roofing of a goat shed not lodged against it in a pileup. Reports are all in favor of the ATSF having upheld all safety standards and employed the latest braking system. After the accident flagmen planted flags and torpedoes and held their stations, up line and down, until relief was at hand. Runners were sent to the towns of Colmer and Springer, and a telegraph from Springer alerted the stationmaster in Las Vegas. The rescue train was sent from Las Vegas and the wreck train from Albuquerque.

Mrs. Simms is the woman in charge here at the Montezuma and she has told people to stop asking me about the accident but that is no use. They will not stay off the subject. I do not want to talk about it with anyone who was not there. I am trying to keep to myself except for talking with Jewell Cartwright, with whom I share a room, and have spent most of my time in the room, but have wandered about some. I am not much use because of my hands. The left is worse than the right.

July 27. I should describe the hotel. It is a gothic place. I do not know the meaning of gothic, but I believe it is a gothic place. It is several miles from the town of Las Vegas, in the mountains—wrongly described to me as hills—an oasis of refinement situated among native vegetation. The weather is cool due to the elevation, the air thin, rarefied, highly electrified. Spires and turrets rise from the walls. It sits on a hillside over a river canyon, a location chosen for the movement of the sun. A veranda runs along three sides, furnished with lounging chairs, so in winter a leisure guest can move from chair to chair and follow the sun all day, or in summer, follow the shade—though I am told it is rarely hot here even at midday. The roofline was designed to imitate the hills and mountain peaks and make the place organic to the eye. But to me it is at odds. It resembles a castle yet is not among the luscious landscape of picture books, but among huge mountainous rocks. The rocks themselves are out of scale from that to which I am accustomed. The sky seems greater, an illusion generated by the altitude. The name Montezuma comes from an Aztec emperor who is said to have journeyed up from old Mexico to bathe in the hot springs here, which are a bluish color and contain minerals curative of syphilitic, cutaneous, rheumatic, and some forms of tubercular diseases. Also gout and dyspepsia. The water is hot in some springs and cold in others.

I wish it could wash away memories.

Mrs. Simms is a small woman with a large head and pale skin but attractive. Her rules are strict. We are to bathe daily at our washstands or down the hall in a tub, but only in cold water so as not to waste the hot, except we are allowed a hot bath once a week on a basis of rotation. At all times on duty we must wear our uniforms and hairnets. No jewelry at all. I am to work six days a week, twelve hours a day in split shifts—better than domestic service in a private home, and nothing requiring kneepads. We are not to be seen sitting. The establishment cleans our uniforms—we are not to wear an item with a stain. The kitchen is equipped with modern stoves, refrigerators, steam wringers and washing machines for the laundry. We cannot fraternize with guests or Harvey employees such as waiters and bellboys. We may talk with railroad employees if we are chaperoned. If I were to find a man to marry I would have to wait a year from now, or forfeit pay and rail pass home. This rule was devised because of girls who use the Harvey ticket to go west and get married, and then quit employment without regard. For all of this, the wages are fair.

The room we share is small and excessively narrow with a view of a courtyard hung with laundry lines and a hodge-podge of utilitarian mechanisms. The several rooflines jut above and below the window in diverse configurations and pigeons strut about. Efforts have been made to stop the pigeons from nesting—there are nails hammered upwards through the ledges. But the pigeons only use these as a base on which to weave their straw.

Two beds are set against the wall on the low side of the room where the ceiling slants down, head to foot, the high side of the room crowded with two dressers side by side and the washstand. My roommate's bed is nearest the window, her dresser covered with jars and bottles of pins and rice powder, which I suppose I am to assume she wears only in private, as it is not allowed. I presume she is excessive. I believe I mentioned her name is Jewell. She is friendly and told me a great deal more than I asked to know. She has worked here for a year. Her first roommate was found out in rudeness to a guest and then shipped home; her second had a broken heart and attempted suicide by eating Rough on Rats and later was transferred to the Harvey House at Lamy. Jewell does not like her own mother, which seems impossible to me. Her family is poor. Her father died from nosebleed, his nose was bleeding for nine days, she says it was because he was a great meat-eater. She suffers from sick headaches when she sews. She has seen Fred Harvey twice, he is English by birth and noticeably nervous by nature she says. He was poor when he came to America as a child, he is quick to lose his temper, he visits his establishments incognito casting off employees with impunity when everything is not perfect. Nevertheless he is thought to be judicious. There is a Harvey establishment every 100 miles or less along the Santa Fe lines, some only boxcars but kept with the same standards—good food and no surly hash slingers. His food is considered superior, though Jewell says she is no judge of this, having never found ingredients interesting. There is a bakery on the grounds, a dairy in Las Vegas; most of the food is shipped here fresh by train and delivered by a spur train that comes up twice a day from town. Mr. Harvey serves no canned foods. This afternoon the spur delivered peaches, shellfish, sea bass and sea celery, all from Mexico. Mr. Harvey won't reduce the quality of food or size of portions even when he is losing money; he will cut his pies in quarters only. The coffee is all Costa Rican or Roasted Java in 50-pound cans. The rice is Japan rice. Jewell said the courtyard under us is often flooded as the drainage system pours the water from the roofs but has nowhere to put it. This creates a difficulty with deliveries to the kitchen, everyone wading about in slickers and rubber boots. She said Mrs. Simms plays the violin and has attended a business college, also a conservatory of elocution, and lives in a suite on the second floor, her husband being dead from influenza, and that Queen Victoria's daughter came here once and aristocrats go about swaddled in bedsheets on their way to the mud baths.

The hotel is built to accommodate eight hundred people but is never more than half occupied, usually less. It is extravagant, with a topiary garden adjacent and a zoo of native animals including a fox and a bear. The halls inside all have fireplugs and hose reels and the rooms have alarms connected to a central system. There are modern amenities and electricity that comes from a private plant over the river and is carried across in insulated wiring. The walls are fireproof, the guest rooms are large with comfortable beds, the lobby has nothing cheap like artificial ivy and is all dark polished paneling and expensive furniture, also stained glass. But people believe the place is cursed; it has burned down twice already and been rebuilt.

July 28. Jewell instructed me how to wait tables this morning. The dining room is large with tall windows and a grand piano and is crowded with three dozen round tables covered in Irish linen and set with English silver. The chandelier cost 1,500 dollars, the guests are mostly friendly and their dress is not fancy though the women do themselves up nicely in the evening. After supper the men go to the arcade in the basement, which has billiards and a bowling alley with eleven alleys, and the women go to the curiosity shop down there, or stay in the parlors and play at cards. The upper floors have sewing rooms with flowering plants and songbirds in cages.

I am supposed to go to Las Vegas tomorrow to the train station to identify my trunk. It was under water in the baggage car, as I recall seeing it there, on the floor, submerged, when we were searching the car for the medical bag. I doubt that anything in it is much good now, and would just as soon abandon it so not to revisit that night. But the railroad is taking care and has been searching the ravine for a great distance downstream to collect any items that might have survived the looters, so I suppose the least I can do is identify my trunk and relieve them of it.

It is strange here in a place so elegant but isolated in the hills. At home I had the isolation in my room, and people outside, but here I have to share the room, relating at all times, and when I venture out into the open spaces I encounter solitude and everything vast.

July 29. I awakened this morning with such a heavy dread and loathing for the task at hand that I lay in bed inventing a conversation with Mrs.

Simms in which I requested someone else to go for my things. But she had already arranged for a driver to take me in the buggy as I would have difficulty returning with my trunk on the spur.

So I left early to get it done with. The drive was ten miles into town, with decreasingly mountainous views. The route appeared new to me, as if I had not seen it before. From the ascent five days ago I remembered only how suddenly the Montezuma rose out of the hills.

There was another passenger with us— a man who wished to be reclusive. We did not bother each other with conversation, so it was not until we arrived at the train station that I realized he had also come for his bags and had been a passenger on the train. We were taken to a large room where the baggage that had lost its identification was set out in rows. The gentleman's bag and my trunk were both swelled and damaged, coated in dry mud. The lock on mine was jammed and the porters had to use a tool to get it open. One of them was impatient and wanted to send me off with the trunk unopened. I was not any help because of the bandage on my hand. When they got the trunk open, the contents were mostly ruined. The clothes were still damp and some of them had started to mildew and the books I believe will warp when they dry. They tied it closed with a rope. One of the girls in the kitchen here has kindly offered to wash the clothes and I have set the other items out to dry in the courtyard. The sun is out. We will see in a few hours how everything comes out. The bag and the book I had with me on the train are lost, though I left a description of them with one of the porters. He promised to let us know if they are found.

My relief when the trunk was loaded into our roofless buggy gave me a sense of happiness, not because I recovered my things—most of them are good as gone. But because of leaving the accident and everything about that night behind me, and having it all done with. There was a feeling of life at the station, such as I have not been able to perceive at the Montezuma as it is isolated. The station, to the contrary, is the source of all that happens here; it is the distribution point for the territory and noisy and badly aromatic. To-day it was chaotic with a herd of beefs in the pens, and about three hundred sheep. There was talk of an old mother of a jailed man who threw herself before a train yester-day in her despondency but was dragged away to safety, also of a man taken to task for growing potatoes in one of the cemeteries. A Mexican woman was suckling a child in open view, clothed in dishabille, she wore no kind of corset, but a white chemise with loose abbreviated sleeves, a negligee style. Her breast was large and made me mindful of the perfumed cream that my friend Agnes once gave me, supposed to grow the size by inches, supposed in fact to feed the tissues and make them fat and plump though it did not.

Our return was livelier than the drive down, and the driver answered a great many questions. He has lived here since the railroad came. It is the lifeblood of the town. He drove us back through an industrial area near the tracks and then through the neighborhoods. There are two parts to the town—the old and the new—divided by the river. The new, American half is closest to the depot and called New Town or East Town and is mostly industrial; buildings are under construction. There are two telephone companies. We passed a skating rink and a wall-paper store, some churches and a Hebrew Synagogue. Some of the larger houses have water piped in from a reservoir, the courthouse is imperious, the opera house will seat six hundred. Presently Japanese acrobats are performing. There are public and private schools. The driver said that a City Hall is supposed to be built and will cost $12,000. An iron bridge separates new Las Vegas from old Las Vegas where the Mexicans live; we crossed it both going and returning. In old Las Vegas the streets are hap-hazard and built around the square, the houses mud and squattish with flat roofs, the likes of which I have never seen anywhere else, and crowded wall to wall on the narrow streets with dogs wandering about. The windows fit poorly into the frames. The industry is all in New Town, but Old Town is the heart. It has two fine hotels on the square. The square is called a plaza.

Now I am back in my room at the Montezuma, about to begin my life here.

July 30. To-day I polished tableware and waited tables and purchased turquoise earrings in the arcade, though Jewell said I could buy these cheaper at the Mexican Depot in town. I went out to the archery range and tennis courts. Four large turtles in crates were unloaded from the spur, sent here by an Indian chief in Mexico under contract with a

Harvey buyer, and put on a flatbed and brought to a pool beside the river where they will live until they become steaks.

July 31. Finally went down to see the springs this morning, across the footbridge, there are forty, with a bathhouse and rooms for vapors built atop half of them. People in swimming costumes stood in the pools inhaling vapors and lay about in tubs of clay in the mud room; they have to pay a dollar for shampoo and manicure and mercurial medical treatments, three dollars for mud-packs, 75 cents for tub and vapors, 50 cents for a tub bath with no extra charge for soap and towels and help from attendants. Mist rises all the time, even in the warmth of day, and creates a heavy bad unpleasant sulfur odor.

My dreams remain frightening, often about the train. I go about the day, but nights are lonely sometimes.

August 1. Jewell has been instructing me with indian clubs to good muscular effect and telling me stories about men. She complains about restrictions at the Montezuma, but her lamentations are not bitter, instead they take the form of story-telling of her promiscuity before she came here. Her voice is nasal and unpleasant, her eyes are dark, her nose large, her face narrow. She eats condensed milk from the can by the spoonful and uses large amounts of Mum, though in general she is not particular about hygiene, and reuses sanitary rags and spends her money on perfumes but will not buy toothpaste, she uses only cheap bicarbonate of soda. I believe she would neglect to change the linens on her bed if left to impulse, and yet she is devoted to her beauty rituals and sleeps in cosmetic gloves filled with soggy oatmeal. She has seen the private parts of two men, though both occasions happened in the dark, the proximity too close for her to get a view with any good perspective. She described the size and expansion factor and where there is hair and where there is not. It is very smooth, she says. The other girls appear to like her. There are twenty of them on this floor, a few more below us. Most are friendly but immoderate. One girl named Charlotte, from Missouri, prefers cold winters to the heat, and while the elevation here keeps temperatures no higher than the 80's Fahrenheit even in the summer, she complains of heat. She carries a handkerchief soaked in lavender water, and on passing near a satin sofa must lie down on it to feel the coolness of the fabric.

Marjory Peters, two doors down, suffers digestive and sexual neurasthenia. She has been treated with electrization of various hideous types, electrodes being introduced into her private parts and the entire region of interest, though this apparently did no good. At night she employs a pocket battery with cables to administer vibrations to her skull.

My favorite of the girls is Lillian McBride, who was put to work at the age of four sorting beads in a factory sixteen hours a day. The factory owner kept the children at their work until they fainted or succumbed to sleep, at which time operation was unprofitable and he would shut the factory down until early in the morning, so the children had only a few hours sleep each night if any at all. Her father was Catholic and believed it was his privilege as the patriarch to use his children's labor as he wanted. Her eyes were nearly ruined from such close work, she wears heavy spectacles, her back is stooped, she suffers spinal pain from ovarian malfunctioning, and the tortures she endured in treatment of her ovaries have not done any good. Leeches were inserted, and one crawled up into her womb, where it was irretrievable and caused agony. The doctor injected her womb with substances including a decoction of marshmallow, and then cauterized the entry, all to no effect. He wanted to remove the ovaries but Lillian refused to let him.

Her roommate is a rude-looking girl who takes supplements of iron and calcium and fluoride and is reading a book called *Microorganisms of the Human Mouth*.

To-morrow in town there is going to be a parade of Mexican girls and a competition of horsemen pulling roosters out of the ground. A girl named Virgie is obsessed with Spanish cruelty and told me how in Mexico the horses are blindfolded and sent into the bullfight rings only to be gored to death. Of course, I have heard of dog fights just as bloody in Chicago where the Spaniards are noticeably rare. It seems to me that blood sports are driven not solely by cruelty, but by cruelty mixed with a need to be empathetic, toward the victor or the vanquished, I cannot say which, I presume it differs by the individual.

August 2. The lobby smelled of kerosene all day because the floors were being mopped. The guests complained about it. The guests are very complaining in general. Apparently I am very complaining too! Though not in general.

August 3. I am about too tired to hold a pencil and feel worse than a stewed witch. A Thomas cat is howling in the courtyard, it keeps me up, I was awakened at five o'clock this morning to work in the laundry because the women supposed to do the wash are all sick with influenza, and then we had to dust the rugs with tea leaves and salt them, I despise the hairnet, and feel unnatural being in motion when my hair is not.

August 4. A family of slobs is ensconced in the bridal suite, the girl is less than eight years old, a pretentious little snip, she ordered me to lace her shoes this morning. "Lace them, not too tight," she said, placing herself in a cushioned chair and extending her foot in my direction. I said I would lace the shoes if she would be less rude, but otherwise she could offer her foot to the wall. Her pout was furious, but she had no one of authority to turn to—her mother was not there—so she attached an "if you please," to her demands.

I spent all after-noon on the second floor cleaning the bird cages, then at dinner waited on a man with a leg made of aluminum, which is lighter and more durable than wood, also another very old man with a masticator whose wife had suction teeth.

August 5. The days are warm but not oppressive, the clouds bring rain and clean air from the mountains with the smell of damp earth and fresh evergreens. I am taking my after-noon respite now, and the cool of a thunderstorm has darkened the bedroom window. We could set our clocks by the thunderstorms that roll in from the mountains every day. In the mornings the air is so transparent if I were to live before the days of science I could not imagine air existed. It carries neither temperature nor moisture. But as the day becomes warm, insects fill the void with rhythmic chirpings, canaries light in the trees by the river and pigeons rise in flocks, circling and then lighting on the rooftops once again, and I am made increasingly aware that something unseen is inhabiting the empty spaces. Haze overcomes the hills. Then come the white clouds, borne by something other than internal industry. A cool breeze brings the musty smell of dirt and the fragrance of wild plums ripening beside the river, and I perceive from instinct, not from science, that a power is surrounding me, invisible but of astonishing intensity. The clouds grow dark. They spread across the sky as if they plan to close us in. Eventually they drop the rain, and afterwards move on, leaving the air scented with pine and wild flowers. There is a bush here called Sage, with an odor so refreshing and pungent I smell it in my sleep. The sun shines lazy yellow for a while before it drops behind the hills, and afterwards the world turns cold and purple and the birds are active in preparing for the night. I am surprised at how this landscape seeps into my thoughts. I find it more a part of them in this short time, than the buildings in Chicago ever were. One would think the more obtrusive setting would create the greatest impact, but instead it is the solitude that presses with more force.

August 6. The body of the woman who washed downstream from the wreck was discovered yester-day by an old man tending goats. She was a woman in her seventies, returning from the funeral of her sister at Raton. I now recall her getting on the train at Raton, as she was wearing black. She was seated a few rows in front of me. I don't remember how she escaped the train when the fire started—I never saw her after that.

Am I, honestly, to believe in God?

August 7. An embarrassing event happened to-day because I wore a pair of drawers with a blood stain from my periodical, in violation of the prohibition on stained clothing. I told Jewell that Mrs. Simms would never know about the drawers, and Jewell found this amusing and informed Sally Porter, who mentioned it to Mrs. Simms, who called me to her office. We sat facing each other over her desk with the American Code of Manners between us—I with a view of the hills outside and she with a view of me, and tried to assess the situation with more scrutiny than it deserved. When I told Jewell later of the trouble she had caused me, she was prostrate with remorse and lay on the bed cursing herself, at which point I had to console her. After this she hurled herself into my arms and cried that her mother had never loved her. What this had to do with anything, I am at a loss to know. I can't decide if she is loveable or too eccentric. I disliked her sobbing, and became as starchy as my uniform, uncomfortable with her emotions, they were so displayed. I think she came very close to a nervous prostration. Later, however, our conversation was normal again and she told me about an episode in the garden here, in broad daylight, in the bushes by the walkway, when a stonemason repairing the wall took his trousers off and put his tongue on her breasts. She did not remove her undergarments, except to show the breasts. She says she is a virgin but I doubt it. I suppose I should strike this entry out.

August 8. Patty M. and Lillian and I will take the early spur to town to-morrow for a sale on flouncings, summer underwear, sateens and woolen challis, all offered at great sacrifice and bedrock prices.

August 9. Burned my right hand to-day with sealing wax while pickling peaches and can hardly write. At least I am rid of the bandage on the left hand.

A company of rainmakers was on the lawn all day discharging balloons to no effect. The sad old riding mules were kept at the door from dawn to dark, but no one wanted to ride them, the weather being too hot. Some of the guests went hunting for bear and mountain lions and an old man disappeared from the group and could not be found—a party has gone out.

August 12. While I was on the veranda this after-noon serving cheese and olives, the wind came up with the smell of rain and laid the grass down flat, it was so strong. Several men hurried out and volunteered to carry in the wicker chairs. A consumptive from North Carolina, named Mr. Hodge, dragged an iron chair up the steps of the veranda, remarking sadly afterwards that he supposed he was mistaken in the effort, as the chair did not need bringing in. I said perhaps it was a sign of the improvement in his health that he was capable of bringing it, and he said No, it was a sign of his desire to impress me. He asked if I have yet been bathing in the springs, and remarked that he would like to see me in a bathing costume. I said I do not wear bathing costumes, meaning it would seem too strangely intimate to have the water flowing over a man's body in the most adjacent way and then flowing up against my own. Jeanette Millford was watching from the window, so I said I would have to go in, but he cared nothing for the rules, and asked me to stay. Jeanette has a reputation for informing. She is plump, from California, always yanking flowers from the garden by the roots to use them in her room, and speaking loudly about nothing of interest. She often exults in her own misfortunes, holding them dear by virtue of the simple common attribute that they are hers. The actual tragedies of her life she tells as if they were a piece of gossip, when in fact they horrify us all—her sister was struck dead by lightning out in California, burnt completely up, and the oldest of her brothers had a gruesome death of meningitis of the brain, his deliriums so strong the family had to tie him in his bed . . .

August 15. Mr. Hodge is on the porch or in the lobby at all times wanting to talk. Yester-day he found me in the garden cutting flowers for the tables, and tonight at a celebration in the lobby with a Mexican string band I was serving crepes and olives, and he kept eating olives just to meet me, and eventually gave me a badly written poem professing love. He is disingenuous. He knows my parents are deceased, and I believe that he perceives me as a person capable of watching death descend without a lot of flinching. Which is not the quality for which I hope to be desired. I doubt that he would go so far as to want to marry me just in hopes of getting a permanent nurse. But I do wonder about the apparent strength of feeling he has managed to develop in so brief a time.

August 17. He lay in wait for me this morning by the palm tree in the lobby. He affords me no consideration. He complimented me, which compliment was overheard by Mrs. Simms, who called me to her office. I would like to be writing something more consequential but have settled on Mr. Hodge because I am not a great thinker and he is everywhere.

August 18. No sightings of Mr. Hodge.

August 19. I saw the ubiquitous man only from a distance.

August 20. He followed me into the drawing room and said he intended to ask Brother's permission to marry me, which is perfectly unthought, as Brother is not old enough to be handing me off. He accused me of avoiding him. I said he jeopardizes my employment when he speaks to me in public. He tried to place me in the role of having wronged him, but I declined on good grounds to comply. I told him I am not inclined to marry him, because I do not have the necessary feelings of the heart. Do not speak of *love*, I said. You do not know me well enough to love me. He said indeed he did, and that my sentiments would happen by-the-by. But why? If affection were a matter of choice, why would I choose Mr. Hodge?

August 21. He hired a buggy early and is gone now. I feel a little sorry for being rude. Pity comes over me. (And yet doesn't overcome me.)

August 22. It is a month now since I arrived here, and late at night. The window is open, the lawns were mowed to-day with the Excelsior, the smell of cut grass reminds me of the times when Papa asked me to place his chair by the window so he could smell the grass. I dreamed of him again last night, though he was nothing like himself. My memories are laid to waste by the ephemeral. I wish that I could talk to him and see his sweet, distracted eye pass over me to settle on the drawing on his board. I knew his habits so entirely, his needs, the amount of spice he liked in his chutney, the amount of starch in his shirts, though I realize that he did not often make me privy to his thoughts, or his feelings much, so I would be a silly girl to say I miss the things that I have rarely caught a glimpse of. I wish my thoughts of him were not so subjugated by the illness; his decline eclipsed our years together, so that in my mind he is still lying on his bed and asking in a whisper if he might have ice.

I suppose I am uncomfortable with chilly August nights. Jewell is asleep and I am writing in bed while the lamp on the dresser lights the page and throws the shadows of the candlewicking on the spread. Insects are hurling themselves against the screen trying to get in, they fill the dark with noise, but when I go to the window and try to locate where a certain sound is coming from, I am only confounded. There are no certain places when it comes to insect noises. Even if I close my eyes and try to follow a strand, it tangles itself outside in the dark.

A breeze blows from the mountains, pressing at the curtains, and I am thinking about the draperies of my bedroom in Chicago, and that room feels so utterly distant, and yet so deeply familiar that I recall a scratch embedded on my dresser from a hairpin.

Out here among the rocks and all the summer storms I often feel exhilarated, and while I am too busily employed to use much time examining my feelings, I am constantly aware that nothing in my life is permanent these days. Out here there is a new astonishing horizon over every hill, and I am often strangely disconcerted.

I have written to Agnes and Rebecca but feel disconnected from them. We lack common themes of interest. Agnes thinks only of bicycles. Rebecca sends me recipes for layer cake.

I hope the light of morning will erase my mood and my—false?—feelings of despair.

August 23. A buyer from the Tiffany company who is here to see turquoise caves in a nearby mountain told me fantastic stories at breakfast, saying that half the mountain was cut away in the old days by old-time Indians and all the caves are haunted. At table with him was a young man who recently coasted Montezuma Hill on an Ordinary and was written of in the papers, also an Englishman from the London Zoological Garden who is studying the effect of perfumes on animals and informed me with a straight face that lions and leopards are partial to Lavender.

Jewell has fallen asleep reading the *Ladies' Home Journal*. To be so lively in the day she is a dead heap at night. We are tired out. Spent all day placing beetle-catchers in the rooms and dismantling beds to put alum and Borax in screwholes. Received a letter from Brother, who has sold the house and paid the debts and put aside six hundred and seventy-five dollars for me, not enough to depend on but more than I had hoped for. I had thought to be nostalgic but decided not to.

August 25. Seven girls are here in our room eating nuts and talking everybody over and going on about beauty, drinking vinegar to purify their skin though Mildred swears nothing will help except arsenic and the absence of electric light; she is telling me to use a borax wash or benzoin and alcohol, also to try vacuum cups or rubber hemispheres to enlarge my breasts—altogether a lot of advice I did not ask for.

Sept. 1. To-day while dusting in a bedroom I knocked a syringe from a dresser and broke it, found the woman in the garden and told her what had happened, she was forgiving but troubled. I talked to Mrs. Simms, who advised me to forget the matter. However I could not. Jewell told me that the woman is an addict and is here from Baltimore with her husband, and has suffered beatings and shock treatments at the University of Pennsylvania in the effort to escape addiction, also antidotes from charlatans, though the antidotes contained morphine and fed the very need they were supposed to overcome. Her doctor is the one who caused the addiction by prescribing medicine containing opium for her female problems; she did not know about the opium until she was dependent. She conceived a child but he was born too early and did not survive. The vial I broke was used for enemas of opium, which she prefers to needles, she has other methods also, a large supply of Dover's, also a bottle of Winslow's syrup which Jewell discovered yesterday in the dresser drawer.

Sept. 3. I feel surrounded by strangeness here and tired of company, there is no place indoors to be alone. I am social all the time and it uses me up. All day long I am encountering persons in every room; I am tired from smiling, I do not like sharing a room. Jewell is always raving about something absurd. She is obsessed with regulating her cycles and having bed rest during periodicals. This after-noon she was in fits about red stockings and French peas, having heard the stockings are toxic and imported brands of French peas have been barred from Massachusetts by the Board of Health because of artificial coloring; she has worn red stockings in the past and consumed the implicated brands of peas. She is tiresome to listen to.

Sept. 4. Jewell has been hysterical all day about ammonia, having heard it is prevalent in food. She has another headache. She had her eye on a man this week, a collector of internal revenue who is gone now. Two weeks ago she was entirely stuck on the man who invented a method of processing census returns, and before that on a writer for the *Wall Street Journal*, a lively gentleman who displayed interest but was found out to be married.

Sept 12. Minerva is sick with influenza and keeping nothing down but ginger beer, and this morning while I was with her she confided that she was married and divorced in Oklahoma Territory and has a four-year-old son living in Wyoming with her aunt. At the time of the divorce, the courts awarded her five hundred dollars from her husband on account of his abandonment of her. She is supposed to be receiving alimony payments of two hundred dollars per annum but has yet to see a dollar; he is to send it to the aunt but has skipped out and gone off to Cedar City where he has married two wives. Meanwhile Minerva is saving pennies and wants to go home as soon as her contract is done. She cries for the little boy, it was pitiful to listen to, but her employment here is respectable and she hopes to do well by him. If she is found out being married and divorced they will send her home. Last year before she came here she nursed her father through his death from dropsy of the heart, the skin on his entire body swelled and the doctor had to tape his legs to force the fluid out.

Sept 14. Jewell has had the grippe all day and is badly run down, thinks she owes it to a box of sardines. Dear Lillian has fallen in love with a man named Vance Tolliver whom she met in the lobby last week while he was discussing the shortness of the world grain markets and she was serving chocolates; he had the courtesy to thank her for the chocolates. He has bad skin and is unhandsome, but they write notes to one another. However she is apprehensive knowing she will have to tell him of the problems with her womb and that she is unable to bear children.

Sept 19. Jewell was up all night again with a sick headache, vomiting in the chamber bowl, very bad off, I stumbled on the vacuum cleaner on the stairs and nearly broke the chamber bowl going down to empty it, the noise woke Minerva and she relieved me so I could get some sleep . . .

Sept 20. I met with Mr. Tolliver beside the river this evening at Lillian's request and told him her misfortunes concerning infertility, which he took very well, though he wants to have children—he is fond of Lillian however. He is employed by the Interstate Commerce Commission in Washington D.C. compiling statistics on injured railroad workers and is going home next week but says he will come back.

TEN

Fat chance of that, Meg thought. Fat chance Mr. Tolliver will come back. Men were not that reliable. She sat thinking about her father. He had not been capable of standing up to Bassie. That had been the root of the problem. Bassie had badgered and criticized him, according to Nina at least, until he had finally walked out on the entire family. But Nina, of course, had had her own hand in the situation: Nina was only attracted to weak men.

Meg looked at the clock beside the bed. It was nearly eleven now. She should try to fall asleep, but the journals had unsettled her. The train wreck had unsettled her. She was trying to get a clearer picture of Hannah, who was—she decided—opinionated like Bassie, but not as selfish as Bassie. Meg could not imagine Bassie emptying anyone's vomit out of a chamber bowl in the middle of the night.

Meg thought of calling Paul but decided against it. He would not want to hear about the Montezuma or the journals; he wouldn't be interested. She was, Meg realized, no more authentically in love with Paul than he was with her. He was annoying to her, actually, with his jaded, careless way of tossing his opinions around. He was spoiled.

September 21. Jewell saw an advertisement in this morning's paper about a Chinaman from Denver named Lee Wing who is at The Plaza Hotel selling vegetable remedies for ailments including headaches, and got permission to go, and I was sent along. We had to wait our turn in the lobby; he had set up shop in a room on the second floor—

The second floor? Meg was jolted by the phrase, and by the odd sensation that Hannah was approaching her, that she had entered the lobby below and was starting up the stairs. She felt disoriented, as if the cluttered pathways connecting her to Hannah had been cleared and thrown open, and she could see Hannah coming down the hallway toward the very room where she sat propped against the pillow, reading in bed. It was possible that this was the very same room where the Chinese healer had set up shop. She sat staring at the door, feeling an intense nervousness. Bassie for years had been shoving the journals at Meg while Hannah had seemed indifferent, posing on the cover in her large hat. Now it seemed as if Hannah had turned full-face toward Meg, and was pursuing her.

Meg set the book aside, got up and walked to the window. The rain had ceased. She wiped the condensation from the panes and stared at the brick wall across the alley. It was illuminated by the light from her own window, her own vague shadow smeared across the bricks. Her room was quiet. She realized that her heart was thumping, and tried to be amused by her irrational apprehension. But she half expected a knock at the door.

She turned and faced the room. Except for the clock and the television, the space was probably not much different from what it was in Hannah's time. She closed her eyes and imagined the Chinese man with his vials and packets of powders spread about, and pictured Jewell and Hannah entering from the hallway in their long skirts, Jewell with a narrow face and a large nose, Hannah looking skeptical about the herbal remedies.

There was the sound of someone in the hall, a man and woman talking. They passed the door, their voices trailing away.

Meg returned to the bed and took up the journal again, skimming hastily, even defensively, over the rest of the entry about the Chinese healer in the Plaza, almost relieved to find no mention or description of the room where he was conducting his business. It could have been any room on the second floor. She felt, as she read, compelled as much by eagerness to be through with these passages, as by the interest that was beginning to settle in.

September 23. Jewell has got up a card party in our room and it is noisy in here, I have difficulty concentrating. I should join in but am irritable and have been so all day, even toward the bellmen, who were placing bets on whether or not the club of people in Connecticut who every year produce a suicide among them will be acting to-morrow, which is the usual date—last year the death was poisoning by cyanide of potash. The guests here are all sick with chills, in Turkish baths all day; one woman, a Thomsonian who believes only in botanic healing has been chewing Osha plant, she is a wild case with a turban scarf and sent the doctor away when he called to her room, and then the doctor came downstairs and bothered all of us at work by distributing pamphlets about bicycles. We are not allowed to ride them for fear that we will tip the saddle up to raise the peak and cause pressure and sensation or stoop in the humped position to enhance speed, in the posture of a scorcher, and irritate the lurid feeling—warmth generated by exertion is said to have the same effect. Then at supper it was my misfortune to be assigned a table of railroad employees who complained throughout the meal about a recent court decision that a landslide in a cut is not an act of God—whether it is or not I don't know, but I resented the cavalier attitude of these people, who have likely never been in a train that was wrecked, and seen the misery involved. I also waited on a Russian nihilist who lost his teeth in Siberia and who was the only person in whose company I felt the least bit easy.

September 27. Received a card from Brother who has been two weeks with salt to his face, the dentist broke his tooth off and his face swelled up so he couldn't close his mouth for a week, but on the eighth day he was well enough to take a walk and watch the unveiling of a bronze statue of General Grant. The widow of General Grant reviewed the concourse from a private balcony.

October 2. The weather has turned cold, rime sparkles on the grass, a washout stopped the trains down south but now the skies are clear. A stillness has set in, no less a presence than the wind. Smoke loiters in the air, I feel I am awaiting something; something in the air withholds.

The Aspens on the slopes have turned to yellow now against the evergreens, sunflowers in the valley have grown tall. I long to be outdoors. I long to write something of consequence. We received our winter uniforms from storage and have hung them on the lines to air, the courtyard smelled of camphor all day long.

Meg skipped over several pages, until an entry on October 12 seized her attention.

A haunting, gruesome incident happened to-day, an ornithologist who was here to collect a nest of eggs of Rocky Mountain birds was killed by a freakish accident. I had just served breakfast to him and to two of his friends, before it happened; they talked of how to get the nest, he was handsome and said he hoped to see me in the dining room at supper, then took his leave and went to his room for equipment and came back down on the elevator carrying ropes and wearing traction shoes and leather gloves and kneepads, and he and his friends went out and climbed the hill. I saw them from the windows of the dining room, it was a brilliant day. He got to the tree that had the nest, and tied two ropes together. The tree was tall and on a steep incline, the branches high—there was none down low to the ground. A few of us and some of the guests were watching from the windows of the dining room; he tossed the ropes up over the limb and tied them around himself and began to climb the tree. The bird on the nest flew off, but then returned, and dived downward, attempting to attack the man's eyes. He fought it off while holding on to the ropes, and secured the nest, and started down holding the nest upright as well as he was able so not to drop the eggs, though it was very large. But suddenly he lost his hold and fell. The rope secured him at his chest, but snagged on a limb so he was not able to swing back to the trunk, nor was he able to get himself free and drop to the ground. He dropped the nest, and the eggs broke on the ground. The bird flew down to them. A waiter named Tom Perkins and several men at table and I all ran out of the dining room and up the hill, where we found the man's friends at the base of the tree trying to climb the trunk, which proved to be impossible as there were no limbs near the ground and there was not another rope. They shouted to us to bring some rope, but Tom had thought of this already, and he was on his way back down the hill, taking a different route and running down a slope toward the carriage house. When the others of us arrived at the tree everyone was shouting or attempting to climb the tree while the poor man hung there with the weight of his body dragging him down and the rope slipping up higher around his chest. His arms rose in the air and he began to vomit, he could not get air. The bird attacked him, pecking at his eyes. We threw rocks at the bird but without effect, and the ornithologist was choking and his face swelled up, his eyes came to rest on mine, but I could not give any relief, as I was not an angel who could fly up to his rescue, though I surely would have done. In the end he raised his face to the sky. It was only then that one of his companions cried out for a shotgun so he could shoot the rope in two, and cursed himself and hit his head against the bottom of the tree for having thought of the solution now instead of earlier. Thought had evaded us all in the awful moments. Someone ran to the carriage house and got a gun, but then it was too late. Tom came with the rope, the gun was brought, the body was shot down. A crowd had gathered around. It is all too clear in my mind—the man's despair. I cannot stop myself from recollecting. I see him dangling from the rope. He will hang in my sight forever. A telegraph has been sent to his sister. His body will be shipped home. His mother is deceased. He was twenty-five years old, a graduate of Harvard College.

October 14. Last night I dreamed the ornithologist appeared at my window standing on a tall ladder with the pigeons on his shoulders and helping the pigeons make a nest on the sill, weaving strands of straw between the nails put there to prevent the nesting. His trouser pockets were filled with straw and he pulled out handfuls and the wind blew some away. In the dream I arose and approached the window, and when he saw me I undid the buttons of my nightshirt to reveal my breasts, and he moved as if to enter the window, but then he fell, and the noise of the fall awakened me. I arose from bed and went to the window and saw the courtyard was deserted. The clouds were vast enough to hide the stars; the air had grown cold, so I closed the window. Light was shining from the hallway through the transom over the door and Jewell was sleeping soundly with her face to the wall. I returned to bed but sleep evaded me, I was so awakened by the dream. My feelings were of a sexual nature and I lay on my back and dared to remove my undergarments and touch my thighs, then to raise my knees and spread them open with the blanket around them. The blanket shielded me, and yet the feeling was of revelation. I resisted touching inside yet perceived a fluid which I hope is not a sign of malady; I am reluctant to wonder why a man who died so horribly with me as witness should elicit such a dream as this, I fear that I have done him a disservice.

When the milk cart drove into the courtyard down below I rose to make my bed. I have never had a doctor examine me in those parts and fear something is the matter, either with the drainage or configuration, as I cannot see how the male physic could be compatible with mine. If it is true the male part becomes stiff and swells straight out from the body, then how would that part enter me unless the man is sitting straight upright on top of me? Which is not the normal way that it is done. The man lies prone on top. I have never heard of sitting. There is something that I do not understand about the way it is maneuvered. I think it is unnatural to have such overwhelming feelings in the middle of the night, precipitated by a dream and having had no stimulants, not even tea, and no flesh meat at all. I should strike this entry from the journal. Agnes said unmarried women examined with a speculum sometimes become enamored of the feeling and start to gratify themselves with the solitary vice or in the most extreme of cases ask physicians to examine them on unsubstantial grounds, only to enhance the prurient desire. Having never had a medical manipulation I cannot imagine what, but illness could create such pressing feelings.

ELEVEN

Meg closed the book, startled by the passage. These pages were powerfully strange to her; the dream was bizarre. Hannah mesmerized her in some new, dark, voyeuristic way. Her own life and her own discovery of sex, as she recalled it, seemed by comparison to Hannah's at the Montezuma to be deprived of texture. Her first sexual experience had happened when she was seventeen, in the bedroom of someone's apartment. She was drunk on salty margaritas, and afterwards had never been able to put the genie back into the bottle. Her mother had cast her adrift long before that night, and Bassie had always been too practical to tell her how to manage the emotional needs related to sex. Her adolescence had lacked the significance and naïveté of Hannah's restless night.

—The dream having commandeered the channels of my thoughts I went to Jewell for information but did not tell her my situation, but discovered all she knows, that sexual impulse comes from the base of the brain instead of from the higher convolutions, and women do not have the same propensity as men because of having fewer convolutions. They do have some propensity however in the same way that they have a part of the anatomy that corresponds but is smaller than the same part in the male. Jewell has actually engaged in the solitary vice—*in actuality and to completion*—and with the reputed paroxysm but no bad consequences. Temperance, she believes, is the only thing that matters, more than several times a year would be excessive . . .

The entry went on. Appended to it was a footnote by Bassie. "Masturbation," the footnote said, the word confronting Meg with a boldness that was disconcerting,

---

—according to pamphlets distributed by physicians and clerics of the day could result in maladies including blindness and mental illness. Women engaging in it were at risk of ovarian diseases that would cause nervousness and irritability, loss of memory, and craving of spicy foods. If a woman obtained orgasm during the time she conceived a child, the child's health would be affected. A few physicians claimed that the genitals were in need of "exercise" for health, but this theory was not generally accepted. Men were said to be at higher risk of "sexual perversion" than women due to stronger desires. Masturbation would drain a man of "life forces," as semen was a "nerve substance" forty times more valuable by weight to a man's health than blood. Devices used to halt nocturnal emissions were widely advertised in newspapers and included electrical alarms triggered by erection, and sheaths for the penis, with spikes that lay flat until the moment of erection. A wooden egg was inserted in the rectum to direct seminal fluid upward in the body and prevent it from escaping. Men secured cords around their penises to prevent ejaculation, though one physician observed that this was "about as useful as trying to prevent a man from vomiting by compressing the throat." Tying the hands to the bedpost was an easier and less expensive remedy. In cases deemed to be extreme, physicians cauterized the urethra and prescribed medications such as squills and digitalis. They administered electric shock and blisterings and attached leeches to the penis to relieve congestion.

In spite of these prescribed treatments and religious views, most Americans were free of sexual neurosis. They discussed sexual mechanisms more openly than is commonly thought. During the same week in which Hannah composed the noted entry, *The Las Vegas Optic* advertised "Dr. Dye's Volcanic Belt," describing it as "an electric suspensory appliance for diseases of personal nature caused by abuses."

Meg disliked the footnote. In her opinion, Bassie's decision to include this particular journal entry was selfish, as Hannah obviously had thought of deleting it, and almost certainly would have done so had she been the one to edit and publish the volumes as she intended. Instead, Bassie had taken Hannah's sensual and whimsical curiosity and flattened it into a clinical explanation. Far from giving it a broader context, she had made it seem irrelevant and antiquated.

She would forgo these footnotes in the future, Meg told herself, and continued reading, settling on a visit that Hannah and Jewell paid to a fortune-teller on Jewell's "natal day."

October 18 . . . our time being circumspect we went directly to the house, where we found a number of children and dogs out playing in the yard and entered through a swinging gate. The air was nicely cool and the sun lay weightlessly, so bright it made the black hair of the children glisten white on top. The porch was strung with garlic and dried peppers and the door was open; a girl came out to greet us but did not speak English. We displayed our palms to show the reason we had come, and she went into the house and returned with the fortune teller, who greeted us in Spanish. Her hair was gray and her skin dark. She had not lightened her skin with chalk as many of the women here do. She brought us in, indicating that we were to sit. The chairs were cow hide, the room dark and smoky with a pleasant fragrance, the walls made of mud that was painted blue, the ceiling comprised of dried branches and sitting low over our heads. The floor was dirt but swept, and along the wall under the window was a bench of dry mud covered in blankets. There was a mirror made from a pane of window glass backed by a black shawl, and also religious paintings on the wall. We sat as instructed, and she turned and left us, departing through a doorway to the back of the house. The smell of roasting garlic drifted from behind the house and blended pleasantly with the aromatic scent of cedar twigs and berries smoldering in an earthen bowl on a high table in the center of the room.

The children were watching us from the doorway and the windows, their shapes dark against the sunlight. The fortune-teller returned with a young boy about ten years of age who greeted us in English, telling us the fortunes would cost a dollar each. Jewell told him we had been informed that they would cost ten cents, and the boy then said "fifty." We agreed reluctantly, as it was more than we had meant to spend. His demeanor was commanding but sincere. He said that one of us should wait, the other was to follow the woman, whom we now understood to be his grandmother, into the back of the house. Jewell went in first, and the boy remained with me. His name was Anthony. He showed me a piece of furniture with rows of minute drawers filled with tools and paints and chalks, and said his uncle was a maker of "Santos,"—"bultos," they are also called—saints made out of wood. The Mexicans pray to these. Two saints in progress lay unfinished on the table, one was only several inches tall but the other, Saint John with his cruciform staff, was more than a foot high when held upright. Saint John was yet unclothed and his torso merely a block of wood but the arms and legs were well-defined and attached by sockets. Paints were spread across the table in small pots, and there was also a bowl of sand as soft as flour which the boy explained would be mixed with the paints to make them shine. He said human hair is often pasted on the Santos, but his uncle chooses to rely on God's artistry passed through his own hand rather than to cut a piece from God's creation and sell it as his own—Therefore Saint John's hair was carved from the wood and painted. The face was delicate and long, with features made intricate down to the nostrils in the nose and a small black beard. The eyes seemed to perceive me. The robes, Anthony said, would be made of cloth soaked in a wash and molded on while wet, then painted when they dried, and the saint would be made to kneel. Anthony got on his knees to show me this, not knowing the word for kneel. I was taken with the notion of how strange it is to carve the joints so perfectly and then to clothe the saint in fabric that would harden him in place so he can never get up off his knees. It reminded me of how my starchy uniform and hairnet do the same as that, and a strange sensation came to me, the hairs rose on my arms and I felt an unfamiliar elevation of my spirit, as if I could transcend my situation at the Montezuma and discover freedoms I have not contemplated. I do not know what freedoms I envisioned—I perceived them more than thought them—they were sensations, not images. Anthony then went outside and I was left alone, watching from the window the children tossing stones in a circle they had drawn in the dirt in the yard. In a moment Anthony returned from down the street, with a large pot of red geraniums. When he entered the house he was shy of me and gave me the geraniums. He told me they were from his home and he had spent the day before taking them out of the garden and putting them in pots for winter. He said if I were to place them by a window they would turn and press against the panes, and said it is a magic thing they do. Then he went to the back part of the house and I heard the fortune-teller greet him, and after a while I heard him translating Jewell's fortune though I did not hear what he said.

When Jewell was brought out I was taken into the room and told to sit opposite the fortune-teller. Anthony sat beside her to translate. The room was lighted by a wick sitting in a tin of oil emitting a bad odor. The window was sheathed with a blanket. The fortune-teller took my hand and studied it before she spoke. Her eyes were fierce, her manner disconcerting. The fortune she predicted was so sorrowful I told myself to disbelieve it, but could not dismiss her statements until I got myself out in the sun again. Her predictions were not firm, but oblique—that my happiness will collapse into ruins, my health will be bad, my heart will be broken. "Is there nothing good?" I asked her, and she replied in Spanish, which the boy translated, "one is the maker of his own destiny."

Jewell was eager to recite her fortune afterwards, and in my own opinion she has not done anything to deserve a life as good as was predicted. The fortune-teller had discerned her character by the shape of her hands and length of her fingers, also by the way her thumbs are prone to bend—I have never heard of telling personalities by finger length and if the fortune-teller were not accurate in her assessments I would have thought she was a charlatan. But her description was correct, that Jewell is moody and impulsive with a long index finger that connotes a fickle character. The ridges on her nails are vertical which means that she is prone to agitation. A flat area on her palm shows a nature lacking in resolve. Yet the line that corresponds with luck is long and deep. This must explain why she will do so well, as her happiness cannot be based on diligence or wisdom in my own opinion. She related her fortune with no mention of the line that corresponds with intellectuality, so I suppose that it was neither long nor visibly entrenched. She believed the criticisms had been compliments, which proves the fortune-teller was correct that she is flexible—as shown by the bend in her joints but also, I think, by the perversity of her excitement in the diagnosis. It is not a character depiction I would welcome. The fortune-teller may be right in many things, but I cannot believe Jewell's palm has very much to do with it: anyone could look at Jewell and know these things about her.

Now there, Meg thought, was another glimpse at the origin of Bassie's critical nature—Hannah's assessment was so like one that Bassie would make. Jewell was the perfect foil for Hannah. She was ridiculous at times, and neurotic. But Hannah had flaws of her own.

Meg read a little further. Hannah returned to the Montezuma and placed the pot of red geraniums on the windowsill. A puppy was killed in the rungs of the "mowing machine." A Canadian who argued that Canada should be allowed to ship produce duty-free to the U.S. but charge duty on shipments from the U.S. was "knocked down" in the lobby. A guest in the hotel, a Boston woman who Hannah claimed believed in "everything Emersonian, and everything occult," and who looked the part, in a turban scarf and gold-rimmed glasses, was trapped in the elevator near the second floor for nearly a day. A few days later, employees of the hotel started to anticipate the arrival of Fred Harvey at the Montezuma.

October 28. Mrs. Simms asked me this evening to remove the flowers from the windowsill so Mr. Harvey would not think we had made the place into a Mexican hotel. "Because of flowers?" I inquired. She said that only Mexicans have red geraniums, to which I told her I had thought that Mr. Harvey had a reputation for admiring the culture, as he makes a point of serving local foods, to which she said that Mr. Harvey is not in the habit of consulting the whims of employees about his décor. She was nervous in the face of my dumbfounded silence, and the falling nature of her aspect only fueled my resolve, so that I told her the flowers were a gift to me and that I was reluctant to remove them unless

Mr. Harvey should ask me to, himself. I then went to my room, but feared she would send up for me, and decided I should go outside to be alone rather than remain in the room and await my fate. Jewell told me I would lose my occupation if I dared to go alone, but I did not, at that moment, care, and promised her that I would sit on the bench in the courtyard and she could summon me from the window if Mrs. Simms should come.

The lobby was quiet, a woman in the music room was singing Finiculi, Fanicula! at the piano, Andrew had closed the desk, the time was quarter past eleven. I went outside and took the path around, and saw that someone had erected an elaborate croquet course on the lawn below. It was made of an extraordinary number of wickets and extended over both lawns and the archery range. The wickets were illuminated with candles and the place looked like a fairyland. I noticed the players' liberty of sentiment and stood a while watching from the avenue, my vantage being elevated and affording me a view. A stout breeze swept the voices up to me with exquisite clarity; one man told a story of a fainting sheep dog. When the story ended and the game ended and the players started snuffing out the candles, I continued around the building to the courtyard and sat on the bench looking up at my window. My mood had resumed its former chaos and resentment; my emotions jangled. The air was biting cold, having come across the mountains and the caps of snow. I had worn my wrap, which concealed my uniform, so I was not afraid of being recognized if someone saw me from the windows. Some of the girls were still awake, I saw them in their windows and a few of the guests moving about in the windows on the far wings. The roofline blocked the moon, the stars were vivid and the courtyard was empty, and though I was surrounded by the people in the rooms, I felt as if I were alone with the walls looming around me, and could not decide if I was apprehensive or exhilarated to be outside breaking all the rules. The pot of geraniums sat in my window in silhouette with the light from inside shining on their petals in patches of red, reminding me of how I used to feel while standing on the walkway outside of our home in Chicago seeing no more than the brick façade of our house while knowing every corner inside—all the places where the cobwebs liked to gather.

And so I sat a while, strangely disconcerted, strangely happy, wanting one of the dogs to come around from the carriage house and keep me company. After a while, a man wearing an overcoat approached from the avenue and said he had seen me enter the courtyard earlier, he knew the back doors to be locked and wondered if I was in need. I recognized his voice as that of the man from the croquet lawn who had spoken of the fainting dog. I assured him I was not in need of any assistance, yet instead of leaving, he sat beside me on the bench. He removed his hat and placed it on the bench between us, and put his hands behind his head and looked up, as if he were looking at the stars above the roofline and listening to the pigeons.

"There are a lot of stars tonight," I said.

"I was looking at the flowers in that window," he replied.

The comment startled me, pertaining, as it did, to the very subject pressing to my mind. "They are my flowers," I told him.

"Then that is your window?" he asked.

"It is."

"Do you work here, then?" he asked, and I replied that I did, though possibly not for long.

"Why not for long?"

"Because of the geraniums," I answered, allowing the statement to end at that, knowing it to be too cryptic for civility but fostering my daring attitude because it seemed the only thing to hold on to, not having much left in the realm of security.

He drew one boot across his knee, and asked me why geraniums should cost me my employment, and I said I had been told to take them down because they were Mexican flowers and Mr. Harvey was expected for a visit. While I said this, it occurred to me that this man could, for all I knew, be Mr. Harvey in the flesh, so I explained that Mrs. Simms had not said unequivocally that Mr. Harvey would dislike the flowers, but had rather asked that I remove them in the case he might.

"I wouldn't take them down if I were you," the man declared—not having any hint of British accent, as I guessed Fred Harvey would, and not seeming to be Fred Harvey, whom Jewell had described as having a nervous nature and being tall. This man was not tall, and had a manner about him that no man who cared about a chip in chinaware would have.

"Even if your job depended on it?" I inquired.

"My dear," he said, "it is an asinine request, to take a pot of flowers off a windowsill."

These words gave me the quietus I had been searching for in solitude and the night air. I felt as if a mandate had been given in my favor.

"You are not Fred Harvey, are you?" I was yet compelled to ask, at which he laughed so loudly that I thought he would awaken someone. "God no," he said.

"And why is that so funny?"

"I don't suppose it is," he said, upon reflection. "Unless you know Fred Harvey."

"Unless you know Fred Harvey, and know you," I said.

"Yes, that would make it even more so," he admitted.

"I take it, that you know him?" I suggested.

"Quite well, in fact," he said.

"So then, in your opinion, would he be the sort of man who would dislike geraniums on a windowsill? My future could depend on your answer."

"I know nothing of Fred Harvey's attitude about geraniums," he said. "Will you take them down if he requires it?"

I said I was uncertain what my course would be.

"Do you have a special reason not to take them down?" he asked. "Other than the frothy nature of the request?"

"They were a gift to me," I said.

"From someone whom you care about," he answered.

"From a boy in town," I told him.

"Ah. Well. What size of boy?" he asked.

"No higher than your chest," I said.

"Well, then," he said. "My vote is, pro geranium."

And I said, "then they stay." I regretted this as soon as I had said it, having, without thought, committed myself to forfeiting my occupation for a principle that showed a stubbornness of character. Here I was at almost midnight, in the cold, seated beside a stranger and having just committed my employment to a pot of geraniums. I said I should be going in, that it was late. He looked to his watch and said it was a quarter after midnight. He stood and put his hat on, and offered me his arm. He was facing me, the light from the windows shone on his face, and I felt a surge of recognition.

"You were on the train," I said.

He became serious, understanding my meaning. He looked to my hands, and when he noted the scars he said, "And you, my dear, were holding the baby." He sat again on the bench beside me. We said nothing, and then I said, "Have you made peace with it? I have not." He did not answer immediately but then said, "I suppose I don't hold peace in very high regard."

"But do you find it possible to achieve?" I asked.

"I believe I find it dull," he said.

"No doubt the people who lost their lives would have given you something for it," I suggested.

He didn't deny it. "Nevertheless, if we were all to find peace," he said, "we would sit in rocking chairs all day. And there would be no progress."

But I am not in the habit of perceiving emotions in terms of their usefulness, and still wanted to come to an understanding of the events, and felt myself in good hands with this man, who introduced himself as Elliott Bass. So we talked of the wreck and how it occurred. It appears to me from what he said, though he is modest, that the number of fatalities unquestionably would have been greater if Mr. Bass had not been on the train. He is the individual who many years ago surveyed the route on which the train was traveling, and mapped where the culverts were installed, and knowing the danger of flooding as we crossed over the initial prong of a forked ravine, he took a lantern to the rear of the smoker and saw the depth of water, the amount of mud sweeping along implying a significant disturbance of soil, and the ominous sign of a portion of the tin roof of a goat shed from upstream being swept along in the muddy flow. From these indications he deduced that heavier portions of the shed would have swept through a wider ravine that had yet to be crossed, and so signaled the engineer to slow the train. But trackage between the two ravines was less than seven hundred feet, and of continuous downgrade, and so there was too little time before the second culvert was reached. While the conductor called for "down brakes," Mr. Bass passed through the train warning occupants of the danger. It was he who woke me from my sleep and he who assisted in the evacuation of passengers when our coach caught fire. He was also with the several men who tried to free the fireman trapped between the firebox and the tender. He knew this man—Joe Gilcrease, he called him—and seemed to have thought a great deal of his reputation and his commitment to his work; he was supporting a large family. He said that Mr. Gilcrease showed a great deal of courage and to the end kept up communication with him and the others attempting to release him, about the danger presented by the ruptured boiler and about the best method in which to try to remove the tender from his legs.

Our conversation restored my memory of that scene to vivid detail, and yet somehow the vision did not trouble me as much as previously. I found the pragmatism of Mr. Bass to be comforting. When I inquired how he knew Mr. Harvey, he said that Fred Harvey sometimes asks for his advice on locations for new establishments and in return offers room and board, free of charge, at his hotels. While we spoke I judged him to be in his early forties, shorter than I when we finally stood but not unpleasant to look at. He has a gap between his teeth.

As we walked around the building to the entrance, he whistled for a dog that came from nowhere, a ratty looking individual of minute build, with short legs, large ears, and a pointed face with prominent eyes. It ran around our heels and tangled itself in my skirts. When we reached the avenue and I asked about the elaborate design of the croquet game, Mr. Bass said he had designed the course, being interested in measurements and liking to knock croquet balls about. We talked of this, and of the recent strictures on croquet and the Boston city leaders who are threatening to ban it. He holds the flat opinion that the moral opposition is drummed up solely by religious people. He does not mind having a woman croquet him, he said, does not consider it emasculating and does not think progress on the court symbolic of pursuit—"that is laughable," he said. But even while we spoke about these superficial topics my mind was in the ravine at the scene of the train wreck. I found myself able to look on those terrible images for the first time without great discomfort.

When we came to the door he asked me to travel with him in the morning to the ice ponds up above the springs. There are nine ponds, which he conceived himself and engineered several years ago; they freeze in winter and the ice is cut and sent down on the spur to the depot for use in refrigerated freight cars. He said the Santa Fe uses twenty thousand dollars worth each year on the main line. His purpose tomorrow is to check the dams. He said he would talk to Mrs. Simms and get approval for me to go—and no matter about the geraniums, he said, as he could smooth over the problem.

I came to the room, and Jewell said she had seen us from the window. She said Cecile McGaffin will be jealous. Cecile is infatuated with Mr. Bass because he once gave her a large indulgent tip when she took his boots to be shined. "*Over* large," Cecile has said about the tip, convinced that he had noticed her, but afterwards he gave no indication he remembered her. Cecile, however, is convinced he does remember her, and that he needs her—though in fact, it seems he needs no one and is only friendly to her, nothing more, and the situation has continued with Cecile living on her hope and chatter, building him into a legend with the girls, always talking up his attributes and what a string of tragedies he has suffered, beginning in his childhood when his family was murdered by Mormons at Utah in the infamous wagon train massacre.

On impulse Meg got out of bed, and got into her jeans and pulled her lime-green sweater on. She put her boots on, and took her jacket and purse, and left the room quietly.

The bar downstairs was open, though it was nearly empty. The restaurant was dark.

Meg left through the front doors; the wind confronted her. She buttoned her jacket and followed the wet sidewalk around to where the car was parked. The clouds were low; now and then the sky revealed a few stars.

Leaving the parking lot, she turned the car onto the road toward the Montezuma. The paving was marred with potholes filled with standing water. She passed a convenience store and a deserted strip mall, noting from the clock on the dashboard that the time was nearly one in the morning. The car radio was on, and she turned it off and drove in silence. Buildings became less numerous, darkness closed in, the road diminished and began to wind up through the hills.

Crossing the river and reaching the college campus, she pulled into the place where she had parked in the afternoon, got out and started up the footpath through the trees. A few lights burned in the dormitory and in the classroom buildings, but the Montezuma was dark, its turrets rising against the gusting clouds.

Breaking from the trees, Meg skirted the veranda and passed the entry to the lobby. The windows of the lobby and the dining room were inscrutable with darkness, and Meg made her way around the corner of the dining room and looked up at the hill on which the ornithologist had died. It was dark now, with evergreens and rocks, the face was steep, tall pine trees clung precariously. Meg could see how someone dangling from a rope from the outside branches of any of the pine trees could be so high above the ground that there would be no chance of rescue. She thought of Hannah running up the hill, and wondered why Hannah had done so. If her account of the scene was complete, then she was the only woman who left the dining room and witnessed the death up close. The ornithologist had chosen her to look to. What was it he had seen in her when she waited on him at the breakfast table or while she watched him dangling from the tree, that had caused him, in his last moments, to settle his eyes on hers?

Meg turned away from the hill and continued around the sandstone walls of the building, until she came to the courtyard.

The dark was more oppressive here, the cold seemed more harsh. The walls of the courtyard shut her in, the pigeons were silent, and the wind was kept at bay.

The old stone bench was there in the center of the courtyard, surrounded by a weed-infested plot of earth. Meg sat on the bench, thinking of Elliott and Hannah seated here. She looked at Hannah's window on the second floor with the single broken windowpane under the eave. It was dark and depressingly empty. She thought of Hannah in the narrow bed, wrestling with the sexual feelings from the dream about the ornithologist, and waiting for the milk cart to arrive. She imagined the dressers shoved against one wall and the beds on the opposite wall, fitted lengthwise foot to head where the eave dropped down. The more she studied the window, the more it began to seem like a window to the past, and knowing how the room was now, as she and Jim had seen it, without furniture, the floor littered with trash, did not ruin the clarity of Hannah's description from a hundred years ago: instead it strengthened it. The present was the paler image. The present was deprived of color, compared to the past.

Meg left the courtyard, circling the building and taking the path back down to where the car was parked. She felt displaced, dissatisfied with her life. She had somehow found a connection with Hannah, the pathways were open now, but she was not sure that she would ever be the better for it. She had spent her life under Bassie's shadow, and now Hannah's shadow was creeping over her also.

She got into the car and drove the ten miles back to the Plaza.

Less than an hour had passed. She went to her room and stripped her jeans and sweater off, leaving on the T-shirt, and pulled on her pajama pants and got in bed, wrestling the blankets over herself.

Half an hour later she was still awake. The journal was drawing her back. She sat up and turned the bedside light on, taking the book in her hands. Hannah was gazing past her from the cover.

TWELVE

As Meg eased the car's hood into the shaggy branches of junipers bordering the parking lot at Pecos Pueblo the following morning, Bassie was criticizing the ratty condition of Meg's sweater. It was the same one she had worn yesterday, lime-green, the hem hanging out from under her corduroy jacket. She was, she knew, not a fastidious dresser for someone who craved order in other areas. Inconsistency was a family trait: Bassie let the black hairs on her chin grow long while plucking her scanty eyebrows and drawing domes in their places with an eyebrow pencil.

Meg got out of the car and went around to help Bassie out. She was dragging Bassie's purse, which was patent leather and as large as a suitcase, off the floorboard when Jim came out of the center.

"Has the crew arrived yet?" Bassie snapped at him.

"Only Tony," he said. "The rest usually get here around eight-thirty."

"Not a very tight ship you're running," Bassie remarked. "Where's Phil?"

"Not here yet. Good morning, Meg."

"Good morning."

"Is he avoiding me?"

"Not that I know of. He never gets here before eight-thirty."

Meg had not given much attention to the visitors' center yesterday when she had hurried through it, and looking around now, as she entered with Bassie and Jim, found it pleasant and functional, with plate glass windows on either side of the double doors of the entryway admitting swaths of morning sunlight. A park ranger seated at the front desk stood as Bassie entered.

"Hello, Dr. Bass," he said. "I'm David Valdez."

"I know who you are," she answered him. "How is your nephew doing?"

"Well, that's a story," he answered with obvious reluctance. "I'll tell you sometime."

"Tell me now."

"He quit school for a while," the man admitted.

"Dropped out," she observed.

"Not permanently, I don't believe," he said.

"Well, I should hope it won't be permanent. I went to a great deal of trouble to get him into that school. What happened? Why wasn't I told?"

Wanting nothing to do with this exchange, Meg stepped into the exhibition room, which was still dark. Jim followed her and flipped the light switch on, making the room disarmingly bright, the exhibits of pottery and other artifacts illuminated in display cases. A linear time line spanning one wall depicted the dates of historical events that had taken place at Pecos.

"Poor guy," Meg said to Jim, referring to the ranger.

"He takes his chances with the rest of us," Jim said.

"She's mean as a snake," Meg said.

"Always has been," he replied philosophically.

"But especially this morning."

"I was hoping to get some work done on the hill before you got here," Jim said. "But something came up with my son, and I just got here myself."

"Is your son all right?"

"He is now. He's a science aide and didn't want to feed live mice to the snakes. He wanted me to talk to his teacher and see if she would let him off the hook."

"Did she?"

"She did."

"He sounds like a good boy," Meg said.

"He's a sweet boy. Not motivated academically. But he'll make his way."

"I met Hannah last night," Meg offered.

Jim raised his brows. "You're reading the journals?"

"I know; I'm surprised too. It was an impulse buy in the hotel. I didn't have anything else to read."

"And I guess they were the only books for sale?" he asked, looking amused, and when she didn't answer, he added, "How far did you get?"

"To where Hannah meets Elliott. I skimmed some."

"So you survived the train wreck."

"Yes." She turned to a glass case displaying an assortment of artifacts carved out of bone, and studied an object labeled as a flute made from an eagle's tibia. Jim was looking at her. "What?" she finally asked him, but before he answered she was aware of a draft of air and heard someone enter the reception area.

Jim turned to see who it was. "Here we go," he said quietly. "Phil's here early."

They stepped into the reception room, and Meg saw that Bassie had ceased to lecture David Valdez about his nephew and positioned herself in front of a rack of postcards. "Hello, Phil," she said to a man standing in a patch of sunlight near the entry door.

"Hello, Claudia."

"I don't like your plans."

"Jim told me."

"You tried to hide them from me."

"Yes, and I wish Jim hadn't decided to tell you about them."

"Belatedly. But that's beside the point. The point is, I want my mother's dogs. This is my granddaughter. Meg Mabry."

Phil came forward and shook Meg's hand, looking bored and making a few inane comments about how kind it was for Meg to bring her grandmother to New Mexico. His chin, Meg noticed, tapered unattractively and the bottom teeth seemed too small for the top ones. His eyes were a pale green, his white hair cut in a stiff crew. Something about him, Meg decided, either his looks or his attitude, was inherently off-putting; she could see why Bassie didn't like him. His mouth turned downward at the corners; his eyes had a jaded expression.

Bassie, by glaring contrast, was rigid with intensity. She was dressed in solid black, draped in the mothy fur coat, her eyes glinting behind the smudged glasses.

Phil attempted to inject a few pleasantries, mentioning the weather and what it had been like when Bassie was last at Pecos, with snow on the ground in April. Then he said, "I guess Jim told you that the project is already under way. We have permission from the Native Americans, as long as we stop digging if we come across any tribal remains."

"I guess he told you that I've come to get the bones?"

"As ridiculous as that is," Phil said. He cleared his throat. "Actually, the Native Americans are very excited about this project. The room is going to house their ancestors' artifacts that have been in storage for decades." He was, Meg realized, addressing this explanation to her. "A lot of the artifacts were discovered by Alfred Kidder, who was a famous archaeologist who did some early excavations out here. And as a matter of fact, the people who live in Pecos—the town—are pretty happy about the plans too, because a lot of the artifacts are Spanish and probably came from their ancestors."

"We know what the artifacts are," Bassie said. "Stop beating around the bush, and tell me your plans for the bones."

"Well, I don't exactly know yet," Phil said. "They don't belong to me. I can't just hand them over to you without a lot of legal issues coming up."

"Then I'll talk to the press about it, and see what they have to say."

"If you do that, I'll close off that whole area to you and everybody else."

"Oh, do it, Phil," she said mockingly. "I would love to pose for photographs with the barricades behind me and my little caskets at my feet."

"Your caskets?"

"My little dog caskets. For the bones."

"You didn't bring any caskets." He seemed alarmed by the idea.

"But I would," she said.

"That's ludicrous," he answered, his voice rising. "What in the world do you want with those dog bones, Claudia?"

"I intend to take them home and bury them in my backyard. What do you want with them, Phil? To put them on display? A hundred-year-old canine femur on display beside a fourteenth-century biscuit-A bowl?"

"They're government property. Everything buried here is government property."

"Oh, for God's sake, Phil. I helped to write that law. Don't go citing it to me. I don't expect to own the bones. I'm going to take them out on loan."

"On what? Are you crazy? You can't take them on loan. Just the paperwork for that, aside from the moral issues—"

"Let me put it this way. Either you can give me the bones, or I'll get the press out here."

"You know damn well what kind of trouble that would cause me. All hell would break loose."

"You bet."

He studied her. "You're going to look foolish if you pursue this," he said at last.

"Nobody cares if I look foolish. They care about my mother, and her diaries. They care if you people out here are cavalier with your attitudes."

"We're not shovel-happy, if that's what you mean." Meg could see that he was losing his temper. Bassie had put her toe on sacred territory: she was threatening his job.

"A matter of opinion," Bassie answered.

David Valdez behind the desk was attempting to appear as if he were not listening to the conversation. He lifted the receiver of the telephone and made a call concerning the price of a history book on something he referred to as the Pecos Land Grant, tinkering as he did so with a screwdriver and the hinge of a cabinet behind the desk.

"Claudia," Phil Barker said, "we've known each other a long time. What are you doing, really? You don't care about those graves. You don't even like dogs."

"I care about my memories, Phil. I'm old. When Mother buried those dogs, she dug deep enough to keep coyotes out. She piled the dirt high enough to keep the ground from sinking. The only thing she didn't figure on was you coming along and erecting a room on top. If that is your intention, I want the bones."

"What if, just say," he offered after a moment, "for the sake of argument, I agree to give them to you. Would you keep the press out of here?"

"I don't control the press."

"But would you summon them?"

"Not if I have the bones."

David Valdez ended his phone call and hung up.

Jim said, "Is that an agreement then, between you two?"

"It's unreasonable," Phil said.

"As far as I'm concerned, it's an agreement," Bassie said.

Jim turned to Phil. "It's fair," he told him.

Phil drew his mouth into a grimace, considering. "It probably would be okay," he said at last. "But I can't promise. It might get out of my hands. I'll do what I can."

"All right, then," Bassie said. "If you want to put it that way, to save face. But if your part of the agreement doesn't work out, mine won't either. That's a promise."

"Claudia, if you would just— "

"Leave it alone, Phil," Jim said.

Phil appeared to be making an effort to do that. "You probably want to go up there and look around," he told Bassie grudgingly.

She turned and began plunking her way along to the back door. "Come with me, Meg," she said.

Jim moved to open the door for them, and followed them out.

"Where are the prints?" Phil was asking impatiently, and Meg turned back to see David Valdez fishing a roll of paper out from behind the desk and handing it to him.

"I'll tell you one thing, Claudia," Phil said as he came out behind them. "The press had better not show up out here. I'd have every Native American in the state out here wanting their ancestors' bones on loan. I can tell you, if that happens, your dogs are going to end up in a storage bin under lock and key."

Outside, the harsh sun had melted the frost. The tension of the conversation seemed to evaporate some in the open spaces. Jim put on his hat. It was made of felt, with a floppy brim, and had replaced the Smokey the Bear hat he was wearing yesterday.

Meg inhaled the crystal air and Bassie slung her cane out toward the shallow valley ahead, where the grass was dry and wiry. "That's where the house stood," Bassie said over her shoulder, and then stopped abruptly and lifted her face to the sun, closing her eyes and sniffing the air. "Sage," she whispered. Her shoulders seemed to settle under the heavy coat.

Farther up the main trail the majestic mesa rose like an island, the red adobe church perched on the edge in stark relief against the pale blue sky. The place, Meg felt, possessed an eerie romance with the rushing sound of wind in the yellow grasses. She looked at the empty valley and imagined the frame house she had seen in the photograph, where Bassie had lived the first four years of her life. She thought of Hannah stepping from the back door onto the porch and moving down the steps with her dogs at her feet, the chimney behind her easing the scent of burning piñon over the valley. She imagined the night scenes Bassie had described—the shots fired, the grave dug on the hill, in the moonlight, in the snow, with Bassie as a small child watching from the porch of the house in the valley below.

Phil was moving on, turning off the main trail onto the narrow footpath leading up Dog Hill, and the others started along behind him. His pants were so starched they appeared lacquered; he carried the roll of prints in his hand. As they entered the rocky areas, Bassie was compelled to jab her cane around between the boulders in order to steady herself. She was breathing with difficulty. Jim helped her along. Buffalo grass and shrubby junipers grew in patches of red dirt nestled between the rocks, and prickly vegetation clung to Bassie's coat hem.

They crossed the narrow trench that Meg had nearly stumbled into yesterday and arrived at the ledge where she had first seen Jim. The uphill slope eclipsed any sight of the mesa and the church.

Two members of Jim's crew came trotting up the hill behind them with satchels over their shoulders, and Jim stopped to introduce them to Bassie and Meg. They were philosophy majors from the University of New Mexico: Victor de la Garza, who was handsome, though broad and bulky in his build, and a fragile-looking girl named Kelly Murphy, with a limp blond ponytail. A third crew member, Annie Pike, whom Tony Flores had described on the previous day as a menace with a trowel, ambled along behind the other two, swinging her bag. A patch of bright pink hair was secured on the top of her head with a rubber band, and she was smacking chewing gum. "Hey," she said, when Jim introduced her to Bassie, "I've heard of you. My mom has read your mom's journals."

Bassie told Annie that she ought to read them herself if she was going to be employed at Pecos, and Annie good-naturedly agreed to take a look at them.

"Excuse me for interrupting," Phil Barker said loudly, "but we need to hurry along here. I have things I need to get back to. Claudia, do you want to just look around up here and see what we're doing, or do you want to see the prints?"

"It must be difficult being you, Phil," she said, turning to look at him.

"I manage," he replied flatly.

"Your looks are against you," she observed.

Jim was talking to his crew, sending Victor and Kelly to resume their work on a test pit that they had started excavating the day before. When they were gone, he called down the slope, past a stand of trees. "Tony?"

"*Qué pasa?*" Tony answered.

"We need you for a minute," Jim replied.

Tony came up from a clump of bushes, picking his way through the brush. He greeted Bassie enthusiastically in Spanish, gave a cursory nod toward Phil, and said good morning to Meg. He ignored Annie, chomping ferociously on her gum, and Meg could tell that he disliked her personally as well as professionally. He was serious about the work on Dog Hill, and quite obviously she was not.

"What do you want me to do today, Mr. Layton?" she was asking Jim, turning to Bassie and explaining, "I'm not very good at the real work, so usually Jim just sends me out on errands."

"If you would be more careful I'd put you to work," he said, assigning her a trip to Santa Fe to an office supply store for some graph paper and other items. He made her get out a pen and write them down.

When Annie had gone, Phil said, "If that girl is that useless, Jim, you ought to get rid of her. We're paying her to drive back and forth to Santa Fe all day."

"No, I'm not going to get rid of her," Jim remarked. He took the prints from Phil and led Bassie and Meg over to the ledge and spread them out. Noting something of interest on the surface of the ground,

Meg leaned to pick it up. "That's a piece of chert," Jim said. "It's what you call 'flint' in Texas." He squatted down and plucked some other objects from the dirt. "And here's a pottery fragment, and this is obsidian, which is volcanic glass the Indians made tools from. It's always surprising how many of these things you can find just lying around on the surface."

Meg took the objects and looked at them and then gave them back, and Jim replaced them on the ground where he had found them. The sun was breathing warmth into the morning. Meg could hear the far-off whistle of a train and the clatter of rails. A sudden sense of the past washed over her. She thought of the hundreds of years of habitation here, lost to her on this sunny day, with Bassie and Phil bickering about dogs' graves. The place, she felt, held its dark mysteries with far more elegance than it could hold the blatant light of present day.

Bassie leaned on her cane to look at the prints while Jim weighted the edges down with stones. Meg got on the ledge to see the prints from above. Jim's face, under the floppy brim of the hat, was visible to her only in glimpses from her vantage as he pointed down to where a corner of the visitors' center was nestled against the rocks at the base of the hill. "At that corner there," he said, "and along that exterior wall, is where the room will be attached. We're going to have to carve a section out of the side of the hill there—which is right here on the plans." He indicated the area to be leveled, his hands, against the paper, callused and blunt-fingered, with dirt under the nails. Pointing out the pin flags on the downward slope, he explained that the blue ones marked the perimeter of the construction site and the red ones were his grid. "I wasn't able to get much of a physical grid, with string," he said, "on this incline, so I've had to tag it instead." The room was going to be tucked into the side of the hill, he told them, so that it would not spoil the view from the mesa. The construction area totaled two thousand square feet, with the test trench running precisely down the middle and pits to be dug on either side of it, to make certain that no sensitive areas would be disrupted or valuable artifacts covered over.

"How do you choose where to look for the graves?" Meg asked.

"We'll excavate some random pits, and then we'll also find signs that make certain places interesting," he said, "—like if the ground has been turned." He pointed out a mark in green ink on the plans. "Tony's working on that part of the trench there," he said. "That's where he found the tray yesterday. And Victor and Kelly have a pit on the slope just below those boulders, where this mark is. We've finished one a little farther down the hill. You can see the edge of it down there if you look. Just under the top of that tree. See that tall limb, with the bird nest? We also need one closer to the center. And then there's the place next to a stand of cholla, which could be one of the graves, and the place I started looking into yesterday, inside a circle of boulders. Over that way." He pointed.

Victor de la Garza appeared suddenly through the bushes, calling, "Look what I found, Mr. Layton," and made his way over, holding out what appeared to be a small sliver of bone that Jim took, and studied.

"Is it bone?" Victor inquired.

"Yes, it is," Jim said.

"I thought so, but I wasn't sure."

"When you're uncertain, there's a way to verify it," Jim said. "You just hold it to your tongue, and if it sticks, then it's bone."

Victor took the sliver and placed it against the tip of his tongue. Letting go of it, he held his hands under it, and it hung suspended for a second before dropping into them. "Cool!" he exclaimed. "How does it do that?"

"Porosity," Jim said.

"So what do you think it is? What kind of bone?"

"Probably a rodent's."

"A rodent's?"

"Probably."

"I had it in my mouth."

"I saw that," Jim said.

"Oh, man."

"It's not going to hurt you," Jim told him.

"Yeah, well." Victor looked embarrassed. "Don't tell Kelly I did that."

"Okay," Jim said.

"So what do I do with it?" Victor asked, holding it in his palm.

"Plot it, bag it, label it," Jim told him.

"Even just a piece of rodent bone?"

"You bet."

Victor left with the remnant, and Jim began rolling up the prints. He tucked them under his arm, and then started to lead Bassie along toward one of the pits. Phil Barker had been waiting impatiently for the last ten minutes, and now fell in step behind them, and Meg got down from the ledge and followed. They made their way through an outcrop of rocks and a dense stand of prickly bushes into an open area where a large boulder sat beside some tall cactus.

"There's a spot on this side of that boulder," Jim said. "Under the cholla." He turned to Meg. "Cholla is that tree cactus. They call it coyote candles out here. It grows in patches. Where you see a stand of it like that, it usually means the soil has been turned there in the last hundred years or so. The rest of that brush is rabbitbrush and it's not a good time indicator. In turned soil, cholla grows at a fairly steady rate, so we can guess a stand of it at that particular height put its roots down about eighty or ninety years ago, maybe a little more. Which would put us in the ballpark for the graves."

Bassie was looking at the cholla, as well as at the larger layout of the rocky slope. She shifted the direction of her gaze down to where the house had once stood in the valley.

"Well, Claudia," Phil pressed her. "Does any of it ring a bell? Could that be where you saw your mother digging?"

"It could be the place," she said coldly.

"Was there a big boulder in your memory?"

"I was watching from down there. How would I remember a boulder?" She waved her cane at the valley.

"You'd better figure it out," Phil said. "Jim can't just dig up the whole hill looking. You're going to have to pick your spots."

She was studying the hill, her cane now planted in a small patch of red dirt, her head shoved forward and turning slowly as she surveyed the landscape. "There—" she said, swinging her cane out toward the upward slope, starting to make her way through the bushes, and then, with difficulty, hoisting herself onto a low ledge. In a few more steps she reached her destination.

Jim said quietly to Meg, "That's where I found the notebook cover. If it's a dog grave, what was a notebook doing buried there?"

He and Meg climbed the ledge and stood beside Bassie over an area of earth and stringy grass about ten or twelve feet in circumference. It was bordered on the uphill side by a row of small junipers growing on a ridge of sharp rocks. In the center of the area, the pit that Jim had been excavating was marked with string into a grid. "I started on this place yesterday," he told Bassie. He had cleared away the surface dirt, a few inches deep, on half of the square. The other half was untouched.

As she stared at the area, Bassie's expression was fierce. Her face puckered into a monkeyish scowl exaggerated by the black rims of her glasses. Her braid had loosened from its knot and was dangling in a loop against one shoulder. "This is the place," she said. "This is the grave."

"Well, that's a surprise," Phil said, joining the three of them, unhurriedly. "That was easier than I thought. Lucky us." He was standing as stiffly as the cholla, his prickly white hair juxtaposed against the soft shades of the sky over the rooftop of the center. He looked as if he had been pasted onto a photographic background, the light not hitting him right, the mood wrong. "Okay, Jim, you've got your work cut out for you," he said. "I would encourage you to get it done as soon as possible and get this out of the way so Claudia can take her bones and go home. If you put Victor and Kelly on it with you, how long do you think it will take?"

"A day or two," Jim said. "The soil can't be more than six feet deep. But I'm going to do this on my own timing."

"I need to go on record here and express that I still don't like this," Phil said. "We're spending time and money just to satisfy Claudia about the dogs."

Bassie continued to stare at the patch of ground, and did not respond.

"Look," Jim said to Phil, "if I need to do this without your approval, I can."

"You can?"

"Is that a trick question?"

"Maybe."

"Then yes, Phil. If you want me to shoulder the responsibility, I'll do that. You've already said you'll let her have the bones. I'll be responsible for the digging. If it makes you happy, I'll be responsible for all of it."

Phil smiled. He shrugged. "Sounds good to me," he said. He looked up at the sky. A flock of cranes was flying overhead. "Not one cloud," he observed. Then he turned to Bassie. "Claudia," he said, "I have to get back to the office. You're in Jim's hands. He's responsible. Meg? It was good to meet you." He turned and started down the hill.

The three of them watched him go, his shadow gliding erratically over the boulders but seeming, to Meg, to move with more conviction than the man himself.

"What a weenie," Meg said.

A noisy bird flew from a ledge nearby and settled in some trees, hopping gracelessly in the branches and bending them into a state of agitation. Jim stood watching the bird. "It's supposed to be bad luck when you see a magpie flying alone," he said, and removed his hat to scratch his head. "Are either of you hungry? There's a place in Pecos that makes good breakfast burritos."

"*Is* either of you hungry," Bassie corrected him. " 'Either' is the subject. And it's singular. And yes, I am hungry."

Jim put his hat back on. "I have to make a couple of phone calls first, but they won't take long," he said.

Meg looked at Bassie, and thought of the ruins on the mesa above them, invisible from here, the old church standing like a sentinel protecting secrets that were not yet uncovered, or a monument to those that were.

THIRTEEN

While Jim was making phone calls from his office across the parking lot from the visitors' center, Bassie settled into the darkened theater with a family of tourists to watch a newly produced film on the history of the pueblo.

Meg went out to the car to read. The seclusion of parked cars had always given her a feeling of safety in some primitive and territorial way; when she had lived with Bassie she had often gone outside after dark with a flashlight and a book and locked herself in Bassie's car to read. The interior of the car had seemed luxuriously spacious compared to the room that functioned as her bedroom and Bassie's file storage room, and she would curl her toes around the dashboard, prop a Big Red on the armrest, and read until she was tired.

A similar relaxed feeling of seclusion came over her now, as she sat in the backseat of the rental car with her legs stretched lengthwise on the seat, the windows cracked open. Sunlight warmed her legs through her blue jeans, and she opened the book against her thighs. For a moment she sat lazily thinking about Jim Layton and mulling over what it was that she liked so much about him. She liked how directly he put things. It was a quality that bridged her usual distrust of men.

October 29. My journey with Mr. Bass to the ponds was eclipsed by a rare discovery that is astonishing and grim—Jewell is in fact a stranger to me if particulars have weight. To put it bluntly she is married. Her husband was abusive and she abandoned him two years ago and came to work here pretending to be unmarried, but now her husband has placarded her face in train stations and is trying to find her. Mr. Bass had seen the placards, and he recognized her when I introduced him to her in the lobby. He took her aside and told her about the placards. They offer a reward and include a likeness of her face and an account of her abandonment saying that she left her home in Oregon disguised in a cloak and hat. Her husband makes a strong plea saying his affection and concern have forced him to appeal to the community at large. She is prostrate with fear, and should find employment in the east in a private home instead of here in the public eye where her face is bald to the world. But she does not want to work fifteen hour days and seven day weeks and take a considerable pay reduction . . .

October 30. This morning Mr. Bass wired train stations to discard the placards and we talked with Mrs. Simms about the trouble. Meanwhile Jewell has attached herself to a man who shows symptoms of derangement and was wealthy but squandered his money in bucket shops and apparently was recently indicted for sending obscene matters through the mail. She is not rational. I spoke with the man and found him gruesome, he talked only of convicted murderers in New York City who will be executed by electrocution; he claims to have a large inheritance, which I believe is why she likes him, she hopes that he might rescue her.

November 2. Mr. Bass was here, we walked along the river, he is intense and animated. He said the wealthy Morales family who has a mansion on the outskirts of town and ranches in the mountains were made victims of a crime last night, that a gang of liberal bandits called the White Caps with hoods over their faces set one of the Morales barns on fire and cut the fences at their sheep ranch near Raton. The Morales family is Republican, all of them opposed by liberals except for a middle son, Vicente, who is Mr. Bass's favorite and a liberal and the founder of the populist Spanish newspaper in town. The family owns a great deal of land, but all of the land boundaries in New Mexico are constantly disputed, having been confused by the transitions of legal systems from Spanish to Mexican and then to American. There is a shortage of legal documents and survey records, and most were imperfect or illegal from the start, others tampered with, wrongly applied, destroyed or lost—there is no steady line of land ownership that can be traced, but rather a web of confusion with strands imperfectly connected. Liberals are opposed to the Republicans for taking control of communal lands and erecting fences around them, as it leaves the common people without a place to graze their sheep and without access to water. . . .

November 7. Mr. Bass is like the wind bringing the outside in, he states his mind without consideration for what is thought to be appropriate and does not kneel to convention, he does not care what others think of him. Walking to-day we found contiguity of sorts, by virtue of his lack of pretense; he talked of monopolies and pools and rates and grants, he is interesting to listen to, he is forceful. He talked about the railroads' bribery of politicians and corrupt subsidizing of newspapers and all the unethical retaliations on the poor farmers who oppose them, but said the worst grievances have ended now that the government is regulating commerce between the states. He said the local people may eventually be glad to have the railroad here, or eventually may not, probably their sentiments will be divided. Before the rails arrived here, half a decade of migration would bring only several thousand people to the territories, but now, whenever a railroad reaches a village, the population doubles within weeks. Mr. Bass is essentially Republican and believes in progress and commerce. I inquired how he felt about the emigrants who spent their money traveling westward in train cars not deemed fit for livestock, who were cheated on arrival into buying lands the railroads had been given free of charge by the government, only to starve and have to burn their corn for fuel. He said people are always going to be caught in the cogs of progress, and spoke of everything that the railroads have made possible. He said most emigrants have profited from coming, and made a case in point of fifteen thousand German Mennonites brought to Kansas from the steppes of Russia by a German-born land agent working for the Santa Fe. He is forthcoming with opinions, but withholding of himself. I am not privy to the tragedy in his past though at times I am made aware of it by a motionless expression that comes over his face, as if he has left the moment, and gone some place, or something in the depths of him has split off. He is animated, and yet I sense there is a mournful side.

November 11. We took one of the hotel buggies to the new branch bank in town and then to Mr. Bass's office at the tie plant. He explained his work and why he preferred his previous survey endeavors to his current duties. I believe he must be a genius at conquering landscape by mathematical equation, such as when he conquered Raton Pass by mapping the ascent and the tunnel through the mountain and the descent into New Mexico though he will not take credit: "Someone was going to get over those mountains," he says about Raton. "I only beat the DRG by twenty minutes." By this he means the Denver Rio Grande. He also once convinced a president of Mexico to subsidize Santa Fe track through one of the Mexican states, and in a single year his crews built more than four hundred miles of track in northern Mexico. His stunts have been reported in newspapers: once, he shot holes into the air hose to stop a train from going over a cliff where a bridge had collapsed. Another time he hired the outlaw Bat Masterson and a hundred armed Texans to protect his crew from sabotage while they were laying track at the Royal Gorge on the Arkansas River, and twice he traveled to Europe to represent the Santa Fe's interests to investors. But now the Santa Fe has overbuilt and is financially unsound and does not need surveys as it is not putting down new track—and has bought too many railroad lines in the effort to acquire right-of-way and trackage. The failure of crops in Kansas and financing with bonds has multiplied the problems. Mr. Bass was laid off by the Santa Fe a year ago, as they did not need any new surveys, and he became the city engineer of Topeka, in Kansas, but disliked the job and hired with the Santa Fe again. When he was doing surveys, he was often in command of several hundred men in locating teams and tracking gangs, while his present job involves only the endless task of keeping up the old main line. His office smells of creosote. The work is dull compared to mapping routes and putting track on virgin ground.

I wish he would disclose more from under the surface.

November 12. I am writing in a meager shaft of light admitted by the transom, to-day I learned more about the wagon train massacre at Mountain Meadows in Utah where Mr. Bass's family was killed. Evie Myers lent me a book by a Mormon woman who left the religion and then revealed the secrets of polygamy and also of the massacre though she admits there is a great deal she does not know about the massacre because the men swore secrecy among themselves.

It happened thirty-four years ago at the time of the Mormon reformation when the people were fiery with religion and ruled by the fanatic Brigham Young. A large convoy of nearly 140 people mostly from Arkansas were traveling to California; they had to go through Utah, and the Mormons did not want them in the territory and refused to sell any provisions to them, and then devised a plan to kill them, thinking that some of the immigrants might have been responsible for murdering one of their prophets in Arkansas and therefore they should all be punished, except for the smallest children who were too young to atone for their parents' sins and too young to relate to authorities what had happened. One morning while the immigrants were camped in a meadow surrounded by hills and starting their morning campfires, a group of Mormon men disguised as Indians, along with some Indians whom they had got on their side, started shooting at them from the hills. The immigrants constructed a barricade using wagons and the livestock that were shot dead, but could not enclose any portion of the stream beside the camp, and so were cut off from water. For four or five days and nights the immigrants fired back into the hills while suffering a terrible deprivation of water as well as food. Several times some of the men tried in the dark of night to take barrels down to the stream but were fired on and most of them were killed. They tried to dig for water inside the barricades but never got deep enough. It is hard to imagine the suffering of the mothers with children—to see their men killed and to have no water for their babies. They were also short of firewood. Everyone who left the fortifications to try to get some was fired on. The dead were buried inside the fortifications. Some of the women fought along side the men, while others cared for the children in trenches along the barricades. A few men tried to escape and go for help but the Mormons killed them. Finally some of the Mormons rode down from the hills with a white flag and said they had just arrived on the scene and would negotiate with the Indians and escort the immigrants safely back to the settlements if they would leave their belongings and lay down their arms. The immigrants were almost out of ammunition and had no choice, the suffering of the children for lack of water being unbearable. The men were made to go separately from the women and children, and as the line proceeded on the road, the Mormons, and some Indians with them, on a command of "Do your duty to Israel," and in the name of God, set upon them, shooting most of the men in the head and then setting upon the women and children with knives, killing all of them in cold blood except for the smallest children, who witnessed it all. A few Mormons tried to show mercy, but the leaders did not allow it; a father shot and killed his own son for refusing to cut the throat of a young girl who was clinging to him for protection. Finally the children that had been spared were gathered up and loaded into a cart, many with their mothers' blood on their clothing—there were seventeen in all. Two were badly wounded, one girl barely old enough to walk had her arm shot nearly off; her sister, only about five or six years old, had saved her life by dragging her to a hiding place during the killing. The children were all taken in the cart to a nearby Mormon household, and the following day they were separated from one another—great care being taken to separate siblings—and delivered to different homes, where they were to be raised as Mormons.

Elliott Bass was among these children, though I have not heard him mention the massacre, nor have I heard him say the word Mormon or in any way show any connection to the tragedy, except that there is a look about him. The Mormons made a pact to blame the Indians for the butchery, but word got out, and a year later the U.S. army was sent in to retrieve the orphans. They found them, not in the hands of the Indians as they expected, but with the Mormon families, who claimed to have rescued and ransomed them from the Indians. Clothing and jewelry from the immigrants was discovered in the tithing offices and Mormon homes. Some of the Mormons asked for reimbursement from the government for boarding and feeding the children. Most of the children could not remember their own names, knowing only the names the Mormons had given them. The army attempted to learn their true identities, and then brought them in a wagon back to Arkansas to whichever family members could be found.

After reading this story there is no empty space in my mind, it is all occupied by the cruel fate of the children—the idea of them takes over with a piteous, despotic quality. I lay my pen down in the hope of sleep, but my heart is bound too tight by the fearful, desperate hold of the helpless orphans.

November 13. Jewell has been attempting to conform the day into a mold it does not fit, her conversation is all "he spoke . . . she spoke," nothing contemplative about it, while I am getting in deep. I have been thinking of nothing and no one but Elliott Bass and how he suffered as a child, and yet when I am with him I cannot reconcile that child with the man he has become, whose strength and humor—when I do not pay attention to nuance and feel the distance about him—makes me think he has never suffered a day. He is dedicated to forward movement, as if he were out laying railroad track. He pours on me a constant flood of questions about myself and listens with great avid interest to everything I say. I am nervous of my feelings. Even now my thoughts are on the edge of promiscuity, where I admit that I desire them to be. They threaten to leap off the edge the moment I turn out the light.

So I am going to write about him, and of the day, all night if I need to, in order to subjugate anything lurid.

We left for town this morning in the buggy, with Jewell between us, and the Chihuahuan dog in Mr. Bass's lap. Mrs. Simms had given us the full day off from work. Mr. Bass talked about the town and mostly about the time when an outlaw named Hoodoo Brown got himself elected justice of the peace and the Morales family had to take over and file charges against crimes that he allowed to go unchecked, such as toting of concealed weapons and public drunkenness, also gambling without licenses and prostitution, profanity in public and operating opium houses. This involved "pounding a number of heads with guns," as Mr. Bass described it.

We stopped at a mercantile store owned by the Morales family—they own a good number of establishments in town—and Mr. Bass met a friend from the east side who told us of his apprehension by police last night for playing poker—he was fined by the justice of the peace because he did not pay the license fee of a hundred dollars a table. He and Mr. Bass talked about the streetlights being changed to electrical and the company that is supposed to do it, and about a German Hebrew who owns a mercantile establishment in town and outlets in other towns and is a benefactor of the community but competes with the Morales family in business. Jewell bought fig syrup and sarsaparilla for cleansing her blood, and afterwards we drove the five miles out of town to the mansion where the family lives. It resembles a plantation house, including servants' quarters, and the area is known as Moralesville and is all owned by the father, Pedro Morales, who is called Don Pedro by everyone in the county and is said to be greatly generous as well as probably corrupt. He is one of the founders of the Plaza Hotel and owns a resort hotel on the Gallinas River. He is opposed by some for having made a portion of his wealth selling lumber to the railroads, some of which is said to have been cut from the disputed lands claimed by the community as a whole. There is a valley in front of the Morales house and a hill in back of it and a train stop and a creek beside the barn. The mansion is stone and two stories and not Mexican in style. Indian servants met us in the driveway and Mrs. Morales came to the door. She is fat with a pleasant face, she is a Navajo, but is called Diana. She was wearing a velveteen blouse and a red skirt and silver jewelry and took us to a sitting room where we sat by a fire and she brought us tea. The furniture was mostly American but for a few hide chairs; the room was an elegant hodge-podge. There were Mexican blankets and taffeta pillows along with woven baskets and pieces of pottery around the room, and a brocade from the Orient and Catholic paintings. Mr. Bass had gone into a different room with the men. Mrs. Morales sat on the sofa and told us about her life. She is quiet and unstriving; her story has magnificent proportions though her English is poor. She was stolen from her family when she was a child and sold to a Mexican rancher and made to be a slave to his wife. Don Pedro met her at a Taos market when she was fifteen years old and he was not much older, and he paid the rancher money for her and then married her and now she is devoted to him and to their children—the children are all boys and grown now. Her parents in the meantime had been taken by Kit Carson to a reservation and Don Pedro later found them, and there was a great reunion, though the parents remained on the reservation and she returned with Don Pedro to Las Vegas. Don Pedro insisted that she learn English, and she is still improving; she studies the Ollendorf lessons from a newspaper. Don Pedro learned English on his own when he was very young, having commerce with Americans. He sent all of his sons to university in Saint Louis.

Vicente Morales came into the room eventually; he is handsome and has a benevolence about him, and warmth and generosity. His eyes are black, he has a broad mustache and is tall. He keeps a shadow of a smile. His spectacles impart a slight appearance of the philosophical. Jewell of course was smitten, as he is not married. Two of his brothers and their wives came into the room shortly after he did, and Mr. Bass with them. The oldest brother is Lorenzo and is solemn and austere, the youngest resembles his mother, being short, broad, and round in the face with serene expressions—I take him for a dreamer. He has made a fortune in pharmaceuticals with a concoction supposed to cure every imaginable ailment, and of which he gives away large amounts free of charge to anyone in need, though his advertisements, Mr. Bass told me later, are condemned as false.

Following this group were three men from the jail who have been declared insane but harmless by the courts. They were released from jail at Don Pedro's instigation as he was against housing them with criminals, as they are not criminals, and so they are living in the Morales house; one is bent and old but happy, another short and grandiose with a great tall hat from thirty years ago, the third no more than sixteen years of age, giddy and solemn at alternating moments. Apparently they are allowed to wander as they please throughout the mansion; their odd behaviors are ignored. I wanted to observe them, but discipline availed me. Eventually we were invited to the dining room with these three individuals among us; no special care was given them, nor was there any chastisement of their bad manners and vulgarities. The youngest laughed happily and often during the conversation, ate quickly, and left early without taking leave. The short gentleman wore his hat at table; the eldest passed wind several times, loudly during conversation, without so much as an eyebrow raised in his direction.

The meal was lavish and Mexican, the room sunny, the courses several, and the service steady. Don Pedro is a lawyer and a member of the territorial legislature and was away with the legislature working on a comprehensive school bill; his place at table's head was therefore vacant. At table were his wife Diana, his second son Lorenzo, his fourth son Vicente, his fifth and youngest son Placido of the pharmaceutical endeavor, the wives of Lorenzo and Placido, neither of whom spoke English, and both of whom had children present with them. The talk was animated, passionate, with frequent disagreements. A parrot in a cage by a window repeated much of what was said and squawked loudly about "Gringos" and "Bolillos" until Señor Vicente carried his cage out to the hallway. The family is apparently what Mr. Bass calls "Agringados," (he says this openly, in their presence, and jokingly) all but Vicente Morales, who is not Americanized, and who has parted with the family politically and become a liberal populist and a Democrat and writes editorials in his newspaper about how natives of New Mexico should retain their culture. His father Don Pedro fought on the Union side of the Civil War and is a United States patriot. Vicente Morales is a different sort of patriot, and wants the native people of New Mexico to accommodate but not assimilate into the American culture, and to welcome immigration from the east and welcome trade with Mexico, and thereby make New Mexico a place of manufacturing and commerce. He believes the United States has mistreated New Mexicans and violated the treaty under which the territory was acquired, but that the people here nevertheless are better off now than they would be if they were still a part of Mexico, where the free press is shut down and people are poor even while the country has obtained stability through foreign investment. "My mother is a testament to the wisdom of this attitude," he said. "She will admit that she is better off, and has a better life, than her family on the reservation. She is loyal to her life as it is, but keeps her soul pure by remembering the Navajo customs."

Jewell asked a number of questions to impress Vicente Morales, and his answers were elevated from her plane of reference though he did not condescend. He spoke of how the citizens of Madrid defeated Napoleon and said conquistadors were greater explorers of our continent than Americans who received the accolades, and that Kit Carson should not be held up as a hero. The children of New Mexico are taught only to admire Americans. "We are ridiculous when we attempt to impersonate Anglos," he said. "It makes us no better than mimics." His brothers took offense at this and other statements and were critical of him for supporting a cousin who has joined the liberals and been elected sheriff. Vicente claimed the cousin had acted on conviction, and was therefore blameless, but the brothers said the cousin should be censured for betraying the family. "Blood is more substantial than conviction," one of them said. "Blood is permanent." Finally Mr. Bass put an end to the argument, declaring that the cousin had got elected sheriff through corruption rather than conviction, and that Vicente knew this and did not respect him any more than did the brothers but continued to defend him in the same way he was known to salvage thieving sheep dogs after they had been discovered bathed in blood. Vicente did not deny this, but thought it humorous and true. Paco the Chihuahuan dog was sleeping under the table and seemed to understand that members of his species had been placed in an unfavorable connection, and began to growl, most likely dreaming of a rabbit chase, and even the brothers laughed at this. They are all fond of Mr. Bass, as he manages to ease the tensions without making light of things. When the conversation had settled on the Indian Geronimo, I accidentally ate a red hot pepper and might as well have shoved a burning candle in my mouth; I got the pepper into a linen but had difficulty breathing, and Mr. Bass presented me a glass of water, while Placido Morales went for a jar of his famous medicinal ointment. The women implored me to eat bread and drink water and offered me some ice. The children all stood around staring at my stupidness. Only Vicente Morales did not move from his chair, but locked his eyes to mine across the table. The warmth and steadfast nature of his gaze seduced me to complacency. . . .

Seduced her, but not to complacency—Meg was thinking when she was interrupted by a tapping at the window behind her head. She turned and saw Jim looking in. He was leaning with one hand on his knee and his face close to the window, shielded by his hat. He stepped back as she opened the door, and then squatted on the asphalt to be at eye-level with her. Seeing the book in her hand, he said, "Where are you?"

"At the Morales mansion choking on a pepper."

"Then you've met Vicente."

"I'd say. There's five inches of print just on his looks. All we heard about Elliott was that he had a gap between his teeth."

"And a certain intensity," Jim added.

"Which he better hang on to," Meg said. "So what's the deal? I mean later. Between her and Vicente. They're just friends?"

"I don't want to ruin the suspense," he said.

She swung her legs out of the car and got out, stretching. Jim stood up. "Are we ready for burritos?" she asked.

"We are. Is Bassie inside?"

"She was in the theater when I came out."

"How do you think she's doing?"

"Pretty well. She's apprehensive. What do you think the chances are that there's something significant in that . . . area?"

He smiled. "We call it a pit."

"What are the chances it's got something in it besides that leather cover?"

"Pretty high."

"Fifty-fifty?"

"A little better. If you want a number on it, I'd say sixty-five percent. More often than not, if you find something like that, in a place where a significant block of soil appears to have been turned, you'll find something else."

"And what do you think the chances are that it's one of the dogs' graves?"

"Well, given she thinks she remembers it, at least fifty-fifty. Of course, if you're doing probabilities, there's also at least a thirty percent chance Phil Barker will find some way to call the whole thing off before we get anywhere."

"So if Phil doesn't stop us, the chance of finding nothing is still about fifteen percent."

"Fifteen percent?"

She nodded.

"You mean, exactly? You did the math in your head?"

"Yes, but it's not hard."

He looked dubious.

"Fifty percent of the time, it's not a dog's grave. And thirty-five percent of the time, there's nothing else in it. That's seventeen and a half percent. But that only works for the seventy percent of the time that Phil doesn't stop us. Seventy percent of seventeen and a half is twelve and a quarter percent. I added a few percent for the magpie you saw flying alone. You said that's bad luck?"

"Indeed."

She smiled. "Should we take your truck, or the car?"

"We can take the truck," he said, still studying her. "I need to clean the seat off, though. Keep on reading if you want to. Those are really the right numbers?"

She nodded.

When she got back in the car and opened the book, instead of reading she found herself watching Jim as he went to his truck and opened the passenger door and cleared off the seat. He pulled out several cardboard boxes and placed them in the back, leaned inside the cab and removed some papers, stacking them on the floorboard, then went into the center for Bassie. Meg watched him until he was in the door.

Mr. Bass stayed inside with Lorenzo Morales after the meal, and Vicente Morales took Jewell and me out to the veranda. The weather was bright and cool and we sat in chairs with a long view of the valley. Vicente Morales remained standing, leaning against the rail, smoking a cigarette and looking handsome in his muslin shirt and linen vest, his corduroy trousers tucked in his boots, the effect being neither Mexican nor Indian nor American but a combination. He has a Hungarian sheep dog that lay around at his feet thumping his tail and grinning. I tried to engage the dog but he ignored me. Jewell tried to engage Vicente Morales, asking why he is not married, and he answered with a Spanish proverb: "He who wants to know his finest qualities should die. He who wants to know his faults, should marry." I asked what faults he was afraid to learn of, and he considered and drew on his cigarette but did not answer.

"Not cowardice," I said, "I hope"—and he said no.

"Not stinginess?"—No.

"Do you have a temper, then?"

"No temper to speak of," he said.

"Not meanness then,"—No.

"Then there's nothing you should be afraid to learn, if you are generous and brave and kind."

He answered only with a smile and then said, "Elliott Bass, on the other hand, has no reservations. Elliott will take a leap if he decides to. If he faces a canyon, he will build a bridge. If he faces a mountain, he will blast a tunnel. Forward is the only direction that interests him."

"But he has never been engaged to marry," I observed, and Mr. Morales answered with another parable, saying that he knew of an exceptional sheep dog whose owner bred her, to perpetuate the line, and afterwards allowed her to work the flock until she had the pups, then locked her in the barn with the pups for the night. The following morning she escaped and went out to find the flock, but it had been moved to another pasture. She followed the scent and found them and worked them until noon and returned to the barn to feed the pups. In the afternoon she went back out again, but the flock was moved and she ran several miles to find them. She returned to the barn that night and nursed the pups, exhausted, but on the next day ran so far to reach the flock that she was nearly dead when she returned. They tied her with a rope that night, to prevent her from running off again, but she chewed the rope in two, and at daybreak was discovered gone. A vaquero found her twenty miles from home following the scent of the flock.

"Is your point that Mr. Bass requires to be far from home?" I said.

"My point is that the dog was equally devoted to the work and to the pups."

That point—I told him—was fairly obscure.

We played dominoes and chess the remainder of the afternoon and departed after dark. I intended to climb up into the buggy after Jewell, so that she would be between Mr. Bass and myself according to etiquette, but Mr. Bass whispered to me, "Step here, and go up first; I intend to keep you warm." I found myself beside him, with the dog in my lap. Vicente Morales handed up some blankets and placed heated stones under our feet, and we started back to the Montezuma. I may perhaps some day forget our conversation on the way, how cold the air was, how numerous the stars, how soothing the rocking of the buggy on the

springs, but I will never—even to the day they bury me—forget the strange and disconcerting power of his proximity.

Meg closed her eyes and rubbed at the back of her neck, noting a sleepy feeling that often preceded a headache. The story of the massacre at Mountain Meadows had depressed her, and the feeling lingered. She fished her sunglasses out of her purse and put them on and leaned her head against the window, trying to relax her mind. But she was restless. She found herself looking toward the center, waiting for Bassie and Jim. Finally she opened the book and skimmed over a page: Hannah speculating about "the silver question" and how McKinley's tariff bill would affect the cost of "the necessaries of life."

But the topics were meaningless to Meg at the moment. She glanced at a few more pages. The world was in turmoil for several passages: there was an earthquake in Japan, Russia was persecuting the "Hebrews," the U.S. Navy was still "mixing it up" in Chilean politics, and someone had been vandalizing the Santa Fe Railroad by placing rocks on the tracks and causing wrecks to "rolling stock."

As for Hannah's private life, she attended a play called *She* with Elliott at the Opera House in Las Vegas, describing it as "a rocky production of transient talent." The traveling players had "skipped out" before the final act to catch the train for Santa Fe.

Meg caught a movement in the corner of her eye. The door of the visitors' center was swinging open; Jim's arm was pushing it. Bassie plunked her cane into the sunlight.

FOURTEEN

The town of Pecos was two miles north of the pueblo, nestled in the valley where the Pecos River tumbled from the Rocky Mountains. Meg sat crowded between Jim and Bassie as they rattled into town in Jim's pickup truck and Jim talked about the area, saying he would have preferred to live on the outskirts of Pecos instead of in Santa Fe if not for his wife, Judith, who wanted to live in town, and his children, who needed decent schools. "Someday I'm going to buy some land out here and build," he said. "I would do it now, if I had the choice."

"You would squeeze your life into a six-inch square if you had the choice," Bassie said.

They entered the town, bouncing over potholes. Jim's elbow grazed against Meg's arm as he swung the wheel to avoid a piece of tire in the road. "Do you have enough room?" he asked, shifting gears.

"I'm fine," she said.

Houses with shabby exteriors were strung out along the road, old grindstones propped in yards for decoration. Trash was smoldering in a fifty-five-gallon drum beside a hog pen.

They drove past a grocery and a hardware store and the post office, and came to an intersection. Meg asked Jim how he had come to live in New Mexico, and he said that after he had graduated from Rice University in Houston he had driven out to look at the University of New Mexico's archaeology department for graduate school. "I'd never even seen the Rockies," he said, "and when I drove in through those passes and pine forests it was like the view behind me just closed. I never looked back."

"Your car broke down; that's why you ended up here," Bassie interjected.

He laughed. "There was that, too," he admitted. "The engine went out and I couldn't afford a new one. So I painted houses for a while."

"At the paltry age of twenty-one, he had arrived where he's been for the rest of his life," Bassie said.

"Which is the good thing about archaeology," Jim remarked. "If you end up in one place for a long time, you can just dig and discover another world underneath you. You don't have to go anywhere."

"Unless you want to get somewhere," Bassie said.

"Get off that, Bassie, would you?" he said, with a discernible edge in his voice.

He turned the truck down a side street and pulled into a graveled parking lot where a tin shed was tacked onto the side of a rundown adobe house.

They entered the café through a screen door that opened into a small tin room illuminated by sunlight through the windows. Booths lined the walls, and several tables crowded the center; apparently the kitchen was through an entryway into the house. A sour-looking woman with gray-streaked hair was waiting on a table, and when she had finished she came over and took some menus off a stand near the door. "Booth okay?" she asked tersely, and without waiting for an answer turned and led them to a sunny booth beside a sliding metal window. Jim sat beside Bassie, and Meg slid into the seat across from them.

"I'm short a waiter," the woman said. "I hope you're not in a hurry." She poised her pen over her order pad and turned to Bassie. "What'll you have?"

"Coffee," Bassie said. "And enough time to look at the menu."

"I think we'd all like coffee, Juanita," Jim said. "Is that right, Meg?"

Juanita put her order pad in her apron pocket, got three stoneware mugs from a stand near the door, and sloshed them full of black coffee.

After she had placed her order, Meg went into the bathroom for the purpose of escaping Bassie's irritability and Jim's lack of response to it—which, Meg had to admit to herself, was beginning to bother her. She had seen that he was annoyed with Bassie on the drive over, but he had continued to tolerate her insults.

When Meg had returned from the bathroom and Juanita had deposited plates onto the table without comment and left the three of them to eat their burritos, Bassie took a bite of hers and announced it was too salty.

"You ordered bacon on it," Meg said. "Bacon is salty."

"Then she shouldn't have salted the eggs," Bassie said.

"She's bound to scramble all the eggs together," Meg replied impatiently. "She can't make your eggs separately from everybody else's. If you order bacon on your burrito, it's going to be salty."

Bassie argued with Meg about this, and Jim sat silently eating his breakfast and watching the two of them as if they were bumper cars charging at each other in a ring. When he had finished his two burritos, he leaned back against the corner of the booth and brushed a dead fly off the windowsill into the rut of the sliding window, then stretched his arm out in the sunlight on the sill and continued watching.

Bassie had, as usual, declined to remove her coat. Meg could smell the musty odor across the table. The sunlight lay glaringly on the speckled Formica of the tabletop and glistened on what was left of the plates of cold burritos and lumpy beans. Meg kept her sunglasses on. She knew how harsh and opinionated she must seem to Jim, with the sunlight glittering on her frazzled hair as she jerked her hands around and then cupped them in her lap under the table and leaned back against the vinyl of the booth and became mute, as if she had retreated somewhere, only to lean forward again and place her elbows on the table and state an opinion that was almost as belligerent as Bassie's, and always diametrically opposed. "You can't have someone like that on the Supreme Court," she heard herself saying dogmatically. "It was sexual harassment."

Bassie introduced the topic of bilingual education, declaring that New Mexico should vote an English-only amendment to the state constitution. Meg challenged her, knowing nothing about bilingual education, and caring even less, but managing, she thought, to concoct a fairly decent case in favor of it.

"You don't believe that," she said to one of Bassie's statements.

"I certainly do," Bassie said, citing several constitutional provisions and case decisions. She quoted an editorial Vicente Morales had written in his liberal Las Vegas paper in 1892, and declared him "dead wrong" on the subject. "I know more about the language controversy in New Mexico than anyone alive," she said, and turned to Jim. "Do you know anyone, other than myself, who has read every issue of *La Herencia del Norte*?"

"I can't say I know anyone, other than you, who's ever read any of them," he replied.

Knowledge was weaponry to Bassie, and she had an arsenal. She began to quote Thomas Jefferson on language and recite sections of the Chinese Exclusion Act of 1882. She quoted contemporary Texas legislators who had stated a few years ago that any legislation attempting to designate English as the official language in Texas would be "dead on arrival." She jutted her chin forward. "When John Marshall was on the Supreme Court he refused to endorse Webster's dictionary as representative of our official language," she said. "And that was a crying shame. This coffee is stone cold." She looked around for Juanita, who had disappeared into the kitchen.

Meg got up and poured a fresh mug for Bassie from the pot of coffee on the stand beside the door. "How is Julie?" she heard Bassie demanding of Jim.

"It's Judith, not Julie," he said. "She's fine."

Bassie clacked her dentures. "Your marriage any better?"

"The marriage is fine," Jim said.

"Kids are okay?"

"Kids are doing great," he said. "Meredith's on the soccer team. She's got a game tonight."

"There's something going on," Bassie said. "You're not happy. Your marriage is in trouble."

"I'm very happy, and the marriage is fine," he said.

Meg returned to the table and set the coffee down in front of Bassie. She slid back into her seat. "What's that fortune-teller sign over the door about?" she asked.

"Juanita's a fortune teller," Jim answered.

"Puh," Bassie responded. "Juanita's a fake. I can tell by looking at her."

"Have you ever had your fortune told?" Meg asked Jim.

"When I was in college," he replied. "But it wasn't much of a fortune. I remember the woman said I'd had intestinal worms as a child."

"Did you?" Meg asked. "Have intestinal worms?"

"I don't remember."

"Every child gets worms," Bassie said.

"I didn't," Meg said. "I don't think I did."

"Humph, ask your mother about that. No, she was drunk. She won't remember it."

"She's been sober for ten years, Bassie. I wish you'd quit being so critical of her."

Bassie leaned back in her dandruff-speckled coat, her wrists emerging with birdlike thinness from the sleeves and her skeletal hands holding the coffee mug possessively, as if someone might attempt to steal it from her. She took a sip of coffee, then glared at Meg and said accusingly, "This is already cold again," as if Meg should be held accountable for the laws of thermodynamics.

Meg did not get up this time to fill the mug. She and Bassie stared at one another, Bassie with the sunlight smeared as white as powder on the black fur of her coat and an obstinate expression on her mouth. Juanita appeared from the kitchen and came over and filled the mug, sloshing coffee on the table without bothering to wipe it up.

Suddenly Meg looked at her watch. "I need to use a phone," she said.

"Can Meg use Mario's office phone?" Jim asked Juanita.

Juanita shrugged. "Go ask him."

Meg followed Jim into the house through the kitchen and a brief, dark hallway. "Is this breakfast stressful to you?" he asked quietly. "I assume it is."

"Yes. It's not to you?"

"Probably not as much as it is to you. She knows all the buttons, doesn't she." He turned and knocked on a door.

"*Hola, pásale,*" someone shouted from within, and Jim opened the door to reveal a small, mud-walled room with a large desk in the center at which a tidy-looking man with a thin mustache was seated. The man stood up when he saw Jim, and came around the desk exuberantly to embrace him, thumping him on the back. Then he indicated the chair in which he had been sitting, a thronelike piece of furniture with a black-and-white cowhide seat, and said, "How do you like my new chair? My kids gave it to me. No, amigo, don't tell me. It's ugly, I know! I would rather have the cow!" He laughed heartily and for a long time, and then looked at Meg. "Who is your attractive friend?" he asked Jim.

Jim made the necessary introductions, and Mario then told Meg a story about how he and Jim had fought together "like lions" against a Greek con man who had tried to buy the ranch near Pecos Pueblo and make it into a resort. "It would be like Disneyland!" Mario exclaimed. "Do you think I'm kidding? I am not kidding! Pecoseños would be selling popcorn! Our friend here—" Mario said, whacking Jim on the back again, "he took on the rich guys while Señor Phil Barker sat his skinny ass on the fence! So, tell me, how are you so lucky to know this man?"

"He's a friend of my grandmother's," Meg said.

"You've probably heard of her grandmother," Jim added. "Claudia Bass. Tony Flores knows her."

"She's famous!" Mario exclaimed. "And I met her once."

"She's in the restaurant," Jim said. "You should go out and say hello. But Meg would like to use your telephone if it's all right."

Meg took her billfold from her purse and located her calling card, but Mario insisted that she sit on the cowhide throne and dial direct. She called Paul at his office in San Antonio. "Good," she said when he answered, "you haven't left yet."

"What's up?"

"We're here. We're settled in," she said. "I left you a key under the pot by the front door. But I need you to do me a favor and fax something to St. David's whenever you get there. It's a price quote on equipment; I left it on the kitchen counter."

There was a second's hesitation on the line. "When do I have to do this by?" Paul asked.

"Tonight would be fine," she said.

"Okay. What's the number?"

She was annoyed that he wasn't more gracious about it, given the fact that she was allowing him to stay in her apartment.

"Are you busy or something?" she asked, challenging him.

"I'm late for a meeting and I'm trying to get out the door," he said.

She fished her bulky address book out of her purse and looked up the fax number for St. David's dialysis unit.

"I'm using someone's office phone," Meg said when she had dictated the number. "I've got to go. If anything comes up, I'm staying at the Plaza in Las Vegas." She paused. "That's New Mexico, not Nevada."

"I know," he said offhandedly, not perceiving the comment as barbed.

"What's the weather doing?" she asked.

"Raining. At least here in San Antonio."

"All right. I'll talk to you later."

When she was off the phone she said to Jim, "Well, that's bad news. It's raining. The ground's already saturated from the rains we had last week, and if we get any floods in the hill country, I might have to go back. You're going to have Bassie on your hands if that happens."

"Would you come back to get her?" he asked.

"If you're lucky."

"What's wrong with the woman?" Mario wanted to know.

"She's mean," Meg said.

"Oh, I know this kind of woman," Mario replied. "I am married to this kind of woman."

They went out into the restaurant and found Bassie in the booth where they had left her, the plates pushed away and a newspaper spread on the table in front of her. After Jim had introduced them, Mario explained to Bassie that he had met her once before, when she was working at the pueblo.

"How is the food?" he asked. "Did Juanita bring you a feast?"

"She brought me a salty burrito," Bassie answered.

"Too much salt?" Mario inquired.

"Taste for yourself," she said, pushing her plate toward him.

Juanita was passing by the table on her way to the kitchen with a tray of dishes, and saw the gesture. "*A la reina le pone la mesa, si quiere comer, y si no, lo deja,*" she said to her husband. Meg understood only that this was an insult.

Bassie scoffed. Mario reprimanded Juanita in Spanish as she turned her back and carried the tray into the kitchen.

"Look at this," Bassie was instructing Mario, jabbing her finger at the newspaper. "The word 'Hispanic' used as a noun."

"It's wrong?" Mario inquired.

" 'Hispanic' is an adjective," she said. " 'Hispano' is the noun. And look here. They're calling the native citizens of Mexico 'Latin' and 'Hispanic.' For crying out loud. Mexicans have got more Indian blood than Spanish blood. Why would eighty million people want to go around impersonating Spaniards? Why not call themselves Tarahumarans or Tarascans or Purapechas? Why Latinos? Journalists these days don't give a ripe fig if they're technically wrong, as long as they're politically correct. Bunch of mealy-mouthed cowards."

Mario said, "My kids use the word 'Hispanic' that way all the time." He shrugged. "I don't see why they shouldn't."

"History, is one reason," Bassie answered. "Grammar is another. If they're talking about New Mexicans, that's different: there's a lot more Spanish blood here drop for drop. But Mexico—"

"Stop nitpicking, Bassie," Meg said.

Bassie swung her gaze to Meg and said loudly, "And you stop showing off for Jim."

Meg glanced at Jim and saw that he had heard this. She had started to slide into the booth across from Bassie, but now stopped midway, speechless, then slid back out again.

"You know what I'm talking about," Bassie said. "You've been trying to impress him. If you don't watch out, you're going to be just like your mother. With no respect for marriage." She turned to Mario. "Kids," she said, rolling her eyes. "How many do you have?"

Before Mario could attempt to answer this question, Meg pulled some bills from her purse and slapped them on the table. She took her rumpled corduroy jacket off the seat and headed for the door, letting the screen slam shut behind her as she left.

Jim followed her out, and found her pacing in the graveled parking lot. "I was intending to buy breakfast," he said, holding out the money she had left. "If that's okay."

She took the money without comment and shoved it back into her purse, then pulled her coat on, angrily, her hand becoming lodged in the sleeve for a moment before she wrestled it through.

"Who knows where she gets that stuff," he said.

A dusty motorcycle was purring slowly down the street, the driver maneuvering between potholes and rolling to a stop before a house with a rotted porch swing. A dog behind the chain-link fence began yapping, and a teenage boy came out and shouted at the dog. Then the boy got onto the motorcycle behind the driver and they departed in a cloud of dust and fumes.

Meg said, "She comes up with things like that. And *why*?"

"I don't know," Jim said. "You have some hot sauce on your chin."

She wiped her hand across her chin. "She's like a hit-and-run," she said. "She'll say something completely offensive, then just disappear behind that goddamn simpering smile. And then I have to decide whether to be big about it. Every day: big, or small? Big, or *microbic*?" She flung her arms out.

"It's a mean streak," Jim commented. "It's my theory she was born with it."

"She's got something against everybody she meets," Meg said. "Yesterday she was ranting about feminists and quotas. And she used to be a suffrage worker! Poor Mario. She's probably in there right now lecturing him about how stupid his kids are to say 'Hispanic' instead of 'Hispano.' An *adjective*. My gosh, who knows stuff like that? And she's so old everybody thinks they have to be nice to her. Then *wham*. She gets you. And what makes me really mad is how she presents herself as this generous old lady concerned with everybody's education, when in fact, she's stingy."

"She's paid a lot of tuition fees," Jim offered. "You have to give her that."

"She sure as hell didn't pay mine," Meg said.

"She didn't?"

"She did until I switched from history to engineering. Then, poof! No more funds."

"She never told me that."

"Of course not."

"You paid your own tuition?"

"I got a job. Don't look at me like it was terrible. It wasn't like a deprivation. It was just nauseating watching all these little students stop by

Bassie's house to pick up their tuition checks. How come you didn't get pissed off at her in there?"

"I guess because I don't care as much as you do. She didn't raise me."

"I thought you said she was like a mother to you."

"I wasn't a child at the time. It makes a difference."

"It makes a big damn difference, apparently," Meg said. "She's been goading you all day, and you've just been passive."

"She's unnerved about the Dog Hill situation," Jim said.

"I don't care what she's unnerved about. I would have snapped back if I were you." She saw Jim contemplating her, and thought she saw a fleeting look of amusement on his face. "Is something funny?"

"To me. Probably not to you. What made you switch from history?"

"I didn't like it. What's funny?"

"I'm just wondering if you abandoned history just so you could disappoint her."

The dog yapping from behind the chain-link fence across the street was grating on Meg's nerves. "Shut up!" she shouted suddenly at the dog, surprising herself with the volume of her own voice. The dog, unexpectedly, complied, retreating beneath the porch. "I can't believe I just screamed at that dog," Meg said.

"Scared the hell out of me," Jim said.

Meg let a moment pass. "I don't know if I liked history or not," she said finally. "I can't separate it from Bassie." Then she flung her arm out toward the café door. "What is she *doing* in there? Is she waiting for us to come back in? She can forget it."

"Well, I'm going in to pay the bill," Jim said.

Meg inhaled a breath, tilting her face up and closing her eyes.

"And I'm waiting here," she said.

"Actually," Jim said over his shoulder as he walked to the door, "I was kind of flattered to think you might be showing off for me."

When he came back out with Bassie, Meg was waiting for them by the door. She had flipped her hair over to brush it out and was tying it back again, slinging her purse strap over her shoulder. "There," she said. "Let's go."

FIFTEEN

They arrived at the pueblo in stony silence. Jim excused himself and went to check the progress on the hill, and Bassie plodded her way into the visitors' center and commandeered the front desk as a work space. She spread her papers out and began making notes on the galley proof of the illustrated history of Pueblo pottery that had been sent to her for promotional comments by the University of Chicago Press.

Meg started up the main trail to the pueblo ruins, a five-minute uphill hike to the top. Midway up she heard Jim calling her name, and turned to see him down at the junction where the footpath leading up into the rocks on Dog Hill joined the trail she was on.

"Wait, Meg, and let me take you up," he called. "I have to check on something in my office first, but I'd like to give you the tour."

She retraced her steps back down, and he explained that he wasn't going to have anyone work on the pit that Bassie had pointed out, where he found the notebook cover, until he was there to supervise and do most of the work himself. Meanwhile he needed to go to his office. He invited her to come with him.

She walked down with him, and they made their way around the visitors' center to the parking lot and up a small path to what appeared to be an old ranch house, and entered through a screen door. Beside the door was a basket of lost and found items overflowing with hats and jackets, a few pieces of toy jewelry and a Tony Hillerman novel. Books and papers were stacked among boxes of bone fragments, and the walls were lined with file cabinets. The far end of the room was divided by a tall stand of bookshelves that stood floor to ceiling in lieu of a wall, forming two separate office areas, each area with a desk, one of them disorderly and the other the only ordered corner of the room. There was no one at either desk. The windows in these two areas allowed a cross breeze to the screen door, and beyond the windows birds were eating berries in the juniper bushes.

"It used to be the foreman's house when this was a ranch," Jim explained, hanging his hat on a peg attached to the wall. "Make yourself at home. I need to check my messages. There's a coffee machine in the back—" he nodded toward a doorway, "—I doubt there's any made, but if you want some—"

"No thanks," she said. She had consumed too much at Mario's; it had made her jittery.

Jim sat down at the untidy desk, which Meg discerned was his, while she browsed through the bookcase beside it. She noticed that he picked up a note, glanced at it, and rifled through a mound of papers, finally pulling an old address book out from under what appeared to be a stratographic chart of Dog Hill.

Meg could see the note. "Dorothy at SHPO wants a 106 instead of triple X—call ASAP," it said, and she watched Jim turn the pages of his ratty address book, which was filled with deletions and insertions scribbled in the margins. She had thought that archaeologists always learned to write in neat, block script because of the need to draw maps and graphs, but Jim seemed to be an exception.

"How do you read that?" she finally asked, about the address book.

"I don't have any trouble," he said, continuing to turn the pages, presumably in search of the elusive phone number for Dorothy at SHPO, whoever and wherever that was. It was probably not a twist of fate, Meg thought, that he had found a job involving the unearthing of prehistoric trash mounds.

When he had located the listing, he marked the place and turned to show Meg a large black-and-white aerial photograph of the pueblo that hung beside his desk. "Charles Lindbergh took it when he was out here in the twenties," he told her. "Here's where the visitors' center is now. And there's Dog Hill."

But Meg's eye had fallen on two framed photographs on the desk. One was the familiar black-and-white of Elliott that was featured in the journals, the other, a faded color image, was of Jim, younger, with two children in a treehouse. Jim was holding the boy upside down by the ankles, and the girl was doubled over, laughing.

"Are those your kids?" Meg asked.

"Meredith and Billy," he replied. "I'm hoping you'll have a chance to meet them."

"I'd like to," she said, and added, "Sorry I was snippy at Mario's."

"Don't worry about it," he said, resuming his search through the mound of papers and at last extracting some forms from the bottom of the pile. "I have to make one phone call. Sorry to keep you waiting."

While he was on the phone she perused the titles on the shelves and saw a hardback set of Hannah's journals. Taking down the first volume, she found it was a 1965 first edition. The flyleaf was inscribed by Bassie to Jim; the pages were dog-eared and water-warped. She carried the volume to the chair by the door and sat down with it while Jim continued his phone call. He was spinning a piece of flint—or chert, as he had told her it was called here—in circles on his desk and discussing something he referred to as "triple-X compliance forms."

Meg found the place in the journal where she had left off in the car, and began reading.

November 20. To-day a conversation with Mr. Bass that was enlightening because of its opaque quality. He is difficult to know. He is more deeply troubled by his past even than I thought; it separates him from me and I believe from all of humanity. He is outward thinking but I believe he is driven to this by inward thoughts.

We were in the parlor during my time off, with only Paco the Chihuahuan dog, and our conversation in the beginning was impersonal—we talked of the emigrant problem and the persecution of Negroes in Saint Louis and a wreck on the C&M Railroad. After awhile he said suddenly, "Does it bother you that I am shorter than you?"

I told him, not in the least.

"That I am forty-one years old, nearly twice your age? The ideal difference, they say, is eight years."

I assured him I am not enamored of ideals.

"The ideal is like the mean," he agreed—"it is the point of least interest."

"Why have you never married?" I asked.

"Because I'm terrified of marrying," he said. I told him I doubted he was terrified of anything. "I'm vaguely terrified of you," he said, and stood up to examine a clock on the mantel that needed winding. He wound it up, setting it by his watch. I remembered I had forgotten to take lavender salts up to a woman on the second floor who had requested them, and excused myself for a moment to go and do so. When I returned, Cecile McGaffin had seated herself in my chair and was talking to Mr. Bass. She had taken her hairnet off, her profile was earnest. She was imploring him, under the guise of affection, to reveal to her the details of the massacre in which his parents and his sister were killed. "I pity you so extremely," she was saying. "Should you ever need to reveal what happened, I would listen with compassion."

I expected Mr. Bass to find some way to send her out of the room, and stood waiting in the doorway for him to do so. I believe he would have done so, but there was, for an instant, a look of desperation about him. He was standing behind a chair as if to use it as a barricade against her, and the very absence of expression on his face is what alerted me to the depth of his emotion. I perceived that he was trapped where he stood, not by Cecile's presence, but by whatever thoughts were going on inside his head. It was strange to see a man so strong appear disconcerted.

"Cecile, what are you doing?" I said.

"I'm having a conversation with Mr. Bass."

"He doesn't seem to be saying anything."

"I was giving him the opportunity."

"Perhaps he doesn't want the opportunity."

"Perhaps, some day, he may," she said, and got up and walked out past me.

Mr. Bass remained a moment in the same position, then brought his eyes to bear on mine, and seemed to repossess himself. "I hope I did not appear incompetent," he said.

I assured him that I felt he was entitled to his privacy.

"I'm not, exactly," he replied. "I'm dedicated to it. Perhaps not entitled to it. Not if I want to know you better." And he began to tell me some of the circumstances of his childhood and his life after the massacre, not with detail, but in a rote fashion, clearly with a feeling of obligation, though I tried to silence him and assured him he need say nothing. He was direct but lifeless in the presentation and did not speak of the massacre itself, but said that when he was eight years old he had been taken from the Mormon family, with whom he was living, and delivered to relatives on a farm in Illinois, where he disliked the farm work and finally at the age of fourteen ran off and joined up in the army under General Sherman by lying about his age. He was along on the march from Chattanooga to Atlanta and Carolina and fought in a number of battles on the way. After the war he found employment working for an engineering firm in Boston and then attended the University of Iowa but did not graduate, as he was expelled for liking Mr. Darwin's theories and having a copy of his book on the development of species. He also had an inability to take the Bible at face value.

"You are not afraid of hell, then," I observed, and he said no.

"So would you call yourself a Christian, then?" I asked, and he said no, he did not believe in God: more evil was done in the name of God than for any other purpose. I knew he meant the murder of his family, though he did not say so.

After leaving the university he had worked for several different railroads, surveying routes across the west and into Mexico, and eventually worked exclusively for the Santa Fe.

When he finished talking, I had the impression I had been involved in a confessional; that Mr. Bass is in the habit of moving forward so not to look back. The animation in his voice when he talks about the future, or even the present, diminished to a blank stare when he talked about his past. Only when he came to the part about the railroads did he have any expression at all, as if the moment when he started building railroads, his life acquired meaning. At that point, it all became about momentum, and progress.

When our conversation ended, we were still standing as we had been; I had not moved from the doorway. I went to the window and he came to stand beside me. It was snowing out. A sleigh was coming up from the river bridge, and we knew that the passengers would disembark and end our privacy. He took my hand and placed it on his sleeve, tracing my fingers and seeming as idle as if he were stroking his dog: he was looking out the window. I was lulled into a stupefied paralysis at the intensity of physical feeling. At last we left the window, and together began to look for his hat, though lamely, as our thoughts—or mine—I should speak only for myself—were much too settled on residual ephemeral impressions to be of much use at anything mundane. In the end, we discovered the hat in the lobby, and retrieved it, with his coat, and Mr. Bass took his leave into the snow with Paco at his heels, though with me there remained an impression of him that will always—

Meg glanced up from the passage, aware suddenly that Jim was no longer talking on the telephone. He was sitting at his desk looking at her.

"Ready to go?" he asked.

She got up and returned the volume to the bookshelves. "So," she said, inserting the book into its slot, "when is Elliott going to tell Hannah about the massacre?"

"He isn't."

She turned around to look at him. "Never?"

"Never."

"You mean they never talk about it? You would think— "

He was nodding, "You would."

"Does she ask him about it?"

"Oh yes." He got up, and pulling down a different volume of the journals, turned the pages until he found a footnote Bassie had included. It was a report by a U.S. Army lieutenant, made when the army came to secure the children orphaned in the massacre from the Mormon families with whom they had been living for nearly a year.

Meg read the testimony to herself.

> The eleventh child I interviewed was living in the house of Elder E. H. Smith along with the girl, aged four, whom the Mormons call Nancy. He is the oldest of the survivors and gives his name as Elliott Bass, his present age as seven. He shows reluctance to talk. He is distrusting, and claims the girl whom the Mormons call Nancy was called Prudence by her parents, but the Smiths require that she be called Nancy. She is not related to him. He says his fa-

> ther was shot several days previous to the massacre attempting to obtain water from a stream outside the fortifications. His mother was killed with arrows during the massacre, which he attempted, at the time, to remove. His sister was shot. The only relative he knows of is an uncle named Myron Tate residing in Rockford, Illinois. He claims that after the massacre some of the Indians washed their faces in the stream, and when they returned they were white men. He believes they were the Mormons, and claims to have seen Mr. Smith, with whom he has been living, at the massacre killing children. He says he wanted to escape from the home of Smith, but would not leave the child, Nancy. He said if not for Nancy, he would have run off and found his way to California. I suspect it is the truth—he appears capable.

Meg closed the book and gave it back to Jim. He returned it to the shelf. She looked at the photograph of Elliott on Jim's desk, standing with his arms crossed in the sunlight in front of the train engine. "Bassie seems to think that he's—" she fumbled for the right description—"sort of your spiritual guide."

"As much as one atheist can guide another spiritually," Jim said.

"What does he mean to you?"

He was thoughtful, looking at her. "He means that it's possible to move on."

"Hannah seems to think he was haunted," Meg said.

"I went to Mountain Meadows once," Jim finally answered. "I walked the route those people were walking when the Mormons laid into them. And I can tell you Elliott was haunted."

The set of his features, the sound of his voice as he said this, clarified for Meg the nature of his connection with Elliott Bass.

Jim, as well as Elliott, knew what it was to be haunted.

SIXTEEN

The mesa rose before them as they ascended the path. It was higher than the valley floor around it but lower than the distant mountains, like a flat rock sitting in a large bowl. A three-foot-high stone wall encircled the rim, and as they came to the top and passed beyond the wall, the trail forked to make its oblong track around the mesa. Meg was carrying a trail guide. The view she encountered was spectacular and the breeze crisp and constant. The sun's warmth penetrated her jacket. To her left was a matrix of ragged rock and adobe walls, only a few feet high at the highest places, the interior rooms formed by these walls open to the sunlight and grown over with buffalo grass. Jim began to explain the arrangement of the ruins. The area in which they were standing, he told her, had been a separate, smaller pueblo from the main pueblo, which was ahead of them, though both had been substantial and several stories high. Meg consulted the trail guide. But even looking at the illustration of the pueblos as they once had stood—elaborate structures—she had difficulty envisioning them, as all that was left were rolling mounds overgrown with weeds and grass and a few remnants of stone walls.

"Basically it was a city with a wall around it," Jim said. "The Pecos were a military power and the mesa was a natural fortress. The river is down over there."

But Meg wasn't looking for the river and she wasn't interested in Pecos Indians. She was looking at a distant row of snowcapped mountain peaks and wondering what Hannah had thought the first time she saw this view, when she had left the Montezuma and come out here to live with Elliott. Meg couldn't help but compare herself to Hannah, and question if she herself would have had the desire to live in this remote place. Hannah had been more ambitious, she decided. At the age of twenty-one she had come to New Mexico to support herself, eager to compose a record of her adventure. The equivalent for Meg, at that age, had been to slog through New Delhi with a backpack and a vegetarian boyfriend on drugs. Hannah was steadier than Meg. She was calmer, more sure of herself. She had a sense of who she was, while Meg's own identity seemed to have evolved simply in reaction to Bassie.

"Those are the Sangre de Cristos," Jim was saying, "the southern branch of the Rockies. The peaks are thirteen thousand feet, so they're covered in snow almost all year. And that's Glorieta Mesa." He indicated a flat, massive wall of rock juxtaposed against the mountains, and explained that Glorieta Mesa was the first in a series of land formations reaching down to central Mexico, and that between it and the mountains was a natural pass used by people as a passageway for the last ten thousand years. "That big bald peak with the snow over there is Pecos Baldy," he said, swinging his arm in another direction. "And over that way, which is west, is the Rio Grande Valley. To the east over there, past the valley, you can see where the corridor opens to the plains."

She was aware of him, but only vaguely listening to his words. It was the air and the light, she thought, that had so powerfully drawn Hannah to this place. The view was mesmerizing, but even with the land formations stretching out until you had to squint to see them, the most compelling feature on the mesa was the sky. Meg thought that even had she been standing in the shadow of the church ruins, on the far edge of the mesa, she would still have felt more connected to the sky than to the land. Even in the past, when the mesa supported a city, the people living here could not have felt exactly grounded on this elevated plain. She could see why they dug kivas. Down was the only place of refuge.

"I guess you're not interested in the period when all of this was under the ocean," she heard Jim say, and turning to him, saw that he was smiling.

"It depends on how many million years that leaves you to fill in," she said.

They continued along the path, Jim explaining how Pecos Pueblo had been the center of trade between the Pueblo and Plains Indians and how the Pecos Indians had managed to stay rooted on the mesa until 150 years after Coronado and other Spaniards arrived, though the arrival of the Spaniards had begun the corrosion of Pecos, creating conflict within the tribe.

They came to a square hole in the ground with a primitive-looking wooden ladder protruding from it, and Jim hung his hat on the tip of the ladder and started down. Meg followed him, the trail guide rolled in her hand. Her hair fell motionless the minute she was below ground level where the air was still, and she felt the coolness of the underground envelop her as she descended. When her feet struck the earth, she removed her sunglasses and became aware of her surroundings; she was standing on the dirt floor of a circular room about twelve feet in diameter and entirely subterranean. The walls were made of stone cemented with adobe mortar, and stood nearly seven feet from floor to ceiling. The place smelled richly of raw, damp earth and was eerily quiet, and a patch of sunlight slanted downward from the entry hole through which they had descended, settling on the ladder rungs and stretching across the stones of what appeared to be a firepit in the center of the floor. The otherworldliness of the place overwhelmed Meg with emotion; the air seemed to be drawn out of her lungs, and she could hear herself breathing in the strange quiet. "Wow," she whispered.

"They believed it was a link to the underworld," Jim said.

Her gaze wandered around the walls and came to rest on Jim.

"A time portal," he said.

Indeed, the past seemed preserved here, in this dim, underground environment, as if the people were still down here and time had lost its linear dimension.

"It connected the realm of the underworld to the world above ground," he said. "Spaniards filled up most of the kivas with dirt and trash so the Indians couldn't come down and worship their gods. So then the Indians built more kivas. And the Spaniards backfilled those, too. That indentation in the floor near the wall is called a *sipapu*. It was reminiscent of a human navel, and symbolized passage from an even deeper underworld at the beginning of life."

The wind wuthered over the opening, but the room itself, as Meg looked around the walls, seemed untouched by motion. The downward slant of light illuminated particles of dust that hung suspended in the frigid air. Jim stood at the base of the ladder, stark lights and shadows from the shaft of sunlight clinging to his face like paint as he spoke.

He talked about one of the kivas at Pecos that he had excavated.

"What was that like?" Meg asked. "To uncover a place like this?"

"Imagine a room filled with dirt," he said. "And every shovelful just might contain a piece of gold. Metaphorically speaking."

"And did it?" she asked. "Metaphorically speaking?"

"We found some potsherds," he said, and she laughed. "We found a soup plate. Two hammerstones. Fragments of oxidized iron. Charred food bones, including those of a domestic rooster. Shall I go on?" But then his expression became serious. "It's like being the first person to walk into a room hundreds of years after the last person there walked out of it."

A lizard was attempting to attain a foothold on the base of the ladder, and Jim gave it a boost with the toe of his boot. "Hannah and Bassie used to come to this kiva," he said, and Meg was taken by the thought of how they had entered this womblike place and inhaled the musty smell of the dirt here, their eyes, like hers, adjusting to the dark. "When Hannah was first here it was only a roofless pit, but Elliott put some old railroad ties over the top so she could bring tourists down. She kept a blanket down here, and at one point got a night-blooming plant to bloom in the dark. Then when she had Bassie, Bassie used to come down here and have conversations with imaginary people."

The image of Bassie as a small child unsettled Meg. She could almost see her, nestled here in her mother's skirt.

But this was not her usual way of thinking. She had descended, somehow, in her thoughts, into another world, just as she had climbed down through this wormhole to the past, and suddenly she felt a need to surface again. The problem with reading the journals, she decided—and with coming here to Pecos and this mesa and this hole in the earth, was that the people who had lived and died here had not left any room for newcomers. Hannah and Elliott were still, in too many ways, determining the course of Bassie's life, and Nina's, and now Meg's. It was one thing to be in conflict with the living. Another to battle the dead.

She turned abruptly to Jim. "About what Bassie said at the café. She's always accusing me of flirting with married men. Because that's what my mother does."

Jim walked over to the wall and settled down against it, his knees propped up in front of him. "Who's this 'Paul' guy you were talking to on the phone?" he asked.

"An architect from San Antonio," she answered. "I've dated him for a while."

"Dated him seriously?"

She contemplated the question. "I guess so."

"Except he doesn't have a key to your home. Sorry, but I couldn't help overhearing."

"I'll put it this way," she said. "He's a guy who gets a sinus headache when I get a migraine."

"Oh, I know that guy," Jim said.

Meg had known a number of them. "One of the drawbacks to being thirty-seven and not married is that you start to know which traits you're looking for, and which ones you don't want to have to put up with," she offered. "And both lists keep getting longer. I have a question." She was still standing, and placed her hand on a rung of the ladder. "Why do you like Bassie? Or do you? Honestly."

"I do, actually. At first, I'm ashamed to say, it was probably because she liked me. I was young, and she impressed me."

A gust of wind blew over the opening, carrying the voices of tourists who were passing on the trail. "We should probably go up," Meg said.

But Jim remained seated for a moment, taking his time and asking Meg more questions about her life with Bassie and her relationship with Paul before rising to his feet, setting flecks of dust in motion in the stream of sunlight.

When they reached the surface, Meg squinted in the glaring light and Jim took his hat from the tip of the ladder where he had left it. They started along the trail and up a gradual rise, looping toward the left to a valley a third the size of a football field. The valley was surrounded by low swells of earth covered in weeds that Jim identified as ragweed and asters, snakeweed and seeding mullein, the profusion of which threatened to destroy the ruins. Crossing the open area,

Meg stopped and consulted her trail map. "So where are we?" she inquired.

"In the center of the pueblo," Jim answered, showing her the place on her trail map. "We're standing in the middle of the quadrangle, which was basically the plaza, or town square. Those areas"—he pointed out the swells around them—"are what's left of the structure. It extended all the way around us. The swells are symmetrical, and from what's been seen of the wall construction, we think the pueblo was probably designed as a unit. Two thousand people lived here at one time. When American colonists were just gaining independence from England this place was already in decline, and had lost three quarters of its population."

She studied the sketch of the pueblo in her trail guide. It was built around a quadrangle with porches and passageways connecting the rooms. There were no exterior doors or windows in the first story; these rooms were accessible only by ladders protruding through the ceilings.

The path along the edge of the mesa was bordered by a three-foot swath of mowed area on each side, the purpose of which, Jim explained, was to keep the snakes away. When Meg and Jim had gone most of the distance around the trail, they could see the treeline of the creek below them, marked by the paler color of trees growing on the banks. Ahead was the massive church, an earth-red color in the sun and standing on the narrow southern end of the mesa. Meg was awed by its size, and Jim began to tell her of the violent revolt of 1680 in which several tribes of Pueblo Indians united and drove the Spaniards out of New Mexico. The Pecos church had been set on fire at the time and reduced to rubble, but later when the Spaniards returned they had built the present one on the ruins of its predecessor.

The church was only a shell now. The entryway was supported by the original carved beams, but the roof beams and the roof itself were gone. Sunlight shone down into the interior, and Jim talked of the experience of excavating the graves under the floor. He had supervised the excavation.

"Did it bother your conscience?" Meg asked.

"I can't say it did," he answered.

"What if it had been your ancestors buried here?" she wanted to know.

"Dead usually seems fairly accurately dead to me."

But not exactly stone cold, Meg surmised, remembering what he had said about the kiva being a time portal and a link to the underworld. It had seemed, when he said it, as much his own opinion as a Pecos belief. She guessed he was less settled in his thoughts about the dead than he wanted to appear.

Studying the uneven, weathered line of red adobes against the vault of open sky, she thought of how the church would look in the evenings, when the shadows brought the textures of the walls into relief. Jim was telling her that Catholic mass was held here once a year, but to Meg the place seemed too empty to hold anything with any more conviction than a draft of air. The air moaned dolefully around the massive walls. The place was filled with a mournful, quiet quality. The structure seemed to have released events of the past when the roof caved in, and it did not seem to be collecting any more. Unlike the kiva, it felt vacant.

He led her from the church out to the ruins of the convent, a series of rock and adobe walls no higher than short hedges, and told her of passages in the journals that described Bassie, as a three-year-old, climbing up in the church window for a higher view. The window seemed impossibly high for such antics now, as the dirt had since been excavated from the base of the walls, but back then, Jim said, the window would have been accessible. Meg stood looking at it, attempting to conjure the picture of Bassie there as a child. But there was nothing in the window now except a patch of pale blue sky from the roofless interior. It was a perfectly blank frame.

A man and a teenage boy wandered up, going in the opposite direction, along the path, from the one suggested in the trail guide with its numbered touchpoints. "What are all the holes in the ground?" the man called out to Jim, seeing his park service uniform.

"Infestation of pocket gophers," Jim replied.

The man and the boy came up to talk to him.

"The bigger holes have been taken over by rock squirrels," Jim explained. "But they're all made by gophers."

"It seems like the holes would be destructive to the ruins," the man said.

"They are," Jim told him. "We try to control the gopher population. It's a battle."

"You kill them?" the boy asked.

"Poison them," Jim answered.

When the boy and the man started off, Meg said, "They're going in the wrong direction."

"It looks like it," Jim observed.

"You don't want to tell them?"

"Not especially. Do you?"

It was strange to her how little control he seemed to need over people, while he would poison gophers to protect the ruins.

"I better go down and see how things are," he said. "If I can get hold of Judith, do you think you and Bassie would be up to driving into Santa Fe to our house for dinner? I can see if Judith could pick up a pizza or something."

SEVENTEEN

The western sun was blindingly low, shooting shafts of light from the roof of Jim's pickup truck and forcing Meg to shade her eyes as she followed the truck on the way to Santa Fe. The drive was a mere twenty-five miles but already, less than halfway, it seemed longer, with Bassie sitting in a mute, hostile posture against the passenger door as the mesas and valleys rose and descended on either side of the road, her thoughts inscrutable. Jim had made little progress in the pit within the circle of boulders; he had spent too much time on the mesa showing Meg the ruins, and then had been unexpectedly detained in his office by a protracted phone call with the contractor who was to build the addition.

Bassie adjusted the heater vent to blow into her face, inhaling the hot air.

"You're searching for a father figure, aren't you?" she said.

"Not that I know of."

"You're playing with fire. Don't you get in the middle of his marriage."

Meg pressed her foot on the brake, harder than she meant to, and swerved the car onto the shoulder of the road. Throwing the gear into park, she turned to Bassie.

Bassie was clutching the door. "Now look at that," Bassie said. "He's pulling over too."

Jim was veering his truck onto the shoulder, and backing toward them.

"I'm going to say this once," Meg said, her hands on the wheel and her eyes on the approaching tailgate. "I'm here because you asked me to come. And I'll leave if you don't back off. And you can get home on your own."

"The worm has turned," Bassie muttered.

"The worm has always been turned, goddammit," Meg said.

Jim was stepping from his truck and starting toward the car. Meg rolled her window down, admitting the cool air, and leaned her head out of the window. "Sorry. There's no problem," she called out. "Bassie and I were just talking. It'll only take a second."

He hesitated. His face was shaded, the sun behind him, the hat sitting back on his head. "Just flash your lights when you're ready to go," he called, and turned back toward the truck.

Meg said to Bassie, "If you could remember how to get there, we wouldn't have to follow him."

"He knows what's going on," Bassie answered. "He knows what we're talking about."

"Of course he knows. You weren't exactly subtle at Mario's."

"You're the reason we're invited to dinner," Bassie accused her. "Judith doesn't like me. Jim put her up to this. And you're the reason he wore that hat."

"What hat?"

"The one he's got on. I've never seen him wear that hat before."

"Well, it's obviously been worn before."

"Not at work, it hasn't. You don't get to choose your hat when you work for the park service. I'll tell you why he wore it. It looks better than his regulation hat."

"That's ridiculous."

But she had to wonder. It did look a great deal better than the Smokey-the-Bear affair.

Jim was getting back into his truck.

"I'll tell you one thing," Meg said. "If you embarrass me at dinner, I'm going to fucking kill you."

"The worm has grown profane," Bassie said.

"Oh, leave me alone," Meg said.

"I'm an old dog. I don't do new tricks."

"Fuck you."

"The worm, the worm is out of control."

"I'm going to flash my lights at Jim, and I'm going to pull out, but I'm warning you, don't you try to be my conscience. I am not my mother. I am not flirting with Jim Layton. In fact, he's getting on my nerves. He's too calm."

"He is not calm. He's repressed."

"Would you stop it."

"Stop what? Stating my opinions? Not until I die."

"If I'm lucky," Meg said bitterly.

She flashed her headlights and Jim's blinker started blinking; his truck pulled slowly out onto the highway toward the glaring, sinking sun. Meg checked her rearview mirror; no cars were approaching, there was only the road stretched out, the hills and mesas on either side spotted with junipers. She eased onto the road and then accelerated with more force than she intended. The car lurched forward; Bassie grabbed hold of the door, her glasses reflecting the sunlight.

Meg drove, enveloped in angry silence. She could feel her face grow hot with anger.

"His wife is an enabler," Bassie said at last.

"I don't know what you are talking about," Meg said.

"She doesn't care one fig about the fact that he has wasted his career. She's enabled him to do it."

"Oh, that is psychobabble."

"He's still got the same job he took when he was twenty-six years old."

"Why shouldn't he? It's a great job. Why is it your business, anyway? He's found something he likes and stayed with it. What's wrong with that?"

"Stuck with it, you mean. Stuck with it, out of fear of the unknown. If he had chosen the job, that would be different. But it fell into his lap. And Julie. Puh. Judith. Whatever her name is. I can never remember her name."

"Oh, you can too."

"She's a river guide. Did he tell you that?"

"Should he have?"

"She takes tourists on rafting trips."

"So?"

"She's glad to have him stuck here. It allows her to do what she wants to. He married her because he got her pregnant. And then she miscarried."

"You told me that already."

"He took the job at Pecos so she could finish her degree. She was an English major."

It was, Meg thought, an unusual combination—rafting and literature.

"He should have married someone who encouraged him," Bassie said.

"That is so incredibly sexist. She's not responsible for his career."

"Of course she is. Marriages work that way. Not that you would know. He's done less, with more, than any of his colleagues. I'm not the only one to say so. They offered him a job at the University of Cairo, and he refused the offer."

"Do you really need that heater blaring in your face?"

"Air does not blare. Sound blares."

"You haven't taken that coat off since we got here, Bassie. You can't possibly be cold." Meg rolled her window down, breathing the cooler air. "I can't tell you how much I am dreading this," she said. "Taking you to dinner. It's like taking a loaded pistol."

"I've got manners."

"Convince Juanita at Mario's."

"Roll that window up."

"You always have to have the last word, don't you?"

Bassie declined to answer, by way of denial. Meg left the window open.

"You're tailgating," Bassie said in a moment.

They topped the roll of a hill, and descended, and when they ascended another hill the sun disappeared at the horizon. They were entering the limits of Santa Fe, and traffic had increased. Meg stopped behind Jim's truck at a traffic light; she saw him glance in his rearview mirror and lift a hand. She raised a hand in response. The light turned green and they started out again.

"He was in the backseat," Bassie said.

"Who was in the backseat of what?"

"Jim was in the backseat when his parents were killed. No one found them until morning. It was a back road."

"You mean he was in the car with them all night? Was he injured?"

"Broken ribs."

"And his parents were already dead? Did he know that?"

"He was a child, not an idiot. I suppose he knew it. The people in the other car were dead too. It was a head-on collision. He won't, by the way, tell you any of this. He won't talk about it. He told me twenty years ago. I doubt he's talked about it since."

Meg drove in silence, trying to picture an injured six-year-old boy spending a night in a car with his dead parents. She could not imagine it, and began to puzzle over the vagaries of the unlikely friendship between Jim and Bassie.

Then Bassie said, in a quieter voice, "Orphans understand each other."

The house was an adobe ranch house in the area known as South Capital, and was hidden on a narrow dirt driveway half a mile from the road, the ground around it studded with cactus and junipers. Jim parked in his garage beside a minivan, wedging the truck between the van and ambiguous bulky items stacked in leaf bags. Boat paddles and life jackets were suspended on the walls of the garage.

He got out of the truck and motioned Meg to park behind him, then came over to help Bassie out of the car. A stone path led from the driveway to the door, and Jim took them along this path, explaining that the area had been undeveloped when he and Judith had first moved here, but the city had since filled in around it, and the house inhabited its original five acres rather defensively now. He told Bassie he had added on to the house since she had been here last, attaching a stone patio onto one side and a room for a pool table onto the other. It was his son, Billy, who had wanted the pool table, so they had built the room together.

Opening the front door, Jim escorted Meg and Bassie into an entry hallway. The end of the hallway, Meg could see, opened to a rustic living room with plate glass windows revealing a view that matched the view in the front—cactus and sparse grass and junipers illuminated by the bluish light of evening. Judith appeared, wearing jeans, and barefoot, flipping on the hall light and greeting Bassie, and then introducing herself to Meg. She was older than Meg had expected, her skin weathered, her short hair bleached reddish by the sun. She was muscular and her face was lively, with luminous blue eyes. To Meg she seemed like a true earth-woman. Her handshake was strong, the forearms muscled and veined. She was as tall as Meg.

Bassie said, "I hope Jim didn't have to twist your arm to make you feed us."

"Only slightly," Judith replied, leaving it unclear if she was joking. She led them into the living room, where the adobe walls were covered by bookshelves crowded with books. The floor was made of stone and blanketed with area carpets, the furniture was unremarkable—a worn leather sofa, upholstered chairs, a television in one corner and a fireplace in the other. A Mexican blanket hung on the wall over the fireplace, and pottery urns and bowls were scattered among the books on the shelves, but otherwise there was almost nothing in the way of decoration. Meg had imagined Jim as living among primitive, exotic objects.

An overweight basset hound lifted his head and watched with bloodshot eyes as Jim settled Bassie into a reclining chair beside the fireplace. Jim stacked logs and built a fire, and he and Judith talked briefly about the dog, which Judith had taken to the veterinarian earlier in the day because of ear mites. Jim then excused himself to change his clothes, and Judith went to open a bottle of wine. When she came back holding the bottle opener and requesting preferences for red or white, Meg volunteered to help her in the kitchen.

The kitchen was a small, low-ceilinged room with a square butcher block for a center island and glass-front cabinets. A plastic lazy Susan stood on the counter, crowded with spices and a large squeeze bottle of Aunt Jemima pancake syrup. An enormous box of Cheerios and smaller boxes of cereals and pancake mix were perched on top of the refrigerator, along with a cookie jar filled with vanilla wafers. It was not a cook's kitchen; there was nothing like fresh garlic strung on the wall and no assortment of exotic utensils and Cuisinarts, but the pots hanging on the rack were obviously well used, and things appeared settled into convenient places. Meg felt uncomfortable, as if intruding on the cozy room, and oddly in need of proving herself to Judith.

"How can I help?" she asked.

"It isn't very elaborate," Judith said. "I picked up a lasagna." She rummaged through the refrigerator and pulled out a jar of Parmesan cheese. Examining the expiration date, she held the container as securely in her hands as if it were the paddle of a raft. She appeared, Meg thought, to fit the perfect image of a river guide. Meg could picture her on a raft descending over rapids, shouting instructions to her passengers over the noise of rushing waters.

"This will do," Judith said, setting the Parmesan on the counter. She opened the oven, and took a knife and plunged it into the lasagna, extracting it to test for heat. "You could go ahead and open those two bottles there," she said, indicating the bottles of wine.

Meg uncorked the bottles and poured red for Judith and for Jim and a glass of white for herself. Bassie had requested club soda with lime, so Meg asked for a lime, which Judith found, slightly brown from age, in the refrigerator. "I'm not much of a cook," Judith said. "Jim does most of our cooking. How is Bassie holding up?"

"So far, pretty well," Meg said. "I guess Jim told you what's going on."

"No."

"Her mother buried some dogs on the hill that's beside the visitors' center, and now they're planning to build an addition there. Bassie wants Jim to find the graves so she can take the bones and rebury them somewhere else."

"Jim could find four-leaf clovers on Pecos Baldy," Judith said. "He'll find the graves. The lasagna is vegetarian. I hope you don't mind." She did not actually seem to care if Meg minded or not.

Meg sliced the lime and squeezed some into Bassie's soda, and took the soda and Jim's wine into the living room. No one was there, and Meg could hear Bassie clunking the cane around in the bathroom off the hallway. Setting the drinks down, she began browsing through the titles on the shelves, and realized as she did so that she did not feel up to Judith. She dreaded the dinner conversation.

When Jim returned, his hair was wet from a shower and he was wearing khaki slacks and a blue cotton shirt instead of the park service polyester. He took his wine from where Meg had placed it and came over to the bookshelves, smelling of aftershave. "Are you doing okay?" he asked Meg quietly.

"Yes. What do you mean?"

"I mean the talk you had with Bassie in the car."

"Oh. Those talks don't bother me like they used to."

She could tell he didn't believe her. She didn't actually believe herself, though she had lived with her defenses long enough to convince herself they were adequate. "She's just hard to be around when she's upset. She takes it out on people."

"She takes it out on you."

Bassie returned from the bathroom and Jim helped her into the recliner and gave her the soda. "I'm going to go help Judith with the salad," Meg said. As awkward as she felt with Judith, she preferred the kitchen to watching Bassie's watery eyes glaring at her from behind the fishbowl glasses, analyzing every gesture she and Jim made toward one another.

In the kitchen Meg washed greens for a salad, rationing her sips of wine so as not to resurrect the headache that she had fought off in the morning.

"So you live in Austin," Judith observed. "I don't think I could tolerate living in Texas. It's too hot. And too politically conservative."

"Austin's not conservative," Meg said, feeling defensive, thinking of the Frisbee golfers on Shoal Creek—fraternity boys and Rastafarians, women with nose rings and beer-bellied cowboys all cussing together when the Frisbees landed in the muddy creek instead of in the chain-link Frisbee catchers.

"Have you lived there long?" Judith asked her.

"Most of my life. What about you?"

Judith reached for a salad bowl in one of the cabinets. "I grew up in California, near where Marineland used to be," she said. "My father taught English at a college out there." She opened the refrigerator and looked inside. "This is a pretty good Italian dressing. I also have French. The kids like French."

"French is fine. Bassie told me you're a river guide."

"In the summer. During the year, I substitute teach at the high school." She took some tomatoes from the refrigerator and placed them beside the sink, and Meg began washing them, looking out through the window over the sink at the rental car parked in the drive beyond the stone path. The night had grown dark; an outside light had come on over the driveway. "Before we had the kids," Judith told her, "I had my own rafting company on the Green River. But for the last two years I've just been doing day trips out of Buena Vista."

"Does Jim go with you?"

"No. He's not much of a rafter. He likes rock climbing better, though he doesn't even do much of that anymore. He's had some problems with his knees." She paused. "We used to raft together, before we were married. A lot of the canyons in Colorado have Indian ruins, and we would beach on the spits and explore the places you couldn't get to any other way."

This explanation brought things into focus for Meg. Judith, she decided, was the sort of woman in beer commercials, who rafted the rapids and camped at night with her lover. Meg had been camping only once in her life, in college, with half a dozen classmates of mixed gender, and she had been so uncomfortable with so much proximity that she had sat up all night stirring the coals of a recalcitrant fire and nurturing her loneliness. And now, she figured, there was little possibility she would ever find her way into remote places with a lover, or sleep on the ground watching the stars glide over a canyon ledge. She was too tied to her work and routines.

"Of course that was back in the wildcatting days, before the companies monopolized," Judith added, starting to count silverware out of a drawer. "It was a great subculture then—the river rats. But it's impossible to live like that after you have kids." She paused from her counting, and added, "I'm trying to decide if they're going to want to eat at the table with us or not. Do you have any kids at home?"

"No," Meg said, rinsing off an overripe tomato.

"We were married for a long time before we had Meredith," Judith told her. "I had a miscarriage early on. Jim was more ready than I was to try again. We had this house for nearly ten years before Meredith was born." She pulled the oven open and tested the lasagna to see if it was hot, then shoved a loaf of French bread in to heat. Meg could see how Judith was suited for Jim: they both loved to be outdoors. The river carried Judith on her adventures, and the ground gave up its secrets to Jim. She could imagine the two of them camping together, making love in a tent on a spit of land along the Colorado such as the ones that Judith had mentioned—whatever the hell a "spit" was—and then awakening in the morning to traipse up a canyon in search of Indian ruins.

But in other ways the two of them did not appear compatible. Jim was more inquisitive, and seemed more intuitive than Judith. He was certainly more likable.

"I'll go see what they're up to out there," Meg said.

When she returned to the living room, Jim was sitting on the floor beside the basset hound discussing with Bassie a new editor at the University of New Mexico Press. "I think the lasagna's almost hot," Meg said, but then, hearing someone behind her, turned and saw a teenage girl entering through the front door. The girl was tall and wore athletic shorts and an oversized gray sweatshirt; her hair was tied in a ponytail. She slung a backpack to the floor.

"Hi," she said to Meg, obviously wondering who Meg was.

"Hello," Meg answered.

Jim got up off the floor. "Meredith?" he called. "Come in here; I want you to meet some friends of mine."

When Meredith came in, he introduced them. "This is Meg Mabry, and her grandmother, Claudia Bass. Dr. Bass."

The girl's eyes fixed on Bassie and widened dramatically, "*That* Dr. Bass?" she exclaimed. "Oh, my gosh. We're reading those journals right now in my English class. Oh, I can't believe this. My teacher makes everybody read those books, every year. I mean, she doesn't make us read them all, just certain parts, but this is great! Wait till I tell her. I knew you knew my dad, but this is unbelievable."

Bassie leaned back in the chair and thumped her cane once on the floor, then directed the point of it to a chair across from her. "Sit down and talk to me," she commanded. "What's your teacher's name?"

"Ms. Rodriguez, Amy Rodriguez," Meredith said, dropping into the chair. "I told her my dad knew you and she almost flipped out. She's read the journals, I don't know how many times, and—"

"Invite her to dinner," Bassie said.

"What, tonight? Wow! She would love that. If I can get hold of her. She would just be so amazed if I just called her up and—oh, I hope I can find her number—"

"Go ask your mother if it's all right," Jim said.

"She can eat *my* food if there isn't enough," Meredith replied. "This is so great. I bet she'll give me an A for this. Where's Mom?"

"She's in the kitchen," Jim replied.

Meredith got up from the chair. "I'll be right back," she said to Bassie, and passing Meg, disappeared into the kitchen. Meg could hear her talking animatedly to Judith, discussing how to find the phone number for Ms. Rodriguez, which she knew to be unlisted.

In a moment, a boy a few years younger than Meredith came in through the front door, lugging a backpack overstuffed with books. He had the same unhurried movements, Meg noted, as his father, coupled with an instant shyness when he saw Meg standing in the entry to the living room. He was shorter than Jim, but resembled him, and had a similar, observant, tolerant expression.

"Hey," he said to Meg.

"Hey."

"I'm Billy."

"I'm Meg. Your mom is in the kitchen. Your dad's in here."

Billy set his backpack on the hallway floor beside the satchel that Meredith had dropped, and walked past Meg into the living room. When he saw Bassie in her mangy coat with her cane across her lap and her cloddish shoes propped on a stool before her, he seemed to think he had made the wrong decision to enter the room. "Hello," he said under his breath. From the kitchen came the lilting voice of Meredith talking into the telephone.

"Billy," Jim said, "this is a longtime friend of mine, Dr. Claudia Bass. You've heard me talk about the journals that her mother wrote."

"Hello," he said again, and Meg couldn't discern from his voice whether the name of Claudia Bass was familiar to him or not. She hoped that Bassie would not say anything to intimidate him. Bassie often demanded a forwardness that Billy obviously didn't possess.

Bassie said, "I met your sister when she was an infant. I have not met you. I knew your father thirty years ago, when he looked about like you would look with a ponytail."

Billy seemed uncertain if he was supposed to take this as a compliment.

"Go tell your mother you're home," Jim said, offering a reprieve, and Billy turned toward the kitchen.

"Wait a minute," Bassie said. "Sit down and tell me what you're studying in school."

Billy dutifully returned and sat in the chair that Meredith had vacated. "Science is my favorite subject," he said hesitantly.

"He likes botany," Jim added. It was obvious to Meg that he was trying to ease the situation for Billy, and she found this endearing.

"Why botany?" Bassie demanded, and Meg grew tense at the question, as it was uncomfortably like those that Bassie had asked of her back in the days when she was making the decision to change her major from history to engineering. Bassie had a habit of making people justify themselves.

Billy briefly related a story about his childhood interest in a certain exotic type of flower he had seen on a camping trip with his father in Holy Ghost Canyon, and then turned back to Jim. "Dad, do you think later you could help me with my report?"

"Meg is the one who should help with that," Jim said. "She knows about hydraulics." He turned to Meg and explained that Billy was writing a report on the Hoover Dam.

"Sure, I'll help you with that," she told him, relieved at the thought of escaping the dinner party, even for a while.

Meredith came out of the kitchen. "She's coming!" she exclaimed to Bassie. "She's on her way. She'll be here in twenty minutes. I better go change clothes."

"Who's coming?" Billy asked.

Meg was the only one to hear him. "Her English teacher," she said, feeling tenderness toward the boy, and knowing that the longer she could keep him from the dinner table and away from Bassie, the better off he would be.

When Amy Rodriguez arrived forty-five minutes later the lasagna, which Judith had left in the oven to remain warm, was dry around the edges. Bassie and Meredith had been carrying on a conversation with the intensity that only people with great self-confidence manage to generate in a short time, Bassie instructing Meredith on how to design the book report on Hannah's journals, and Meredith responding, "This is really great . . . this is just perfect . . . that is such a fantastic idea." Judith was in the kitchen, and Meg had retreated to Billy's bedroom with Billy and was seated on the bed with him—the bed being the only place to sit—with a laundry basket full of unwashed clothes at her feet. They were discussing the Hoover Dam, and Jim loitered in the doorway, listening, seeming reluctant to interrupt them but apparently preferring their company to that of Bassie and Meredith.

Meg had not had much experience with boys of Billy's age, even when she was that age herself, but she found that she liked him. He came quickly to be at ease with her. With encyclopedias and library books spread between them on the bed, they formed a kind of refuge on the stained patchwork coverlet, and were reluctant to leave it when Judith called them to dinner.

Amy Rodriguez was a young, ferociously vivacious woman, unmarried and overweight, with luxurious black hair. In Meg's opinion she was a sycophant to Bassie, dragging a yellow notepad to the table—apologizing loudly as she did so—and taking notes on almost everything Bassie said. Bassie spoke of her futile search for Vicente in Mexico, where he had disappeared after Hannah's death, and of her search for information on Hannah at the sanatorium in the last year of her life. Bassie had always believed that Hannah must have kept a journal during that year at the sanatorium, as it was unlikely that Hannah would have ceased writing, abruptly, without any indication that she intended to do so. But if a final journal had once existed, Bassie had not, in spite of all her searching, ever found it.

Meg sat quietly listening, now and then exchanging a look with Jim. They both knew that the notebook cover Jim had found on Dog Hill could, by a long stretch, be the remnant of a journal kept by Hannah. But it made little sense that this would be the case when the only writing in it—on the endpage adhered to the leather and recording a purchase of fruit—was not in Hannah's handwriting. Also Hannah had died at Las Vegas and the scrap of leather had been unearthed from Dog Hill at Pecos Pueblo, nearly fifty miles away.

When the conversation settled on the exhibition room to be constructed on Dog Hill, Amy Rodriguez was, or pretended to be, as outraged as Bassie about the prospect, appealing to Jim to intervene. Meredith said, "Daddy, you can't let them do that!" until Jim explained the politics involved.

Bassie, Meg noted, was more herself at dinner than she had been in the last three days. Her hostility vanished, and she seemed invigorated. Meg wondered briefly what her own relationship with Bassie would have been like had she simply given in and read the journals when Bassie had first asked her to—if Bassie might have come to respect her more or respect her less. It was troubling to Meg how affirming Bassie was toward Meredith, when she had never been this way with Meg. She was complimentary toward Meredith, whereas she had always demolished any confidence that Meg had managed to cobble together. Meg had often felt like a rat in a scientific experiment receiving an electric shock regardless of which way it turned in the maze until finally it just crouched in one place, resigned to having no control over its own fate. Only in adulthood had she pulled herself together and fought back.

"I've always thought it would be interesting to know more about Hannah's parents," Amy Rodriguez was saying. "I saw their graves when I went to see Hannah's in Chicago—I was there for a teachers' convention and just took my afternoon off to go to the cemetery. Really fascinating, actually to be there at her grave. I suppose you've been there a lot of times?"

A moment passed before Meg realized that the question was addressed to her.

"No, never," she said belatedly. "Bassie and I talked about my going with her one time, but something came up."

"Meg has never read the journals," Bassie added.

"You're kidding me," Amy said, looking from Bassie to Meg. "You have got to be kidding."

The following moment was familiar to Meg from similar ones in the past, in which she could defend herself by exposing Bassie and revealing how destructive Bassie's obsession with Hannah's journals had proved to be for the family. But Meg did not like public scenes, and intuition told her she would end up looking worse than Bassie if such a scene occurred. "I just never got around to reading them," she said.

The silence after this was broken by Jim. "Strange as it may seem to those of us who live in the past," he said, "some people actually live in the real world. While we're trying to piece together other people's lives, these people, like Meg, are living their own. Seems strange to us, doesn't it? They go to work. They make a difference." He paused. "They're the ones who make history for the rest of us." He smiled across the table at Bassie, and then rose from his chair. "I'm going to make a pot of coffee."

"I saw you," Bassie said as Meg pulled out of the driveway and turned onto the unpaved road, the headlights sharply illuminating blades of grass and the long ears of a jackrabbit. "I saw you watching him and Judith. Sizing it up."

"You were too busy lording it over the teacher to see anything," Meg said.

"The teacher was delightful," Bassie observed.

"The teacher was an egomaniac and a sycophant. If it's possible to be both of those. She was full of herself."

"You didn't like Judith, either, did you," Bassie answered.

"No, I didn't. I think she's self-absorbed. I liked Billy, though."

"Of course you liked Billy: he had nothing to say. You two were peas in a pod. Botany, puh. He's going to find a patch of dirt to hoe, just like his father did. Only not as deep. Why isn't this heater getting hot?"

"It takes a minute."

"Meredith has promise," Bassie said.

"You mean Meredith is the one that likes the journals."

They drove in silence. The heater began to grow warm, and Bassie closed her eyes. Meg looked at her and hoped that she was falling asleep, but after a moment Bassie spoke with her eyes closed. "I'm sure it didn't help their marriage that Jim had his eyes glued on you, and was insulting the rest of us to take up for you."

Meg rolled her window down.

"Close that window," Bassie said.

"It helps me stay awake."

"You're not sleepy. You're trying to drown me out."

"And who would blame me?"

Bassie opened her eyes. "Don't act as if you didn't notice he was watching you."

"I didn't notice."

But she had. Several times she had turned to see him looking at her. She wondered if Judith had noticed, and decided she had not. Judith had seemed complacent toward Jim. Almost oblivious of him.

"You're mulling it over," Bassie said. "You think I'm too far gone to know what's going on. But I can read you. I know exactly what you're thinking."

"What I'm thinking," Meg said, "is that I'd pay you a thousand dollars to shut up."

EIGHTEEN

December 10. Received a letter from Mr. Bass this morning and spent an hour poring over penmanship which so exceeds mine in distortion, being no better than crow tracks, that at times I lost the meaning of a sentence before I reached the end of it, though on the second reading the words began to sing in my ears. It was a wonderful letter. I read it while sitting under the footbridge for privacy, forgetting the unpleasant rocky frozen ground beneath me in my concentration. Mist from the water secluded me. Even Mr. Bass with his left-handed writing in my lap seemed far away and off the point, though his potential felt near. His words had the same exactness he would use to add up figures in mathematical equations. He is still in Santa Monica installing track, but intends to be here by Christmas.

Editor's note: The previous entry refers to this letter written by Elliott Bass to Hannah Troy in December 1891.

My dear Miss Troy,

I hope that you are well and not besieged by ingrates there at the Montezuma. I also hope that you are not besieged by too many handsome men. Do not look at them, my dear, think only of your poor old friend in California who has got a toothache. It is, if I am honest and do not devote myself to getting your sympathy, better to-day. Yesterday a dentist filled the tooth with amalgam and enjoyed the process rather more than I did.

It is a rough set of men I have got on my hands here, all of them consumed by grumbling fits, nothing happens to their liking. Last night they rolled ninepins until three in the morning and then had a rumpus, which I had to mediate or else lose several men for several days if not for good. They had got their knives out.

Graybacks in our bedding have been keeping us up all night. When I am not thinking of you I am shaking out my blankets and pondering the nature of the railroad business. The boom in California has collapsed and California fallen off the map. Tickets are not selling; no one wants to come here. Freight business is increased, but due to rate cuts and commissions, profits remain low. Labor and materials are high, while shipping rates decline. Ten years ago we made a dollar a mile for a ton of freight, and now make less than a cent. The Kansas drought has doomed us for a while. Southern P. telegraphers are striking which will compromise passenger safety. My superiors (in many ways but not including common sense) are trying to force our own dispatchers to handle the surplus work. Of course they refuse to do it. Weather and human nature still determine profits more substantially than all the labor policies and regulations and restructuring of debt.

Pay no attention to my penmanship. It is bad in the morning because of this rheumatism, and bad at night because I am saving fuel and writing in the dark. The truth is, it is bad in general. I had hoped to find at least a page of vellum, but you see, I did not.

Write to me. I want to know what kind of time you are having and if Miss Jewell Cartwright is safe and not annoying you too much. Write to me on subjects such as this; be honest; I hope you will. You may tell me anything. I will write to you from Colorado. I intend to see you before Christmas.

Your sincerest friend,
Elliott Bass

December 12. The snow will not let up, the pipes have broken, there are not enough plumbers. Over in Colfax County people are trapped in their homes without food and the roads are snowed over, but everyone here at the Montezuma is skating on the pond and sledding and the spur has been getting up the mountain with the mail. A Mexican arrived today, escaping the volcano in Colima, also a woman from Arkansas who says the Salton Sea is drying up, and five judges of the territorial land court and a group of New Yorkers who are funding the building of a mausoleum in New York where people will be buried under glass. New Yorkers in general are bad tippers. Jewell has got a sore throat and is walking about with flannel bandages soaked in Pain Balm tied around her neck. We have taken six counterfeit coins in the last two days; the sheriff was out to warn us, but too late. The coins came out of Trinidad.

My dear Miss Troy,

I am en route by train but will soon be at a place where you can write to me. I want to hear from you. The words I hear out here are all below your standards. Last night I had a hostile conversation with a lazy government inspector whom I discovered sleeping on the job and who insisted that the track was adequate, his only evidence being the fact that he was able to sleep. If the track were faulty, he said, the jolting would have awakened him. I put him off the train this morning. There are too many miles of shoddy track with bad ballasting and faulty grading left over from the Great Race when they were building track on ice—We have more accidents in this country than they do in the United Kingdom; our trains are faster but not as punctual and have been losing nearly 7,000 lives every year in accidents due largely to idiots such as these.

At any rate, I am loyal to the corporation and see horizons just as vividly as corporate leaders do, but there is a difference between us: they can only put their mark on the map, while I can find the way to get us there. By necessity I have to deal with the people living on the route; in Mexico they trust me, and while I have not lost much sleep worrying about corruption and corporate infidelities I will not look the other way when my work is compromised or when my word to people is violated or my figures treated casually. I don't like making promises the corporation fails to keep. Safety for the passengers is paramount, and if the government inspectors won't do their job, then I am left in the awkward position of being a liar. I cannot spend the rest of my life riding the rails I have built with an eye to maintenance; if I did, then there would be no more advancement.

December 13. I would have thought that squinting so long over his previous letter might have given me a knack for his left-handed crow tracks, but I was cost an hour in deciphering what I had thought would be his intimate reflections, but instead was a declaration of opinions on the subject of corruption in the railroad kingdom. He is optimistic and does not doubt himself and is not afraid of censure. He is devoted to his work; I like this about him.

The book club honored Mr. Whittier's birthday with a reading of his poems, he is eighty-four, the poems were badly read, prohibition was discussed at length, Republicans should drop the cause or it will sink the party . . .

December 16. A sad dream concerning Mother last night haunted my sleep, it was a desolate, unwieldy fabrication and has hung in my mind all morning giving me a blackish mood. At noon I was called to the desk and given a letter from Mr. Bass that he will not return for New Years but will stay in Colorado and then go to New York for meetings with the traffic association and the likes of Jay Gould. He wanted me to write him at the Windsor, but I am not in the mood. I am anxious. His work in Colorado is risky and he is not careful. He suspends himself from bridges to correct his measurements.

December 18. It is too quiet here, almost everyone has gone home, only a few of us have stayed, we pass each other in the drafty halls with hardly a greeting at times, very down at the mouth, having assumed the attitude of somnambulants. I am reminded of poor Lucy Snowe in *Villette* wandering the halls of Madame Beck's Pensionnat de Demoiselles in the Rue Fossette, and though we are not as alone as Lucy Snowe, or put to the task of caring for cretins, we are certainly cut off from the world by weather and the hills. Our usually noisy place is now too quiet, though the fires are kept burning in the public rooms, which is a little cheerful, and the air smells like narcissus and hyacinths that bloom all winter here. A gaudy Christmas tree and plumes of Pampas grass have imposed themselves on the lobby. Only a few guests were ill-advised enough to come this time of year, and most of those who have stayed here are tuberculars who sit on the porch all day with spit-cups, breathing sage and cedar to try to clear their lungs. It is fairly dismal, very sad. They eat raw eggs, take creosote in hot water and drink milk. Jewell is nearly the only one here who is cheerful.

My dear Miss Troy:

I would prefer to call you *Hannah.* May I, my dear girl? Your letter was waiting for me at the Windsor. I was glad to know you are well, but thought the letter formal. You will reduce yourself to phantom status if you will not risk your thoughts. Please give me *thoughts*. Forgive me that I am not a model of divulgence myself: I am attempting to do better on that front. I want to know you better. Write to me again, with less discretion and more heart.

Yours faithfully,
Elliott Bass

December 21. If I had the nerve to bare my thoughts and send them off to him—an almost stranger still—to be read in a place I have never been, and at a moment when his mood may not be quite so hungry for my thoughts, then I might be diminished. Why should I disclose myself when he does not?

They are trying to be festive downstairs but it is mostly tuberculars and they are not happy, most of them are sick.

December 22. The snow does not let up; a track inspector near the town of Colmor, not far from the place where our train was wrecked, was lost in a five-foot drift but found alive. Brother sent me a Christmas gift, it was a large fringed wrap of iridescent silk which has on it an embroidery of peacock feathers. A committee of men from an organization of health resorts has settled into the club room to talk about statistics on the weather here and how it affects the respiratory organs. A Texan rancher and his wife arrived, he likes boxing and Beethoven and talks incessantly, they came to escape the Mexican revolutionaries marauding around the Texas border and foraging the cattle. Also we have three goldminers who have come up from White Oaks and are paying room and board with pieces of raw gold. The waiters and bellboys are betting on whether the world will come to an end next Friday as Adventists in Kansas City predict. Walt Whitman is said to be dying. If he could have heard Cecile McGaffin puffing *Leaves of Grass* out of her rosebud lips as a tribute to him in our book club meeting, he would have died at once.

Christmas night. I am not in my room at the Montezuma with Jewell as usual, but reclining on silk pillows in a stuffed chair by a fire in a bedroom of the old Morales Mansion and Jewell is sleeping across the hall. We were working in the dining room at the Montezuma this morning when Vicente Morales appeared and said that Mr. Bass had telegraphed Mrs. Simms and made arrangements for us to go to the Mansion. We packed our bags and Vicente brought us in a fancy barouche with an Indian driver—there were children knocking on doors in town and singing for treats as we went through, and candles everywhere. We arrived at the mansion in the afternoon, with hundreds of people already here, including the lunatics the family has taken in, and almost a hundred orphans. A Mexican band played in the hallway and Vicente Morales's father, Don Pedro, greeted us, he is handsome like his son but with gray hair. He said a number of fine things about Mr. Bass. He did not seem overjoyed to see his son Vicente however. Don Pedro has sided with the Anglos and the U.S. Congress in passing a bill for public education in New Mexico; this was opposed by Catholics who up to now have run the schools, and also by some of the native population who dislike the idea of paying taxes to support the schools. Vicente Morales, like his father, supports the idea of public education, but several days ago published an editorial saying the schools should teach in Spanish as well as English because the loss of language would be detrimental to the culture and prevent the people from speaking either language well, and would in other ways impede international business on which New Mexico ought to profit. Therefore Vicente had a disagreement with Don Pedro, which is only one of many. He does not live at the mansion but at the family's sheep ranch at Raton; he also has a house in town and usually comes to the mansion only when his father is not home, and yet on Christmas day they are together. Don Pedro resents that Vicente operates the liberal newspaper called *La Voz* on some of the profits made from the family's ranch, yet Vicente feels entitled to the money as he is the one who manages the ranch.

We had only been at the house a few minutes when one of Vicente's political friends arrived, and Don Pedro asked him to leave, and started shouting at him in Spanish, and Vicente grew angry in defense of his friend. One of the brothers got involved and there was a terrible argument without any resolution, though the man did stay. Later several printers from *La Voz* arrived, looking poor and badly dressed, and Mrs. Morales allowed them in. Don Pedro grumbled about their presence: he is not against the poor—he is a great benefactor—he is only against *La Voz*.

When most of the guests were gone, Vicente invited me to the carriage house with him so he could feed and put away the horses. The servant supposed to do so is an ancient Indian who every Christmas drinks a bottle of bourbon and leaves the horses to put themselves away. It was late at night by now and so we took a lantern with us, snow was on the ground, the wind had extinguished most of the candles on the roofs and pathways; the moon was not yet up. We did not see the Indian in the carriage house, but saw that he had left the horses unattended in the stalls. At least a dozen cats took refuge in the hay and watched us, the lantern light reflecting in their iridescent eyes. Vicente hung the lantern from a hook; it cast its light around the walls and steadied to a glow that intensified the depth of shadows. The barouche in which we had traveled and several other vehicles were parked at the end of the room, partitioned from us by a half-wall, and while no sound came from that area except the wind through cracks between the boards, Vicente told me that the Indian—a man whom he called Tío—was asleep in the barouche. Vicente lit a cigarette, and went about with hay and buckets of grain from the bins. The dusty smell and quiet was calming after so much social intercourse extended for so long a period without a space to breathe. Vicente saw that I was cold and had not brought my coat out, so he returned to the house for a blanket while I waited alone and watched the dark barouche for any sign of the Indian though there was nothing to suggest that he was there. Vicente came back after a while with a woolen blanket called a poncho and took the liberty to dress me in it, pulling it over my head as comfortably as if he were placing a blanket on a horse.

He entered a stall and removed the saddle, placing it on the rail, and began grooming the horse, and told me he had gone the back way to the house instead of through the front door on his errand for the poncho to avoid his father and also Jewell. I asked—was Jewell in search of him?

"Unless my instincts are bad," he answered, and when I inquired why, he said, "You know why."

I tried to explain her behavior, saying it was due to a propensity—and I was going to say "for drama," but Vicente interrupted me. "For men," he said. "A propensity for men." He stopped grooming the horse, and looked at me, his cigarette between his lips. He is intense when he is serious, with an aspect of profound well-meaning.

"It isn't necessary to avoid her," I told him.

"Like a rabid dog," he said.

I admitted that she is excessive, but said I hardly thought she was demented, and he said that if he were to invite her to the carriage house, then she would come, but not for conversation. I suggested she would soon drop off if he did not express an interest, and he was amused. "She is not a tick," he said. I asked if she appealed to him, and he said she did not. I told him women have perceptions and always know if a man is interested, or if he is not interested, and he said "Do they?", and stopped brushing the horse to look at me. I told him that they do unless their instincts have been subjugated by their thoughts—I meant by too much thinking—and that some women do rely on reason, and yet Jewell was not one of those.

"Are you one of those?" he asked, inhaling from his cigarette, and my heart did make a beat beyond the ordinary, though I resisted answering. We talked of Mr. Bass and the dangers of his work; Vicente remained in the stall with the horse, leaning on the rail to talk to me—the light was vivid on his spectacles, I could not see his eyes though I perceived their focus. He told me Mr. Bass could walk through flames and come out alive, and that I needn't be worried about his safety. "Listen, my friend," he said, "God has whims that no one can account for, but Elliott Bass, left to himself, would live forever." He said that Mr. Bass can walk on ledges like a mountain goat and fifteen years ago surveyed through the Indian areas without a military escort while other surveyors required protection, and that the only injury he suffered was some creaking in his bones from winter winds. During the conversation he asked if I would take a horseback ride with him to-morrow, and when I admitted my lack of experience with horses, he offered to instruct me. We agreed that Jewell would have to come along.

We also talked of how he first met Mr. Bass, who was very young at the time, though older than Vicente, and plotting the route for the Santa Fe to get over the treacherous pass at Raton. This was long before Vicente was in conflict with his father. The Santa Fe and Denver Rio Grande were competing for the pass; they each had spies to watch the other's movements in the area. Mr. Bass called on Don Pedro to help the Santa Fe, and Don Pedro arranged for him to meet Vicente, who was managing the family's sheep ranch in the mountains near the pass. They met at the ranch and invented a ruse—they disguised themselves as shepherds and rode out to Vicente's flock of sheep and for two weeks Elliott went about surveying the landscape in a serape and sombrero and copying his notes at night by firelight. In this way he secretly mapped the pass, and when the race to build track finally began, he was able to beat the DRG because his route was already finished. He started grading before daylight one morning with the help of a make-shift crew of people from the area, which Vicente and the keeper of an inn had put together on an hour's notice when they were told that men from the DRG were on their way up. So the Santa Fe got the pass by right of prior construction, and Mr. Bass and Vicente have been fast friends since then.

Vicente was done with the horses by the by, and took the light down from the hook, and as we were leaving spoke in Spanish, and a voice answered—It was Tío, the Indian. Vicente told him that the horses had been taken care of.

In the house he took me to the library and gave me a Christmas gift of an English Spanish dictionary that he had used when he was seven years of age. He said that he would teach me to speak Spanish.

Jewell found us then and sat on the sofa and took the dictionary and read aloud shamelessly and badly, wanting Vicente's attention, but then Mrs. Morales came and showed us to our rooms. Later Mrs. Morales returned to my room and said that Jewell had gone to sleep prone across the bed without pulling back the covers, so we went and put her into bed and returned to my room together and sat for a while by the fire, and talked about Mr. Bass. She is grateful to him for keeping the peace between Vicente and Don Pedro, as much as possible, and for reminding Vicente that when he aligns himself against Don Pedro, he is at risk of losing the very continuity and tradition that he advocates. Mr. Bass counsels tolerance on both sides, and speaks his mind bluntly, and so keeps their mutual trust. I believe he is invigorated by disagreement; he is certainly not afraid of discord; life to him is an experiment based on calculations and revisions of calculations. While he keeps his eye on the future and on landscapes in the distance, he is still attuned to conflicts between the farmers and the railroads, the rich and poor, Republican and Populist, Don Pedro and Vicente.

Mrs. Morales left the room two hours ago, I have been writing steadily, the wind is blowing audibly outside and whistling through the branches, the draperies are open, the moon is rising over the hills.

December 26. This morning we borrowed riding clothes and blankets, and Mrs. Morales gave us hats. Don Pedro came with us a distance but argued with Vicente, also his horse favored a leg, so within no more than fifteen minutes he turned back. This left the three of us; the morning was overcast, the ground covered in snow. My mount was supposed to be a tame old gelding but took me at a hard trot across an open field, his destination appearing to be a large tree the size of a fortress with branches low to the ground, and Vicente had to come alongside me and get hold of the reins. Jewell, of course, then also needed rescue, by design.

The trail was obscured by snow but Vicente knew it from memory; it wound its way uphill between rocks and prickly bushes. Vicente talked about his sheep dog that trailed along behind us; he said it has a natural herding talent and that when it was a pup it often herded chickens around the yard. It was suckled to a ewe and thereby bonded with the sheep. He also talked about the Raton ranch. He is the only one of his family who likes the ranch—Don Pedro and the brothers have not sheared or dipped a single sheep, nor do they care to be involved except in the accounting and profit. Don Pedro watches expenditures, therefore Vicente is not autonomous but does not care, as long as he can secure the money he needs to operate his newspaper. He talked of toxic weeds and scab and foot and mouth disease and anthrax. He is interesting and animated, though Jewell and I learned more than we had ever wondered about pustules and the chemical composition of dipping medications and Great Britain's ban on U.S. livestock because of contagious diseases. In some ways he is easier to know than Mr. Bass; he doesn't shut off pockets of his life in secrecy, but offers his opinions without provocation. He is devoutly Catholic, a patriot of democracy, but laments injustices to his people under U.S. laws and is defiant toward Republicans even though his father is a party leader: he says that he has seen enough of sheep to know sheeplike behavior.

December 28. Vicente took us to a concert by a Mexican band at the opera house and Jewell and I argued afterwards, she is jealous of my friendship with him, and says he is in love with me. She has gone to sleep now finally.

December 29. I wrote Mr. Bass and told him about Christmas and the horse ride and hearing the Mexican band with Vicente. But should I try to explain the whole unwieldy truth before it even settles into shape? It is too elusive. I cannot explain it. I am certain of what I feel for Mr. Bass. My intuitive affection for Vicente is more complicated and more difficult to grasp. I feel as if it exists on its own terms, and while I know I should settle it in my own mind, I feel impatient with my conscience, and confused.

I don't know when this letter is going to go out, as the mail has been held up—trains are blocked by snowdrifts, one collided with a bear before it plowed into a drift and carried the bear in with it.

Everyone at the Montezuma is complaining. There is a group of Englishmen who talk of nothing but wild headhunters in the Solomons who are attacking Englishmen, and there are Texans here talking of nothing but neutrality laws and problems with Mexican insurgents. . . .

New Year's Eve—Vicente came unexpectedly to the Montezuma tonight. He was meant to be at a celebration ball hosted by the hose and fire company because his family is a benefactor of the company and pays for their equipment, but instead he came here and found me serving eggnog in the lobby. Some of the girls had got up card and board games and were mixing it up with the guests, Vicente was the champion at chess and took second place in checkers and made some money at whist. I played a game of twenty questions and waited tables, watched a few *tableaux vivants* and helped the children perform shadow plays in one of the rooms. The piano and victrola were at odds with each other all evening, the men were intoxicated, the women drank sarsaparillas and opium concoctions—prohibition is all talk and no conviction here. One woman who pretends she is devout uses uterine morphine wafers in her private parts, supposedly to relieve painful monthly periodicals though I would guess her to be nearly sixty years of age. At midnight we sang Auld Lang Syne, and Vicente and I stood on the stair landing and watched the people below crushing eggshells of confetti on each other.

January 1, 1892. Vicente took a room and stayed the night; we rode this morning, following the frozen treeline of the river. Jewell was angry. I cannot live my life by her emotional presumptions, they are transitory. Last night she was cavorting about with a small man from Connecticut with a biting humor and cutting wit and no patience for those he thought on a lower social plane—except that he was drunk last night. Why Jewell likes him I don't know, perhaps the money, or possibly she was hoping to make Vicente jealous; I do not care, and don't suppose her feelings are substantial no matter how intense, she is too silly.

January 5. DEAR JEWELL, If you are reading my journal you had better stop. And do not come talk to me about it. The thought of discussing your feelings about invading my privacy makes me furious. I dislike drama just as you dislike circumspection—these have been in conflict from the beginning with us—but to READ MY JOURNAL—Jewell! What on earth possessed you? You had better not confess to me, or anyone. I will never trust you again. I will find out if you do it again. Now put it back.

January 6. Jewell has got a headache and avoids me, I am surrounded by strange people here, some of them have come from town to hide out in the mud baths from the sheriff who is knocking at their houses trying to collect a penalty of 25% on their delinquent taxes, others are downstairs armed with guns in protest of an editorial the *Optic* printed saying people should not have to arm themselves in these modern times, as it is not likely they will be called on to defend themselves at a moment's notice and there are a lot of decent men locked up in the penitentiary for shooting someone on impulse out of anger, who would not be locked up had they not been armed. Indeed—I might fire on Jewell Cartwright if I had a gun. There is also a group of strange women downstairs en route to a suffrage meeting in Washington, they have been trying to incite our feelings on the vote, and argued with a doctor in the dining room who said that women's nervous systems are already overstressed and that the vote will overwhelm the female constitution. His own, male, constitution has been overwhelmed by Germans lately, he is surly about the Germans, he is off all Germans—they are all he talks about. The German son-in-law of the German who discovered that consumption is an organism says that sputum is the method of contagion for the influenza, and the doctor calls this nonsense.

I wrote to Mr. Bass but have no idea where I should send the letter, or where Mr. Bass is staying, or if he is en route from one place to another. . . .

My dear Miss Troy:

I found your letter of December 29th to-day awaiting me at the Windsor. I was in Topeka and am back now in New York, and stopped at the Windsor to see if any mail had come for me, thinking, of course, of mail from you. The reason I am in New York is this: While I was in Topeka I met an old friend who is employed here, an odd character who several years ago was involved with an effort to make contact with the "other world" by means of the wireless—a scheme that Congress considered funding with $40,000 but thought better of—and who now has got himself into a more reasonable project— He is working on the plans for the underground. He asked me to review the plans, and offered me a significant fee to do so, which I could not easily refuse as I am not in the chips at the moment. So here I have returned, though on my own expense and staying at a boarding house. We dined at a shabby restaurant to-day in a part of town where there are many unfortunates who are homeless. I will leave to-morrow, and be back to see you soon. I want to see you. But I will have to make some stops along the way, so do not look for me until I come.

About your letter. I hope my friend Vicente Morales is not trying to replace me. I have no doubt he would lay out his life for me, but this, of course, is another matter. He has seen more of you, and you have seen more of him, in the last two months than either of you have seen of me. At the risk of spinning things out along this strain too long, I will say that any man worth anything would head toward home at this point, and I am on my way. Meanwhile thank him for me—I had asked him to look after you—and ask him not to overdo it. He is also caring for my dog, but I doubt that Paco has received the same attention.

I see that Congress has again denied us statehood. I'm sure Vicente has something to say on the subject. They have based their arguement on the premise that residents of New Mexico are aliens because most of them speak only Spanish. However the argument is full of holes, as there are patches of people down in Louisiana who speak only French, and in Pennsylvania who speak only German. New Mexico has been part of our country for more than forty years and everyone living there who is under the age of forty, which is most of the population, ought to be considered as a native-born American no matter what he speaks.

I had a suit of clothes made. The material is good. I also saw an oculist; my sight is better than I thought.

Yours as ever,
Elliott Bass

January 29. Lillian and Minerva and I were in town for a matinee performance of *The Count of Monte Cristo*, and encountered Vicente by accident. We had just come out of the theatre and were discussing whether or not we had time before the spur at five o'clock to walk to the Bazaar, and I was looking at the sky over the roofs opposite to see if it would snow, and noticed Vicente entering a tack shop. I sent Lillian and Minerva on, saying I would meet them later at the depot, and went over to talk to him. He was looking at a piece of hardware and was surprised to see me, and apologized for being in his work clothes and unshaved. He had come to purchase hardware for a gate that he had joggled loose in the middle of the night when chasing a pair of thieving dogs out of his pens with a Base Ball bat. The dogs belonged to a neighbor and were known as good sheep dogs but had started running off secretly at night and stealing poultry from the neighboring ranches. Vicente had lost some hens, so he and one of his men decided to sit up late and watch to see what had carried them off, and shortly after midnight the dogs arrived and Vicente sent one of them limping to the hills and locked the other one in a coop. Early this morning he drove the captured dog on a flatbed back to its owner, and so the mystery that had plagued the area was solved. The dogs had been every night soaking off the blood of their kill in a water trough and returning home in the mornings to assume the mantle of protectors, and therefore they were not suspected until Vicente caught them in the act. They had not killed so much as a rat in their own yard.

The neighbor shot the dog that Vicente brought to him and will shoot the other one if it returns home, as it likely will because of its devotion to the sheep. I thought this pitiful, but Vicente said it is common to shoot dogs that become killers, as the instinct cannot be undone.

He made his purchases and stored his belongings under the counter and we took a walk through the American neighborhoods. The houses are large, most of them built after the railroad came; the train station was placed a mile from the Old Town plaza, and New Town grew up around it. We must have looked conspicuous together as I was dressed for the theatre and he was dressed for wrestling thieving dogs. One man gave us a look of hatred and came riding a large horse slowly toward us from the opposite direction with a menacing expression, and pulled his hat over his brow in a threatening way. Vicente watched him and instructed me to turn left down a walkway toward a house, as if I were going into it, and I complied though he did not come with me. He stayed directly on his course, not veering an inch to the left or right but meeting the mounted man face on. Only when the nostrils of the horse came in contact with Vicente's chest did the man rein to a stop. He spoke to Vicente in Spanish; Vicente did not answer, but stood where he was, until at last the man jerked the reins and turned his horse aside and went his way, at a slow and ominous pace.

A moment later, we continued walking. "He is a Gorra Blanca," Vicente said. "A White Cap. These men are liberal bandits who ride about the countryside at night with sheets over their faces destroying the property of rich people. To him, I am a rich Republican who has stolen his land and starved his sheep and made his cattle go thirsty."

"But you are not a Republican," I said, "and you have not."

"I am a Morales," he replied. "We have made money while others are losing it, so who can say we haven't written history in our favor?"

He said the mounted man who had confronted him had raided a ranch last night with twenty men disguised in hoods; they had killed the milch cows and entered the house and threatened the family, and injured a caballero. Sheriff Lopez, who is Vicente's cousin, knows their identity but is a sympathizer and will not arrest them.

A silence passed between us after this discussion. I wanted to ask him where he was leading me, as we had crossed the railroad tracks. There was no path to speak of, but a mood had settled on us that precluded reason, and the route began to seem as clear as a trail. We ascended a hill, and I thought the summit to be our destination, that he intended to show me a view of the plains. The climb was steep, and my shoes not made for walking uphill over rocky, muddy ground. The cold was harsh; the sky withheld the snow; behind us was the town. A heaviness had fallen on Vicente's face. There was no sound except the rustling of my skirt. No trains came whistling down the tracks behind us, no noise came from the streets of town. When we reached the summit, the view struck me speechless; it was not a landscape of flat plains spread out in front of us, but moors. Each hill rolled out beyond the one before it, as far as we could see, the perfect image I had conjured from the ruminations of the Brontës, the grass turned brown and lumped with patchy snow, the bushes widely scattered, nothing taller than my knee. I was astounded with the strange and barren feeling of the area unfolding like a sea under the heavy sky, and could only stand and stare at it in silence, overcome with an emotion I could not identify.

But Vicente took my arm and led me down toward the moors, and at last he said, "I should tell you I have no idea where I am headed."

I stopped and turned to face him, and he looked at me directly. We had come to a level place, but another downward slope was rolling out beyond us. His eyes revealed his sadness, and I understood but vaguely that we had arrived somehow, at a place of some kind. We stood apart from one another, and yet the open spaces bound us to each other.

"We should go back," I said.

"Or further," he suggested.

I asked what purpose there would be in that. He looked away from me. I asked if he would look at me, but he would not. I moved to put myself within his line of vision, and when he looked at me, he said, "To be together. We could be together."

If I had known him less, I might have thought he was suggesting something he was not. He only needed time to state his own conclusions. I asked him to consult his conscience, but he consulted, instead, my face, and at great length, and when he spoke, his voice was so distinct against the solemn, quiet weather and dark overcast of sky, it seemed to lay itself emphatically on my psyche, as if the clouds had dropped a stone down on my head. "My conscience tells me you belong to Elliott," he said. "And that I'm walking on an edge."

I told him he was not the sort of man to fall from edges. He did not readily concur. He agreed at last to trust my judgment on that theory, and we turned and started back. The weight of my emotions burdened me as ominously as the weight of pending snow, but the threat is always black, and snow falls pure and white. We did not speak for a while. An understanding had descended on us. I'm not disquieted by honesty. On this occasion I was briefly soothed, knowing the connection that it gave us.

It was long after dark, after my return to the Montezuma, that the snow began to fall in earnest and my mind to shadow over with the day's events—to conjure up the rolling land and pending clouds, the solemn look in Vicente's eyes, and to think what circumstances can befall when the truth is severed from its moorings and allowed to find its way in open skies.

NINETEEN

When Meg and Bassie made their way up the rocky incline at eight o'clock in the morning, they found Jim with Tony Flores in the roped-off square inside the ring of boulders, consulting a large book on soil composition. The area was about six and a half feet long on each side, but as yet was dug only inches deep. Jim was wearing gloves and kneepads and had obviously been working. The sun was breaking through a stratum of thin clouds, but the air remained cold.

"Have you heard the weather forecast?" Bassie growled at Jim as she approached. "It's supposed to sleet."

"Good morning," he replied cheerfully, closing the book. "We've got a full day before the sleet gets here, if it does. And I've got tarps, to cover things up if we have to. Good morning, Meg."

Bassie settled herself onto a low ledge.

"How's the Texas weather?" Jim asked Meg.

"So far so good. No rain where it matters."

"So you don't have to go home?"

"Not yet, anyway."

While Bassie sat on the ledge with her legs extended, crossed at the ankles, her cloddish orthopedic shoes scuffed in the morning light, the laces frayed at the ends, Jim described to Meg the work yet to be done. He led her down the hill through a series of low ledges and a number of tall junipers, through roped, pin-tagged areas, and showed her where he and Tony had used a plumb and line level and something called an "idiot stick" to rope the pit that was under the stand of cholla. They had cut the cholla early in the morning with a chain saw, and cut the bunchgrass as close to the ground as possible, discovering so far nothing more interesting than pieces of broken glass and three aluminum pull tabs, left over from construction of the visitors' center. "I'm sorry that Bassie was so rough on you last night," Jim remarked, as they stood looking at the roped, denuded square, the chain saw lying on the ground at their feet.

"You don't know the half of it," Meg told him. "But thanks for taking up for me. Guess what. I finished the first volume last night."

"And what do you think?"

"I think I'm paler than my ancestors. I think we're getting watered down."

"Nah. Every generation thinks that. We're supposed to. It's why we have legends."

"To make us feel like losers?"

"To make us try harder."

"Do you think you're a paler version of your ancestors?" she asked.

He seemed thoughtful. "No. I think I'm a paler version of yours."

"Very funny." She actually thought it was.

"Hannah isn't perfect, you know," he said.

"No, she's intolerant and judgmental. Like Bassie. Am I that way?"

"Well." He didn't say she wasn't. "Some traits are better watered down."

"I am that way?"

"I wouldn't like you as much if you weren't."

"I'm going to assume you intend that as a compliment," she said.

A strand of her hair blew across one eye, and Jim reached and tucked it behind her ear, then seemed to feel embarrassed for having done so, and looked away, and said, "Intolerance isn't the worst that Hannah pulls off. Keep reading."

Meg was touched by his gesture of taking the hair out of her face. "What do you mean?" she asked.

"Just keep reading,"

"What does she do?"

"You'll see."

"Tell me."

"Takes her clothes off for Vicente. For one thing."

"She does what?"

"You heard me."

"You mean she undresses? On purpose? She knew that he saw?"

"I believe that was the idea. He asked her to."

"When?"

"Well, she was married to Elliott."

"And then what?"

"That was pretty much it."

"And she wrote about it?"

"Volume two, page sixty-five, paragraph two, line six—"

"Oh, come on—"

He laughed. "It does happen," he said. "I don't actually know if it was line six."

"Does she describe it in detail?"

"Interested?"

She was. She was also aware of the attractive shape of Jim's back; he had squatted down nearly at her feet to pull from the soil a handful of grass that had escaped his earlier labor. His gloves were tucked in his back pocket, the fingers flopping out. "Nevertheless, Hannah still seems like a lot to live up to," she said.

He tossed the grass aside, then stood up and dusted his hands off. "Yes, and Bassie is too," he said. "Of course Bassie is also a lot to live down."

"Speaking of which," Meg said, "do you have any Excedrin in your office?"

"No. Do you have a headache?"

"It started yesterday. I've used up my Excedrin."

"It's the altitude. I'll find someone who's got something. We're almost seven thousand feet here, and that can cause dehydration and a headache. Are you drinking enough water?"

"I think so."

"You should have said something yesterday."

"It wasn't that bad yesterday. It got worse."

His eyes were deep brown against the backdrop of the sky. "I forgot that you're descended from a family of stoics," he said. "Out of curiosity, what do you think would happen if you started complaining?"

"I'd turn into my mother."

He laughed. "There has to be some room between Bassie and your mother."

"Just where anyone would want to be," she said. "Between Bassie and my mother. We better go up," she said. "Bassie's probably looking at her watch right now."

When they arrived back at the ring of boulders, Bassie was still seated on the ledge, waiting for them, the fur of her coat blossoming in the wind.

The crew began to arrive. Tony went down to start digging on the pit beside the decimated cholla, while Jim instructed Annie to go to his office and make some phone calls, and assigned Victor and Kelly to help him in the pit inside the ring of boulders. He reviewed with Victor and Kelly how to bag and label discoveries and note them in the field book, and how to carry the dirt in buckets down to the screening area by the center, and sift the fill through a screen. Then he gave them each a pair of kneepads and put them to work.

At nine-thirty Meg asked Bassie if she would like to go down to the center where she would be more comfortable, but she refused. When Annie returned from making the phone calls, Jim sent her to get a lawn chair for Bassie from a closet in his office. She returned with the chair and a blue ball cap, which Bassie accepted, as the wind was picking up.

An hour later, Jim went to place a phone call to Phil Barker, who was in Santa Fe transporting his diabetic mother home from the hospital. Temperatures were dropping and Bassie decided she wanted a woolen scarf from the car. Meg went down to get it for her, loitering in the car for a moment and relishing the solitude, thinking about her conversation with Jim.

She returned through the center, started up the hill with the scarf for Bassie, and halfway up met Victor running down toward her. "Where is Dr. Layton?" he asked excitedly. "I've found a bone!"

"I think he's in his office. What kind of a bone?"

"Tony says it's a rib. It's near the surface and it may just be a deer rib or something, but it could be a dog's. Tony said I had to wait for Dr. Layton before I could dig anymore, so we don't know yet if it's just a piece, or if it's whole, or if it's attached to anything."

"Go look for him in his office."

But Jim was coming up the hill, carrying an open box filled with smaller chipboard boxes. "What did you find?" he asked.

"Tony says it's part of a rib," Victor said. "It's on the second level—about where we were working when you left us—about twenty centimeters deep. I saw this change in the soil like you talked about, and I told Tony, and he got the Muncell to check it against. And then I hit this hard thing. I thought it was a rock, but when I brushed around it I could see it was porous. So I did your trick of putting my tongue on it, and—sure enough—I felt it kind of stick. Come look. It's pretty big."

Jim shifted the boxes and reached into his pocket, extracting two Excedrin he had scavenged from somewhere, and handing them to Meg. She took them and swallowed one, forcing it down without water, and put the other in her coat pocket. They continued uphill and found Bassie within the circle of boulders, seated in the lawn chair at the edge of the roped square, the baseball cap shoved so low on her forehead that it rested on the black frames of her glasses. She was close enough to the rope that her shadow, in the morning sunlight, appeared to have crawled into the pit, and now lay across the place where the bone tip protruded from the soil. Kelly was leaning against a boulder, drinking bottled water from a jug, and Annie was sitting cross-legged on the ground at Bassie's side with a bag of Oreo cookies in her lap. "Go look," she said enthusiastically, waving her hand at the square. "Victor found a bone."

It did appear to Meg, as she propped her hands on her knees and leaned over the pit, that she was looking at the tapered point of what was probably a rib. It was embedded in the dirt in about the center of the square, which was approximately six-foot-by-six-foot and at present dug less than a foot deep. Jim fished a trowel from a bag of tools and got into the pit and started digging carefully around the bone. Bassie watched him closely from the lawn chair, Annie ate Oreos, and Victor and Kelly crouched beside the pit to watch Jim work.

"Tony?" Jim called loudly, in a moment.

"*Sí*," Tony answered from somewhere below, screened from sight by the succession of ledges and junipers.

"You got the camera with you?"

"Yes, I'm coming," Tony called.

"Do you think it's a dog bone?" Victor asked.

"I don't, but it could be," Jim replied, and went on digging. When he was finished, he had pedestaled the bone about three inches above the ground around it. "If you look here," he said, "you'll see it's not articulated."

"What does that mean?" Annie asked.

"It's not attached to anything. It's a fragment."

Bassie sat staring at it, the scarf Meg had brought her knotted like a noose around her neck.

Tony took photographs while Jim made calculations in his notebook and marked the placement of the fragment on a grid map, after which Jim tugged gently at the bone and freed it from the soil. He studied it. It was about four inches long. "It's a rib, all right," he said. "But it could have belonged to almost any large animal. Possibly a dog, but probably not. This close to the surface, it probably wasn't buried by anything but the elements."

Tony was the only one of the crew indifferent to the discovery; leaving the camera with Jim, he returned to his work downhill.

Bassie demanded a cup of coffee, and Annie set aside her bag of Oreos and trotted off to get it. She appeared to have voluntarily assumed the role of Bassie's personal assistant, which Meg found herself glad to relinquish.

Feeling conspicuously useless, Meg inquired of Jim if there was anything she could do to help.

"I think we're all right," he said, continuing to gouge out lumps of dirt with his trowel. "The best thing you could do right now is to convince your grandmother to go down to the center and get out of the cold."

"I'm not going down," Bassie said.

Victor and Kelly continued shaving the dirt an inch at a time, and Jim pointed out several features to them, including a demarcation in the soil in one corner of the square where the dirt was more compact and lighter in color. If something had been buried in this area, he told them, the digging had not extended to that corner. The soil in most of the square was slightly darker, more homogeneous, and less compact, indicating it had been turned sometime in the past.

Kelly, it appeared to Meg, had a better eye for these details than Victor did. She was a pretty blonde with a thin, flat-chested figure and an old-fashioned way about her.

They had been working only a few minutes when Kelly took a bucket of fill down to screen, in the area set up behind the center, and returned with a metal item, a fraction of an inch in size, conical in shape and corroded, which she had screened out of the fill. Jim said it appeared to be the screw tip of a mechanical pencil. He thanked Kelly for the care she had taken, as the screw tip could have fallen through the quarter-inch screen unnoticed, and then stored the tip away in one of the small white chipboard boxes that he had brought up from his office.

"But it's not a very important discovery, is it?" she asked.

"Probably not," he said. "But you never know."

A few minutes later Victor, who was working near Kelly, sat back on his heels. "I think there's something metal here," he said.

Jim crawled over to examine the spot. Bassie leaned forward and watched him.

Annie came up the hill with a plastic cup of coffee for Bassie. "I brewed it fresh," she said. "What did you find?"

"Something metal," Victor said. "Conquistadors, here we come!"

"Just because it's metal doesn't mean it's Spanish," Annie said, rolling her eyes, vigorously chewing on a large wad of bubble gum.

Jim brushed the area around the object, exposing it to view without extracting it from the soil.

"What is it?" Annie asked, standing at the edge of the pit.

"I think it's a mechanical pencil," Jim said.

"A pencil?" Victor echoed, with obvious disappointment.

"Yeah," Jim said, examining it further. "A rubber-barreled mechanical pencil. Come here."

Victor crawled over to look.

"See," Jim said, "the rubber's in bad shape, but otherwise the pencil's basically intact. This knob caps the bottom end, but the tip is missing. You can see this little cylinder of lead coming out here. Kelly, hand me that screw tip, will you?"

She got up, retrieved the screw tip from the chipboard box and brought it over to him. He studied it and held it to the pencil in the dirt. "It fits," he said. Cutting the soil with his trowel, he extracted the pencil, still embedded in the sheath of hard soil, and placed it in a separate box.

"I don't guess anything made of rubber is very old," Victor observed.

"Rubber has been around longer than you think," Jim replied. "This pencil probably has a story." He got to his feet and turned to show it to Bassie.

But her expression stopped him. She had stiffened herself in the folding chair and was staring at the box. "Give me that," she demanded hoarsely, dropping her cane clumsily and reaching for the box. "Give it to me."

Jim handed her the box. She was drawing the cold air into her chest with an audible sound. Her head appeared small, with the baseball cap jammed down onto it and the woolen scarf knotted under her chin. The wind creased waves into the fur of her coat; she cradled the box in her lap and stared at the object, then looked at Jim.

"It's my father's," she said.

"Your father's?"

Meg went over to look.

Victor and Kelly had not heard what Bassie said, and were joking about conquistadors using mechanical pencils. Tony could be heard sharpening his tools down near the pit where he was working; the grating sound carried uphill on the rising wind. Annie was smearing lip balm on her mouth.

"Mother ordered a box of pencils for his birthday," Bassie said flatly. "It's in the journal. There were twelve of them. They were called pocket pencils. Slide pencils. She got them from the Ward catalog. I looked them up for the footnote. They had rubber barrels and gilt tips and were three and three-quarters inches long. Measure it." She offered the box to Jim.

He carried it to his tool satchel, and kneeling on the ground, took a metal ruler from the satchel. "This is centimeters," he said as he measured, mentally changing the numbers into inches. "Three and three-quarters inches exactly."

Bassie, Meg thought, looked frighteningly old. Her features seemed harsh and exaggerated. She had become more like herself over the years, in every way, her worst traits magnified by the refraction of time. Jim took the pencil from the chipboard box, intact in its cocoon of soil. He wrapped it snugly in a strip of rag that held the dirt in place around it, and placed it in a plastic Ziploc bag, into which he punched air holes with his pocketknife. He put the bag into the chipboard box.

"So here's the question," he said, setting the box on the ground beside his satchel and turning to Bassie again. "If this is a dog's grave, what is Elliott's pencil doing in it?"

Bassie was looking down toward the valley to the place where the house had been. Meg leaned and retrieved the walking cane from where it had fallen and propped it against Bassie's chair. As Bassie took hold of it, Meg saw that her hand was shaking.

"Look at this," Kelly said suddenly, on her hands and knees with her head inclined over a metal object about the size of a thumbnail.

Jim turned from Bassie and stepped back into the pit to inspect the object.

"It's a jewelry charm," Kelly said. "Shaped like a hunting dog."

"Would you mind handing me my camera?" Jim asked her. "Victor, I need you to mark this on the graph. You know how to do that, don't you?"

Kelly stood up to get the camera, and Victor rose and began looking around for the record book, pausing inadvertently between Bassie and the pit as he did so. Bassie jabbed him in the back with her cane. He swung around. "What the hell—" he said.

"Move," Bassie ordered him, leaning forward in her chair and getting unsteadily to her feet. "That jewelry charm is mine." She had fixed her eyes on it. "I remember it."

It glimmered from the red soil. Bassie stared at it, then lowered herself back into the chair with a look of disorientation. For a moment Meg believed the unimaginable would happen and Bassie would dissolve into tears. But then Bassie spoke in a steady voice. "It makes sense that it would be buried with Argus."

"Why is that?" Jim asked her quietly.

"It's a dog charm," she said.

"Ah," he answered.

But it did not make sense. A mechanical pencil and a jewelry charm were not the kind of things one usually found in a dog's grave. Nor was the leather cover of a notebook.

Jim photographed the item, plucked it from the dirt, and placed it in Bassie's hands. The dog's tail was extended, the front paw lifted in the pose of a pointer, the eye sockets empty of tiny jewels or bits of colored glass that they apparently had once held. The metal was discolored and corroded.

"Is it silver?" Kelly inquired, still kneeling near the place where she had found it.

"It's aluminum with gold plating," Jim said. "Most of the plating's worn off."

Bassie's hand continued shaking. She gave the charm back to Jim and turned away.

The sky still held its blue color, and no ominous clouds had appeared yet, but the wind was tossing the limbs of the junipers and the birds had become restless.

"This storm isn't going to give us a lot of warning," Jim observed, studying the sky. "It's going to drop on us from over the mesa." He looked at Bassie. "I think you and Meg should start on back to the hotel before long. We're going to work a little longer and then I'm going to send everyone home."

"I'll leave when you do," Bassie said. "Not before."

"You and Meg have a longer drive than I do," he replied, and turned to Meg. "You shouldn't be on the road if there's ice."

But Meg knew it was pointless to argue with Bassie.

Jim continued to work with Kelly and Victor while Meg settled onto a boulder to watch them, and Annie stood at the edge of the pit, chattering about a horror movie she had seen the week before.

"Are you drinking enough water?" Jim asked Meg. "The drop in air pressure can make your headache worse."

She climbed down from the boulder and filled a paper cup from a water jug and swallowed the second Excedrin.

Victor soon uncovered a single small vertebra, too small to be associated with the rib, then took a break and sprawled on the ground beside the pit, drinking water from the jug, his hands blistered from working too much of the time without gloves. "I smell rain," he observed.

Kelly tinkered with her trowel; the handle was coming loose, and though she had taped it, it wasn't holding.

Tony appeared with a plastic tarp to be used later to cover the pit. He dropped it in a pile, and went back down through the trees to resume his work.

The boulder where Meg was sitting had become cold and uncomfortable. The wind had drawn the sun's warmth out of the stone. Meg was about to climb down, when she saw Jim strike on something. He plunged his trowel in the dirt, then hesitated, throwing a look at Meg, then shifted his position, turning his back to Bassie so she could not see his work. The jewelry charm had troubled Bassie; her life was strangely closing in a full circle; the items that her parents had buried or dropped in the dirt here almost a century ago were being hauled out, one by one, for her observation.

An eroded slide pencil. A child's jewelry charm. What kind of markers were these?

Jim was working quickly. "Bassie?" he said over his shoulder at last. "Do you happen to know what kind of shaving razor your father used?"

"A safety razor," she said flatly. "It's in the journals. What have you found?"

"What did a safety razor look like?" he inquired.

"Like a modern razor," she said.

"What kind of blades?"

"Steel."

He was scraping around the object. "Here it is," he said. "A piece of a steel blade."

Kelly crawled over to look at it. "It's rusted," she said.

"Steel used to have a lot of iron in it," he replied, and sat back on his heels to look at Bassie. "Any reason we would find Elliott's razor in Argus's grave?" When she didn't answer, he said quietly, "Bassie, what do you think is down here? Could this be a trash dump? Do you remember where your mother dumped the trash? I don't suppose she would have carried it uphill."

"There was lead in the pencil," Bassie snapped. "So it wouldn't be a trash dump. Would it."

"That would depend," he said. "On how expensive lead was. Or how wasteful the owner was."

The faintest rumble of thunder rolled over the ridge. Angry clouds were starting to darken the sky. Through the stone on which she sat Meg could feel the deep vibrations of the thunder; the hairs rose on her arms. This felt like something more portentous than autumn blowing in. She watched Jim take his gloves off and flex his hands and put the gloves back on. He adjusted his hat on his head and continued working. Victor and Kelly began to work more quickly, sensing the increasing urgency.

"I would kill for donuts," Victor said at last, wiping a hand across his forehead.

"I've got some Bubble Yum," Annie offered.

"No thanks."

"I saw powdered donuts in the machine by the bathrooms," Kelly observed.

"I love powdered donuts," Victor exclaimed. "Those Mrs. Baird's ones?"

"I don't know if they were Mrs. Baird's," she said.

"I'll get you some," Meg offered.

"Oh, man, would you?"

She climbed down from the boulder, and Victor got up and went to his backpack in search of money, but Meg was already starting down the hill.

"But I want three packages," he called after her.

"I can spring for three," she told him over her shoulder. "Anyone else need anything?"

"My jacket from the car," Kelly said. "Would that be a lot of trouble?"

"No," Meg called.

"My car's a green Toyota. The door that has the big dent is unlocked."

Meg made her way down to the center and purchased three packages of rank-looking powdered donuts. On her way to the parking lot for Kelly's jacket she talked with David Valdez at the desk; he wanted to know when Jim was planning to stop working. She thought it would be soon, she said.

When she arrived back on the hill, Jim had put Annie to work at the opposite end of the pit along with Kelly and Victor. Victor was asking Annie about some recent movie releases, as she had a night job at a video rental shop in Santa Fe. She was expounding on a remake of *Of Mice and Men* when her trowel struck something. Jim took over, extracting it from the ground. It was a black rubber comb, missing nearly a third of its teeth. To Meg it looked like a comb that could be found in any contemporary drugstore, but Bassie, from her lawn chair, stated that rubber combs had been in common use before the turn of the century.

They had deepened the pit by half a foot when Tony called for Jim to come down to the area where he was working. Jim asked Meg to come along.

Bassie started to rise from her chair also, but Jim said, "We're running out of time, Bassie. If it's anything important, I'll come get you."

She hesitated, and then lowered herself into the chair again.

They made their way down through the brush, shoving branches out of their faces. "I have about an hour before I have to send the crew home," Jim said. "And then I might keep working."

"Can you, if it sleets?" Meg asked.

"I have a tent I can set up over the pit," he said.

Tony was sitting on a rock beside the area he had been digging, smoking a cigarette. He nodded toward the hole, and Jim and Meg approached it to see what he had uncovered. He had dug the pit to nearly a foot deep, and revealed a portion of a skeleton and skull of a medium-sized animal, the arch of the ribs protruding from the dirt.

"A dog," Tony said, drawing on his cigarette and exhaling the smoke up toward the darkening sky. "But look at it."

Jim stepped into the pit and got on his knees beside the bones. He ran his finger over several of the ribs. "You know," he said, looking at Tony, and then at Meg. "It's one of the dogs all right. It's the one they called Milton."

"How do you know?" Meg asked, feeling her pulse accelerate. She stepped down into the pit to look at the bones.

"They're abraded," Jim said. "See here? And those are tooth marks. A lot of times rodents chew on the bones for calcium, but these abrasions are too deep to be that." He tugged his hat lower against the wind.

"And these bones were gnawed before they were buried," he said. "Do you know how Milton died? Wild dogs killed him." He picked up Tony's trowel and scraped around the edges of the bones, loosening the dirt around them and then dragging it away with his hands, exposing more of the hip and shoulder and a few more inches of the rib cage. When he sat back, looking at his work, the wind was tugging at his hat brim. Meg secured the buttons of her jacket.

Jim said, "I should go tell Bassie."

"I'll get her," Meg told him. But something held her where she was. The scarred bones lay placid and still while the wind whipped over them. Dark clouds gusted in a sky that earlier had been stunningly blue through a lacy gauze of cirrus.

"What do you think she'll say?" Meg asked.

"I don't know. There's something about it that's unnerving."

"I feel that too."

"*Yo también*," Tony added, stubbing out the butt of his cigarette.

To Meg, the place felt like a crime scene, the bones like those of a murder victim. Tony drew a box of matches and a pack of cigarettes from his shirt pocket and lit another cigarette, shielding the match from the wind.

Jim brushed more dirt away from the bones. "Hannah described what happened to Milton, but apparently it was more violent even than she said, now that I see the bones. He was basically torn to pieces." He pointed to the bones of the front leg. "See this gap? It's too big to have happened after the dog was buried. Bones can separate after they're buried, but that's not what happened here. This leg was separated from the body earlier. And see here? The vertebrae are severed. In other words the neck was torn off, probably by the dogs chewing on the throat." He paused. "Hannah mentioned that the dogs fought over the body."

"Did she witness that?" Meg asked.

"She heard it. It was in the middle of the night, and Elliott wasn't there. She heard the fighting and went out barefoot in her nightgown with the shotgun—I don't know how she got up the hill like that, but she did. She described how she couldn't see the dogs too well but she could hear them, and fired the gun a couple of times to scare them off. But then she could see them hiding around in the rocks. She didn't know if Milton was dead, or where he was, so she went back to the house and got a lantern and came back looking for him. She said she could see the dogs' eyes watching her from the rocks. When she found Milton's body she got some tools and a lantern and came back up and buried him where he was. Which I guess would be right here." He paused, then added, "She reassembled the body when she buried it. She didn't write about that."

"She put it back together," Meg said.

"Every piece. The only thing missing"—he said, scraping the dirt away from the end of the exposed front leg—"is this paw." He pointed to the vertebrae along the neck. "She put the head on here."

Meg imagined the nightmarish scene of Hannah reassembling the body parts of her dead dog. An eerie feeling was imparted by the wind and lurid sky and the wild motions of the juniper branches, and Meg felt the odd connectedness of time. The immediacy of the place troubled her. She had seen other places where Hannah had been—her room at the Montezuma, and the lobby of the Plaza in Las Vegas, and the valley below, where the house had stood. She had felt her presence in the kiva. But she had not seen Hannah in those places as graphically as she could see her here, digging with the shovel by lantern light, with Milton strewn in pieces and the wind tugging at her nightgown. It was the gruesome quality that made the scene so potent. She remembered how Hannah had described the saintmaker as assembling the limbs of the saint and then freezing them in place with the lacquered clothes. Hannah had done that same thing here. She had put the pieces of her dog together and sealed them down with dirt.

Jim brushed the dirt off his hands and stood up. "This answers one thing, though," he said. "She wrote in the journal that after she buried Milton, she burned her nightgown in the stove, and now I know why. It must have been covered in blood." He settled his eyes on Tony for a moment, and then looked at Meg again. "Let's go tell Bassie," he said.

Bassie hoisted herself onto her cane.

"Can we go see?" Victor asked.

"Come down in a minute," Jim replied, "and then you'll have to make it fast. Just down and back."

Jim took the camera. Tony was back on his hands and knees in the pit when they arrived, but ceased to work and got up and moved out of the way.

Bassie stopped beside the pit and stood looking down at the bones. She gave Meg the handle of her cane while she took her glasses off and cleaned them with a rag from her coat pocket and put them back on. She took the cane back again, and leaned against it heavily, holding her coat around her with the other hand. "Well," she said at last, "there's one of them. One of the dogs."

Victor, Kelly, and Annie could be heard coming down through the trees. They reached the grave, and with a few deferential glances at Bassie stood exclaiming over it.

Jim began instructing Tony to take the necessary photographs before he dug any further, and to get the bones out of the ground before the storm arrived. "I don't want to leave them exposed, even with the tarp," he said.

Tony assured him he could get the bones out in time, and said he would prefer to have no help from the crew.

"Guys," Jim said, though his voice was almost lost in the wind, "that means he wants us out of here. Come on. Back to work. Bassie, you're halfway down to the center. You won't go on down?"

"No," she said.

He took her arm, and started with her laboriously up the slope toward the pit in the circle of boulders.

Half an hour later Victor, his face still speckled with powdered sugar from the donuts, came across an area of soil that contained several small, seemingly related objects. Jim took over the work of uncovering them while Meg sat on her boulder watching. Bassie inched her chair so near the pit that Jim told her to move back.

In twenty minutes more, racing the storm, Jim had revealed a metal latch, a circular piece of clear glass about half an inch in diameter, a thin, rusted metal bar, the remnants of a small wooden box about two by two inches in size and mostly rotted, with a hinge at the bottom and a latch at the top, and a corroded metal key that resembled a clock key.

Bassie got up from the chair and stood by the edge of the pit, her blunt-toed orthopedic shoes extending a half inch over the edge. She leaned over and planted her cane on the dirt in the pit, and her coat hem brushed Jim's neck. "It's a camera," she announced.

He turned to look at her over his shoulder. "Did your parents own a camera?"

"Elliott used a Kodak for his work. But that's not what you're looking at. That's a Brownie camera."

"They had Kodaks back then?" Victor asked.

"I thought Kodaks were Japanese," Annie offered, jabbing her trowel at a stubborn tangle of roots. "It sounds Japanese."

Bassie straightened, placing the tip of the cane on level ground. "Elliott used a twenty-five-dollar Kodak with roll film of a hundred exposures. Brownies were smaller. Portable. Children used them."

"Could this one have been yours?" Jim asked.

"I was three years old, for God's sake. Of course not."

"So how big were they?"

"Small."

"How small, Bassie?"

"Three by five inches."

"And they were around by 1900?"

"Yes."

"Did they have roll film? Is this the film box?" he asked, pointing to the small, decayed wooden box pedestaled above the ground around it, its interior caked with dirt.

"Yes," she said. "Roll film. Paper or transparent. Six exposures to a roll."

"There's no camera casing here," Jim said. "Only parts."

"The exterior was cardboard."

"Oh," Victor said, "I know what she's talking about. That kind of cardboard that was made to look like leather. I've seen pictures of cameras like that."

Jim examined the parts in the dirt. The camera had been lying on its side. "It's tricky," he said. "We're going to have to get this film box out without exposing the interior to light, in case there's film inside."

"If there's film, this isn't a trash dump," Bassie said.

"Or a dog's grave," Jim replied.

"Could celluloid last that long?" Kelly asked. "Underground?" She looked skeptically at what was left of the film box, one side almost completely disintegrated and the interior packed with dirt.

"We'll find out," Jim said. "Victor, get some pictures of it. I want all the pieces photographed separately and then as a group. Annie, you take my notebook and write down what I say."

She took the notebook and poised her pencil over it, and Jim rattled off descriptions of the camera parts and their relative positions in the soil, taking measurements as he did so. He instructed Annie to take the notebook to his office and make a phone call to a professor named Michael Prentis in the department of photography at UNM. She was to tell him that something resembling the film box of a Kodak Brownie had been discovered buried in nearly two feet of loamy soil on the hill near the visitors' center at Pecos, and to read the descriptions of the parts exactly as Jim had dictated. She was to ask Prentis where the film box could be taken for examination.

Jim looked at the sky again. The clouds by now had formed a solid blanket of gray. He shoved his trowel in the soil beside the film box, prying underneath it, and encountered something.

Meg saw him stiffen. She saw him lean back, then lean forward again and scrape the soil with his trowel.

"You're onto something—not the camera," Bassie said, still standing at the edge of the pit.

"Yes, and I'll figure out what it is a lot faster if you'll sit down," he told her.

"You suspect something," she said.

He looked at her. "Will you sit down?"

"You think it's bone, don't you?" Bassie said.

"Yes." He continued his work.

"How can you tell?" Kelly asked.

"I can't, for certain," he said. "Bassie, I need you to sit down."

Bassie started to return to her chair, but a sudden gust of wind flung the chair on its side and scudded it against one of the large boulders in the ring surrounding the pit. Victor retrieved the chair, Bassie settled into it, and Jim resumed his work. Meg sat on the ground and hugged her knees for warmth.

Within a few minutes Jim had removed the film box from the soil, unharmed by the procedure, the interior still packed with hard dirt. He placed it in a chipboard box and sealed the box, then dug down deeper to where he had encountered the resistance he believed to be bone. Victor and Kelly were working steadily at the opposite end of the pit to keep the levels even.

Meg could not, at first, make out what Jim was uncovering, but eventually it showed itself to be a very small snout of some sort, with sharp incisors. The more of it that Jim revealed, the more grotesque it looked to Meg, vicious in its placement, snarling out of the soil as if to fight off intruders, the bottom half of the jaw dislodged from the top. Meg almost expected the teeth to start snapping at Jim. The strangest thing about the snout was its size. It was small enough to be a rodent's. It was certainly extraneous to the large rib fragment Victor had uncovered near the surface, but it might be associated, Meg discerned, with the tiny vertebra that Victor had found.

"Your mother only had two dogs?" Jim inquired of Bassie.

"That's right," she said, her eyes fixed on the exposed snout. "Milton and Argus."

"And Argus was large," Jim said, looking to Bassie for confirmation.

"That's right."

"Any chance your mother might have buried a dog as small as a Chihuahua up here?"

"No."

"You're sure of that?"

"It would be in the journals."

"Could this possibly be Paco?"

Bassie's expression remained fixed.

"Who's Paco?" Victor asked, tearing open his third packet of donuts and bending to look at the snout.

"It's not Paco," Bassie snapped at Jim. "Paco was with Elliott in Mexico when Elliott was killed. You know that. Neither of them came home."

"But someone might have brought Paco back," Jim said. "Elliott probably had people working with him who might have done that."

Bassie struggled up from the chair.

"Could it be a puppy?" Kelly was asking.

"No," Jim said.

"Why not?" Victor asked.

"The teeth. Bassie? Are you all right?"

She didn't answer. She had propped herself against the wind.

"I wish you'd sit down."

"No."

Jim measured the snout while Victor photographed it, using a flash now. The wind had begun swirling dirt into their faces in spite of some protection from the boulders. Bassie pulled her scarf up over her mouth, and Annie came up from Jim's office, smacking on a mouthful of chewing gum, her tuft of pink hair bobbing in the wind. "Ugh," she said when she saw what Jim had uncovered. "What's that?"

"It's a snout," he said impatiently.

She squatted near the edge, at Bassie's feet, and leaned over the pit to look more closely at the jaws protruding from the soil, and as she opened her mouth to comment, her wad of chewing gum fell out onto the snout's small row of pointed bottom teeth. "Look!" Annie exclaimed. "Gross! It looks like he's chewing gum. Could you get that for me, Jim?"

"No," he said. "You get it. And don't touch the teeth." He was losing his patience.

Annie got on her knees and leaned into the pit, plucking the bubble gum from the teeth carefully, as if she were stealing it from the jaws of a shark. She placed it in a wrapper that she then inserted into her coat pocket. "I couldn't get hold of Michael Prentis," she reported, opening her notepad and seating herself at the edge of the pit. "He's out of town until tomorrow. But I talked to somebody named Mickey. I don't remember his last name, but," she searched her notes. "Well, I thought I wrote it down. Anyway. Mickey somebody. He said if you bring the film box to the lab, then somebody can analyze it for you. He looked up Brownie cameras and said . . . let me see . . . I wrote this down . . . oh, yeah—they started being sold in February 1900. The film speed was ten ASA. You didn't hold the camera up to your eye, but down at your chest. So you had to look down through the lens to see what you were taking a picture of." She paused, skimming over her notes. "Oh, yeah," she said. "He said there was a problem with the first model—that the outside box kept flopping open—so in March of 1900 Kodak put a latch and a hinge on the box. So he said the one we've found, if it's a Brownie, was made in March of 1900 or afterwards, since it has the latch. But he said it could have been made a long time after that, because they sold Brownies like that for a long time."

Bassie's lawn chair, without her weight to anchor it, tipped for a second time in the wind and scuttled across the ground. Victor righted it again. "Elliott went to Mexico before that," Bassie said. "The camera wasn't his. So don't try to tell me that the dog is."

"The camera wasn't his unless he bought it in Mexico, which is possible, Bassie," Jim said. He turned to Annie. "You help Victor and Kelly out for a while, and we should be able to pack up here in a minute." He went on digging. "Bassie," he said over his shoulder, not turning to look at her. "Would you please, for my peace of mind, sit down?"

Bassie took her seat again.

Meg could see that something else was emerging from the soil under Jim's trowel, only inches from the snout, but she could not make out any feature of it, and saw that Jim did not want to call attention to it; he was working discreetly, scooping away the dirt. Suddenly he stopped, and she saw a look come over his face, not one of puzzlement but something more deeply felt, and more grim. He looked closely at his work, for a second only, and then, with a swipe of his hand, dragged the dirt back over the place. "All right, everybody," he said, standing up and pulling off his gloves. "Let's pull the tarp over this. I want you guys on the road."

"We're quitting?" Kelly asked.

"We're quitting," he affirmed.

"I thought you said we were going to work some more," Kelly said.

"Changed my mind," he told her. "Come on. We've got sleet on the way."

Meg stood up. The wind was bitter cold. The sky was as dark as evening and the birds had ceased dancing frenetically in the junipers and taken refuge somewhere. The sky appeared to be swirling around Bassie's head; she had pulled the ball cap off, and her braid was blowing free, coiling like a snake around her neck. She seemed to Meg like the apparition from some dark fable in a children's book of witches, her dry lips painted a vivid red, and it appeared that she was trying to speak, but her craggy voice was blown off toward the valley.

The others started packing up the tools.

Phil Barker appeared suddenly on the slope as if the wind had tossed him from below, his shoulders hunched around his ears against the cold. "There's an ice storm coming!" he was shouting frantically against the wind. "You guys better cover things and come down!"

Jim supervised the spreading of the tarp across the pit, wrestling it down and calling instructions against the noise of the wind. He insisted that it be securely anchored, and Meg could not tell if he intended to leave the tarp in place for the night, or return later with the tent he had mentioned and continue digging after everyone was gone. She didn't have the opportunity to inquire without Bassie overhearing, so she helped spread the tarp and anchor it, without asking any questions.

The crew started down the hill as the first few drops of rain dropped suddenly from over the mesa. Meg helped Bassie over the rocks. Victor carried the lawn chair over his head; periodically it caught the wind and nearly tugged free of his hold. Jim went to help Tony remove the last of Milton's scarred bones from the dirt, and Meg didn't have the chance to say good-bye to him before he disappeared between the tossing branches of the junipers. Together she and Bassie and the crew crowded through the back door of the center and into the reception area, where they sorted out their tools and bags. Annie headed for her car; Victor and Kelly hurried to Kelly's Toyota. David Valdez was eager to lock the building and go home, but he was waiting to talk with Jim. Phil had left already.

Meg took Bassie out to the parking lot, bundling her into the rental car. Bassie was cold and exhausted. "I'll be right back—" Meg said, and closed the door. With a glance at Bassie's face through the speckling of rain on the windshield, she ran back toward the center.

David was turning the lights off and locking the doors to the exhibition room when she ran through. "Forget something?" he called after her.

"No—" she said. "I just need to ask Jim something—" and hurled herself through the back doors and out against the scattered drops of rain. She turned onto the narrow path leading up the hill, the air dark and cold around her, and then made her way between two boulders, into the brushy trees. "Jim?" she called. "Are you still here?"

He appeared out of the bushes before her, his face blurred to her vision by the raindrops and the wild movement of the branches. His hat was gone, his jacket zipped tightly under his chin.

"What did you find?" she asked him breathlessly.

He hesitated, then took her arm as if to brace her against the wind.

"Just tell me what you think it is," she urged him.

"Human bones," he said.

The wind was whipping through her hair.

"And if Bassie's right, and that's the grave she saw Hannah and Vicente digging, then there are things that we don't know."

It was a moment before his suggestion became clear to her. Elliott's grave had never been found in Mexico.

"Could it be Elliott?" she asked.

"It could be anyone."

"You're going to keep working, aren't you," she said, knowing he was.

They spoke hastily in the spattering rain, and then in the windy obscurity of falling darkness, Meg turned and started hurriedly down the hill.

TWENTY

When Meg and Bassie reached the Plaza the rain was falling heavily but had not yet turned to ice. Meg ordered room service for Bassie then went across the hall to her own room and made several phone calls to Austin. Carolyn Stott informed her that the weather in central Texas was still holding, though a front had been predicted and rain could be expected in the hill country within the next two days.

A message from Paul was waiting on Meg's home recorder, saying he had faxed the papers to St. David's as Meg had asked him to, and had spent the night in her apartment. He appreciated her hospitality "in absentia," he said.

" 'In absentia,' " she grumbled, hanging up the phone. How pretentious he was.

She ran a hot shower and stood for a long time under the stream of water, recalling the day's events. She considered ordering room service, but the thought of staying in the room all night seemed too depressing at the moment. Going down for dinner alone did not seem any more appealing, nor did sitting in the bar.

She wanted to be on Dog Hill with Jim. He would need to put the tent up if he was going to continue working, and she imagined him making his way up the hill in the storm, toting his equipment and wrestling to secure a tent over the pit.

When she had finished her shower, she found herself dressing in blue jeans and the green wool sweater instead of pulling on her T-shirt and pajama pants. She opened the door and stood looking across at Bassie's door, then stepped over and listened. The television was on.

Downstairs at the restaurant she ordered two turkey sandwiches to go, and while waiting on them went back upstairs and knocked on Bassie's door and found it unlocked. She cracked the door open and found Bassie seated on the edge of the bed with a dinner tray. A prime-time comedy show was on the television, but she did not seem to be watching it.

"You in for the night?" Meg asked.

"I am."

"Okay. I'm going to bed," Meg said. "My headache is not any better. I just wanted to see if you needed anything."

"I don't. Thank you for checking."

"All right, then." But she was hesitant to leave. "What are you thinking about?"

Bassie was quiet, and then said, "I've spent my life resurrecting the past. But today disturbs me." She tore a piece from a bread roll on her tray. "Now go to bed," she said.

Meg went across to her room, closed herself inside and stood for a moment. Then she got her coat and left, locking the door quietly behind her and moving quickly down the hallway.

The receptionist at the front desk was a slight woman with heavy black eyebrows and a tag with the name "Monica." Meg asked if she would hold any calls that might come in, thinking that if Bassie were to call and find the phone on hold she would be less likely to knock on Meg's door than if she simply got no answer. "And if my grandmother, Claudia Bass, comes down looking for me," Meg said, "tell her I've gone to a drugstore to get something for a headache. I may actually be a while, but you don't need to tell her that."

At the restaurant, she received the sandwiches in a paper bag along with a plastic container of fruit salad, and minutes later was in the car on her way to Pecos with the bag of food beside her on the seat. The rain was rapidly turning to sleet, bouncing in the road and seeming to swarm at her headlights. By the time she neared the Pecos exit, she was in a state of doubt about her reasons for coming and the wisdom of having done so, knowing that she might end up being trapped at Pecos by the weather.

Turning onto the narrow road that led to the visitors' center, she saw that the situation was actually even worse than this scenario. She was locked out of the park. The metal gate was closed and secured with a padlock. She got out of the car and ran through the sleet to test the lock, then returned to the car and sat with her headlights shining on the metal wire of the gate and illuminating the sleet as it fell. She tried to recall the distance from the gate to the parking lot, and wondered if the sleet would damage the car.

At last she eased the car onto the shoulder of the pavement up against a thick group of brushy junipers, switched the motor off, looked at the clock on the dashboard—it was only nine in the evening—and sat in the dark, assessing the situation.

She could climb the gate, she thought, then sprint to the parking lot and around the corner of the visitors' center and up the hill. If she didn't find Jim on the hill, she could cut back through the parking lot and up the path to the offices and see if he was there.

Tucking the sack of food up under her coat, she flung the car door open and launched herself onto the glistening pavement and toward the gate, sleet peppering her face. She nosed her hiking boots between the wires and cleared the top, landing on the far side on her feet. In only a moment she had reached the parking lot and was dashing around the corner of the center. The building was entirely dark. She sloshed into a puddle near a drainpipe and was glad that she had waterproofed her boots when she had purchased them, recalling, as she ran, how she had stood at the counter of a shoe store in an Austin mall deliberating about whether to buy the can of leather-guard.

She grappled her way up the hill, protecting her face from the sleet with her arm slung over her eyes, catching hold of the slippery surface of rocks along the trail with her other hand for balance. Pebbles of sleet were bouncing off the ground and beginning to accumulate in the crevices between the rocks. She turned into the brush and headed toward the ring of boulders, and saw the tent erected over the pit: a bright blue structure in the shape of a geodome, glowing with interior light. She saw some movement from within, a shadow thrown against the wall, and then a burst of light, as if from a camera flashing.

"Jim? It's Meg!" she called as she reached the tent, but her voice was drowned by the noise of falling sleet. Calling again, she unzipped the tent flap and pulled it back. Jim was on his knees in the pit; he turned his head and saw her, but her presence seemed to register slowly. He was holding a camera and wearing a red child's scarf around his neck that Meg remembered seeing in the lost-and-found box in his office, and an orange down-filled jacket. She stooped to enter, zipped the flap behind her, and turned again to face him. There was a stillness inside compared to the noise of the storm. The room that was formed by the tent extended just beyond the borders of the pit, with the space for a narrow ledge along one side. Tools and a lantern and a stack of boxes lined the ledge; beside the lantern was a Thermos. The lantern's flame warmed the room, sputtering light against the walls and creating a mood of isolation. The center of the tent was high enough for a person to stand in the pit without stooping, but the edges sloped to the ground, and as Meg stood, bent over slightly, beside the entry, the tent leaned in a gust of wind, rippling fantastically around her with the pattering of the sleet.

"Hey," she said, unable, at the moment, to think of anything else to say, "—I brought you a sandwich."

She spoke before she saw the skeleton. But then she saw it. It was partly revealed in the dirt, from the kneecap to the pelvis. Jim had been working upward from the knee. His flashlight lay in the dirt, directed at the pelvis, the surface of the bones absorbing the light and the neon blue of the tent, their porous texture vivid in the stark beam.

Beside the human knee, the small dog's skeleton discovered earlier was now entirely uncovered and open to view, snarling out of the dirt. Some of the bones appeared to be missing and others were out of place. The spine was disassembled, but enough remained in place to reveal how the dog had been positioned in the grave, stretched out on its side with its head upturned in the dirt, the snout resting at the highest elevation.

Meg's initial instinct was to wish she had not come. Here Jim was, unearthing a human being, and she had arrived with a picnic.

"Is it—whole?" she asked.

He lowered the camera with which he had been photographing, and was quiet, looking at Meg and then at the bones. At last he said, "My guess is that it is. This bone, the femur, is attached here to the tibia." He indicated where. "And the kneecap's floating over the joint. Which means the bones were buried before there was any dismantling. People don't usually bury only part of a person."

"What can you tell about who it was?" she asked.

"It was an adult male," he said.

"The dog's skull looks like it's crushed," she observed, and then noted a small hole in the opposite side from where the bones were shattered.

"The dog was shot," he said.

"Shot?"

He nodded.

Neither of them spoke for a moment, and as the silence lasted, it grew eerie and disturbing. The confined area, with the wind pressing against the walls, made Jim's intense demeanor all the more apparent. The flamelight and seclusion of the working space seemed to draw the oxygen away.

"I shouldn't have come," Meg said.

Jim switched the flashlight off and reached for the lantern, turning the knob to lower the flame. "I'm trying to conserve the batteries and fuel," he explained, his face thrown suddenly into shadow, the movement of the surrounding walls exaggerated by the flicker of the flame. He pushed his fingers through his hair and shook his head, his eyes now fixed on hers. "I don't have a lot of fuel here to work with, but the Office of Medical Investigations is sending someone out in the morning as soon as the roads are passable and I want to be finished by then."

She assumed he had a theory of how long the body had been buried, but if so, he did not seem to want to share it. She pulled the bag of food from under her coat and dropped it beside him. He didn't open it, but remained in the pit, looking at the bones.

"Then I should go back," she offered at last.

"You mean to Las Vegas? Not in the sleet," he said.

"I got here all right in the sleet."

"Did you climb the gate?"

She nodded. He looked at her for a moment. "You can't drive back in the sleet," he said.

"What should I do, then?" she asked. "You don't want me here."

"Oh, I want you here," he said.

Their eyes held before he looked at the bones again. "You could stay in my office," he said at last. "There's a couch in one of the back rooms."

Without his gaze to hold her she felt detached from the scene in front of her, too conspicuous, her head touching the low blue nylon ceiling, the sleet pattering against her skull. It seemed that Jim was more connected to the bones before him than to her. "Bassie gets up early," she said, "and I don't want to have to explain to her where I was."

"That's not enough reason to risk driving," he said. "If you stay in the office I'll drive you back in the morning."

"I could stay here and keep you company," she offered.

"I've got company," he said, gesturing toward the skeleton.

"Are you going to work all night?"

"Probably." He stared at her. "Yes. I'm going to work all night."

She looked around at the tent walls, smelling the dank rich odor of the raw earth, and settled her gaze on the bones, and then on Jim. He was still sitting back on his heels looking up at her, his hair oily and swept back from his forehead where he had pushed it with his fingers, and the child's red scarf wound around his neck. Flamelight threw the shadow of his profile on the wall.

"I'll walk you over there," he said.

He retrieved the flashlight from the pit and switched it on, then gathered up a sheet of plastic from the narrow ledge and handed it to her. "Put this around you," he told her, and she tossed it over her shoulders, unzipping the flap of the door. He followed her out into the cold, the rain and pebbles of ice pelting their faces. Meg pulled one end of the plastic over her head and offered the other end to Jim; it billowed around them in the wind. They followed the beam of the flashlight to the path and down the incline, taking hold of rocks and also of each other, and made their way down to the center, then skirted the building and ran through the parking lot, up the incline, and to the door of the old ranch house where Jim's office was. Jim opened the door and they went in. Dropping the plastic on the floor, he flipped the overhead light on and switched the flashlight off. The cluttered room came into sudden focus, the lost-and-found box on the floor, overflowing with items. Jim escorted Meg through a door down a hallway to a small concession room. An old fake-leather sofa was shoved against a wall opposite a Coke machine and a snack machine. The room was grubby with a warped linoleum floor, but comforting to Meg nevertheless, with its bright fluorescent lights and the incessant humming of the Coke machine.

Jim left her there for a moment and returned with a jacket. "You can use this for a pillow," he suggested, handing it to her. "There's a coffee machine there." He indicated a countertop with a stained coffee machine and a can of coffee beside it. "If you can't sleep, and want to read, you know where my books are."

He went into the bathroom and Meg could hear him urinating and then washing his hands. She sat on the sofa and waited for him to come back out.

He surveyed her when he did. "You don't look comfortable."

"I'm all right. Are you all right?"

He was quiet. "Can I get back to you on that?" he finally said.

"Yes," she answered.

"I'm going back out there," he told her.

"I'll see you in the morning?"

"Yes."

She sat on the sofa for a moment after he had gone, then got up and wandered around the offices, taking some of the books from the shelves and sitting at Jim's desk turning the pages. She studied the photograph of him with his children in the tree house. The three of them looked happy.

At last she took a volume of Hannah's journals back to the concession room, but she was too unsettled to read. She sat on the sofa, wishing she had never left the hotel. Wishing, in fact, she had never set foot in New Mexico. Short of either of those things being true, she wished she had not left her purse in the car and could buy the bag of pretzels staring at her from the window of the snack machine. She had left the sandwiches in the tent. She was tempted to go to Jim's desk and search his drawers for quarters, but didn't feel she should.

So she sat wondering if it could possibly be Elliott in the grave. And what it would mean to Bassie if in fact it were.

She got up and switched the light off, then returned to the couch and rolled up the coat that Jim had given her to use as a pillow. But the room did not go dark. The snack machine was lit internally, and its items continued to entice her through their individual windows. A red light on the Coke machine blinked at intervals. Meg reclined on her side, nestling her head into the coat, and stared at the numbered food items, thinking about Jim and wondering what she would tell Bassie in the morning.

If the roads were not too slick with ice, she decided, she could drive back on her own at daylight and be in her room when Bassie called or knocked on her door to wake her.

She closed her eyes and tried to allow herself to be soothed by the humming noise of the Coke machine. She could not get Jim from her thoughts. When she finally began to dream, it was of him, though his face was skeletal and his voice incomprehensible and hollow. In the dream she was with him in the kiva on the mesa and they were standing to their waists in murky water. He led her down a secret passageway out through the kiva's walls and along dirt corridors into unexpected rooms.

She thought she felt a sudden presence, and awakened, startled, and lay listening, but no one was there. "Jim?" she called, in case he was in his office. She raised herself onto her elbow and consulted her watch. The time was four fifty-five in the morning. The dream was in her mind. She thought perhaps she could free herself from it by reading for a while, and dragged herself up off the couch and went to turn the lights on. When she returned to the couch, however, she did not pick up the journal, but sat slumped, groggy and disoriented, still wearing her coat, her hands shoved deep in her pockets, staring at the relentless blinking red light on the Coke machine. At last she got up and went into the bathroom and splashed cold water on her face. Her eyes in the mirror were swollen from sleep.

She went out to Jim's office. The lights were on, as she had left them. He apparently had not been back. But the room felt different now, and she realized slowly that the sound of falling sleet had ceased. She opened the door to the outside. The night was still and quiet, and the wind had lessened.

She ventured out a few steps. Small pebbles of sleet had collected on the ground, mostly in crevices where the wind had blown them. She decided the roads might be navigable.

Returning to the concession room, she turned the lights off and took the volume of Hannah's journal back to the shelves beside Jim's desk.

Outside, the sky remained overcast, without a hint of dawn. Starting for the hill, she discovered more wind than she had anticipated, and pulled her hands into her sleeves for warmth, avoiding the patches of ice and trying to think of what to say to Jim.

As she approached the tent, she noted that the glow from the interior was dimmer than before. Apparently Jim had lowered the flame on the lantern further still, to conserve the last of his fuel. She made her way to the entrance and saw that the zipper had not been tightly closed. Peering in through the gap, she saw Jim seated on the ledge, his feet dangling into the pit, which was about four feet deep now. His profile was to Meg, his elbows on his knees. He was holding the flashlight. The beam, though weak, was directed at the skeleton lying under a sheet of plastic. Meg could see, through the haze of the plastic, that the skeleton had been revealed and yet was lying exactly as it had been in the dirt. She could see the structure and the skull but could not make out details; the arms seemed to be crossed on the chest, the hands and fingers curled instead of lying flat. There was a disturbing quality, a sad, denuded aspect to the appearance of the bare bones under the plastic.

Beside Jim on the ledge the bag of food was still untouched. The lid of the Thermos was off. Nearly a dozen small white chipboard boxes were stacked and labeled with black writing. Mounds of sifted dirt were piled against the walls: it appeared that Jim had finished his work. He seemed to be keeping a vigil of some kind. The flamelight and the stillness and seclusion had absorbed him in some way. He blinked tiredly, rubbing the back of his hand across his eyes; his hands were scratched and dirty; he had been working without his gloves. A draft of air found its way beneath the anchors of the tent, tossing the light wildly around, and yet Jim's focus remained fixed on the skeleton in the thin beam of the flashlight.

Meg placed her hand on the tent flap, and almost drew it open. But she hesitated. Jim's solitude seemed impenetrable. She forced herself to turn away. Without a word to him she made her way in the darkness back to the path, down the slippery incline, and around the center, toward the locked gate and her car.

TWENTY-ONE

Slowly, she drove back to Las Vegas and the Plaza, pulling to the shoulder of the road to avoid icy places. There was no traffic, and the sky remained dark. The clouds were low and threatening, but no precipitation was falling. For a while she drove in silence listening to the sound of the wheels crunching on the ice, but this, along with her thoughts, became depressing to her, so she turned on the radio and listened to an NPR interview with a woman who had written a book about her experience working on the boat docks of New Zealand.

She was trying to corral her feelings. The strange night and the vision of the skeleton shrouded in plastic and illuminated by the fading lantern light, with Jim keeping his strange vigil—his face shadowed with stubble, his hands scratched and dirty—these images troubled her. Numbed by exhaustion, she arrived at the Plaza and trudged up the wide old staircase and down the hallway to her room. Bassie's room across the hall was dark and quiet. Meg changed into a T-shirt and got into bed, willing herself to sleep.

She was awakened by the telephone and was holding it to her ear before she was fully aware that it was ringing.

"It's Jim," she heard him say. "I'm downstairs in the lobby. I'm glad you're here. I was worried."

"I should have left a note," she said. "I'm sorry."

"Is Bassie awake?"

Her eyes moved to the window. She had not drawn the curtains, and could see that dawn had hardened into daylight. "I don't know," she answered.

"What time does she usually get up?"

Meg looked at the clock. "Before now."

"I'm going to call her room and call you back. I need to talk to you together."

He hung up, but called back in a moment. "She's awake. Can you meet us in her room?"

When Meg stepped across the hall, Bassie was already in the doorway letting Jim into the room, and Meg noticed that his face was still unshaven, his hair uncombed, though he had washed his hands.

Bassie let him into the room without a word, and Meg went in also, closing the door behind her.

"It isn't just a dog's grave," Jim said, looking at Bassie. "There's also a human skeleton. I uncovered it last night. I believe it's Elliott's."

She opened her mouth to draw a breath, her shoulders slumped forward, her hand clutching the handle of her cane, which wobbled back and forth. Meg reached to take her arm, but she pulled away. Jim stood watching, his own shock at the news he had just delivered seeming almost to equal Bassie's.

Bassie stepped back and lowered herself to the bed. Then she stood again, as if to leave the room, but looked distractedly around and lowered herself onto the bed again. "It can't be," she said, bringing her eyes to bear on Jim. "He died in Mexico."

"I found surveying tools in the grave, Bassie," Jim said. "A barometer and hand level. And the cover of a notebook with a record of some fruit purchased in Mexico. And there were other things. But that's not how I know it's Elliott." He paused, seeming to collect the words. "It's his face, Bassie. There's a gap between the teeth. There's also osteo and rheumatoid arthritis all over the body. The hips and spine are lipped in the joint margins, and there's pitting. The lower vertebrae are eroded, and higher up they're compromised by friction. I don't know how much you know about this kind of thing and about how it affects the bones."

She was shaking her head.

"Rheumatoid is systemic and affects mostly the hands and feet," he said. "But it can also be in the larger joints. It's symmetrical in the body and doesn't fuse the bones, so it's easy to tell it apart from osteoarthritis."

"What about the hands?" Bassie said.

"They have osteo and rheumatoid both. And he was left-handed, if that's what you mean. There's wear on the hip joints, too, so he was a horseman. Not Indian; there's no bend in the femur. And the skull is Caucasian. So are the artifacts. I found fly buttons, suspender buckles, jacket buttons, shirt buttons. Eyeholes and nails from the shoes. There was a U.S. dime and some Mexican coins, all dated between 1863 and 1900." He looked at Meg, then at Bassie again. "There's something else," he said. "There's a bullet hole in the skull."

Silence enveloped the three of them.

"I don't know a lot about forensics, but the hole is less than an inch in diameter, and beveled on the outside. The bones on the opposite side are in pieces, a perfect exit wound. The OMI can do a reconstruction. There's a bullet hole in the dog's skull, too. I wanted you to know before I talk to Phil. I've talked to Jake Montoya over at the Maxwell. Do you know him?"

She shook her head.

"He's director at the museum, a forensic anthropologist. I went to school with him, so he's a friend of mine. He said he'll handle this himself. He's got a good rapport with the OMI."

"Why have you called the OMI?" Bassie demanded.

"It's routine," he said. "When we can't put a date on a body. You know that, Bassie."

"It's routine where murder is suspected," she replied. "Is that what you are thinking? It was murder?"

"I called them before I saw the bullet hole."

"There's no statute of limitations on murder," she said.

"No."

"They'll investigate," she said.

He nodded.

"I want to see him," she said.

They were on their way in Jim's truck in fewer than fifteen minutes, Meg in the middle with her legs crowded to the far side of the stick shift. Jim admitted, as they drove, that he had known from the moment he first laid eyes on the kneecap floating free above the joint, while the storm had been approaching, that the bones were human, and probably male, being robustus and knobby, distinctly pitted, with sharp planes.

But he had not believed they were Elliott's bones. This had come to him only gradually as he revealed the rest of the skeleton and the skull. He had looked at the teeth and the dental work only superficially, noting two gold fillings and one of amalgam. He had left the forensic work for Jake Montoya, whom he referred to as "Montey."

Bassie asked if there had been a dental device made of vulcanized rubber replacing two of the back upper teeth, but Jim said he had not explored the mouth cavity deeply enough to know. He had wanted to keep the placement of the lower jaw intact, as it had separated from the skull. This kind of separation, he told Meg, was usual in skeletons buried for some time, but Montey would need to see things exactly as they were.

Bassie inquired of the sex of the dog.

"I couldn't tell," Jim said.

"And what if they find it isn't Elliott?" she asked him.

"I don't think that's going to happen," he said. "But I have to tell you, Bassie, until Montey makes an identification and the OMI accepts it, and writes up a death certificate, they're not going to want you to have any say about anything. They're going to want you to stay off the hill while Montey takes the bones out. He's going to have to take them to his lab."

They arrived at the park at nine-thirty and went first to Jim's office, where the chipboard boxes of artifacts were stacked on his desk.

Bassie handled the artifacts, turning them over and studying them, requesting a magnifying glass, which Jim produced along with the leather notebook cover that he had shown to Meg three days ago when she had first arrived at Pecos. He speculated that this might have been Elliott's ledger book, as Elliott had referred to such a notebook in his letters. The only discernible writing in the notebook was the record of purchase, in Spanish, of fruit from a company in what appeared to be Juárez, Mexico, and this was not in Elliott's handwriting. It was undated. But the paler, less visible pencil markings on the page could have been Elliott's, Bassie said as she examined them. The size and slant of the letters was familiar, though the words themselves were illegible, faded as they were on the dirty and damaged page.

Bassie was handling a set of jacket buttons made of black horn when Phil Barker arrived. "Don't you get involved in this," she warned as he entered the room, but her voice lacked venom, and she appeared more shaken than menacing in the cold gray light from the window.

Phil said nothing in return. He was agitated and distracted. He asked Jim to go with him to his office. The office was in the back of the building, near the concession room where Meg had spent the night. Meg went to purchase a 7-Up and the pretzels she had stared at in the middle of the night, and while standing in front of the Coke machine overheard their conversation.

"No chance it's Native American?" Phil was pressing.

"No."

"Thank God," Phil said. "I'd have to call everything to a halt."

"You're going to have to do that for a while anyway," Jim said.

"For a while, yes. What do you think—a few days?"

"At least."

"But not permanently. You're sure it's Caucasian?"

"Positive."

"And you don't think Jake Montoya is going to find anything different?"

"No, I don't."

"Well. If you're sure—"

"I'm sure, Phil. Okay? I'm sure."

"What about the OMI? Will they make their own finding about this? About whether he's Caucasian?"

"Goddamn it, Phil, he's Caucasian. He's a white guy. Okay? I know who he is, he's Elliott Bass. Now try to have some respect for the situation, will you? Put yourself in Bassie's place."

"It's not like 'a white guy' gives me a perfect scenario," Phil snapped. "I mean, it lets us build the room, but we've still got Bassie to deal with. And the OMI. Jake Montoya is no piece of cake, from what I hear."

Jim held the tent flat open for Bassie and Meg to enter, and then followed them in. Bassie stood at the edge of the pit as Jim climbed into it and lifted the sheet of plastic off the skeleton. The highest elevation of the bones was three feet down, the dirt around swept as clean as a floor, with bedrock showing on one side. The skeleton lay with its hands folded across its chest, a posture—Meg thought—that should have seemed restful but oddly did not. For bones that had inhabited the same place for so many years, these did not have a restful look about them. They seemed uncomfortably placed. The ankle bones and those of the feet extended beyond the boundary of the original square; Jim had dug out the area around them. He had removed the string that previously had enclosed the square, leaving the corner stakes in place as he carved out the nook for the feet. The skeleton did not appear to fit the place appropriately.

The skull was grotesquely compelling, with the eye sockets staring vacantly upward. Meg recalled the photograph of Elliott. The intensity of that gaze looking unblinkingly into the bright sunlight was not evident here in the cold and muggy gray-blue morning filtered through the neon blue of the tent. The bullet hole was more apparent than the eyes. The skull was cracked around the hole, and shattered on the opposite side, with the fragments held in place by dirt. The lower jaw was loose, the mouth cavity packed with dirt; holes gaped where the nose had been. An elbow was raised slightly in the soil, and the skull was tilted back. Whoever had dug the grave had not taken the care or the time to level it.

Bassie requested to be alone. She swung her gaze to Jim, her head wobbling on her neck, and leaned heavily on her cane. "I want," she repeated a second time, when he did not agree at once, "to be alone."

Meg could see that the request was against the rules of the situation. But Jim acquiesced.

Meg followed him out of the tent. They stood together, outside the ring of boulders, in the cold wind. Meg jabbed her boot against a patch of ice. "Who do you think buried him?" she asked.

"I'm wondering who shot him," Jim said.

"And there's no casket," she said. "I just wish I knew if this was the grave Bassie remembers them digging."

"All I know," he said, "is that Hannah's dog Argus isn't in it." After a moment he added, "And Bassie's hunch about the place was pretty strong."

The wind was whipping Meg's hair around. She tried to capture the hair and hold it still. "Suppose that they confirm it's Elliott. What happens next?"

"They try to figure out who killed him."

"I hate that she's shaking so much. It's like she has some kind of palsy."

"I noticed that. I can get her in with my doctor if you think it's necessary."

"She won't go."

A train was wailing in the distance. The sound seemed to eradicate time. This moment could be ninety years ago, Meg thought, and she could be Hannah Bass standing on the hill in the cold and listening to the train.

A gust of wind came up, tugging at a juniper nearby, and the sound of the train grew distant.

Bassie was standing in the grave when they entered the tent, her cane planted beside the skeleton. "This is my father," she said.

When the park employees began to arrive, Jim kept them off the hill. Bassie refused to leave the tent, so Jim carried the lawn chair up for her and created a space inside, on the ledge beside the pit. She sat with her cane across her lap, her eyes fixed on the skeleton in the filtered blue light. Her hands were chapped and blue. Jim found some gloves and brought them to her, but she declined to put them on. He drove to Pecos for propane and filled the Coleman and set it next to Bassie to warm her, but she shivered so strongly her dentures clattered together.

Meg went down to the offices and brewed a pot of coffee. She filled Jim's Thermos and took it to Bassie.

Jake Montoya—Montey, as Jim called him—arrived at noon. He was part Navajo, according to Jim, broad-chested, large-boned and full-faced. He was dressed in boots and a bolo tie and wore a turquoise bracelet, displaying so many ethnic stereotypes that he seemed to transcend them all. His blue down jacket made him look as stocky as a snowman; his gray hair hung in wispy strands around his ears and fluttered in the wind like feathers. It was he whom Jim had called last night before unearthing the grave, and he who had spoken with the OMI and gained permission for Jim to prepare the skeleton for removal.

Jim admitted him into the tent and introduced him to Bassie and Meg. Phil appeared at the entry and stood holding the flap open, watching Montey remove several small tools from a bag and climb into the pit. Squatting on his heels beside the skeleton, Montey studied it, then switched a flashlight on and leaned over the skull, directing the light into the oral cavity.

"Who's been digging at the teeth?" he asked.

"I have," Bassie told him.

Phil Barker turned to Jim. "You let her do that?" he demanded.

"I didn't know she had," Jim said, but unapologetically.

"I saw a dental piece that proves this is my father," Bassie said. "I want those bones left where they are."

Montey rocked himself cumbrously back on his heels to look at her, then leaned forward again with the flashlight and studied where the dirt had been dug from the mouth cavity. "What were you digging with?" he asked.

"A hairpin," she replied.

"The good news is," he said, "you haven't dug out anything that didn't need it." He sat back on his heels again and looked at her. "The bad news is, I'm going to have to ask you to leave."

She shoved her shoulders back, and straightened herself, but looked fragile, as if she had outlived any power she had once had, and retained only belligerence.

"I realize, Dr. Bass," Jake Montoya said, "that these may be the remains of your father, and probably are, which is all the more reason for you to let us do our work here. We'll keep you informed."

"You may look at the bones all you want," she said. "But don't take them out of the grave."

Phil cast his eyes to the ceiling. "Here we go again," he muttered.

"I hope you're not equating dog bones with my father's," Bassie said.

"Look," Phil told her, stepping further into the tent and dropping the flap behind him. "I don't mean to be insensitive, but even if that's

Elliott, the bones have got to be removed. We're building a room here. We're blasting this whole area. And officially, for now, this is a crime scene anyway. You don't have permission to be up here."

"You would rob my father of his grave, without a second thought," Bassie accused him.

Phil crossed his arms on his chest. His head was bent forward with the slope of the ceiling; his flat-hat rested on his ears. "These bones are not your father's until Jake says they are," he said. "And Jake won't know that for sure until he gets them out. And even if they are your father's, it's not going to affect our plans. If he was Native American—yes, you just might have a case. But he was Anglo, for God's sake. And he's on federal property. I'm telling you, you can have the bones if they're his. But you can't leave them here."

"That's right," she said. "You fall back on legalities, Phil. Forget human decency. Forget history. You don't give a fig about history. All you care about is your Boy Scout badge."

"Look," Phil said, dropping his voice, "I'm not trying to steal anyone's grave, but I have a job to do, and none of this is going to stop me from doing it."

"The press might stop you," Bassie said.

"You're going to start on that again?" he answered.

Montey stood up, brushing the dirt from his hands. "Dr. Bass," he said, "what the press has to say about this, at the moment, I'm afraid, is not going to be very relevant. These remains have been discovered, and they have to be exhumed. That's not Phil's decision, or Jim's, or mine. It's the law. This skeleton, for that matter, isn't even dead by law until I say it is. You can make all the trouble you want; you can drag the press in on this, and they can record you making trouble. But my job, right now, is to take the bones out of this grave and take them back to my lab and wash them up and figure out who they belong to. And see what I can figure out about the bullet hole. That's what I am going to do. And after that, if they're your father's, you can have them. You can bury them anywhere you want."

"Except this hill," Phil said.

"We have the artifacts, and the dog," Bassie answered emphatically. "We have the dental evidence. How much evidence do you need?"

"It's not a matter of what I need," Montoya said. "It's a matter of exhausting what there is. Aren't you curious about the bullet hole?"

Bassie thumped her cane on the ground.

When Meg had settled Bassie at Jim's desk to use the telephone, she went back up the hill and found Jim in the tent with Jake Montoya and Phil.

"I'm going to need more light in here," Jake Montoya was saying as she entered. He was squatting beside Jim in the pit with the skeleton, examining something on the skull. "Or else we can take the tent down. What do you think, Jim?"

"Whatever you want," Jim answered. "It's easy to take it down. Hello, Meg. Is Bassie calling the press?"

"She was talking to a news station in Albuquerque when I left her."

"Then leave the tent up," Phil said sourly, having seated himself in Bassie's chair on the ledge. "Unless you want the whole procedure on the nightly news." No one responded to this, and Phil added angrily, "Can't the OMI keep the press out of here?"

"I doubt they care to try," Jake Montoya said.

"I could declare this hill off limits," Phil answered. "People aren't supposed to get off the trails anyway."

"People and the press are two different animals," Jake Montoya observed. "You're going to make an even bigger stink trying to keep this under wraps." He paused, looking up at Phil. "If we're going to leave the tent up, somebody needs to rig me up some better light." He chuckled. "She's a cat, Phil. She has got you by the balls. If she gets the feds up here, they'll want to know what's going on." His chuckle escalated to a wheezing laugh. "Whew-whee," he said, "I tell you. You better polish up that scout badge, Phil. Them feds will check for shine."

TWENTY-TWO

Jim drove Bassie and Meg to Las Vegas as evening began to settle over the road, the hills turning azure in the early twilight. His face was still unshaved; Meg watched him from the corner of her eye. She watched his hands on the steering wheel. When he pulled the truck to a stop outside the Plaza, he didn't offer to come in. He helped Bassie out, but allowed Meg to take her into the hotel, saying he had better go home.

Meg took Bassie up to her room, then went to her own room and locked the door and dropped herself onto the bed. For a while she lay staring at the ceiling and trying to assess the day, then dragged herself up to turn on the television for the last half of the five o'clock news.

The discovery of the grave was featured on two stations. Bassie was pictured standing in front of the tent, bent slightly in her fur coat with her cane planted in the red dirt, stating that the bones were those of her father, Elliott Bass, who deserved to keep his grave. "This was not federal property when he was buried here," she stated to the camera, her voice tremulous in the wind. "My father brought the railroad to New Mexico, and the railroad brought commerce. Before that, the people here were goat farmers. And now the government thinks it can have his grave, just because it owns the land."

Phil was shown briefly on one of the broadcasts, seated in his office wearing a coat and tie. He appeared more reasonable than Bassie had on the windy hilltop. Meg was surprised that the story nevertheless was weighted in Bassie's favor. A famous old woman opposing her father's exhumation was more appealing than a sour-faced, equivocating bureaucrat who said the bones could well be those of any white male in his early fifties.

Jim had declined to be interviewed, as had Jake Montoya, though Jim appeared in one of the camera shots, his hand sweeping the tent flap open as he stepped out into the muggy light, the child's scarf from the lost-and-found flapping around his neck. He had worked with Jake Montoya throughout the day, removing the bones from the grave and packing them in numbered boxes.

When the news was over, Meg tried to call her mother. She dialed her apartment first and then her office, leaving messages on both recorders.

The phone rang a few minutes later. "Hi!" her mother said. "What's up?"

"Don't sound so happy, Mom. It's not good news."

"What has she done?"

"It's not Bassie. They think they've found Elliott's grave on the hill where they thought the dogs were buried."

"What?"

"While they were looking for the dogs' graves they dug up a human skeleton, and they think it's Elliott's."

"Elliott died in Mexico."

Meg started at the beginning.

"That is just astonishing," her mother finally responded, with more than her usual note of theatrics. "I have to catch my breath. How is Mother? Is she just behaving horribly?"

"Don't you think she has the right to behave horribly?" Meg said defensively. "You always make these judgments, Mom. It's a lot more complicated when you're here in the middle of things."

"Yes, you're right about that. I should be there. I'm going to see if I can get a few days off, and—"

"Don't," Meg said. "I can't tell you what a bad decision that would be. It would just put Bassie under more stress."

"You think that's all I would contribute to the situation? More stress?" She was not—Meg knew—as hurt as her tone implied: it could hardly be a surprise to her that she and Bassie didn't get along.

"Basically, Mom, yes. That's what happens when you two get together. It's not your fault, it's just what happens, and—"

"And I suppose you're a calming influence?"

"Not really. But I'm a generation removed. That makes it easier."

"On you, or on her?"

"On both of us."

"Well, lucky both of you," she said sarcastically. "I'm going to think about it."

"About coming? Please don't, okay? I just need to handle this, for a day or two anyway. All we're doing at the moment is waiting for the OMI report, and I'll call you as soon as we know something."

"What's the OMI?"

"The Office of Medical Investigations."

"What on earth are they going to report on?"

"On whether it's Elliott. And if so, on how he was killed."

"You said it was Elliott, and you said he was shot."

"That's what it looks like. They have to confirm it."

"And if they do confirm it, that means he's my grandfather. And I have a right to be there then."

"What's that clicking sound?" Meg asked. "Are you clipping your toenails, Mom?"

Nina hesitated, and then said, "What if I am? Do you have a problem with that?"

"Not a big one, no. It's just weird."

"Cutting my toenails?"

"At this particular moment."

"Well, then, I'll stop. If it will make you happy."

Meg heard one more click of a toenail, then silence. "To answer your question," she said, "if it's Elliott, then Bassie's probably going to want to bury him somewhere here. I'm just guessing, but that's what I would assume. She wants to bury him on the hill in the same place where he was, but that's not going to work. It's in the middle of where they're building the addition. Anyway, whenever it's time to bury him, that would be a good time for you to come."

"Well, fine, but it seems like we should have a plan for between now and then," Nina said, and it occurred to Meg that her mother actually had no desire to come. The argument had been for show.

"The plan is that I'll call you the minute we know something," Meg said.

"Well. Damn. So what's the deal? How are they going to know if it's him? Is there DNA or something?"

"No, I don't think so. I don't know how it's done."

"They'll reconstruct the face with clay, I bet," her mother said. "I saw a program on how they do that. But I don't understand why they have to be so sure it's him. Why don't they just give Mother the bones, if she wants them? Does anybody else want them?"

"I think there are laws about this kind of thing, Mom. You can't just give somebody's bones to anyone who wants them."

"Don't be sarcastic."

"It's hard not to, when you make ignorant statements like that, Mother."

"Well, then, I guess I should curtail my ignorance," Nina said loudly. Meg did not respond, so she added, "How long is it going to take? To do the identification?"

"I have no idea."

"What about your job? I thought you couldn't leave your job. That's what you always tell me when I want you to come see me."

"I have people filling in. I'll have a problem if it rains, but otherwise everything's okay."

"What does rain have to do with it?"

"Everything."

"Why is that?"

"Mom."

"What?"

"It doesn't matter. I'll go home if I have to. And I'll come back and get Bassie."

"And who's going to take care of her in the meantime?"

"Since when did you worry about that?"

"Oh, that is ugly of you, Meg."

"It is ugly. But come on. You know I'll take care of Bassie. And I'll let you know if I need to go home."

Meg heard another click of the toenail clipper.

"Is she eating enough?" her mother asked.

"She's eating plenty."

"Does the Plaza have an elevator?"

"You know it does. You've been here."

"Well, I don't remember the elevator. Don't be so rough on people, Meg. You sound like Mother."

"Sorry. It's been a long day."

"Well, I've been *offering* to come out and help. If you want to be rough on yourself, that's just fine with me. But the rest of us don't have to put up with it."

"I just resent you asking me about the hotel accommodations, as if I wouldn't be looking after Bassie. I always look after her. I always have." She resented, even more than the questioning, that her mother always seemed to need to keep her tied up on the telephone. She did this at pressing times. It seemed to Meg that a mother who had essentially abandoned a child at the age of nine didn't have much right to need her later.

Yet after Meg had finally extracted herself from the phone call, she felt lonely and cut off. She took a shower with the bathroom door open so she could hear the phone if it should ring, then got in bed with the journals and started flipping pages. She wished that Jim would call. She wasn't in the mood to settle in and read: instead she picked her way through passages here and there, watching Hannah's relationship with Elliott deepen. She envied the relationship, and also the friendship with Vicente. Hannah seemed to have everything. Yet it was strange, Meg thought, how things dissolved over time: Elliott was only a skeleton now. The Montezuma was in ruins. She found it disheartening in a way, but also liberating, how everything seemed to be leveled by time. It meant that she eventually would be on equal footing with Hannah and Bassie and all the other people who lived richer lives than she was living at the moment.

Nevertheless, she began to feel depressed. She skimmed quickly over a number of passages about the wedding plans and about how Hannah missed her parents during this time.

I wish Papa had known Elliott, they would have had some common themes of interest. . . . Brother has kindly offered to give me away but I am going to tell him not to come, as we will see him in Chicago afterwards . . . I will not need six of everything as Mother would have

thought, but I hope we will not be living out of traveling trunks and eating off aluminum dishes as Elliott would think perfectly fine.

There was a passage about Elliott's attempt to overcome, for Hannah's sake, a tendency to "nickel-nurse."

He has stood the cost for pillow slips but sees no use for them, he does not own any pillows himself . . .

Meg turned the pages rapidly. Hannah reported on events from the newspaper, including a number of train wrecks across the country, and wrote extensively of the precarious financial state of the Montezuma, which from the beginning had teetered on the edge, having, as Bassie explained in a footnote, lost an average of $40,000 a year by now. With the national economic depression, the Montezuma finally closed down. Because Hannah was getting married, she did not intend to keep working, but most of the women at the Montezuma were transferred to other Harvey establishments. Hannah did not send out wedding invitations, only "at home" cards, as she did not have many friends who could attend: Jewell had taken a job at a Harvey hotel in Kansas, Minerva had moved to Wyoming to live with her son, and Lillian, as Hannah wrote, "has gotten in the soup when we had not thought it possible: she is due to be sick in the summer . . ." She also heard from Cecile McGaffin whom she had never liked and who, Hannah reported, "has found a man to marry and is living out in Idaho where I suppose that she can wrap her rosebud lips around a few potatoes. . . ."

Local businesses began to fail. Hannah wrote of a farmer who committed suicide by eating an insecticide called Paris Green and a carpenter who killed himself by drinking carbolic acid. The world seemed to be darkening around her; she dutifully summarized news stories in the name of chronicling the times, writing of a woman found wandering in the train station with her dead baby in her arms. The woman had disembarked from a train, begged money for a ticket to California, and taken the dead baby with her.

Hannah and Elliott were married at the Morales Mansion in the presence of Vicente and his family, and stayed that night at the Plaza

Hotel, leaving by train the next day for a honeymoon in Chicago, where they rented a suite in a boardinghouse on the south side near Lake Michigan within walking distance of the World's Fair. They attended the grand opening of the fair, with President Grover Cleveland presiding, and spent their days at the fair and visiting Hannah's brother, who had inherited the father's architectural firm, and with whom Elliott engaged in discussions about business and economics.

On one occasion in Chicago Hannah took Elliott to see the house where she had lived and where her parents had died, but the experience troubled her. She sat at the curb in the rented buggy and tried to describe to Elliott her memories and was bothered by his inability—almost his unwillingness—to comfort her. "He dislikes the past," she concluded, "—and not only his own. I believe that he would shut it off entirely if that were possible, and I am beginning to understand that his passion for progress is based on a flight from the past. His childhood is the key to him, and because of this, by the nature of time, and by Elliott's nature, I am locked out."

In the mornings they dined with boarders at the house and then walked to the fair. Reading Hannah's accounts of the fair, Meg found herself amused that Hannah was thought of as a feminist by contemporary readers when in fact she had been more interested in the hootchy-kootchy dancer and the body builder than in displays on women's issues and on "New Women" themselves. Hannah was fascinated by prototypes of household equipment; she devoted pages of text to describing washing machines, carpet sweepers, electric stoves, and doorbells. She liked the "palace" of horticulture but was not interested in agriculture, forestry, and electricity. Real-size reproductions of famous ships failed to capture her imagination, but she was mesmerized by an enormous replica of the Statue of Liberty made of salt, a life-sized wax Pocahontas and Buffalo Bill's Wild West show. She described a new invention, called a "Clasp Locker or Unlocker for shoes," which Bassie's footnote explained was a precursor to the zipper, and refused to ride "Mr. Ferris's large bicycle wheel which revolves in the air like a paddle wheel supporting thirty-six cars."

When Hannah and Elliott returned to Las Vegas in June, they settled into a small, rented house in east Las Vegas, or "New Town," near the depot. The national economy continued to flounder: seventy-four railroads were placed in the hands of receivers, including the Santa Fe, which according to Bassie's footnote possessed, at the time, more than eight thousand miles of track. Six hundred banks in the United States closed their doors, and people marched on Washington demanding relief for the unemployed.

Las Vegas politics became violent. Hannah's writing was impassioned and flew across the pages with dashes and dots and every possible kind of irregular punctuation. "It is worse here than before we left," she wrote.

Vicente's cousin the sheriff is in league with the violent populist White Caps and even Vicente has written him off. Of course the entire Morales family have declared against him. His deputies are thugs. Everyone is armed. The owner of a bar on the old plaza operates a gang of murderers that steals from the wealthy ranchers, and three of his men are deputies who work for Sheriff Lopez. Don Pedro and Vicente's brothers are trying to take the law in their own hands. Old Town, on the west side, is divided: there have been brutal beatings and several murders. Don Pedro was shot at twice last week but walked away unharmed, he will not allow Vicente at the mansion though Vicente of course had nothing to do with the shooting and wrote an editorial the next day calling on the populists, who are his followers, to condemn the violence—the priests have joined him in this effort for peace. Our home is now Vicente's refuge. He comes to Elliott with his doubts and deliberations. Elliott is the voice of reason; he believes Las Vegas will soon stabilize. The west, he says, remains the field of opportunity and the gate of escape, anyone with nothing can come west. . . .

November 12, 1893. Vicente has been sleeping on our sofa on occasions when he sleeps at all, which are not often, he is up at every hour scribbling notes, at times I see him from the doorway in the middle of the night and would keep him company if I could. His newspaper now has three thousand subscribers and plenty of advertising revenue and a large printing room; they have bought a new press, have nearly a dozen employees and plenty of writers, but Vicente carries most of the load himself and writes about language and literacy, history, culture, politics, always controversial with an eye to all the possibilities for nativos to maintain their social standing through industry and education. He is widely read and very respected though targeted by all because he is a spokesman for the poor but is not poor himself. His affiliations on all sides are suspected. Yesterday he wrote about the controversies with the land grants, and the cheating involved, of which his family is known to be part, and his brother pounded on his office door this morning and demanded a retraction, which Vicente did not give. The story implicated Don Pedro and apparently rightly so.

November 30. Vicente has been writing a history of New Mexico in order to correct false interpretations made by eastern journalists, it will take him years to finish if in fact he does, it is very ambitious and I believe is more a passion and diversion than a real endeavor, as he uses up his research in his editorials and I think there is very little that he has not already printed, he is not patient and not one to hoard information; though he loves to gather it up, he throws it all out there again immediately. He has been in Santa Fe this week looking at archives and off to interview a priest in Albuquerque, this with Elliott gone too, and I have been alone with a head cold and all the household chores to do, fairly morose, the weather very cold. . . .

December 13. Señor Elfigo Baca came to our house with Vicente tonight, he is one of Vicente's few friends left, other than ourselves. The Republicans all think Vicente is a turn-coat and the liberals think he is not extreme enough—Vicente remains in a down mood, tonight he consumed nothing but Cracker Jacks and beer. Señor Baca is interesting. When he was nineteen years old he was deputy sheriff here and fought off eighty drunken Texans who cornered him for arresting one of their friends and trapped him in a mud house for two days, shooting approximately four thousand bullets into the house; Mr. Baca was miraculously unhurt even when the house caved in; the Texans blew up half of it with a stick of dynamite. When I inquired how he survived the dynamite, he said that he was in the other half. The group of us had a good laugh about this, but then Vicente brought up politics and talked about the falling price of wool, and there was discussion of how the loss of tariff protection has ruined the native farmers who in the past earned decent profits from local sales but now are forced to go off to work in the mines in Colorado or in the western harvests, while their wives cross the river to this part of town and work for the Anglos. Vicente also talked about his father's corruption, how Don Pedro gains control of county offices by buying people's loyalty; he is afraid his father will be killed now that the populists are regaining power, and he had been negotiating with the liberals, in the effort to protect him. His only distraction from politics is at the sheep ranch in Raton. The Rambouillet sheep that Vicente and Elliott bought together—after Elliott saw the breed at the World's Fair—seem to be a good range sheep and are thriving well.

February 6, 1894. Vicente was with us again to-night ranting about race controversies, and Elliott told him to go to the ranch to get over his anger, that his beliefs are too controversial to impose on a town at war with itself, and his message is too paradoxical, and his following, while a mile wide, is only an inch deep. Vicente hardly listened, but smoked cigarettes and talked incessantly.

February 9. Elliott left early this morning for Denver. He has, sometimes, a look in his eyes that separates him from me, and I think from everyone; this morning I felt he had departed, somehow, long before he was gone.

Vicente came at noon. He was a comfort as always and we talked about Elliott and how he seems to exist on a different level—he seems to be higher up somehow, perhaps because he is older. Vicente is always assuring me of how much Elliott needs me, but exactly how he needs me is not evident. In every basic way, he is independent. He is certainly self-sufficient. I don't know what his emotions would be without me, but his life would be about the same. He is so stoic with his feelings—he tells his thoughts but keeps his feelings under the rug.

Vicente is very different from that. I would be lonely without him. He sat in the kitchen smoking while I roasted coffee beans to-day; he sharpened all my knives and talked about progress on his history book, and went on about Hidalgo and Bolivar, smoking so many cigarettes that when I went outside to get the wash I saw the smoke through the window and thought the kitchen had caught fire.

June 15. Too hot to-day for doing the wash. I ordered from an Albuquerque newspaper four books Vicente recommended, they are all in Spanish—*Don Quixote de la Mancha*, a history of Mexico and a book of poems by a poet named Manuel Acuna. Also a text on how to judge men by their looks.

September 15.

My dear girl,

Your letter of last week arrived on Monday. Gracias, dear heart. I hoped for another to-day but was not so lucky. Write to me more often if you can.

Have you finished Don Quixote? I am proud of you for trying. You are adventurous, my dear.

As for the basket social, you should go. Never mind that you don't like the Methodists, you ought to have some women friends. Vicente will do in a pinch, he has done fine by me, but don't you think it is a little odd, my dear, for you to have no female friends to pass the day with?

We are pressing along on schedule as I said in my last letter, which I hope you have received. So I will be home on time. Now that we have got some national laws mandating air brakes we will have a chance to bring our safety record in this country up a notch or two. I intend to do everything possible in that regard. I am always thinking about mishaps such as happened at Ashtabula when the bridge collapsed and eighty unfortunates fell to their deaths. I will never have that kind of blood on my conscience. I cannot prevent head-on or rear-end collisions caused by timetable errors or inattentive employees, nor prevent derailments due to misplaced switches or too much baggage or obstacles on the tracks, but I can make the grades safe and build well above water-flow and make sure my trusses hold.

As for your recent idea about becoming employed as a teacher, please put it aside, dear heart. I can stand the cost of everything we need. And about my being too directive toward you, you will have to forgive me for that, (or in light of the subject I suppose I should say I will have to ask your forgiveness)—the reason is that I have become accustomed to making decisions and having them followed. But it cannot be so in marriage! Allow me to adjust myself in this regard. I will certainly do it.

Take care of yourself my love. Don't fret about anything. Remember that Señor Vasquez will deliver firewood; have Vicente tell him when you need it.

Your devoted husband,
Elliott Bass

October 25. An event took place here at the house three nights ago, Vicente had come for the evening and was with us at table when a shot was fired at him from the street, shattering the window but missing Vicente and breaking a sconce on the wall. Elliott required me to get on the floor, after which I crawled into the kitchen while he and Vicente went outside. They did not find anything out of the ordinary.

October 29. All these months I have been tossing circumspection to the winds and crossing boundaries with my friendship for Vicente—except the basic ones which apparently are not enough to dictate conscience, not to me anyway, and now when I share too many of my thoughts with Vicente, and the same for him—so that we are both always going and coming all day with our thoughts—and *feelings,* by the general way of things, were certain to follow. We cannot rely on instinct when it takes us the direction of our thoughts, as the thoughts are of the kind that should not even be alluded to except to say they are despotic in the night. I have been feeling cut off from Elliott, and lonely, he is unreachable and has sealed off parts of his life. I want to understand him, but he stops me. He seems to live above me, while Vicente is on the same level and gives me more of himself. But he should not be coming here so often, sitting at the kitchen table, smoking, stating his thoughts about every trouble under the sun and how many lambs his Rambouillets are having and what his father said to him the day before.

Feelings are not as easily penned up as sheep, and wrongs will extend themselves and slide into other wrongs as certainly as shadows will grow longer—we cannot stop shadows from lengthening, except to remove ourselves from the light. All of this to say Elliott has not been gone two days and I have made a grave mistake. I was ironing this morning and burned myself, and Vicente came to the house and found me in the kitchen salving the burn and began to help me and then took me into his arms and kissed my face. I wish for the sake of my conscience I could pretend the moment surprised me, but I have known our feelings. If that were all that happened I could live with myself better, but I felt as if my soul dropped out of me, and at the time I wanted nothing but to break the barriers and be up close to Vicente, and that is what happened—he said things to me that I can never forget and have played in my mind since. He unfastened the buttons on my dress and asked me to remove it, which I did, and now I am ashamed and yet would not go back and alter the moment or give it back—that is the truth of it, I would not, the memory is too comforting even while I understand the danger it threatens. Vicente is nearer to me in a thousand ways than Elliott, we are living at least on the same plane, and guilty of the same wrong, though perhaps not equally unrepentant, as he seemed to be filled with remorse and said he would not forgive himself, and afterwards left directly. I am not so much in search of forgiveness, only despondent now with the passage of hours and a growing sense of the fact that I have forfeited any claim I had on honor. I am telling myself that nothing has to be different, and yet of course it is, as I have become a person not to be trusted. Elliott has so kindly, with affirmation and example, freed me from convention—and to what end? He himself at least has wisdom and experience to guide him in his independence from God. To the contrary, I have lost myself in the open spaces.

October 30. Vicente came to the house and said he is going to Guadalajara to research his history book and will be gone a month or more. He did not talk about yester-day but we both knew why he is going. He stayed no time at all, and hardly crossed the threshold, but stood at the door holding his hat. I have never doubted myself as I do now, with a week of lonely solitude before me in which to cherish the memory and examine my anguish.

What I want, is to be in his arms again.

November 7. For a week I have been trying to get hold of my feelings and think of a direction and now have found one, possibly—Elliott surprised me by arriving a day early and not alone, but with Mr. Harvey, who is here on business, and I prepared supper, and the conversation came to this: Mr. Harvey wants to make the west into a tourist draw. The idea came to him during the World's Fair, when he and his son saw an exhibit of prehistoric artifacts from California and thought of marketing pottery, jewelry and weavings—reproductions—as art. He intends to hire Indians to make these and will sell them in his western lodgings and establishments. The railroad will profit from ticket sales if the plan is successful, so the Santa Fe has got involved. The first place Mr. Harvey intends to convert to a tourist stop is the ruin of an Indian city called Pecos on a hill just west of here, along the route to Lamy. The place is abandoned now, the train runs just beneath it. Mr. Bandelier the famous ethnologist studied the ruins of Pecos many years ago and discovered artifacts there—Elliott knew Bandelier when he was in New Mexico but he is gone now. Mr. Harvey said he wanted to hire a tour guide to lecture about the ruins and sell art objects made by Indians who are blood descendants of the Pecos tribe. He said the guide would greet the tourists at a train stop under the ruins and drive them up to the pueblo, show them around and then return them to the next train. I said I would like to do this. Elliott at first thought I was not serious, but came to understand I was, and said it would be impossible as we would have to live there. I wanted to make the argument directly, with Mr. Harvey present, and so put my thoughts before them, and talked about my willingness and my ability with Spanish and said that I could learn the history of the place and we could build a house there. Elliott said the pueblo was too isolated, I would be alone when he was working. I would be alone when he was traveling. But Mr. Harvey said that he would have me, if Elliott would allow it, and meanwhile I should go and see the place. He recommended a book by Mr. Bandelier about the prehistoric cultures that lived in the area; it was published in German but now has been printed in English with a decent distribution as there seems to be a lot of interest in the ways of the past and mysterious cultures. . . .

November 11. . . . We took the train to the stop below Pecos and got off and walked up to the ruins. When we reached the top of the mesa, the air was purely electric, the sky blue, the wind coming from a long way unencumbered and I felt the elevation in my blood and also in my spirits; there was a *rising* feeling, having nothing to do with industry or leg-work, but rather with the lightness of air. The view from there was utterly fantastic, of plains and mountains in the distance. Frost sat in patches at our feet. We walked through the ruins of a large and roofless church—all that is left of the pueblo but for a fallen wall and spiritual rooms underground. It is made of blocks of dirt, each wider than I am tall. There is no sign of recent habitation, only mounds of earth where structures used to be, and scattered pieces of pottery. The place is powerful. The church admits a howling wind. The hilltop was a place of habitation longer than anywhere else in the territory according to Bandelier, and the bones of most of the people who lived there are still buried on the hill. They are said to have been strong and determined people. They tricked the Spaniard Coronado and his soldiers by leading them eastward away from Pecos in order to be rid of them, promising a richer city made of solid gold over the plains and beyond the horizon. The last of the tribe, fewer than fifty, after the others were dead, are said to have stood about on the walls, like stone statues, staring eastward without movement except for the wind blowing their clothes. And then one day they packed up their belongings and went away.

We had our picnic in the bright sun, sitting on the stone wall near the church with a view of a sloping hill below us and a valley, and distant mountains; Paco ate our cheese. Elliott talked about Bandelier and how he traveled thousands of miles on foot, unarmed, making measurements of ancient cities and composing notes on Indians and the terrain. Bandelier was fluent in four languages and always taught himself the language patterns of the people whom he met, including Chinese working for the railroad and cowboys on the ranches. He could speak with Indians of any tribe within a month of having met them.

We talked of this and made our plans, the land stretched out around us—the plains on the horizon were as level as the sea. We walked about the mounds where structures used to be, and entered a sacred hole in the earth and spoke across a shaft of light admitted from the opening above us. And peace came over me. I knew my resolution to be right, no matter what the heartache for myself and for Vicente. I felt concurrence from the dead.

Meg closed the book, and closed her eyes. So that was it—that was the reason Hannah had come to live at Pecos. She had been enchanted with a place that seemed to offer clarity. Even the light was pure there. She could study, she could educate the tourists. Vicente, and the threat he represented to her marriage, would be far enough away. Pecos was a place of safety, an island of rock. A literal fortress. Hannah was taking refuge.

Meg turned off the reading light at ten-thirty, and sat in bed, the light from the bathroom cutting a swath through the darkness. She allowed her mind to drift back to the kiva and the moments she had spent there with Jim. She thought of the quiet, with the occasional gusts of wind whistling overhead, and how the specks of dust had glittered in the shaft of sunlight. The kiva had possessed the same damp smell of earth as in the grave, but had such a feeling of life. A link to the underworld, Jim had called it. A time portal.

She was still attempting to wrestle herself to sleep when the telephone rang. She hoped it was Jim calling, though she told herself it was Bassie, as Jim would be at his home this time of night.

"Hi, it's me," he said. "Were you asleep?"

"No," she answered, sitting up in the dark. "Trying, but not having any luck. Where are you?"

"My office."

"Are the roads bad?"

"Not too bad."

"I thought you were going home."

"I changed my mind."

"You've got to be exhausted."

"Was Bassie on the news?"

"Oh, yes. Very convincing. Scary as hell. What do you hear from Montey?"

"Nothing, yet," he said. "I doubt he's going to make any progress over the weekend."

"What about the film box?" But it wasn't the film box on her mind, it was Jim as he had looked while he was excavating the film box.

"That's going to take some time," he answered, "—and I doubt it's going to yield much."

"I called my mom. She wants to come out here, but I asked her not to. It would be a disaster." She switched the bedside light on. "I'm afraid the OMI is going to think it was Hannah or Vicente who killed Elliott, since Bassie remembers them digging the grave. If that was the grave. Especially if we don't find Argus buried anywhere near it."

"I don't think the OMI is going to put very much thought into it," Jim said. She pictured him in his office, unshaven, at his desk. "The readers are the ones who might jump to conclusions if this gets too public."

"It's going to make the journals seem sinister," Meg observed.

After a silence, Jim said, "That time I went to Mountain Meadows, I was doing an excavation at Zion National Park and just decided to drive over there. It was a long time ago; Billy was just born. Which may be why it affected me so much. It was fall—the same time of year that the massacre happened. And I kept trying to imagine what those parents had experienced, spending four days being shot at from somewhere in the hills. Without any water to give their kids. I looked for the place in the ground where they tried to dig for water, and I thought I might have found it, but I wasn't sure. The land had pretty well healed over. As if nothing had happened. The stream that had been outside the camp had dried into a dirt gully." He was quiet, but Meg didn't feel he wanted her to say anything, and at last he said, "Bassie could be right that one of the reasons I feel connected to Elliott is because we lost our parents at the same age. But a lot of it was just that experience at Mountain Meadows. I don't believe in ghosts, but I'll tell you, after that, I did believe in Elliott Bass."

"I'm glad it was you who found the grave," Meg finally said.

"I almost wish I hadn't. I used to be envious that Bassie knew so much about her parents. But I doubt she'll want to know whatever we find out from here. It's bound to be problematic information. You and Bassie and I may not believe that Hannah and Vicente had anything to do with Elliott's death, but the shadow of a doubt can get ominous. Meg?"

"Yes."

"Tell me about your father. If you would. How old were you when he left?"

"I was three."

"And since then?"

"Since then he died. He was diagnosed with cancer when I was nineteen. Pancreatic cancer. I went to stay with him in the hospital in Ann Arbor. He taught economics at Ann Arbor. I think we both had some idea that there might be some kind of reconciliation if we just spent time together. But I was too . . . young, I guess."

"And too hurt and resentful," Jim said.

"That also."

"And Bassie hasn't done anything to smooth things over; I can see that," he said. "It wasn't subtle, the way she was playing Meredith against you at dinner."

"That kind of thing doesn't bother me as much as it used to. It's just her way of trying to improve me. Whoever's around can do no wrong, and I can do no right. I'm pretty immune to it by now."

"No, you're not," he said.

TWENTY-THREE

She could not sleep after the phone call, and became restless with the effort, finally getting up and taking the journal from the table by the bed and beginning to read rapidly, pouring herself into Hannah's life and Hannah's escape into the refuge of an abandoned ruin.

The frame house in the valley beneath the ruins of Pecos Pueblo was built by railroad laborers and Pecos villagers under Elliott's supervision. Meg imagined Hannah standing on the back porch on a windy spring morning when the house was completed, the smoke of piñon logs rising from the chimney, Hannah's skirt blowing around her legs, her eyes fixed on the jagged slope of Dog Hill rising beyond the patch of grassy flatland, and towering above Dog Hill the mesa enclosed by the low stone wall, with the massive adobe church looming close to the edge.

Hannah had written numerous descriptions of the house, and Bassie had expanded these with meticulous footnotes. It was a single-story cottage with a parlor, a small kitchen, two bedrooms, and a bathroom in the back with a sink and bathtub. Elliott devised the plumbing—an outdoor cistern with pipes running into the kitchen and bathroom. The parlor was covered in popular wall-to-wall carpet and the kitchen in linoleum; the bedrooms had area rugs. Hannah draped the windows in "plain white scrim"—whatever that was, Meg thought—and hung potted plants from the ceiling to humidify the air. Instead of "bric-a-brac" and "whatnots," she displayed chert and shards of pottery from the ruins. She placed Indian baskets and Mexican flowerpots on the porches, between the rocking chairs, and in the parlor hung Mexican lace mantillas beside Indian shields made of buffalo hide—replicas of originals.

Many of these items she offered for sale to tourists when Pecos was opened for business, along with turquoise jewelry displayed in a glass case near the entry door, and hundred-year-old blankets from the village, dyed with indigo and sage.

Elliott stabilized the roof of the kiva with railroad ties and constructed a sturdy ladder so that Hannah could take the tourists down into it.

In several passages Hannah referred to Elliott's attempt to reconcile the legal aspects of inhabiting a plot of land that neither he nor Fred Harvey had paid for. Bassie had clarified the effort in footnotes. The Pecos Grant encompassed more than eighteen thousand acres and was owned, at the time, by a bank in Queens, New York. It included the old ruined pueblo and Pecos Village. But the paper trail was messy. Pecos Indians had sold sections of the land several times over, courts had passed conflicting judgments, speculators from New York, New Mexico, and Colorado claimed overlapping portions. Hispanic inhabitants of the village attempted to have the land appropriated as a Spanish Community Land Grant rather than an Indian Grant, and to incorporate themselves so they could keep their titles and water rights. But industry was starting to creep into the area: a tie contractor from Las Vegas leased sections for timber cutting, and wagons filled with logs rumbled out of the hills en route to the railroad stop below the ruins. The Pecos Grant was placed on county tax rolls, but no one was paying the taxes. The American Pueblo title, the Mexican Pueblo title, and the American tax title all made different claims, but nothing came of them.

It appeared that everyone and no one owned the pueblo on the mesa and the valley where the house was built, in the very center of the grant lands. The paper trail of ownership was so confusing that even Bassie, in her footnotes, referred readers to other sources.

After consulting attorneys and the San Miguel County deed book, Elliott had finally shrugged the matter off and relied on Fred Harvey and the Santa Fe railroad to settle it. The railroad owned a narrow patch of right-of-way just below the ruins, and without any money changing hands, they simply widened the patch to include the pueblo. Profits could be made from tourists, so the Santa Fe desired to have Elliott and Hannah living at the pueblo. In legal terms they were about as authorized as squatters, but no one was complaining and no one could have proven whose property it was they were squatting on, and no one seemed to care. Certainly no one else had tried to set up house in the valley under the ruins.

I have been all day in the sunlight on the church walls reading *Commerce of the Prairies* and also a fine account of a young man's early travels through the Rocky Mountain West. . . . I am in love with the weather here. And solitude. . . . I have been to Santa Fe searching through the Spanish records for anything pertaining to the pueblo. . . . I have hired a woman named Cleofita Ramirez, she is older than I, with a calm manner, a homely face with broad eyes, claims to be a healer and eats juniper berries to aid digestion, therefore smells of junipers. She does not speak any English. She is teaching me to grind corn in the metate and make tortillas and will stay the night when Elliott is gone, which has almost satisfied his reservations, so I hope I will hear nothing more about them. . . . An ancient man named Mariano Ruiz came wandering up the road from the village this afternoon and sat in the shade of the porch with Cleofita and me—he is a friend of hers—we drank lemonade and watched the rabbits. He talked about the old days here and I took notes that someday I will incorporate into the account of life here, as I think the information will interest people in the future. It is a magical place. It holds me . . . We don't see the trains from the house but hear them night and day, a doleful sound as sad as the mourning doves, as eerie as the wolves and coyotes. . . . I have been listening all night to coyotes, who have a strange and chilling way of howling, with ghostly skill, sending their voices over the hills. They modulate and amplify and resonate so that a listener never knows for certain where the ghoulish sounds are coming from—scornful and disloyal creatures, even to each other; they set up ruses and slaughter wantonly and I am told often eat but one lamb for every six they kill. They have the worst traits of domesticated dogs but none of the better qualities, being soulless shadows. . . . Cleofita made hot chocolate and gorditas and leche quemada and sweet custard for the tourists, there were only three tourists to-day. . . . To-day we had six tourists, all interested in nothing, why they came I do not know, they did not care about Pecos or the people

who once lived here; they referred to them with a great deal of laughter as "redskins." I took the merry little band down to the train earlier than necessary and left them waiting in a drizzling rain. . . .

Hannah was twenty-five years old and reading *McClure's* and *Cosmopolitan* as well as more expensive periodicals such as *Harper's* and *Scribner's* and *Atlantic Monthly*. She wore white blouses and plain brown linen skirts loose enough for hiking, and low-heeled, front-laced boots. Her favorite boots had metal toe-caps. Her favorite hat was a floppy straw Bolero that she purchased from the Jordan Marsh catalog, but on hot days in the summer she wore a hat she called a Mountain Leghorn, bought for fifteen cents in Santa Fe. She did not like "brilliants" or buckles or items she considered "Frenchy." Her nightgowns were white flannel without lace. Bundled in a blanket, she and Elliott would sit in the swing on the back porch watching the stars glide over Dog Hill.

With sixty-five dollars of her own earned money, she purchased through a catalog a bicycle fitted with mud and chain guards and a dress guard to keep her skirts from getting tangled in the spokes. It arrived by train and transported her in more ways than the literal. From the *Ladies Standard Magazine*, out of New York and Chicago, she purchased a hat constructed of dried seaweed, which, she remarked, was lighter in weight than felt or straw. Tacked to her hair with a Japanese pin, the hat remained secured to her head even downhill in the wind. She wore divided skirts—"bifurcated," as she called them—but declined to wear bloomers, thinking they would look ridiculous to the villagers. She returned from her bicycle rides exhilarated, and rubbed cold cream on her face and splashed her forehead with water and ammonia. Her home was her absolute haven. The doorknobs were ornamental bronze; the front door had colored "border lights" around the center pane, the iron "cook-stove" in the kitchen was fitted with nickel and tile trimmings and flue capacity enough to burn soft coal. The refrigerator had a double door and was forty-seven inches high, its exterior made of solid ash, the interior having seven walls to preserve forty-five pounds of ice and "keep foods fresh in cold storage." Each bedroom contained a freestanding oil-burning heater, and the kitchen and bathroom had water heaters fueled with gasoline. The house was lighted with paraffin lamps and candles. Geraniums grew in pots on the sills. Hannah nurtured a flower garden in the back; it had a sundial in the center, and no shade trees. Hannah had no reason to grow fruits or vegetables, as Fred Harvey sent them by train.

It was not as isolated a life as Meg had imagined. Elliott went by train to Las Vegas every day or two when he was not in California or somewhere else restructuring old track, and often stayed overnight at Vicente's small house in Old Town or at the Morales mansion, and on these occasions Cleofita stayed with Hannah. Often, Señor Ruiz slept on the back porch or in the parlor on the sofa.

Employees of the Santa Fe came to Pecos to consult with Elliott. Jewell Cartwright came and stayed for a week.

Vicente did not come. His journey to Guadalajara for research on his history of New Mexico included a stay in Mexico and extended months beyond the expected time. When he returned, he resumed work on the newspaper and compiled his notes for the history book. Elliott invited him to come to Pecos, but he provided reasons why he couldn't. He spent more time than ever at the sheep ranch near Raton. Hannah had no contact with him at all.

However, his name appeared frequently in her journal.

October 3, 1895. . . . Vicente's editorial was about the Spanish invasions of Mexico and was perfectly crafted and impassioned if sentimental and too florid. . . .

October 10. . . . Elliott was all morning in Las Vegas with Vicente talking over their experiment involving ewes with extra teats and if the ewes will bear more twins than average, a supposition posed by Mr. Bell who is famous for inventing telephones—Vicente is trying it on the Rambouillets.

October 29. . . . Elliott came home with a story about Vicente, that he encountered Don Pedro near the printing office yester-day and they argued on the street, and nearly struck one another; it caused a public disturbance in which others got involved. Elliott was there and afterwards tried to reason with Vicente in the office but Vicente would not listen and became angry, and Elliott is always so impatient with displays of feeling, that I imagine Vicente was a little frustrated trying to get his points across. I am mystified how the friendship has lasted as long as it has, or become as significant, to both of their lives, as it apparently is; they seem somehow to gain something from the other's weaknesses—Vicente shows too many of his feelings, and Elliott too few. It is hard to know exactly how I fit with them. I am not like Jewell, displaying everything, but I cannot bury my emotions as Elliott does. Vicente causes me to reveal too much, while Elliott appreciates my silence. He is often distracted, and withdrawn, and while I am safe with him, I always know there are things under the surface that I have not yet caught a glimpse of.

November 3. . . . This evening is too melancholy, I am alone, the sun has gone down, the air is cold, the light is silver. Cleofita has gone home for the night.

After this passage a new thread began to wind its way through the journal entries. Hannah wanted to conceive a child, but the attempt was undermined by Elliott's frequent absences. "His dedication to his work is seamless," she wrote.

He can hardly look to left or right of his work sometimes, and of course everything exists in these peripheral spaces, not on the main line, so to speak. The more conspicuous I am in his presence, the more absent he seems to become, as if he is afraid at some deep level to commit himself to me. We talked again last night about the idea of the baby. I have begun to doubt that he will lose a week of work to stay at home and increase our chances. He is leaving again to-morrow. He promises that I will have a baby by-the-by, but meanwhile he will be in California at the crucial time this month. I have got the timing perfect by the books, just after the periodical, two months in a row now, and been disappointed. I hope there is not a problem. So many women use douches and condoms and sponges and diaphragms and pessaries and even so conceive babies left and right, and here I am with no preventative and not conceiving. Cleo thinks it is the Junipers around here. The berries are preventative, and possibly the smell of them is working against us. . . .

December 2. Elliott returned to-night having come through Topeka where he met with Mr. Ripley, who has grown too sure of himself by saving the Santa Fe from financial ruin and has started resurrecting the old ways, planning to expand and build more track, and now has offered Elliott a powerful position as the chief engineer of the Mexican Central Railroad, which is an ally of the Santa Fe, in which Elliott would lay a thousand miles of track in northern Mexico, an opportunity that he has dreamed of, and yet I found myself angry, looking out the window at the stars untethered over the hill and thinking that my husband is no more grounded than they are. He will be in the wilderness, so I cannot go with him. I suppose he would rather spend a night with howling wolves than a dozen nights with me. He apparently needs to be at risk, if he is to be happy. He claims that he can love me from afar but cannot lay track from a distance. I told him he should go. I would only make him miserable by insisting he stay. His silence was an acquiescence. He knows I am opposed. There was nothing to say. I wish he would be more sedentary. And less adventurous? Less ambitious? Less himself?

It is so difficult to let things fall where gravity puts them.

TWENTY-FOUR

From a deep sleep Meg became aware of a loud, rhythmic sound, and heard Bassie's voice break through, demanding that she open the door. Slowly she began to realize that Bassie was pounding on the door with her cane, and lifted herself onto her elbow to survey the room and the digital numbers of the bedside clock: 7:23. The events of yesterday came belatedly to her consciousness.

"Hang on," she called, peeling off the covers, swinging her feet to the ground and making her way sleepily to the door. She unlatched the chain, pulled the door open, and saw Bassie in the hallway in her nylon robe, her bristly black hair fallen around her shoulders, her face appearing pale without the definition of black eyeliner and painted eyebrows.

"They've found a photograph of Mother," Bassie said. "A reporter just called."

"What do you mean?"

"A photograph of Mother. With Jewell and Vicente. At Saint Anthony's hospital. Where she died. Get dressed. We're going to Santa Fe. The reporter wants to talk to me about printing it. Let me tell you I intend to talk to him. He had a story in this morning's paper about Dog Hill. Quoting Phil. With the facts wrong. He tried to pretend he was calling me out of courtesy and could print the photograph without permission from me. We'll see about that."

"Where did he get it?" Meg asked.

"A woman named Myrna Spitz came up with it this morning, after she read his story. I've never heard of her. I don't know any reason she would have a picture of Mother. Now get some clothes on. I want to leave by eight o'clock. He doesn't know we're coming. He thought he could interview me on the phone at seven o'clock in the morning. My phone's been ringing off the wall. Reporters are coming out of the woodwork." She turned and clomped across to her room.

Meg went into the bathroom to wash her face and brush her teeth, then dressed in her jeans and a sweatshirt and called Jim's office number.

There was no answer, only the machine, and she didn't leave a message. She went downstairs for a newspaper and read the story about the exhumation of the grave. It was long for a newspaper story, and in Meg's opinion was overwritten; it stipulated that the grave exhumed yesterday was believed to be that of Elliott Bass though the identification was not yet conclusive. The author was a writer named Manuel Medford. Beside the story was the photograph of Hannah in the plumed hat and the one of Elliott posed in front of the train, as well as one of Bassie taken yesterday on Dog Hill, in her fur coat, pointing her cane toward the tent over the grave.

Meg read the article standing in the lobby drinking a glass of orange juice that Martin Estes handed her. When she returned to her room, the light on the phone was blinking.

The message was from Jim, but the number he left was not his office number. It was nearly eight o'clock now, and Bassie would be thumping on her door again at any moment. Meg called the number and Jim answered.

"Where are you?" she asked.

"At home."

"Did you see the story in the paper?"

"That's why I called."

"Well, the reporter just called Bassie a little while ago. He said somebody brought him a photograph of Hannah this morning—not the one in the hat. This one was taken at the hospital where she died. Here in Las Vegas."

"Saint Anthony's," Jim said.

"Yes. I assume it's no longer around?"

"No. It was torn down."

"Well, that's where the picture was taken. Vicente and Jewell are in it too. The reporter wants to publish it, and Bassie is going to try to stop him. She wants me to drive her into Santa Fe right now to the newspaper office. There she is, she's banging on my door."

"I'll meet you at the newspaper here in Santa Fe, then," Jim said. "Bassie knows where it is. I'll be inside by the front desk when you get there."

He was waiting where he had promised when Meg and Bassie entered the building. "Manuel Medford has been on the phone since I got here thirty minutes ago," he said. "I haven't tried to talk to him. The AP put his story out on the wire and he's getting a lot of calls."

The three of them went to the window that showed a view of the newsroom, a large area divided into cubicles by waist-high metal partitions that were a bright turquoise color. It was difficult to tell how many reporters and staff were at their desks; half a dozen people were walking around with coffee mugs.

"Which one is he?" Bassie demanded.

"Over there," Jim told her, indicating a large man at a desk near a corner of the newsroom. From the distance of the window he seemed hardly old enough to be out of college, he had red hair and ruddy skin pitted with acne scars, and was leaning back in his chair, smiling, holding the phone receiver to his ear and apparently enjoying the attention that the Dog Hill story had brought him.

Bassie started to enter the newsroom. "You'll have a better chance of getting the photograph if you're nice about it," Meg said.

"Finesse it," Jim told her.

"Finesse it," Bassie sneered. "I'll finesse it." She hooked her cane over her arm and shoved the door open with both hands. The woman seated at the reception desk rose to stop her from going in, but Bassie was already inside, with Meg and Jim behind her. The woman called after them, but did not follow or make any real attempt to stop them.

Bassie went directly to the reporter's desk. As he saw her coming, his face registered recognition. He ended the phone call abruptly and stood to greet her. Meg could tell from his demeanor that he was already intimidated. Bassie stood before him in her oversized coat, her head thrust forward, her glasses magnifying her eyes. Her expression implied something close to hatred.

The man gathered himself together and smoothed a hand over his wiry hair.

"You're Manuel Medford," she said.

"Yes," he admitted. "Are you Claudia Bass?"

"Show me the photograph," she demanded.

He seemed about to do so, but then hesitated, and Bassie lifted her cane and brought it down forcefully across his desk, splintering a pencil.

Jim stepped immediately forward, extending his hand to the man and introducing himself. "Dr. Bass just wants to see the photograph," he explained, giving her a warning look. "She'll give it back."

"I will not give it back," Bassie said. "If it's of my mother, it belongs to me. I'll talk to your editor, young man. I know Vernon Sanchez very well. And he will see that I get that photograph."

"But it isn't his," the reporter protested. "I promised Myrna Spitz I would return it. She didn't tell me I could show it to anyone. I don't have permission to do that."

"Get her on the phone," Bassie said.

"If you'll call her up, I'll talk to her," Jim offered. "Dr. Bass has only one photograph of her mother, so you can imagine why she's anxious to see this one."

Bassie's eyes swept the surface of the desk, and Manuel watched her nervously. When she began plucking up items to look at them, Manuel protested, trying to gather them back from her. Before Jim or Meg could intervene she had got hold of an envelope and was extracting a small, rectangular picture. Her face froze as she looked at it; her eyes became fixed and staring. She turned the photograph over, and scanned the words printed in ink on the back. Her mouth opened, then closed; a murmuring sound came from the back of her throat. She fumbled the picture clumsily back into the envelope and then slowly began to sink toward the floor. Meg realized suddenly that Bassie was falling. Jim caught her as she slumped forward. Meg grabbed a nearby chair and shoved it toward Jim and he settled Bassie into it. A spasm clenched the muscles of her face, as if an invisible hand had gripped her jaw and squeezed it, puckering the lips. Her cane clattered to the floor. She smeared her palm over her mouth and drew it away. It was smudged with lipstick that Meg briefly believed to be blood. She seemed to be trying to speak. Meg knelt, helping Jim to support her so that she would not fall out of the chair.

Manuel Medford hurried away, then returned with a paper cup of water. Meg noted distantly that twenty or so reporters at their desks were staring at the spectacle, some of them standing up to peer over the waist-high walls of the cubicles. One had covered the mouthpiece of the phone into which she had been speaking and was observing Bassie with a look of fascination and disgust. Another sat holding a plastic fork with a soggy strand of lettuce trailing from it. Bassie remained collapsed in the chair, clutching the envelope to her fur coat, her scuffed black shoes splayed awkwardly on the floor.

Manuel Medford offered Bassie the cup of water, but she knocked it aside with her arm, and it splattered against his desk. Bassie buried the envelope in her moldy coat so deeply that she might as well have eaten it, it seemed so thoroughly consumed. Her expression was horrible. Her eyebrows arched nearly to her hairline, with specks of dandruff clinging to them, and the garish smudge of lipstick seemed to split her face in two. "I'm going to keep it," she gasped at Manuel, straining for breath like a fish yanked out of water.

Jim said quietly to Manuel, "Call Myrna Spitz, or I will."

Manuel reached for the phone.

Bassie was trying to stand. "Don't get up," Meg said. But Bassie took hold of the cane. Her feet did not seem to be working correctly; her boatlike shoes glided around on the floor. At last she steadied her feet and hoisted her weight and stood with her spine bent forward and her head unsteady on her neck, the blue veins throbbing at her temples. She flung her gaze back toward the door, and Meg realized she intended to turn in that direction and walk out with the envelope buried in the coat.

"You can't take that!" Manuel Medford cried. "I told her I would give it back to her! Today!"

Bassie, however, had started for the door.

Jim moved to her side and stepped in front of her, solidly blocking her way. She lifted her cane as if to strike him with it, and made small chopping motions in the air, seeming frantic and disoriented, twisting her neck around as if in search of another exit. But Jim was in her way, talking steadily to her, asking her to give him the envelope. Her balance shifted and she almost fell, staggering against her cane, and Jim's arm went out to support her. He became more forceful, telling her to give him the envelope, and his insistence seemed finally to break into her consciousness, producing an effect like a dam giving way. She reared her face back and wailed a shattering, unintelligible sound, then shrank into her coat and made another noise that Meg identified, in that stunned moment, as weeping. Jim kept his hold on her, guiding her back to the chair and taking the envelope from her. "I need Myrna Spitz's phone number," he told the reporter. "And a phone that I can use in private. Is there a pay phone or an empty office somewhere?"

"I'll call her myself," Manuel said. "Give me the photograph."

"You'll call her?"

"Yes."

"Tell her what the situation is," Jim said.

"Okay. But I don't want her listening." He swung a glance toward Bassie.

"Why not?" Meg asked. "You better not be angling for another story out of this."

His silence implied that he possibly was.

"Put yourself in her place," Meg said angrily. "She's only got one photograph of her mother, and now another one has turned up and you won't let her have it. I doubt Myrna Spitz even cares."

"I have every right to talk to Myrna Spitz in private," he responded. "If she tells me it's all right to give her the photograph, that's fine, she can have it. But I'm not just going to hand it over. I'll give it back to Myrna, and she can hand it over. Otherwise this is a legal issue."

"I doubt that," Meg said, though she did not, in fact, know much about the legalities of the situation, and was aware that her resentment toward the reporter was irrational and overly protective of Bassie.

Jim placed the envelope on the desk, and Manuel picked it up.

"How reasonable is Myrna Spitz?" Jim asked him.

"Compared to whom?" Manuel responded with hostility.

"How reasonable is she?" Jim repeated.

"She seems reasonable."

"Ask her if we can meet her somewhere," Jim said.

Manuel said he would make the request. He took the envelope and a notepad with phone numbers written on it, and vanished into an office cubicle at the far end of the room.

Bassie sat staring in that direction, awaiting his return. Meg stood beside her to steady her if she should begin to slump out of the chair or attempt to stand. Jim stood beside the desk. People around them began slowly to return to their work, clicking away at their keyboards and making phone calls. Nevertheless, the room seemed unnaturally subdued, with everyone speaking in hushed tones and averting their eyes from Bassie. When Manuel Medford returned, he addressed Jim. "Okay," he said, taking his coat from the back of his chair. "You can follow me."

Myrna Spitz's house was in the old South Capital area on a narrow, unpaved alleyway off a street called Don Gaspar. The houses in the area were adobe dwellings crowded around small courtyards, as many as five houses jammed onto a single lot and sharing a courtyard and cramped parking area.

Manuel managed to find the address with a minimum of backing up and pulling into the wrong parking places. Jim had to park farther down on the street, and Manuel stood waiting in the dreary cold, and then led the way into the courtyard. It was paved with flagstones, and an olive tree shed its slender leaves over the walkway to the entrance. Smoke was drifting out of the chimney. Myrna Spitz opened the door even before Manuel knocked. Her appearance flooded Meg with relief. She was elderly, with a sweet expression. Her skin was an amber color, her hair combed into a tight knot. She appeared to be part African American. She spoke first to Bassie, taking her by the arm and leading her into the house. "Come in," she said. "All of you. Hello—" She extended her hand to Meg. "I'm sorry the house is a mess. But I've made a pot of coffee. I also have tea, if you like. Come in and sit down."

Meg could feel the welcome heat from the fireplace even before she stepped inside. The room was small, with adobe walls and narrow windows. A modern skylight in the ceiling admitted a dull light from outside, but the orange of the flames filled the room with motion and animated light.

Clocks were everywhere. "My father was a clock repairman," Myrna said by way of explanation. "I inherited his clocks, but no passion for them," she added apologetically. "I hardly ever keep them wound." She considered Bassie for a moment. "I guess the photograph has upset you," she said.

Bassie seemed distracted by the clocks, suspicious of their silent faces. Her eyes wandered around the room. Myrna indicated a rocking chair beside the fire, and Jim took Bassie by the arm and steadied the chair while she lowered herself into it. When Myrna went into the kitchen, Manuel Medford tried to fill the silence left behind, sitting awkwardly in a chair that seemed too small for him and asking Jim about the recent rise in crime in the town of Pecos. After a moment Jim went into the kitchen to help Myrna Spitz with the coffee. He brought the tray out, but Bassie refused a cup when Myrna poured it.

"My mother must have known your mother at Saint Anthony's hospital in Las Vegas," Myrna said to her, presenting the coffee cup to Manuel and then offering coffee to Meg and Jim, both of whom declined. She poured herself a cup, and took a seat beside Meg on the sofa. "I haven't read your mother's journals," she told Bassie. "I actually had never heard of them, which I am ashamed to admit, now that I know how famous they are." She took a sip from her cup. "At any rate, when I read Mr. Medford's article in this morning's paper, I recognized your mother's name. I had seen it on the back of the photograph when I was going through a box my mother left me. My mother died twenty-three years ago, and I went through the boxes then, but I hadn't looked at them again until recently. Most of the photographs didn't have names on them, so I got rid of a lot of them. The one of your mother is the only one from Saint Anthony's. Mother worked there for a while—when she was in her early twenties, I think. I understand your mother was a patient there. Mother was a caretaker—a volunteer." Myrna looked at Meg, explaining, "That's what you did back then, when you had tuberculosis and recovered. You helped others who had it. My mother had it as a child, so she wasn't at any risk of becoming infected as an adult. The Sisters who ran Saint Anthony's relied on volunteers to help them." She addressed herself to Bassie again. "She worked there, until she married my father. Her name was Betty Turow. I don't know if the name is familiar to you. She was related to a Black man whom you might have heard of, as I think he was fairly well known in Las Vegas. His name was Montgomery Bell."

Bassie nodded, and spoke the only words she had uttered since she had arrived, saying that she knew of Montgomery Bell. Even so, she seemed detached from the conversation, her eyes flickering to the envelope in Manuel Medford's lap.

Myrna spoke briefly about Montgomery Bell, a prominent rancher and real estate tycoon in Las Vegas at the turn of the century. She stood up and took from the wall near the door a framed photograph of his mansion that he had built in Las Vegas; the photograph was old and speckled with silvering and depicted the mansion after it had fallen into disrepair, with the balcony railing broken and the yard full of weeds, most of the fence pickets missing. "It burned in 1982," Bassie said, when Myrna held the photograph before her.

"Was it only that recently?" Myrna said. "It's amazing, that you know the date offhand. I couldn't remember when it was." She hung the photograph back on the wall. "Your friend Mr. Layton told me in the kitchen that you would like to keep the photograph of your mother," she said. "Of course that would be fine with me. I'm only glad I didn't throw it away. I think it's wonderful it has survived all these years. I suppose you were intended to have it." She returned to her place beside Meg on the small sofa and took another sip of coffee, then turned to Manuel Medford. "Would you give it to her, Mr. Medford?"

"Yes, but I was thinking she might give us permission to print it in the paper and—"

"I doubt that," Myrna Spitz quietly interrupted. "Given the situation." She leaned forward and held her hand out to Manuel for the envelope.

He handed it to her. She thanked him, stood, and carried it to Bassie. Bassie received it and without a word or even a glance at Myrna, pulled the photograph from it, and leaning closer to the fire, held it to the wavering light. She turned it over and read the writing on the back, as she had done before.

"That's my mother's handwriting," Myrna said.

Bassie turned the photograph back over to study the image. Her head began to shake slowly, from side to side. Meg stood and started toward her, but before Meg could reach her, Bassie had thrust herself forward in the rocking chair and stood halfway up, supporting herself with the cane. With a flick of her wrist she dropped the photograph into the flames.

Meg was stunned by the inexplicable action. With almost a sense of panic she rushed to the fire and attempted to reach for the photograph, but it withered before her eyes. She saw it in the burning embers, beginning to curl at the edges, and saw on the face of it, through the smoke, the figures of Hannah, Vicente and Jewell, standing on the steps of a large building. She took an iron poker from beside the hearth and scraped what remained of the photograph out of the glowing ashes. A flame was flickering through it; she put her boot down on the remnant. But when she moved her foot there was nothing left but a smear of ash and a thin, transparent vision that disintegrated when she leaned to touch it.

"Why would you do that?" she cried, swinging herself around to face Bassie.

Bassie had lowered herself back into the rocking chair, from where she sat staring at the ash on the hearth, as motionless as if she had been propped up dead.

Meg suffered a rush of uncontrollable anger. It seemed that Hannah had never been so close to her, and so within her reach, and ultimately so beyond it, as she was at this confounding moment. It occurred to her that everything she had come to know about Hannah had been filtered through Bassie first, and that now she had lost her only chance to see Hannah unedited by Bassie. Bassie had stolen it from her. She felt a claim on Hannah and a deep sense of loss, and fought the sudden urge to cry. She wanted to leave and seek out privacy so she could manage to get her emotions under control, but Bassie seemed to have faded to a shadow, and to be in need of Meg somehow.

Meg swung her eyes to Jim. He was leaning forward, staring at Bassie. Manuel had risen from his chair; Myrna was still on the sofa, looking at the flames and at Meg standing before them with the iron poker in her hand. No one spoke a word. Finally Myrna Spitz said quietly, "It was hers to burn."

Meg dropped the poker to the hearth and leaned over, plucking the transparent sheen of celluloid off the stones. She could see that it was not worth salvaging; no discernible image remained. The substance turned to almost nothing in her hand. And yet her instinct was to try to save it. She started toward the kitchen, and heard Jim stand and follow her. In the kitchen she began to open drawers and look for something to place the remnant on—a piece of foil or plastic. "There's nothing left of it, Meg," she heard Jim say from behind her. "Myrna's right, Meg. It was hers."

"It *wasn't* hers!" Meg turned and almost shouted, not caring if Bassie might hear her. "Bassie isn't going to live forever. It was mine as much as hers. She's spent her whole life *saving* history; why would she want to destroy this? Is she hiding something?" She was holding the sheen of celluloid in her open palm, but could tell through the watery glaze of her tears that the image was utterly gone. Closing her hand around the remains, she dusted them away.

Jim stood watching her. "Are you all right?"

"Not really."

"Should I leave you alone?"

"There's the difference," Meg said. "You're willing to let her get by with this. You let her do whatever she wants. I can't even tell if you care. I can't tell what you care about."

He continued to look at her. "No, you can't," he said. "I think I'll leave you alone."

When he was gone, she stood in the kitchen. It was small, with a tiled floor and an old stained wooden countertop; the appliances were rusty. A narrow window above the sink displayed a bare garden enclosed by a fence of upright sticks lashed together with baling wire. Confusion overwhelmed her for a moment, and she leaned her face into her hands. Her hands, she found, still held the smell of ashes, and for several moments she did not compose herself, but cried into her hands.

When she left the kitchen, she was no longer crying.

TWENTY-FIVE

Meg drove Bassie back to the Plaza in Las Vegas with hardly a word spoken. It was three o'clock in the afternoon when she entered her room and the message light confronted her: Carolyn Stott, her office assistant, had been calling since eight-thirty. The town of Conroe, in east Texas, was flooding and the dialysis clinic at the hospital was threatened with a shortage of purified water.

Half an hour later, Meg was battling a severe headache and awaiting a call with the latest news from Carolyn when Jim knocked on the door.

"About our conversation," he said when she opened the door. "Were you accusing me of being passive? Because if that's what you were saying, I'm going to have to deny it."

"You drove all this way, to tell me that?"

"And to talk about Bassie."

"Bassie's fine. I've got an emergency on my hands. And I've got a migraine." She let him into the room.

"What's the emergency?" he asked.

She told him about Conroe.

"How bad is the headache?"

"I'm about to throw up."

He looked at her, deciding she was serious. "Tell me what to do," he said.

"There's nothing. I just need to get in bed and handle these phone calls."

"Okay." Instead of turning to leave, however, he walked over to the window.

"What do you make of Bassie burning the photograph?" she asked.

"I think the picture scared her. I don't know why," he said.

"Did you see it?"

"Not up close."

"What about the caption on the back?"

He shook his head. "I've tried to call Myrna Spitz to ask her about that, but she wasn't home. Have you taken anything for the headache?"

"Excedrin."

"That's a lot of caffeine," he said.

The phone began ringing, and Meg answered it.

"Here's the latest," Carolyn told her. "Most of the roads into Conroe are shut down, and nobody's getting in. Michael left a couple of hours ago to try, but since then I've talked to the highway patrol again and they say nobody can get in until the rain lets up and the water recedes a little. It isn't supposed to let up until tonight."

"What about the treatment plants?"

"They're flooded. Flooded and evacuated. The machinery's underwater. The hospital doesn't have any water."

Which meant dialysis patients were in critical need of treatment.

"How many are waiting for treatment?" Meg asked.

"Apparently only six have made it to the clinic, plus another eight in the ICU and CCU," Carolyn answered. "They usually have about forty-five by this time. It started raining last night, and everybody tried to wait it out this morning. Then the roads got flooded. The fire department brought a couple of people in, but the water was already off before they got there. They're saying they're going to have to life-flight people out of town if we can't get the water going."

"Are their phones working?" Meg asked.

"They were working an hour ago. That's the last time I tried to get through."

"All right. I'll call you if I need you. Stay by the phone."

"Okay."

She hung up and looked at Jim. He was waiting near the window. "Here's what's going to happen," she told him. "I need you to stay for a while, if you can. I'm probably going to start vomiting, and I have some things I have to take care of." She dialed the dialysis clinic at the Conroe hospital. "It's something to do with the nervous system; I throw up when I get a headache," she explained as she waited for someone to answer the line. "But I can't get out of commission at the moment. I have to get some people dialyzed." She squeezed her eyes shut and rubbed the bridge of her nose. "I can't believe I'm not there," she moaned, still waiting for the line to be answered. "I should have called in this morning. The patients can only go so long without getting treatment. Can you bring me a Coke? Why don't these people *answer*?"

When Jim returned with the Coke, Meg was talking with a nurse named Mary Tromby whom she had met on several occasions and found capable. She was a single mother of four, no stranger to emergencies. "Is there any pressure at all?" Meg was asking.

"The faucets only dribble," Mary said.

"Is Jerry there?"

"He's on vacation."

Jim set the Coke and a bucket of ice on the bedside table. He went into the bathroom and returned with a glass, filled the glass with ice, and left it beside the Coke. Meg drank from the can, scribbling on her notepad, then said, "Hold on," tossed the phone receiver on the bed, and brushed past Jim on her way to the bathroom. She shut the door and flipped the fan on, but she knew he could hear her retching. She flushed the toilet, rinsed her mouth at the sink, and came back out. Jim had seated himself in the chair beside the window. She picked up the phone receiver. The pain in her head was excruciating. "Okay," she said, "so Jerry isn't there. How about Spice? Is he there?"

"Spice didn't make it in. He tried to get over a low water crossing and his car stalled out. He called a while ago. He's all right, but he's not going to make it in."

"So who do we have?"

"Alex."

"Alex is an idiot."

"Well, that's who's here this morning."

"Then put him on the line." She tapped her pencil on the notepad and sketched a diagram, calculating figures as she waited for Alex. Her hair was in her face; she pulled her knees up and unlaced her hiking boots to take them off, but before she had pulled them off, an idea came to her and she went back to scribbling on the notepad. At last Alex answered in his slow east Texas drawl. Meg had never liked him or found him competent, but now he was her only hope. "Listen," she said to him, "here's what I'm thinking. I'm not sure if it'll work, but we're going to have to try. Who's your maintenance person?"

"Darrell Simon. I don't think you know him."

"Sam's not there?"

"I don't know where Sam is. They may have got him over at some other unit. I haven't seen him all day."

"Well, is this guy, Darrell, familiar with the physical plant?"

"I would guess he is. He should be."

"Does he know anything about the hydraulic circuit in the fire main?"

"I don't know. Want me to ask him?"

"Has he ever done the inspections?"

"Yeah."

"Then he knows. Here's what I'm thinking. We may just be saved by the fact that you're on the bottom floor. We can tie the booster pumps into the fire main system and open up a bleed valve on the third floor. You've probably got several thousand gallons sitting in the mains, and if we gravity-flow it to the booster pumps we can probably pick up about seventy p.s.i. by the time it gets down to you. The problem is going to be finding a hose to connect your main with the booster pumps. We need about thirty feet, if I remember right. I can't remember how far the main is from the pump."

"It's around that corner of the hall. Remember? Probably, oh, I'd say—well, definitely more than thirty feet. You want me to go measure it?"

"Do you think the drum pump hose would reach?"

"No. I'll try it if you want me to, but it's not long enough."

She pushed her hair out of her face and pulled off one of her boots. "Is there a garden hose outside?"

"I would think there would be. Yeah."

"Then send somebody out to get it."

"You're not thinking of using a garden hose—"

"Yes, Alex, I am."

"The bacteria—"

"That's what the water refining system is for, Alex. Remember? The water system?"

"Not for cleaning out a garden hose—"

"It can handle it. I inspected it last month. It was working perfectly."

"This can't work."

"Do you have a better idea?"

He was silent a moment. At last he said, "How much water could we get through a garden hose?"

"Probably twelve gallons a minute," she answered.

"But can it handle the kind of pressure you're talking about?"

"Look," she snapped, "don't you think I know about pressure and vacuum?"

"Yes, but—"

"Then that's a chance we're going to have to take."

"The only hose I ever remember seeing out there is a skinny one."

"Then find me a *fat* one, goddamn it, Alex. Why are you trying to make this impossible? It's possible. Okay?" Her nausea was coming again. "Go across the street and take a hose from the Burger King. I doubt they're watering right now."

"You want me to go out there and—"

"Just give somebody a goddamn umbrella and send them out for a hose," she said. "And listen, you don't have the coupling that you need. Your maintenance guy is going to have to rig something. Let me talk to him."

While she waited for the maintenance man to come on the line, she talked with Mary Tromby again about the patients.

"Three of them are supposed to get here on a fire truck any minute," Mary told her. "The National Guard is bringing somebody else—Hilda Martinez. She hasn't been dialyzed in three days. She missed her last visit and she's in bad shape. I don't know what I'm going to do with all these people when they get here."

"You're going to get them dialyzed, that's what."

"I hope you're right," Mary said. "It's risky for them even to come. And they won't be able to get back home. They're going to have to camp out in the waiting room. That's where everybody is right now. Maybe we'll send Hilda up to intensive care. Here, hang on, here's Darrell."

The maintenance man got on the line, and the conversation shifted to bleeder valves, disinfection lamps, submicron filters, and booster pumps. Meg rubbed at the back of her neck as she spoke; her teeth began to chatter between sentences as they often did with a headache. Twice she rushed to the bathroom, vomited, and returned, one boot off and one still on; she tried to breathe more deeply and hold the nausea back. She was hardly cognizant of Jim's presence, focused as she was on the frightening fact that a number of people were counting on her ingenuity, in several cases to save their lives. She would have to control the chattering of her teeth so she could talk about adapters and bushings from the crash box and tell Darrell Simon how to make fire hose thread fit a garden hose.

Jim left the room for a moment, and while he was gone a wave of nausea hit Meg so unexpectedly that she leaned over and threw up in the ice bucket. When Jim returned, he carried the bucket to the bathroom and washed out the ice and the sour-smelling bile. He brought her a towel to wipe her face, and went to get some fresh ice. Returning the bucket to the bedside, he took his seat in the chair by the window again.

During the next ten minutes it began to seem that Meg's scheme with the garden hose was going to work. The couplings fit. The garden hose did not collapse. The water pressure, gained by gravity as the water in the fire mains flowed downward from the third floor to the first and to the booster pumps, rose to seventy-five pounds per square inch, and the water system worked as designed, which meant the water was pure. When Alex told her of the readings from the boosters, Meg gave a yelp of joy through her chattering teeth. "It's working," she said to Jim. "It's going to work."

A few minutes later she settled the phone receiver into the cradle and made her way, aching and nauseated, to the bathroom, trailing the laces of the single boot that she was still wearing. "It takes twenty pounds of pressure for the dialysis machine to operate," she said as she closed the bathroom door, "and we've got that."

She heard him come to the bathroom door. "It's done?" he asked her through the door.

"It's done."

"You are amazing, Meg. Do you know that? I am . . . dazzled."

She turned the faucet of the sink on to cover the sound of gagging into the toilet. "I should have been there," she said, when she had rinsed her mouth. "I would have been in Conroe before they closed the roads and the water plants were flooded. Jim? You can go home, now that it's over."

"I don't mean to be too personal," he told her through the door, "but it doesn't sound over."

"The emergency is over. I can deal with the headache." She waited a moment, and heard no response. "Are you gone?"

"No."

She lay down on the floor on a towel mat beside the bathtub.

"Well, go."

"You think I've never seen anybody throw up?" he asked. "I've got kids, Meg."

"I'm not one of them."

"You sound like you're on the floor."

She didn't answer.

"Can I come in?"

"No."

"So what do you do when it gets like this?"

"Sometimes it stops."

"If it doesn't stop, what do you do?"

"I go to the hospital and get a shot of Demerol and Phenergan."

"How are you planning to get to a hospital?"

"I don't know. I'll find a way." But she wasn't sure. She doubted there was a hospital in Las Vegas. She was very nearly incapacitated by the shaking and the nausea, and the pain was becoming unbearable.

"I think there's a clinic near here," he said. "I'm going to take you," and he opened the door.

She was lying curled up on the towel mat. He helped her up and walked her to the bed, then pulled her boot off, stacked the pillows behind her, pulled the covers up to her chest and told her he was going to go downstairs and get directions to the clinic. She turned on her side and lay shaking. He handed her the ice bucket and left the room. When he returned a few minutes later, she was folded on her knees, gagging over the ice. "It's five minutes from here," he said. "Let's go."

"What about Bassie?"

"I talked to Martin. He'll get her anything she needs."

Jim emptied the ice bucket and helped Meg out of bed and got her purse. Shoving her feet into her boots, he laced them up, then put her coat over her shoulders and walked her to the elevator. She cradled the ice bucket in her arms. In the elevator she leaned the side of her face against the cold metal of the wall and closed her eyes. Jim had asked the bellman to drive his truck to the side entrance, and it was waiting with the motor running. The overcast of the afternoon and the briskness of the humid air were a relief to Meg despite the intermittent chills. She got into the truck and lay her head down on the seat, hugging the ice bucket, while Jim handed the bellman some dollar bills and got behind the wheel.

They arrived at the clinic within moments. It was a single-story structure, contemporary, crowded between stone buildings in the historic district. They pulled up to the emergency entrance at the back, and Meg went in alone while Jim parked the truck. When he came inside a moment later, she was at the desk attempting to fill out registration forms. He persuaded her to wait in the reception area and allow him to deal with the paperwork. She gave him her insurance card. There was no one else waiting, and she was admitted quickly. Jim stayed in the reception area, flipping through a sports magazine.

The doctor was a thin young man with a heavy brown mustache. He took Meg's medical history and administered injections of Phenergan and Demerol. "You need to stay here for a while, and give it time to take effect," he said.

Meg could feel the pain begin to dissipate almost immediately. She lay on the bed in the examining room and closed her eyes under the bright lights, and tried not to think about Jim, concluding vaguely that if her own father had been more reliable she would not be lying face-up in a clinic with a migraine, thinking of a married man.

When she left the clinic with Jim half an hour later, she was feeling the restful influence of the Demerol. The dampish wind refreshed her;

the gray sky had the feel of evening, though it was not yet evening. Meg slumped in the seat of the truck and lay her head back.

When they reached the hotel, Jim went up to the room with her. "Do you want another Coke?" he asked her, standing at the door.

"No, thanks," she said. "I guess it's too late for you to call Montey."

"I'll call him tomorrow. Do you want me to check on Bassie?"

She sat in the chair beside the window, unlacing her boots to take them off. "I'll do it in a minute," she replied, trying to seem casual and detach herself emotionally from him. "Thanks for all your help."

"Will you call me if you need me?" he asked.

She looked up, pulling one of the boots off. "I don't want to call you at home."

"Then I'll be at my office," he said, and turned, turning back to add that he would call her in the morning if he hadn't heard from her. Then he left and closed the door behind him.

Meg remained sitting in the chair. The evening grew darker. She tried to summon the strength to go across the hall and see if Bassie was all right. She wanted simply to climb into bed and go to sleep. The Demerol had freed her mind to drift, and after a while she found her thoughts meandering aimlessly through the depressing hallways of various past deplorable relationships that she had had with men. She wondered if she might be dating Paul only because she did not care enough about him to be hurt by him.

When evening had fully descended and a light came on in the alley, she roused herself and went to her door and looked across the hall at Bassie's door. No light was emitting from underneath. She stepped across and knocked. When Bassie didn't answer, she knocked more forcefully, and called out, then returned to her room for Bassie's key and opened the door enough to look in.

Bassie was propped up in the bed with her glasses off, staring across the room toward the windows over the plaza. She could not, Meg knew, be seeing much without her glasses, in the near darkness.

"Bassie?"

Bassie turned to look at her. Her eyeliner had smudged, making her face appear as if it were bruised. Her cheeks were slick with tears.

"Are you okay?" Meg asked, taking a step toward her.

"No."

"Can I do anything?"

"No."

"Do you need some food?"

"I said no." The voice was emotionless.

"Have you just been sitting there in bed all this time?"

"I guess that isn't your business."

"Why did you burn the photograph, Bassie?"

She turned her eyes back in the direction of the window. Only a portion of the plaza was visible—the branches of bare trees tossing in the wind against the darkening sky, and light from the old-fashioned streetlamps shimmering on the tin roof of the gazebo.

"Do you want me to call a doctor?"

"No." She stared blindly toward the windows, her hands folded on the covers at her chest, her hair loose over her shoulders. "I want you to know," she said, without turning to look at Meg, "that in my opinion you have been better to me than I have been to you. I'm sorry it's that way. I'm sorry to have to admit it. I was lousy to your mother, too, for that matter."

Meg stood in the doorway, making no attempt to answer. She realized through the cloud of Demerol that she should feel more humbled by this odd admission than she had felt by any of the insults Bassie had hurled in her direction through the years. But the confession was, in her opinion, too late to matter. She took another step into the room. "It's all right with me," she brought herself to say halfheartedly.

She waited a moment more.

"The problem with the dead," Bassie said, "Is that they don't keep secrets. Eventually they tell on themselves."

Meg waited for an explanation of this strange pronouncement, but Bassie flicked her wrist in a dismissive gesture.

Meg retreated to her own room and locked her door and stood leaning against it. She realized that it was not just Bassie's disapproval that had weighed on her so heavily all these years. It was her own unwieldy anger.

She pictured Jim rattling along in the dark in his pickup truck, and sat down on the rumpled bed. She ought to try to call her mother. But she didn't want to. She thought of calling Paul but saw no point in doing so.

At last she took a shower, washing the smell of vomit from her hair, and got in bed and pulled the covers up.

TWENTY-SIX

Two hours later, Meg awoke in the glare of the bedside lamp, feeling drugged and deeply depressed, awed and troubled by the memory of Bassie's confession. For a moment she sat bleary-eyed on the edge of the bed. The clock registered 9:15. Disoriented as she was, she might have thought it was 9:15 in the morning had the window not revealed the same cold darkness in the alleyway outside. She knew she could not sleep, and considered reading more of the journals, but lacked desire to do so, feeling a need to anchor herself in the present rather than lose herself to the past.

She thought of Bassie across the hall and wondered if she had fallen asleep. The longer she pictured her in the bed with her hair loose and her face glistening with tears, her eyes fixed blindly on the windows, the more anxious she became. Something strange had happened to Bassie when she saw the photograph of Hannah on the steps of the tuberculosis hospital with Vicente and Jewell—a vital link of some kind had been severed. Meg could only conclude that the photograph presented some ominous, unnerving theory.

She pulled her blue jeans on and crossed the hall to Bassie's door and knocked. When there was no answer, she returned to her room for the key, then let herself into Bassie's room for the second time that night.

Yet this time Bassie wasn't there. The light was on, the curtains were open, the bed was unmade and empty. The old black leather purse was missing, and Meg decided that perhaps Bassie had gone downstairs for dinner. She had not taken her coat.

Meg left the room and went downstairs. Bassie was not in the restaurant, but Martin Estes was there, seated alone at a table with a notepad and a calculator. "Have you seen Bassie?" Meg asked.

Martin looked up from his work. "No. I thought she was in her room."

"She's not. I was just in there."

He set his pen aside and went with Meg out to the lobby, where a sleepy-looking young man was at the desk.

"Have you seen Dr. Bass?" Martin asked him. "You know who she is, don't you?"

"The woman with the glasses, and the cane?"

Martin nodded.

"I saw her an hour ago. She left in a taxi."

"Did she say where she was going?"

"Not to me."

"Did you call the taxi for her?"

He shook his head. "She must have called from her room."

Martin turned to Meg. "Any idea where she would want to go?"

"I can't imagine anyplace. She didn't mention anywhere."

"I'll call the guy who owns the taxi," Martin said. "There are only two taxis in town, and the same person owns them both. He's usually closed on weekends, but sometimes he'll answer. Bassie must have talked him into coming." He turned to the young man again. "Was it Guillermo driving?"

"I don't know. Maybe Antonio saw."

Martin called the bellman over from the door. "Did you see Dr. Bass leave?"

"She was with Carlos Sifuentes. He was driving for Guillermo."

"About an hour ago?"

"*Sí.*"

"Did she say where she was going?"

"No. She came down. She was waiting maybe two minutes for Carlos. She didn't say nothing."

"Did she seem all right?" Meg asked.

The bellman shrugged. "She seemed the same. But she wasn't wearing the coat."

"I'll call Guillermo," Martin said.

Meg went upstairs for Bassie's coat, taking the stairway instead of the elevator for expediency. She was dizzy from the Demerol, but the exertion of climbing the stairs energized her. When she returned downstairs she found Martin in his office at the back of the building finishing the phone call.

"Bassie called Guillermo at seven-thirty and said she needed a taxi," he told Meg after he had hung up. "Guillermo sent Carlos over here to get her. This is Carlos's day off, and Guillermo said he wouldn't have asked him to do it if Bassie hadn't been so dogmatic about needing someone. She wouldn't take 'no' for an answer."

"Did he say where Carlos took her?"

"He doesn't know. He didn't talk to him afterward. He's going to try to get ahold of him, but doesn't know if he can. He wasn't expecting to talk to him again until Monday."

"I can't think where she would go," Meg said. "That was two hours ago." She could hear the alarm in her voice.

"The police chief is a friend of mine," Martin said. "I'm going to give him a call."

While Meg waited, Martin called the chief of police, who radioed the officers on duty to see if they had seen one of Guillermo's taxis anywhere in town. None of them had.

"Will you call Jim for me?" Meg asked when he hung up. "He's at his office. If you can reach him, I think he can get here in less than an hour. Tell him the situation, and that I'm going to look for her at the Montezuma." She hesitated. "The problem is, if she's in trouble, she might try to call my room."

"I'll take your calls," Martin said.

Meg circled through the main streets of town, crossing the bridge and driving out past the railroad tracks, but saw no taxi. The town itself seemed almost deserted, though on the outskirts a McDonald's and a couple of convenience stores were open. She left town on the road to the Montezuma, and ten miles out, on the right-hand side of the road, saw the spires rising from the hills, the ruined old building appearing like a relic from a different world. Crossing the river and passing the campus soccer field, she drove around the cones and barricades intended to block the drive, parked in the lot beside the Montezuma, and got out, calling for Bassie. She tried the doors, but they were locked. "Where *are* you?" she cried. She peered in through the dusty windows to the lobby and the dining room and saw nothing but unnerving darkness. Eventually she made her way along the path by the red stone walls to the old kitchen and into the dilapidated courtyard, where she could barely make out the cluttered arrangement of rooflines and rusty drainage pipes that she and Jim had looked down on from Hannah's window on the third floor, as well as the black shapes of the pigeons strutting on the eaves. Not until she focused her sight on the stone bench in the center of the courtyard, where Hannah had sat looking up at the geraniums in the bedroom window, did she discern a movement and the form of a person seated there.

Meg approached, saying Bassie's name. She found her hunched over, clutching herself, her head tilted up toward the window. The contrast of her age and crumpled posture with Meg's lingering image of Hannah seated on the same bench seemed to Meg like a terrible trick of nature, a distortion of time. As she drew near, she realized the wailing sound ascending from the courtyard was not an eerie progression of wind whistling around the corners. It was Bassie, making a noise more like a dog's whine than a human cry. She was rocking back and forth, and seemed to be crying to someone in the window. But the window was blank. The pane was broken. A pigeon on the eave below it settled down against the wind.

Meg pulled her jacket off and tossed it around Bassie. She sat on the bench and put an arm around Bassie's shoulders in the attempt to warm her. Mucus ran from Bassie's nose, her glasses were smeared with tears. "I believed"—she cried out strangely, pointing toward the window—"I believed I might find Mother here." As she spoke, her eyes sought the window again, as if looking for someone or for a hint of movement, anything that might have sealed itself in time and lasted for a hundred years.

"Hush now. Stop," Meg said. "We have to get you out of the cold." Bassie's teeth were chattering, her head was wagging from side to side. She was not wearing stockings, and her legs in the darkness looked grotesque and swollen; her lips appeared blue.

A sudden gust of wind blew bits of straw from the pigeons' nests, and there was a muted sound, a flutter of wings. "They killed him!" Bassie cried, looking toward Meg. "They killed my father!"

"Who did, Bassie?"

"Mother and Vicente—"

"No, they didn't, Bassie—they didn't."

"But you don't know—you don't know!" Her voice fell. "The dog was in the photograph."

"What do you mean?"

"Argus," Bassie repeated in the same voice. "He was on the steps, at Hannah's feet. At Saint Anthony's. Do you understand? He was alive when they sent me to Chicago. He isn't buried on the hill. I never saw them dig his grave. I saw them dig my father's grave. I heard the gunshots—I saw Mother crying. I saw her remorse. I had thought the memories were separate. They were the same." She threw her head back, gripping her face with her hands, her voice ascending to the high-pitched wail of a child. "Do you understand? They shot him! And they shot his dog so no one would know my father had come back. And then they buried them, and *lied* that it was Argus in the grave. They had to account for the grave. And Vicente took Argus away—"

"It isn't true, none of it is true," Meg said as calmly as she could. "How can you know the dog in the photograph was Argus? If it was just—"

But her logic, in the face of Bassie's loss, was worse than ineffectual; it was offensive. "Do you think I *want* to believe this?" Bassie shouted at her, "—that I would *choose* to believe this? His name was on the back of the photograph!"

Meg recalled the expression of sudden shock on Bassie's face when she had stood before Manuel Medford's desk and looked at the photograph, and turned it over, and then folded to the floor. She recalled how Bassie had looked at the photograph a second time while seated in the rocking chair at Myrna Spitz's house, and turned it over once more to read the writing before dropping it into the flames.

"Bassie, it's cold out here," she said with as much authority as she could cobble together, unable at the moment to weigh the facts and disprove Bassie's unwieldy theory. "And it's late. You can't convince me that what you are saying is true. We need to get you in the car."

"How dare you," Bassie growled, "to presume you know what's true! You have never read a single word my mother wrote! You can't know her!" Her voice was heavy with outrage and the angry impatience of a person unwilling to be reasoned out of a dark truth. Drawing her hand back, she slapped Meg hard across the face. "How can you think you know her?" she screamed, her face contorted with emotion, her glasses askew. "I've spent my life trying to know her, and I don't know her!" She threw her hands over her face again and sobbed violently into her palms. "She has broken my heart! She has broken my heart!"

Meg's initial shock at the blow she had received turned to a surge of anger, which she fought down. She resisted the urge to lift a hand and smooth the pain, but sat, dumbfounded. Bassie's grief was horrible to her, and for a moment it was all that she could do to remain on the bench as a witness. But she took hold of Bassie, drawing her head against her shoulders and feeling the terrible sobbing at her neck, the wet of her mouth and her tears. "She hasn't broken your heart, Bassie—she hasn't done anything. All you've seen is a dog in a photograph, with the same name as the dog your mother once had."

Her own tears were disruptive now; her voice was giving way. The feel of Bassie's face against her neck and the sound of her hopeless sobbing seemed to be draining the strength out of Meg. She willed herself not to cry, though she had begun to tremble from the cold and the emotion. Her own voice had begun to shake, but she forced herself to speak. "And I do know Hannah," she said. "I've been reading the journals. I was reading them last night, and today. She wasn't capable of killing. She wasn't. I promise you, Bassie—I promise. She didn't do that."

After saying this, Meg perceived a slight hesitation from Bassie, an interlude of stillness that settled Bassie's body, fragile without the bulk of the fur coat, against her own. But then Bassie's shaking turned harsh and began to resemble convulsions. Meg became aware of a tremor, an undercurrent of vibration. "You're too cold," Meg said firmly. "We have to get you to the car."

Her thoughts about Hannah were eclipsed by the growing realization that something was seriously wrong with Bassie. The tremors had increased, and Bassie's head was shaking. Her hands had begun to grope at the edge of the bench. Meg took the cane and placed the handle into Bassie's palm, and coaxed her into standing. Bassie's purse was lying in the darkness at the base of the stone bench, and Meg picked it up and looped her arm around Bassie, supporting most of her weight, managing to get her out of the courtyard and around the side of the building. The ground was littered and rocky here; the wind blew hard against the walls. Bassie stumbled and cut her knee on a stone, and Meg dabbed the blood off with the lining of the jacket. When she was on her feet again, Bassie wept and plunked her cane along, passing the dark and dusty windows through which Hannah had witnessed the ornithologist hanging by a rope from an evergreen on the side of the hill. When they finally reached the car, Meg tugged the back door open, helping Bassie to get inside and propping her up in the seat, covering her body with the old fur coat that lay there. The interior ceiling light shone on the ashen gray of Bassie's skin, revealing the perspiration on her forehead. Her breath, out of the wind now, in the stillness of the car, made a shallow, rasping noise; she turned her eyes to Meg, and then her jaw dropped open, her tongue moved in her mouth, her upper dentures tumbled to her lap. She flung the coat away and clutched her chest.

Meg slammed the car door closed, flew to the driver's side and started the motor, knowing she could drive to the emergency clinic in Las Vegas in less time than it would take an ambulance to reach the Montezuma.

Within seconds she was leaving the campus. She looked in the rearview mirror and saw Bassie in the backseat struggling for air.

"We're going to an emergency clinic," Meg said. "I know where it is." Her own purse lay on the seat beside her and she yanked it open and dug inside for an aspirin bottle. Fumbling open the lid, she poured the contents—an assortment of painkillers—into her lap, and in the light of the dashboard identified an aspirin and handed it over the seat to Bassie, instructing her to chew rather than swallow it. She cracked the window open to admit fresh air. "Are you nauseated?" she inquired.

Bassie was shaking her head, but Meg could not discern if this was an answer to the question or only uncontrolled movement; she was trying to get the aspirin to her mouth, but her hand was shaking violently and she dropped it on the floor. Meg plucked another from the mound of pills, attempting to identify it while trying to watch the narrow road and keeping one hand on the wheel. She reached over the seat and placed the aspirin into Bassie's gaping mouth, a terrible image coming to her mind, perversely that of the lacquered, wide-mouthed bass suspended over the fireplace in Bassie's home, there in the dark now, in the quiet of the house, as it had been for decades. She turned the interior lights on and watched in the rearview mirror as Bassie attempted to chew the aspirin. But her mouth was sunken and deformed. She gagged on the aspirin and vomited, the vomit spilling to her lap. A pair of headlights approached from the opposite side of the road, and Meg recognized the vehicle as it passed. She shoved her palm hard on the horn, and in the rearview mirror saw the truck begin to swerve onto the shoulder, the tires tossing gravel in the headlights. It wheeled in a half circle and pulled out again, accelerating behind them. "Jim's behind us," Meg told Bassie. "We're going to have you there in less than seven minutes now."

She was driving eighty miles an hour on the winding road, and had to remind herself to breathe. She tried to think of the best route to the clinic. She was grateful to have been there, but wished that Jim could take the lead. She knew that he would do so if she could find a way to communicate to him where she was going. She waved her hand across the mirror to acknowledge that she had seen him, hoping he would catch the gesture in his headlights. When she shifted her eyes, she saw in the mirror that Bassie had slumped sideways against the door. Her eyes were open, her hands were limp. "Bassie?" Meg called back to her. "Bassie!"

There was no movement in the face, only in the strands of Bassie's hair blowing in the cold air from the window. Meg slammed her foot on the brake and jerked the car to the shoulder. She threw the gear into park, flung the door open, and emerged into the cold as the car rolled to a stop. Yanking the back door open, she climbed in next to Bassie. She thought that Bassie turned to look at her, but then realized that the movement had been caused by the jolting of the car. Bassie's head was thrown back, her throat was pale and exposed, her eyes stared upward. Meg pulled the glasses off and looked into her eyes, which were cold and sightless. The aspirin had crusted on her lips, there was a smudge of vomit and an absolute, absolute stillness. Meg threw her arms around Bassie and pulled her prone onto the seat, gripping her jaw and prying her mouth open, pressing her own mouth over the gaping hole of Bassie's and forcing a hard breath deep into the lungs. She tried to remember how many breaths she was to force into the lungs before she pumped the chest. She could taste the aspirin and the vomit—"Breathe—"she almost screamed, lifting herself and shoving her weight, palms down, onto Bassie's chest, "Breathe, breathe, breathe . . ."

But she had lost the battle before it had begun. She knew this when she started screaming Bassie's name in a horrifying, screeching sound that seemed to echo on the hills. If there had been hope left, she would not have lost control like this; she knew this, and knew that Bassie was gone by the fact that she had lost herself at the same time.

TWENTY-SEVEN

Jim was on the far side, getting in. He climbed inside on top of Bassie and took her face in his hands and began breathing into her mouth, pumping her chest and feeling for breath, but Meg could see that Bassie's eyes, illuminated by the small overhead light, were lifeless and clouding over. She flung herself from the car and stood in the cold wind wrapped in her own arms and sobbing without any attempt to stop. She saw Jim laying Bassie down across the seat and closing the lids of her eyes. She saw him get out of the car and come toward her. He put his arms around her. "Don't"—she cried, pulling away—"Please don't touch me—" and for several moments she cried aloud, leaning against the car. Reality seemed lost in the open spaces around her. She could not accept the fact of Bassie's death—could not accept that she had failed to save her.

Jim said, "We should drive her to the clinic. There's nothing else to do. We can leave my truck here."

She got into the backseat next to Bassie, lifting Bassie's head and placing it in her lap. She did not look at her face. She watched the shape of the hills along the road and felt the weight in her lap.

When they arrived at the emergency room of the clinic, Jim got out and went inside. Meg remained in the car until he returned with the physician who had treated Meg for the headache only hours before. Behind them were two orderlies with a stretcher. Meg got out of the car, and the physician leaned inside to examine Bassie. He stood and asked the orderlies to take the body inside. They covered Bassie and rolled her away on the stretcher, Meg walking along beside.

In a hallway, after the body had been rolled away, under the shocking brightness of the lights, Meg spoke with the physician and the clinic administrators. Jim called Martin Estes to tell him what had happened, and Martin arrived at the clinic moments later. The local justice of the peace was called, and arrived in half an hour, apologetic that he could not issue a death certificate without an autopsy as there had been no doctor in attendance. The medical examiner would therefore have to come from Santa Fe, and the process would delay burial until Wednesday, as this was a weekend.

Jim at this point placed a call to Jake Montoya, who telephoned the medical examiner in Santa Fe and convinced him, as a personal favor, to hurry events so burial might take place on Tuesday.

When at last Meg returned to the car with Jim and saw Bassie's cane and the dentures lying on the floorboard in the back, her grief was knocked loose again. She sat with the heater blowing on her face and tears rolling down her cheeks, and wondered how the death of someone Bassie's age could be so profoundly shocking. As Jim drove her to the hotel, she thought of things she might have said to Bassie when she had the opportunity. The chance to say them was worse than lost now; it was wasted. She wanted to describe to Jim those moments in the courtyard, how Bassie had come to believe that Hannah and Vicente had murdered Elliott. It seemed that Bassie's long attempt to resurrect her mother had, at the end, resembled more a search for some lost remnant of herself, folding into those inhuman, cold, strange moments.

"Argus was in the photograph," she told him. "He isn't buried on the hill. It was Elliott's grave she saw them digging."

But Jim was quiet, and unresponsive. He hardly seemed to follow what she was saying.

When they reached the Plaza, he walked Meg up to her room, and offered to call her mother. But both of them knew that Meg would have to call Nina herself.

Martin Estes brought a steaming pot of coffee to the room; he poured a cup for Meg and left her nursing it in her hands. When he was gone, she put it aside and picked up the phone and called her mother. Jim remained beside the window. "Mom," Meg said when Nina answered, her voice dissolving uncontrollably to that of a plaintive child. "Bassie had a heart attack. She died."

A silence followed on the line, then "Oh, my God—" the voice said, low at first, then escalating. "Oh, my God—"

"I guess you better come."

"How could this possibly happen?"

"I don't know, she—"

"I should have been there," Nina wailed. "I should have come when I wanted to, I shouldn't have let you talk me out of it! If I had been there—"

"I'm so sorry," Meg said, breaking down again, digging her palm into her eyes.

"It wouldn't have happened if I had been there—"

"Please don't say that, Mom—"

Hearing the defensive note in Meg's voice, Jim spoke from the window. "She could have come, if she had decided to. Don't let her blame you, if that's what she's doing."

But resentment, which had been Meg's anchor for so long, failed to hold her now. She felt adrift, and terrified, and poured her emotions into the phone as a child would do. She tried to explain coherently the death, the photograph, the assumptions Bassie had made about the grave. But Nina was not interested in these details. She was trying to pacify her conscience and convince herself that if Meg had not stopped her from coming to New Mexico, events would have been different.

"I'm coming in the morning," she said at last, tearfully. "I'll call and let you know what time to pick me up at the airport. I'm going to see if Ed can possibly come with me."

"Who?" Meg asked.

"Ed Williams. I've been dating him—"

"Don't bring someone you've been *dating*—I don't see how you can think it's right to bring a *date*—"

Nina continued to weep. "I don't even know where she wanted to be buried," she cried.

"She never talked to me about it," Meg said. "I know she left a will, but—"

"We should bury her in Las Vegas," Nina concluded.

"We can't just do what's easiest," Meg answered.

"Are you accusing me of that?"

Jim turned from the window; his eyes were wet; Meg saw that he had been crying. She had forgotten he cared about Bassie. Behind him, the window revealed the bricks of the wall across the alley, illuminated by light from the room, Jim's shadow smeared across them. "Do you want me to stay?" he asked.

She shook her head, still listening to her mother on the line.

"Is there anything I can get you?" he asked.

"No."

He took his coat from the chair.

She wondered distantly how he would manage to retrieve his truck. It was still on the road to the Montezuma where Bassie had died.

TWENTY-EIGHT

Meg awoke early but could not, for a long while, bring herself to get out of bed. She lay in the darkness listening to the occasional passing of people in the hallway—the wheeling of breakfast carts and distant knocking on doors. Memories of the night before dogged her mind like the inevitable shadows that they were. She tried to think about the day that lay before her and the days to follow, but doing so proved more disorienting even than surrendering to the memories. Returning home to Austin and resuming her life without Bassie seemed absurd and pointless. Bassie was the person who had made her emotions valid—frustration and resentment not the least among them. There would be no way to fill the void.

If only—she thought—she had persuaded Bassie to see a doctor yesterday. If only she had been more even-tempered and not so angered by Bassie, or stronger and not so controlled by her, things would have happened differently. As it was, she had been too average to cope with Bassie's perversities and overpowering personality; she had let Bassie dominate, and impose, which had made her susceptible to Bassie and also contemptuous toward her—the worst possible combination. It was no wonder that Bassie had felt Meg was lacking in resolve and wisdom. Meg had never been her strongest self when Bassie was around.

There had been so many crucial moments last night that might have turned out differently. Meg recalled forcing her breath into Bassie's mouth and how resistant Bassie's lungs had seemed, and wondered if she had simply made the choice to die.

She thought of the house perched on the slope under the spreading oak tree on the quiet street in Austin, and the lacquered bass over the fireplace, and hanging from the mantel the metal puffer Bassie had always used to bring the flames back from ashes.

Today would be nearly unbearable. She could not fathom how to go about it. She tried to settle on a plan. She would have to call the attorney and see if Bassie had left any funeral instructions; surely, Meg reasoned, she had. Bassie was too dictatorial to leave her burial to other people's judgment. And yet Meg could not remember a single instruction Bassie had ever given on the subject. Nina was likely to oppose anything that came through the attorney, who years ago had represented Bassie in her threats to take legal custody of Meg if Nina did not overcome her drug addictions. The situation had never escalated to litigation, and Nina eventually had cleaned herself up, but her hatred toward the attorney remained volatile. What she had not blamed on him and Bassie, she had blamed on Meg, because Meg had not asked, at the time, to stay with her mother. In Meg's experience, choice had never been a part of anything when Bassie was involved.

She should get herself out of bed, she decided, and go downstairs and ask Martin Estes about local funeral homes and cemeteries. She wondered if funeral homes were usually open on a Sunday. It would be a pathetic little ceremony, she decided, if it were held in Las Vegas. Who would even attend?

If Bassie were buried in Austin, at least colleagues from the history department and former students might come. Bassie also had a friend in San Antonio who was a fellow member of the American Ethnological Society, and one in Houston who had been a classmate of hers at Columbia but had since, Meg knew, had a falling-out with Bassie over budget issues in the American Folklore Society. Meg remembered Bassie stomping through the front yard of her house, whacking weeds with her black cane and muttering about corruption.

Everything, at the moment, was unresolved. There was Bassie's suitcase still in the room across the hall. There were Elliott's remains—assuming they were Elliott's—to be decided about. They would have to be buried also. And Nina was arriving today, possibly with her boyfriend, about whom Meg had never heard a word before last night. Nina would only hinder the effort to make decisions. She and Meg would disagree.

It occurred to Meg that she should call the hospital in Conroe and see if the water was running again. At last she forced herself out of bed, made the phone call, verified that the clinic's machines were operating effectively, and went about the room putting things in order. She turned the television on and watched a local morning news show, hoping to escape her darker thoughts. But her mind kept turning to Bassie. As strong as Bassie's presence had been, her absence felt even stronger.

Meg telephoned downstairs to Martin Estes. "I need to get a room for my mother," she told him. "She might have somebody with her. He might need a separate room, I don't know."

After she had dressed, she took the key and let herself into Bassie's room. The open curtains revealed sunlight sparkling in the bare branches of trees in the plaza below. The scent of Bassie and her perfumes and the musty smell of her fur coat lingered, but the room was bright. She packed up Bassie's belongings and stood looking at the scuffed blue suitcase, wondering if there was a way to avoid taking it home. She had no idea what she would do with the items when she got them to Austin—the frayed toothbrush, the used cosmetics and threadbare nightgowns and old black shoes.

Dragging the suitcase across the hall to her room, she stored it away in the closet. There was nothing among the clothes, she realized, that Bassie could be buried in. Perhaps Nina would have a suggestion about that.

At the sound of the housekeeping cart in the hallway, she opened her door and placed the DO NOT DISTURB sign on the knob. Then she sat on the bed, and realized how completely she had always relied on Bassie's plans to structure her time.

She puzzled over the statements Bassie had made in the courtyard at the Montezuma last night. Somewhere, obscured by time, was the truth of the story. What was it, exactly, that had happened that night in the moonlight when Hannah plunged her shovel into the frozen hill, and Vicente, beside her, swung the pickax? Was it true that they were burying Elliott? Argus wasn't buried on the hill; Argus, it seemed, was still alive when the grave was dug. Bassie had heard the gunshots. She had seen Vicente enter the bedroom, and seen her mother crying. She had thought these events were separate, but now they appeared connected: the gunshots, the remorse, the nighttime burial that Bassie had watched from the distance of the back porch of the house.

Her thoughts were interrupted by a phone call from a reporter with the Albuquerque newspaper, wanting to know if it was true that Claudia Bass had died.

When her mother arrived at the airport in Albuquerque, Meg was there to meet her. She had come without the boyfriend, but during the long drive back to Las Vegas Meg almost wished that he had come along after all, as the old, entangled emotions closed around her and her mother like a sticky web, holding them hostage to each other. The sunny weather only seemed to throw their complicated feelings into more detailed relief. If Nina's boyfriend had been present, Meg decided, Nina might have been more composed and less punitive toward Meg.

Meg had stored the fur coat in the trunk of the car, but its smell lingered, and every glance Meg cast in the rearview mirror conjured Bassie in the backseat with her head tossed back and her eyes staring blankly upward. She suffered the impression that Basssie was actually back there, her presence, as always, destructive to any tenderness that Meg and Nina might have felt for one another.

Leaving the city limits of Albuquerque and entering a vast terrain spotted with occasional strip malls, Meg and Nina discussed funeral arrangements. Meg had spoken with Bassie's attorney and confirmed that Bassie had not left any instructions, having always meant to do so at some later date. It seemed as if it had never occurred to Bassie that there would ever be a time when she would not be in command of things and able to impose her will on the situation.

Nina sponged her eyes with a tissue, recalling that Bassie had once looked into the possibility of purchasing a plot in the Chicago cemetery where Hannah was buried, and which Bassie had often visited, but had found the plots available unsatisfactory and too distant from Hannah's grave.

As they drove, Nina became increasingly dogmatic that Bassie would want to be buried in Las Vegas. But there was no one in Las Vegas to look after a grave, Meg said. She had made a number of phone calls and discovered that there was only one cemetery in Las Vegas where the graves were cared for—and not with what was called perpetual care—not by contract. One of the Catholic churches had simply assumed responsibility and could at any moment cease to maintain the graves.

"What does it look like?" Nina asked.

"Martin Estes says it's nice. It's been around a long time. It has elm trees. But it's Catholic. Mostly Catholic. You know how she'd feel about that."

"You're acting like I'm being selfish just because I think she'd want to be buried in Las Vegas," Nina said. "It's not like it's going to benefit me—in any way—to bury her there."

But it would, Meg thought. Mandating Bassie's burial place would allow Nina a kind of control over Bassie for the first time in her life.

"I talked with the director of the funeral home that Martin recommended," Meg explained. "He said that if we decide to bury her in Austin, it's no problem getting her there. She can be flown or taken in a transport van, whichever we prefer. He can coordinate with a funeral home in Austin, and they would take care of things on that end."

"I don't know why you are even talking about that," Nina said, "when I think she should be buried in Las Vegas."

"But Mother, come on," Meg pressed her. "You don't know that's what she would want. Are you making this into something about me? About the fact that I've been taking care of her and you resent that, so now you're going to take over?"

"What is the matter with you?" Nina responded. "How can you even say that?" Her eyes, normally a resilient blue in contrast to the red of her hair, at the moment were reddish themselves from crying and lost in the splotchy tint of her face.

"What is the matter with *you*, Mom?" Meg countered. "If we bury her in Austin I can look after the grave. I don't see any reason to bury her here. Hannah's in Chicago, who knows where you'll end up, or I'll end up, but probably not here. And as far as Elliott goes, we can bury him anywhere we bury Bassie."

"Elliott never set foot in Austin."

"It doesn't matter where Elliott *set foot*. This isn't about Elliott, it's about Bassie."

"You are acting just like her!" Nina exclaimed. "You are just as *controlling* as she is! And you want it all your way. You think you know what's best and you won't listen to anyone else. Believe it or not, I'm entitled to decide where my mother will be buried. She chose to die here, didn't she? And I don't think that was an accident. She had come full circle, and this is where she ended."

"You're talking about *symmetry*? Oh, for God's sake. You're talking about New Age stuff. Bassie hated New Age stuff. She would have laughed at that idea."

"Don't you make fun of me like that. I have put up with that attitude my entire life from Mother, and now I don't have to put up with it from you."

"What, the worm has turned?" Meg said.

She had spoken the words before their familiarity struck her. She could hear them in Bassie's voice, directed at herself. Nina was right about this: Meg was too like Bassie. She and Bassie had always been condescending toward Nina. Maybe Meg had sided with Bassie just in order to be on the winning side, or possibly it was to please Bassie, or to state her anger toward Nina for having failed her. Whatever the reason, the balance was certain to shift with Bassie gone. Meg might be superior to Nina in intelligence or capability, but Nina, at least, was less of a cynic than either Bassie or Meg. She had a better heart.

"I'm sorry," Meg forced herself to say.

But her mother was looking out of the window. "I need to admit something," she said. "I'm jealous, that's what. She trusted you. She always trusted you, and not me. She liked you better. I know she's left everything to you." She turned to look at Meg, the bright window framing her. "It isn't the *things* I care about. I wanted her to trust me." She drew a tissue from her purse. "And if I were her, I would have felt the same way and done the same thing. I would have left everything to you." She rubbed her eyes with the tissue. "Ed and I are getting married."

"You're what?"

"We're getting married in December."

"When did you decide this?"

"About a month ago. I was looking for the right time to tell you."

"I don't think you found it."

"I know, Meg, but I couldn't be here and not tell you."

"Why not? How long have you known him?"

"You're not happy for me."

"I'm happy for you. But you've been married three times. And you just met this guy."

"I've known him for a year."

"Who is he?"

"His name is Edward Williams. He works with computers."

"What does that mean? He works with computers. What does he do with computers?"

"It's something to do with the parts."

"Where did you meet him?"

"My boss set us up. You remember Curtis."

"Yes, I do. Where does *he* know him from?"

"He knows him from his church. He—"

"He goes to church?"

"It's not a traditional church, it's a—"

"Great," Meg interrupted.

"No, it's not New Age. He's a very stable person. He's got two grown children about your age. They're married and one of them has kids. I think you'll like them."

"Oh, that's terrific. A ready-made family. Those seem to work like a charm. I thought I'd lost my grandmother, and instead I've gained a whole family. And a new father. What more could a girl want?"

They drove for a while in silence. The hills opened and closed around them, the land rose up and flattened. Traffic increased on the outskirts of Santa Fe, then grew sparse again when they had passed the city limits. The landscape, pale with sunlight, fell away behind them.

Nina pulled the visor down and surveyed herself in the mirror. She tacked her thick hair back with a large barrette. She flipped the visor up and spoke to the windshield instead of to Meg. "The only thing that gives me any comfort about what a rotten mother I have been to you," she said, "is that Bassie was a worse one to me."

. . . . .

While Nina dogged the bellman along the hallway to a room on the first floor, Meg collected her telephone messages from the front desk clerk named Monica. "Let's see," the woman told her, flipping through a pink notepad, "there's one from Carolyn Stott in Austin: 'All still okay in Conroe.' Four from reporters, and one, two, three, four calls from Jim Layton. Here's the number—"

He had given his office number. Meg went up to her room, but delayed calling Jim. She felt that talking to him would only complicate her emotions. It seemed simpler just to take some action—to drive her mother out to look at the cemetery, then go to the funeral home. The funeral director had said that he could meet with her this afternoon. The funeral would take place on Tuesday. She could keep herself propped up until Tuesday.

She was in her room for just five minutes before she went downstairs to get her mother and go to the cemetery.

It was not until the following morning that she called Jim. "We have the autopsy report," she told him. "It was a heart attack."

"Are you all right?" he asked. "I've been trying to call you."

"Sorry. I've had Mom here."

"How is she?"

"Up and down."

They were quiet, and then Meg said, "We've been working out the funeral plans, and were wondering if you would give the eulogy. We've scheduled the funeral for tomorrow, here in Las Vegas. That's what Mom wanted."

"Why Las Vegas?"

"It's a long story. It's complicated. It was Mom's choice."

"All right," he said.

"It's going to be at two o'clock at the San Jose cemetery. Do you know where it is?"

"I can find it. There's no church service?"

"No. We're just going to meet at the cemetery."

After a silence, he said, "What kind of eulogy? What do you want me to say?"

"Whatever you think is right. I guess you should just be honest about her. There won't be anybody there who didn't know what she was like."

"There won't be anybody there who didn't care about her," he said, and she understood that he meant for the comment to be barbed. "You're impenetrable right now, Meg."

"I'm just trying to keep my head above water. Have you talked to Montey?"

For a moment she thought he was not on the line, but then he said, "I talked to him this morning. He said he'll be ready to file a report with the OMI on Wednesday. Have you thought about what to do? With Elliott?"

"I think he should be buried near Bassie. I talked to the funeral director about it. He said we could arrange it."

"Montey will turn everything over to you when he files his report."

"You mean the bones."

"Yes. You'll probably want to go and see them at the lab, and talk to Montey, and then the funeral home can get them and take them anywhere you want. When are you going home?"

"I haven't made the reservation yet. If I leave Wednesday afternoon I could go by Montey's lab on the way to the airport."

His answer was not immediate. "I'll ask Montey if he'll set aside some time Wednesday morning," he finally said. "Meanwhile I'll see you at the cemetery tomorrow. Unless you want to get together before then?"

She almost accepted the invitation. But if she were alone with Jim she would let her emotions loose.

"I probably have to be with Mom," she said.

It was, at any rate, true. Nina had asked if Meg would take her to Santa Fe. They needed to purchase a dress in which to bury Bassie.

TWENTY-NINE

The San Jose cemetery was on the southwest side of Las Vegas, a short drive from the highway, down a pitted road and past a residential area. It lay in a rocky valley between two low hills, serene in the rain that started early on Tuesday morning. Birds were flocked silently in the dripping elm trees of the cemetery like a gathering of mourners when Meg and Nina arrived with Martin Estes. Martin drove the car within the gates and cruised slowly to a stop, seeking a place that was free of mud.

A canvas tent, drooping with pools of water, stood over the empty grave. Meg and her mother got out of the car and walked under an umbrella to the tent. The heels of Nina's black shoes dug deeply into the sodden earth, making sucking noises when she drew them out, so that she seemed to make her way along impeded as if crippled, and Meg was forced to take her arm. Martin followed under a separate umbrella. The rain had painted the trees so sleek and black that Meg could not imagine that these trees, with their dark austerity, would ever shield anything from heaven. In the summer these same limbs would spread a canopy over the tombstones, thick enough to block the sun, but on this dreary afternoon they provided less protection from the drizzling sky than a group of upright sticks.

The casket, Meg could see as they approached, had been closed as she requested. Nina had wanted for it to remain open during the service, but on this one point Meg had been decisive. She had returned to the room in the funeral home where Bassie lay in the open casket, after Nina had left it, and had placed the old fur coat alongside Bassie's body. She had loosened the braid of Bassie's hair, applied more black eyeliner to the lids and more red lipstick to the lips, so that Bassie looked more like herself. Then she had asked the funeral director to close the casket.

"They've closed the casket," Nina said as they approached it.

"I asked them to," Meg answered.

She took some satisfaction in having done this. In this small way at least, she had aligned herself with Bassie. They had lived together in the undercurrents of mutual turmoil for most of Meg's life, and if Bassie had been more willing than Meg to keep the waters churning, Meg had done her own amount of thrashing about. Still, unpleasant as it had been, Meg did not now, looking back, regret her time with Bassie.

Jim was standing near the casket, talking with the Episcopal priest whom Martin had recommended to perform the service. Phil Barker was seated in one of the plastic chairs. Bassie had always had as many adversaries as followers, and it seemed appropriate that both be represented.

The funeral director stood to the side, speaking with several assistants. Meg had grown reliant on him during the past three days, allowing herself to receive more comfort from him, as a stranger going about his routine business, than she did from her mother or Jim. He was a thin, soft-spoken individual and had a face with a slack look about it.

The priest turned and noted Meg and Nina approaching under the umbrella through the drizzle. He had talked with them yesterday about the service, and now came forward and greeted them, placing a hand on Nina's shoulder as she entered the shelter of the tent. He spoke with them about the rain, and suggested Nina let him know when she was ready for him to begin the service. The funeral director came over. Phil rose to speak with Nina; Meg exchanged some words with Jim about the rain and nothing else, and introduced him to Nina, whom he had never met. Nina was wearing sunglasses in spite of the weather.

Another car arrived, and two elderly men, one of them in a neck brace, got out and sloshed their way to the tent. They were Bassie's former editor from UNM Press and an ancient colleague from the history department whom Meg had talked with on the phone. She went to greet them; they spoke with her, and then with Jim, and settled themselves with difficulty into the chairs, which sat unsteadily on the soggy ground. Martin Estes and Phil Barker took their seats beside them, on the second of two rows, and the funeral director seated Nina in the front. Meg sat down beside her mother, Jim on the far side of Nina, and the service began.

The sound of rain and the occasional slush of tires in the street beyond the fence muted the priest's words of consecration so that the words, however forcefully delivered, did not seem to carry much emotion. "Make us, we beseech Thee, deeply sensible of the shortness and uncertainty of life; and let the Holy Spirit lead us in holiness and righteousness all our days; that, when we shall have served Thee in our generation, we may be gathered unto our fathers, having the testimony of a good conscience. . . ."

It was not a day, Meg thought, conducive to the examination of good conscience or bad. It was too cold. She felt isolated in a grim, unfathomable way, as if she were alone with the casket. She could not divert her thoughts from the body lying within. The notion of a lifeless form having replaced Bassie seemed deeply absurd. She thought of Bassie sealed away with the cane and the coat, her large hands with flat nails and the skin draped thin as a sheet over the knuckles.

When the priest had finished speaking, he moved aside and Jim stood up and took his place beside the casket. He did not seem prepared to speak, and had a lost, distracted look about him. He was wearing a suit, and his hair was combed down over his ears but had kicked up in places because of the humid weather. He was not holding a script of any kind and appeared uneasy, settling his eyes only briefly on Meg. He spoke just loudly enough to be heard over the water dripping from the tent into puddles on the ground. "Meg asked me to talk to you about Bassie," he said. "I doubt there's much I can say about her in a general sense that most of you don't know. We know what she was like. Probably most of us know where we stood with her. So there's nothing we have to figure out, other than how to deal with the fact that she's gone." He paused after saying this, and settled his shoulders. "I don't think it's our job to chisel out a more acceptable image of Bassie, as if we're setting it in stone," he continued. "That would involve filing away the rough edges, and those are what made her who she was. She was opinionated. She was cantankerous and intolerant. She was critical of each one of us here at one time or another, and of some of us almost consistently." His eyes settled on Phil Barker. "That would be you, Phil," he said, and a small ripple of laughter, lighter than the rain, passed through the gathering. "But when I was twenty-three years old," he continued, his face becoming serious again, "and still trying to figure out what I wanted to do with my life, Bassie gave me direction. She taught me how to measure myself against my better self." He paused, and shifted his weight. His gaze seemed to move involuntarily toward the casket, and then he drew it back and said, "I hope none of you mind if I'm personal here. You see, my parents were killed in a car accident when I was six years old, and I spent a lot of my life trying not to deal with that. Bassie figured this out about me. She had a way of seeing people's weaknesses. And she took it on herself to get me on a better path than the one I was on. It was a backwards path that she put me on—not the direction I had expected to be going. I had thought the trick was to keep moving forward. But Bassie had grown up without parents just as I had, and she had dealt with that reality longer than I had, and she had come to terms with it better. So one day after she and I had been working together at Pecos for a couple of months, she convinced me to get in the car with her and drive for nearly a week, from New Mexico to Kentucky, so that I could face what I had been running away from. She told me about the time when she had done that in her own life. She was seventeen years old, she said, when she read her mother's journals. She had had them all of her life, but she was seventeen before she had the courage to read them. And when she did, she found that her mother wasn't the person she expected. She was more flawed than Bassie wanted her to be. More sexual. More perversely accessible and more authentic than Bassie's memories of her. In many ways she was unfamiliar to Bassie, which made Bassie feel betrayed by her and abandoned a second time.

"That's why Bassie went back to Pecos, eventually—to reassemble the facts of the past and reconcile her memories with the real story.

"She talked to me about all of this and convinced me—" he paused here. "Well, I can't really say she convinced me, she *told* me—to go back and face the most difficult parts of my own history. So we spent the week on the road together. She was like a doctor when it came to getting information; she could ask invasive personal questions without any apology or embarrassment. We got to know each other pretty well. She gave me some bad advice and some good advice. I was usually better off for having heard both kinds. It helped define things for me. She thought my hair was too long. There were times I thought she didn't like me. But then I realized it was mostly the people she cared about that she bothered to criticize.

"When we got to Kentucky we spent a week going around and seeing places that had been important in my childhood and in my parents' lives. We found the home in Russell Springs where my mother grew up and the church where my parents were married. Then we drove around and found the minister who had married them in 1933. We also met my black sheep uncle whom I didn't know existed, and Bassie set him straight about how to fertilize his tomatoes and told him he needed a shave." There was a spattering of laughter at this, and Jim smiled and seemed to relax some, but then his eyes brimmed suddenly and he lifted his face to the canvas roof. His hands, which had been clasped before him, separated, and he crossed his arms at his chest. "After that we bought a map at a filling station outside Bowling Green and found the curve in the road near Nolin Lake where my parents had been killed." He stood as if uncertain where to go from here. Meg felt her own tears spill, and grow cold on her face. She felt as if Bassie had been a stranger to her. With everything that Bassie had told her about Jim, she had never mentioned this trip to Kentucky.

She waited for Jim to go on. She was uncomfortable for him, perceiving the level of his emotion and seeing how he held his tears in check by staring now and then toward the corner of the tent from which most of the rain was spilling. She doubted he had ever told this story to anyone before, and she could see how difficult it was for him to do so now. She feared that he would explain that he had been in the car with his parents on the night the wreck occurred, and that he had stayed the night alone with them, waiting for help to come. She hoped he would not lay himself that bare.

But either he had not intended to tell the rest of the story, or he found himself unable to do so now. "I made that trip because Bassie made me make it," he said. "She connected me to something that I had cut myself off from. She forced me to ferret the truth out of history, and in doing so, she helped me to know my parents. And she expected the most from me after that. In fact, she expected the most from everyone she cared about. She wanted us to measure up not only to her expectations about us but to the expectations she made us have about ourselves. Some of us are living the lives she wanted us to, and some of us are living the lives we chose in defiance of her wishes. But her influence is still there. She was the unyielding anvil that hammered us into shape. It wasn't until I stood beside the curve in the road near Nolin Lake as a grown man that I was able to come to terms with what had happened there when I was a child. Bassie forced the past on nearly every one of us. She lived her own life based on the lessons of the past. She knew it was important to look back before going forward, and then to go forward fearlessly. I know for a fact it was not until Bassie came back to New Mexico as an adult that she found a life for herself that did not exclude the tragedies of her past.

"We all know that Bassie was difficult to get along with. She was often punishing. But what we have to realize is how productive that could be, and how important it was. When I think of how little I wanted her advice most of the time, I realize just how much I needed it, and how much I'm going to miss it in the future. All of us have tried to escape Bassie—to get away from her insistence that we be better than we wanted to be. When our ambitions for ourselves failed, her ambitions for us goaded us into action. We have all dug in our heels against her, and pitted ourselves against her at one time or another, and as a consequence we have all lost some battles. But during that process she sometimes shamed us into being our best selves. She has used our own personal histories as tools with which to change us. She badgered us until we measured up to some standard of her approval. She made us examine our motives, and account for our actions. She usually created as much resentment as admiration, and she could be destructive. She divided people instead of uniting them. Except, of course, with the dead: she connected us to the dead. She manipulated us through her criticism and continued to see what was lacking in us, but always in relief against a backdrop of what she thought our capabilities should allow us to become. When we were lazy, she let us know it. When we excelled, she made us aim higher. I doubt a day will pass when I won't think of her, and measure myself against what she would have thought of me. On the days when I accomplish something, I am going to wish she were here to know it. On the days I disappoint myself, I am going to feel relieved to be out from under her judgment. Eventually I might come to miss her less, but—" He stopped; his voice splintered. "I guess I'm always going to miss her." He took a breath and then said, "I guess that's the kind of tribute one generation owes to another." He seemed as if he might have more to say, and Meg expected him to continue, but then he turned and sat down in his seat and leaned forward, placing his face in his hands, and sobbing aloud. Nina reached an arm around his shoulder. They cried together for an awkward moment, which was silent but for their crying and the water dripping from the tent.

THIRTY

Meg drove her mother to Albuquerque after the funeral, dimly aware of feeling impatient toward her and eager to leave her at the airport. It was not until Nina, probing a dilapidated Kleenex up under her sunglasses to dab at her eyes, began to chatter about Jim and the eulogy that Meg realized how much she resented the way her mother had handled the last few days. She had talked Meg into driving her to Santa Fe to buy what she repeatedly referred to as a "burial outfit" for Bassie, and then had turned the excursion into a shopping spree, purchasing for herself a new suit for the funeral. She had gone about selecting the casket and the cemetery plot with the same self-centeredness, as if everything were stage dressing for the drama of her grief, choosing everything to her own taste, not Bassie's, making Bassie's death into a tragedy in which she was the star. Now she was attempting to enlist Jim as her costar.

"He was perfect," Nina said tearfully, "he didn't try to whitewash Mother, but he still described her very . . . well, lovingly. Don't you think? In spite of all her terrible faults. He was just so noncondemning in the way he represented her. I think we did exactly the right thing to ask him to give the eulogy. I certainly couldn't have done it myself. Not without breaking down."

Meg didn't respond as Nina talked on, but her irritation increased. She felt that Nina's grudge against Bassie was coming to the forefront now that it was safe to voice it, and that her ways of attempting to even the score were underhanded and childish. Meg would have preferred to be dealing with Bassie's combative directness instead.

"He seems like such a good guy," Nina was saying. "Do you know if he has children?"

"Two," Meg said tersely.

"I remember Mother telling me something about his wife," Nina said reflectively. "I believe Mother didn't like her. Is he still married?"

"Happily," Meg answered.

"What does that tone in your voice mean?"

"Nothing," Meg said wearily, not interested in hearing her mother take up Bassie's refrain and accuse her of having an interest in Jim. "I'd appreciate it if you wouldn't start in on that."

"I don't know what you're trying to insinuate," Nina said. "I happen to be engaged, and anyway he's too young."

It took Meg a moment to realize just how flabbergasted she was. Nina's self-involvement was so monumental it had never occurred to her that Jim might have an interest in her daughter and not in her.

"What?" Nina demanded, obstinately clueless.

But Meg was too drained emotionally to take the conversation down the path it was heading.

"Nothing," she said.

A memory came to her mind, in which she was seven or eight years old, still living with her mother in a small, unkempt house in a south Austin neighborhood inhabited largely by hippies. Her mother was dating an emaciated man with a glass eye, whom Meg rather liked, as he had demonstrated a wry sense of humor and would sometimes remove his eye and let her handle it. On this particular night, he and Nina went out, and Meg, when they did not return, went to bed, as it was not unusual for her to put herself to bed. But when she awakened several hours later to peer out of her bedroom window and discover that the driveway was still empty, she became frightened, and called Bassie, who arrived soon afterwards in a car the size of an airplane and sent Meg back to bed, stationing herself in the living room to await her daughter's return. Meg awakened later to the sound of angry voices—Bassie demanding to know where Nina had been, and Nina, in a slurred voice, drawing out a long excuse having to do with car trouble that Meg knew, even then, was not true. "What are you doing—are you drunk?" Bassie demanded. "For crying out loud, it's four in the morning." Bassie had threatened—for the first time, as Meg remembered it—to take legal custody of Meg, and in spite of being drunk, Nina rallied and fought back, saying "Oh, *now* you want to be a mother!" Throughout the conversation Meg lay in bed listening, at first thinking that the glass-eyed man was merely silent and cowed by Bassie, and then realizing that he wasn't there at all, that he had merely, on seeing Bassie's car parked at the curb, dropped Nina off and driven away.

She thought now, on the drive to Albuquerque, about how incompetent these two women had been in the roles they were playing. How little tenderness there had been between them, how inept they were, and how incapable she herself had now become at handling her feelings.

By the time they reached the airport, even Nina seemed too tired for a display of emotion—or perhaps, it occurred to Meg, she simply perceived that her audience was not in the mood. Their good-bye was perfunctory, and on starting back to Las Vegas Meg felt relieved to be alone.

When she was back in her room at the Plaza, however, with Bassie's empty room across the hall, she was uneasy with the solitude, and dialed Paul's home phone number in San Antonio.

"Hey, where are you?" he asked. "I just tried to call you at home."

"I'm still in New Mexico," she answered, and then said bluntly, wanting it over with, "Bassie died. We had the funeral today."

"Bassie died? Oh. My God. That's terrible, Meg. I'm sorry. I can't believe that. What happened?"

"I don't want to go into it," she said. He had at least—she told herself—made an effort to respond. It was only that his reservoir of feeling was too shallow. Still, he had disliked Bassie, and Meg could not help but hold this against him. "I'm dealing with it fine," she told him.

He took the statement at face value and did not pursue it.

"I just wanted to let you know I wouldn't be home when I thought."

"Is there anything I can do?" he asked, and she was almost touched by the offer, except that she felt it was hollow.

When she was off the phone her thoughts turned once again to Jim, and how utterly sad he had seemed during the service. He had been the first to leave the cemetery, having gone before the casket was lowered into the grave. The rain had increased by then, and he had walked off through the downpour with his raincoat slung only partially over his head. In spite of what he had said at the funeral, it did not seem to Meg that he had overcome his past. He still appeared, in essential ways, to be an orphan. And now he had lost someone who had been, at least for some period of his life, a touchstone. He seemed to be casting about.

As night deepened, the room became eerily quiet. Meg ate some crackers she had stored away, and then sat on the bed looking around the room at the furnishings of a hundred years ago—the oval mirror over the chest of drawers, flowered wallpaper and lacy curtains. It all gave her a feeling of displacement, as if she had been transported back in time to a place that was neither comfortable nor familiar to her, and was immensely lonely. These few days with her mother had proven to her how little besides a relationship with Bassie they actually shared. Their lives seemed small and uninteresting compared to the tragic mystery of Hannah's life. Even Bassie's image had begun to grow dim when held up to her mother's, the years spent in a moldy old house poring over ragged notebooks in the obsessive attempt to reassemble all the pieces of the past, even as the pieces, in the passage of time, began to fade and the picture to lose its focus. In contrast, Hannah, whatever her failings, had lived in the bright sunlight of Pecos.

After a while, Meg pulled the last two volumes of Hannah's journals onto the bed. She sat looking at Hannah in the ridiculous hat, and wishing there were some way in reality to connect with the dead. She regretted that she had not read the journals years ago. The past had always seemed lugubrious and deceptive to her, yet turning from it had resulted in this feeling now of being homeless and cut off. Until just days ago Hannah had seemed like nothing more than an irritation—an image posed in a strange environment and demanding, for brief moments, when Meg's eyes settled on the spines of the journals clustered on the shelves in Bassie's home or in her own apartment, her unwilling attention. And now the image, once annoying in its ubiquitous presence, had become elusive and desirable.

She opened the fifth volume and began reading where she had left off, in December of 1895, with Elliott leaving for Mexico to work for the Mexican Central Railroad as their chief engineer. She read of the appearance one day at the house in the valley of a large, stray dog, his black coat matted with burrs, and a smaller dog—white and missing an eye—traveling with him. Hannah fed the dogs and picked the burrs from their coats, and several pages later she was lying awake listening to the two of them barking at varmints on the hill.

Meg read about Hannah's fears for Elliott's safety in Mexico, her frustration with his absence. She read of Jewell coming to Pecos to visit Hannah a second time, bringing cans of condensed milk and boxed cereals and bottled relishes, and refusing to eat a bowl of Cleofita's chile con carne without adding to it several ounces of Heinz tomato ketchup. Jewell's abusive husband had been killed in an accident involving a runaway carriage, liberating Jewell.

Elliott wrote to Hannah from Mexico.

February 26, 1896.
Dearest Wife

I have only the fewest minutes before the mail leaves here. We are done with the bandit regions and morale is better. My health is good but for the toothache. The joints are improved. Don't judge my health according to my penmanship, as it is not an indicator. I am not exhausting myself. I am invigorated, Paco suffers however. He is getting old, and shivers and walks with his back in a hunch. I hope the dogs you have taken in won't eat him alive. I have a name to suggest for the black one. Ulysses' dog, I believe, was named Argus, and that sounds appropriate to your description.

I have fifteen men with me, mostly Mexicans. Two of my engineers are Mexican and familiar with the area and agricultural potential. We are in the saddle every day at daylight and ride to the end of the line. We are back in camp by sundown except when selecting line. On those occasions, we often stop at isolated ranches for the night.

I am reading the penny dreadfuls a second time. Send me more if you can get them, to the Mexico City address. Anything expensive will not find me.

I wish you would get away from the house more often. You have fettered yourself too tightly to that place. Take the train to Las Vegas on a Saturday and buy yourself something. If you see the Morales family tell them I can say my r's like a Mexican now. I received Vicente's editorial; it is bound to have got the family angry. He is probably at his ranch now, living the life of a true monastic. If you see him, ask him if the Sanitary Board is making progress or if the Indians still prefer to let their sheep go on infecting everybody else's. I heard about the Wyoming cattlemen slaughtering sheep and running them off the cliffs. Send me clippings if you have them. Send me all you can about everything.

I want you to give up the idea of coming here to see me. I do not expect to hear any more about it. It would be impossible sweet girl. I will be in Mexico City only twice next month, and briefly, and would not for anything bring you to these camps in these temperatures to sleep with graybacks in a bedroll and wake up scratching to bathe in a rationed cup of water. Bear with me dear heart, I am rushing to get home to you. In the meantime, have Cleo stay with you at night.

Your loving husband, Elliott

Hannah's brother came from Chicago and pressed her to come home with him and stay until Elliott returned from Mexico. But she concluded she would only be his "cook and nanny" in Chicago, and declined to go. "He thinks I am trying to impose civilization on the wilderness out here instead of letting the wilderness impose on me," she wrote in early March of that year, 1896.

He does not like Argus, Argus growls at him, Argus is not a very good dog though he is devoted to me. Brother spent the morning in his cattletrail boots and Fedora hat eating Tootsie Rolls and swinging his swagger stick and chatting it up with honeymooners from Chicago who were stopped here on their way to Los Angeles. They are rich and purchased a lace mantilla with travelers cheques and will be returning to Chicago on the Limited which can make the trip from Los Angeles in only sixty-six hours. . . .

Elliott wrote to her,

Dearest wife, I am writing with my gloves on because of the cold, please do not attribute my bad penmanship to rheumatism as I think you will—I am very hardy. That is in answer to your question. Set your mind at ease. I have in the past scouted thousands of miles on foot with fewer men and fewer provisions than I have now, and once ate only tree bark for a week without much suffering. We have some shortages but nothing so severe, though I am low on lamp oil and will have to be brief. Poor old Paco is stealing my warmth. I probably did not do him any good in bringing him along. Yet he would be woebegone if I had left him. Please do not, sweet girl, accuse me of projecting my own wanderlust onto the poor old dog. I know you—you are likely to read more into the words than I have put there. I had better close now.

Your devoted husband, Elliott

March 21

My Dear Little Wife,

Your letter of three weeks ago has just now found me. It is raining here and has been for three days. Work is at a halt. We are all in the tents, wrapped to our chins in our buggy robes. I have been darning my socks all morning though the rain has got my hands stiff. If the rain does not stop we will have to go to the village for supplies, though at least our water barrels will be full. I would pay a great deal for a plate of fried chicken. Tortillas cooked in burro fat have lost their novelty. I am bored enough to go to the gaming tables were I able to find any, but instead will have to settle for cards with Toribio Vasquez, who plays day and night with anyone willing to lose. Everyone else, at the moment, is sleeping the sleep of the righteous, though it is only midday. You may be glad to hear that I do not allow the men to play for money. It causes too much trouble in the camp.

We had an accident here yester-day, a man forfeited a finger while repairing a wagon wheel in the rain. I was up with him all night. His morale was very low. He has pickled the finger in vinegar and will not give up hoping a Mexican doctor in the village can sew it back on.

I am sorry to be morbid. I do not have any cheerful news and feel that I should fill the paper to the bottom. We don't have paper to waste. I will use the space to tell you, dear heart, how I dreamed of you last night—a rather sensual dream and one I will not soon forget. But if you saw me at the present moment, you would not dream of me. I have not bathed in weeks but to stand out in the rain, and I only shave my beard to feel worthy of you; no one here would care one fig if I should grow it to my knees.

I should go out and mend the wagon wheel. The page is almost used. I will write again to-morrow and send the letters to the village when the rain lets up. I never put too many pages in a packet as I never know if it will find you. Forgive the use of lead, it is all I have.

Your loving husband, Elliott

My dear girl,

I will be leaving here on the twenty-seventh and intend to be home soon. We will be back in Mexico City next week. This letter should precede me by a week but with the sluggish mails I may be home at Pecos to receive it, if in fact it comes at all. I hope my letter before the last has finally reached you. It was longer than the last, and more suggestive of my feelings, with less about the weather and a good deal more about my longing to see you. As for poor old Chester, it must have been hard for you, sweet girl, but you have done the only thing you could to put him down, given his condition, and we will get another saddle horse not near so old. You do still have the dogs to keep you company, and you will have a baby some day also. I personally will see to that. I never made a plan that failed.

Your devoted husband Elliott Bass

"I suppose that he is doing all the work himself up to the last moment," Hannah wrote.

He would lay the rails himself if it were possible. He would save the price of mules and turn his horse to pasture and haul the rails on his shoulders over the desert, which is supposed to be 120 degrees in the shade when summer comes, and in that way would be assured the rails were laid correctly. He is bound and determined to put himself in barren places under poor conditions and require too much of himself.

When Elliott returned, his joints were badly inflamed. "Travel is the bane and balm of his suffering," she concluded.

He is driving himself too hard and is suffering but is stoic. The territory he has covered is so vast it would blur in the mind of another man, but Elliott is perfectly attuned to separating hills from valleys. He talked all last evening about descent of slope and maximum grade on tangent and the least radius of curve, and I could see how the sway of the hills and stretch of the desert are imprinted on his brain in the same way the rhythm of songs or words of poems implant themselves in other people's memories. He has been living on hardtack and jerky and Mexican beans and thinking only of his progress on the line, appraising the timber and the agricultural and economic possibilities. Paco has suffered physically almost as much. His muzzle has gone white. Elliott is going out to-morrow to inspect the surveys for a newer tunnel at Raton, he is familiar with those mountains and his old switchback is still winding among the trees, his tunnel there still holds, but a new one has to be built for the larger trains. He is a genius with topography, his initial routes are nearly as true as the final lines, though he uses nothing but his pocket compass and the hand level and barometer to calculate. The grade ascending to the tunnel is just about the steepest ever used for a standard gauge, which of course is why it needs the pusher service.

Elliott talks mostly of gradients and radii and tunnel dimensions and rock composition—he is oblivious to anything he cannot calculate. When he won the pass, he won New Mexico, and has managed to construct his life according to his calculations and to bring us all into his sphere. He maps the routes and carves the trails and keeps himself at the end of the line and is always planning where to go next, while I am looking backwards into the past and am giving tours to people in the Audubon and Sierra clubs who think themselves adventurous for touring around the ruins, and to government officials who have come out here from Washington to create what they are calling a "reserve" up in the mountains because too many Texans have been bringing cattle here that overgraze pastureland intended for the sheep. If this "reserve" should be successful, they will do it elsewhere also.

April 10. All day I have been trying to convince Elliott to see a doctor about the rheumatism before he leaves for Mexico, yet he believes in nothing but willow bark powder and hot salt bags and mostly his endurance—he keeps his range of motion by continuing to move. I would admire him if I cared nothing for him. His health is nearly ruined. His stamina is not. We got the timing perfect for a baby.

April 20, Mexico City

Your letter followed me by just two days. I will keep my fingers crossed. If the baby does not happen now, then soon, I promise you that. In the meantime your devotion to that place is touching, my sweet girl, but I hope that you won't turn yourself into a hermit again while I am not there to coax you out. Fill your lungs, but please do not forget that there are other places you can breathe. I wish you would go to Las Vegas more often. It is such a brief ride on the train. Go and see a play. Visit Señora Morales.

I have taken care of all my business here and will be starting for the mountains in the morning. I will be within your eyesight by the middle of next month. If only for a week or two.

Be happy, dear heart. And hopeful.

Your devoted husband, Elliott.

Meg sat with the book splayed open across her knees and imagined Hannah, at Pecos, receiving these letters, sitting in a wicker chair on the back porch, on a spring day, having exiled herself from Vicente, reading the scrawl of "crowtracks" and hoping to be pregnant. She looked at the dates and calculated the months, concluding that in fact this was the month that Bassie was conceived. It was odd to know of Hannah's pregnancy and Bassie's life and death before Hannah, in her own time, knew of Bassie's existence. The journal entries had transformed these fleeting moments into episodes of history, keeping Hannah's life as fluid in print as it had been in reality, with nothing to inform one day of the next. There was no foreshadowing in the journal, no omniscient narrator to hint at things to come. Bassie had yet to be born in Hannah's time. And in Meg's time, her life had ended.

The following entries involved a bizarre sequence of nights related in a poorly punctuated, apprehensive style.

Cleo found one of our hens dead on the porch this morning and we do not know how it got there, there was no blood, the coop remained secure, it was not coyotes or a predator—the dogs had not been restless, they were sleeping inside—.

On the following day another hen was discovered, this time with a note tied around its neck, the note, oddly, addressed to Vicente Morales and inscribed with the Spanish epigram, "One who is born fat, even though he is tied as a baby, will remain fat." The note apparently referred to Vicente's wealth. It was written in cheap lead pencil on a torn piece of wrapping paper, with incorrect spelling. Hannah and Cleofita stayed awake that night, watching out the windows as the moon traveled over Dog Hill and sank behind the ruins of the church on the mesa. Argus and Milton, uneasy with the vigil, ran about the interior of the house sniffing at doors and windows. Nothing strange was seen, but after dawn, when Cleo went outside to gather eggs for breakfast, she found a note tacked to the door of the coop. "*No es el león como lo pintan,*" it said: The lion is not the way it is painted.

Hannah placed the two notes in an envelope and took them to Pecos village to be sent by mail, with a letter of explanation, to Vicente in Las Vegas. She had not communicated with him in more than a year.

That night she and Cleofita watched again from the windows. It was an eerily windy night. They kept the dogs inside. The moon was nearly full, casting shadows from the junipers over the boulders of Dog Hill. From Hannah's bedroom window the valley stretched a long way in the moonlight, and the peaks of distant mountains glowed white and iridescent, otherworldly in their cold indifference to the wind. The chicken coop could not be seen from the windows of the house because of a stand of trees, but the barn, beside it, stood in stark relief against the blue night in the valley. At nearly three o'clock in the morning Cleo came whispering into Hannah's bedroom where Hannah sat in an armchair by the window with a pistol cocked in her hand. Cleo had heard something. She had seen nothing, however, from her watch at the parlor window. Argus rose from the floor at the foot of the bed and moved his large black head from side to side, sniffing at the air; Milton yapped fretfully, but Hannah hushed him. The dogs then left the room and hurried about the house, scratching at the doors and rising on their hind legs to peer out of the windows. The deep baritone of Argus echoed through the hallway; he began to lunge at the back door, snarling, but Hannah refused to let him go out. The women went through the hallway, into the parlor, and waited on either side of a window, hidden from the outdoors but alive to themselves and each other, hearing each other's breathing. Hannah was holding the gun. She swung her gaze across the yard and her heartbeat stuttered. Something was moving along the path outside the fence. The shape seemed less than human—the head not like a head, the body lurching forward. This creature glowed in the moonlight, and the shape took form in the wind, emerging as a person draped in a white hood and carrying over its shoulder the lifeless body of a dead goat. It entered through the gate in the picket fence. As it ascended the porch steps, casting shadows in the moonlight, Hannah drew back from the window and listened to the thumping of the boots. Argus sniffed at the smell of blood and ran about the room, in and out of the hallway, barking fiercely, with Milton at his heels. The figure dropped the goat, Hannah's nanny goat, which lay in repose on the porch with its head flung back, the throat slit open wide and the hair caked black with blood.

The shape of the man now straightened, seeming to become more human, though the hood disguised the face and was smeared with the goat's dark blood, circles cut from the cloth through which the eyes could see. The hood jerked left to right following Argus's barking as he rushed from the door to the window and back again. But then in a quick movement, the empty eyes fixed on the window where Hannah and Cleo stood. Hannah felt the moonlight on her face grow cold. She knew the eyes within the hood perceived her, though she could not see the slightest glimmer through the black holes of the hood. The eerie figure lingered; Hannah stared at it, mesmerized with curiosity. It had a stocky form, and stood no taller than she. The hood hung to the waist;

the shirt beneath was flannel, the skin of the hands dark, the trousers sewn from canvas.

The boots then shifted on the porch in a movement that seemed nervous. She saw that they were hide, like any of dozens of pairs that she had seen in the village. Her eyes were drawn back to the hooded head, and she knew what she was facing. It was the costume of the Gorras Blancas—the White Caps—the gang who rode about the countryside vandalizing property of wealthy ranchers. He had come, she knew, because of Vicente. No matter what Vicente's sympathies for the dispossessed of his people, no matter what his liberal views, he was still a Morales by blood. Hannah realized for the first time, as she stared at the hooded man in the slant of moonlight on the porch, the strength of Vicente's convictions. And the danger they brought to her.

She looked at the nanny goat. A string had been tied around its nose and into its mouth; the lower jaw hung limp and the tongue had flopped to the boards of the porch. Blood dripped from the tip of the tongue. From the string a parchment dangled, tumbled about by the wind.

Hannah raised the window up an inch. She knelt and pressed the barrel of the pistol through the crack. She intended to speak, but found herself only staring at the hooded apparition, watching it stare at her, the empty eyes directed at the mouth of the gun. She angled the barrel in its direction, and saw the apparition turn and make its way deliberately down the porch steps. It crossed the yard, passed through the gate, and started toward the road. Hannah remained kneeling at the window. Cleofita dropped to her knees also, whispering to the saints. At last the two women spoke to each other, and tried to calm the dogs.

Not until after daylight had crept in through the window did they clutch their blankets around themselves against the chill of the morning and go out onto the porch. The note lashed to the jaw of the nanny goat was composed in Spanish. "He who walks among the wolves will learn to howl."

Cleofita went to the village and returned in the afternoon with Señor Ruiz. Hannah and Cleofita and Señor Ruiz kept watch throughout the night. No one came at all. The following night, exhausted, they alternated in their watch, but again no one appeared.

On the next morning Vicente came, having received the letter. "Vicente is sleeping in a blanket on the porch with Señor Ruiz," Hannah wrote in the journal that night. "He came on the early train. He wore his hat down low, so not to be known and endanger us further." More than a year had passed since she had seen him.

They sat in the bold sun behind the shed. The valley stretched beyond them. The peaks of snowy mountains glittered in the distance, and the day was warm. Hannah removed her shawl. Vicente was remote, Hannah uneasy. He asked her to pack her things and go to Las Vegas and stay with his mother until Elliott could return. He said he was no friend to Elliott if he should let her stay at Pecos.

But Hannah refused to go. In the light of the sun, with the smell of earthy spring around her and the fear of the nights over, Hannah convinced herself, and tried to convince Vicente, that the hooded man had never intended to harm her. His hands, she said, resembled farmers' hands. She had seen the nervous movement of his boot. She had seen the stocky paunch of his stomach. He was an old farmer.

"A farmer who has drained the blood out of your nanny goat," Vicente answered her.

But Hannah had married herself to Pecos, for better or worse. She had grown to love the shifts in weather, the purity of air and changes of light, the daily movement of the sun across the mesa. The place had been her refuge, and had changed her. She felt an obligation to her home and her work. And if she had been singled out by the Gorras Blancas because of her friendship—and Elliott's—with Vicente, then going to Vicente's family for protection could only pose a greater danger to her later. All of this she said to Vicente while they sat in the sunlight behind the wooden shed, a spring breeze tossing Hannah's hair about, Vicente holding his hat and letting the light shine so directly on his face that Hannah could see the nuance of expressions, the clenching of the jaw, the crow's-feet clustered around his eyes.

The conversation, after a while, descended into the deeper realms. Vicente admitted that he had taken a lover since the last time he had seen her. Hannah tried to accept the fact, saying she had no claim on him. But then she broke down into tears. Vicente slammed his fist against the shed, demanding to know if she had expected him to castrate himself for her sake. The words flew out of Hannah as unstoppable as bats flying out of a cave, and she could not, later, remember all that she had said.

But by evening, Hannah was dining in the kitchen with Vicente and Señor Ruiz. She lit the candles. Cleofita joined them at the table. Vicente declared that he would sleep on the porch with Señor Ruiz, and stay as long as necessary.

A feeling of safety settled on the house.

THIRTY-ONE

June 18, 1896
My dear Girl:

I returned from the mountains yester-day and found your letters waiting at the Mexico City office with such overwhelming and great news that I could not sit down for the whole day, and have only just now done so in a dark and rather oily little cantina near the Plaza with six strangers who speak only Espanol but are happy enough to celebrate with me as long as I am buying the tequila. I have been blazing away with them in Espanol for an hour, and they have offered impressive toasts to you and to your welfare and that of baby to be. I will not be maudlin but will ask you to forgive me for not being home to learn the news from you. I feel I am farther away from you just now than ever since I met you, though in fact our link is stronger and I hope will overcome the miles of road and rail between us.

I should tell you I dislike your thought of lying in at home. I do not think much of Cleo's medical talent. Suppose that you need laudanum at the time? You should have all medical options open. If the Queen of England can have her babies without pain then so should you, and I am going to be there to see to it.

Sweet girl, I intend to crack ahead so I can come home soon and see for myself that you are well. Meanwhile I will write to Señora Morales and arrange for you to stay at the mansion when the time should come.

And now for the other matter. I should have been there to look after you. I'm glad Vicente is there. He is right that you should not go to the sheriff, as the radicals are all connected. Do not spend a night alone there.

My dear, I am sorry to hear you have an appetite only for raisin toast and Postum. We want the baby big, not small. And I will be home sooner than you think, in order to be with you and "dejen el camino abierto," as they say in Mexico—if you will forgive my lack of manners.

Much love to you, sweet girl.

Your husband, Elliott

Sept. 15. Dear Heart,

I received your letter of August 9, though I think I am receiving only one of every three you write. I am sorry the blue devils have got hold of you. I will run them off when I get there.

Now about the lying in. You must go to Las Vegas when the time comes. I don't know why you are unwilling about it if Señora Morales invited you. You would be more comfortable there. I hope you do not make me have a long discussion on the subject when I see you. I want you in safe hands no matter what. We will want Dr. Middleton if there is trouble.

My dear, stop blacking the stove yourself. And if Fred Harvey has suggested that you stop the tours for a while then by all means do it.

We are just about done with the present stretch. I will visit the city a few days after that, and be home by the end of the month.

As for the nonsense that your mood might hurt the baby, I presume you have your own head and the baby has his—quite separate. Divest yourself of pamphlets! Our baby will be fine.

Congratulate Vicente for challenging the Land Grant Board. I doubt the farmers are as grateful as they should be.

Have the fleas not given up the roost? Do not shake the rugs, dear, let Cleo do it. And put those dogs out of the house.

Your devoted husband, Elliott.

Meg turned through the next few pages, scanning over passages about the pregnancy, about Elliott's return from Mexico, Vicente's visits, Jewell's side career of selling Avon products. The birth itself she hardly looked at, reluctant to read the story of Bassie's birth on the night after her funeral. She hardly let her eyes settle on the words, but turned the pages quickly to glean the essentials—Bassie was born on a snowy night a few days after Christmas at the Morales mansion under the care of a doctor, with Elliott present. She was named Claudia Eugenia—Claudia for Hannah's mother and Eugenia for Elliott's. Hannah was euphoric, transfixed by the child. Claudia was a noisy baby, disquieting to look at, having an unnatural focus to her eyes.

Vicente's mother, Mrs. Morales, cared for Hannah at the mansion for a week, persuading her to drink cinnamon tea to increase her milk production and to remain in bed. Hannah wrote about nursing and changing "nappies." Elliott came and went, sleeping at night on a sofa beside the bed where Hannah slept with the baby, and working during the days at his old office in the tie plant. Vicente also came a few times, when his father was not in the house.

In early January Hannah and Elliott took the baby home to Pecos. They kept a cradle beside their bed, but Hannah had become accustomed to sleeping with Claudia, and while she often wrote in the journal about her intentions to let the baby sleep in the cradle, this never actually happened. "Her tiny feet are always lodging themselves against my belly and waking me up, and poor Elliott has been sleeping in the parlor every night for more than a month now," she wrote in February. "Tonight I will try to put her in the cradle." The resolution, however, was not even mentioned in the entry of the following day, which began "I awoke to Claudia's little face pressed up against mine, her eyes wide open and staring at me so closely that both of us went cross-eyed. She melts my heart with her snuffling and sucking and breathing noises, she is such a small lump of warm weight beside me. When she is a grown woman, I will miss this baby. 'Where is Claudia when she was little?' I will say. 'Where *is* she?' "

Elliott left for Mexico in the middle of March, but returned to Pecos in May and stayed until July, sleeping good-naturedly on the sofa in the parlor most nights, as Claudia had taken his place in the bed.

Hannah's journal entries in these months were prolific and almost exclusively about Claudia. "Claudia was agitated by the storm . . . Claudia picked her first flower . . . Claudia still does not like the dogs." Claudia spent her first birthday vomiting from having swallowed kerosene out of a table lamp. A week later her thumbnail was demolished when she caught her thumb in a washtub wringer. For half an hour she screamed in Hannah's arms, until Vicente fished the nail from the soapy water and gave it back to her.

"Argus is jealous of Claudia," Hannah wrote, "—and snapped at her to-day. Milton tolerates her better though she is authoritarian. If Argus is aggressive I will have to give him up, which I hope not to do. He is a good watchdog."

This ended the fifth journal. The intensity of Hannah's infatuation with her child intrigued Meg and filled her with longing as she read, as she had never experienced this depth of love herself, either from a daughter's or a mother's point of view.

The mood of the journals turned at the start of the final volume. Vicente began to talk of the war in Cuba, and Hannah was afraid that he would volunteer to fight. For him, the war's legitimacy was not merely the moral question it was for other Americans, but a personal issue. While his father was outspokenly in favor of U.S. involvement in Cuba, Vicente found himself offended by the bigotry that began to surface because of the war. Anglo prejudice against Spanish nationals in Cuba extended to a prejudice against anyone with Spanish ancestry, and Vicente, who as one of the founders of La Prensa—the Spanish-language press association—had worked for years to refute the stereotyping of Spaniards that had become prevalent among eastern, Anglo journalists, now had to face the fact of his own prejudice. Because of his heritage, he felt aligned with the Spaniards, no matter what their culpability in Cuba, but he disliked what they were doing there and knew the only effective way to prove to Anglos that he and his people were loyal to the U.S. was to join them in fighting the Spaniards in Cuba. His father had fought in the United States Civil War on the Union side when the war had come to New Mexico, and now Vicente could prove his own patriotism by volunteering to fight in Cuba. He had managed, so far, to give his Spanish heritage equal weight with his U.S. citizenship, but now he was going to have to take one side or the other.

Theodore Roosevelt, a former secretary of the navy at the time, began recruiting troops from the marksmen and horsemen in western territories. Vicente was an able horseman, educated and bilingual.

April 20, 1898
Dear Heart.

Write to me and tell me what Vicente is doing about Cuba. My own opinion is that he will go to try to please Don Pedro, and that is a lost cause. The two of them are never going to see the same view down the same path. They are like fighting cocks when you put them together—you can disengage them, but they will go back at it. If Vicente should ask about my opinion, tell him I believe the war is reasonably just, though we have made our fingers too sticky in the pie. Nevertheless I don't think he should join the fight. They will have plenty of younger men for that.

Now about our girl. Isn't she old enough to have some friends? She has only Cleo and Señor Ruiz and Vicente. If she is talking to the goats she must be lonely. I know the dogs are tired of having her hang about with them. Paco I think was happy to be rid of her. Don't get mad at me for saying so. You know that I adore her, but you yourself have said she is a bossy little thing. Very cute however. Maybe you should take her to the village and find her some friends. Cleo is bound to know some children. At any rate, do give the little scamp a kiss for me. I think about her all the time. And you have done the right thing to have her vaccinated, I'm sorry she got the fever, but better that than smallpox.

Take care, dear heart, and I will too. I will write to you soon.

Your loving husband, Elliott

April. Vicente is going to Cuba and I have nothing to say to him about it, I have said too much, am very melancholy, at least the mosquito net over the bed shuts me off from the world as I cannot stand it at the moment. Claudia has fallen asleep beside me. I have got her up against me, there is no space between us, she is my refuge and the blessing of my life—everything within the net is clear to me, but on the outside everything is unfocused. He was here last night to say good-bye. Claudia was inconsolable. I will not forget how she cried and wrapped her arms around his neck in the moonlight and had to be pried off, asking time and again why he was going and when he would be coming back. Her usual hard-headedness turned plaintive. Vicente held her against him like a limp rag doll. Cleo took him in the buggy down to the station at Rowe to catch the latest freight train back to Las Vegas. In a week he will leave for Texas where Roosevelt is drilling troops in San Antonio. My poor child has seen too many departures.

June—

Dearest Girl. I do not even know what day it is out here. We have lost track of everything we can't calculate in meters. Now about your letter. I suppose Roosevelt is overjoyed to have got so many volunteers. I am not surprised to hear Vicente will be leading the Las Vegas bunch, and am relieved that there are only twenty of them, as he is not too talented at unifying people, the opposite is true. He is divided in his own mind and will talk about the conflicts going on within, which makes him a good writer but is likely to make him a poor militant. Was he still as dubious when he departed? I am sorry he has gone.

Kiss my little girl for me. Expect me home within the next ten days as promised. I can only stay a week or two this time but have been missing you, and will make the trip no matter what the jefe in Mexico City has to say about it. I have found a toy train for Claudia and am making an iron track. She will want to tell me how to construct it.

Your loving husband Elliott

July 7. The weather was threatening all morning, the tourists did not get off the train, rain started by two o'clock in the afternoon and I intended to stay indoors and figure accounts, but Cleo remembered she had not put the goats under cover. By the time I got my mackintosh, Claudia had disappeared. I left the dogs in and went out after her and found the gate to the pens open and all six goats, including the kid, nowhere in sight, and Claudia gone too, as she had gone looking for them. I was frantic, calling around the barn, and came back to the house for Cleo—she started for the road while I went up to the ruins.

The lightning was continuous, the wind nearly strong enough to knock me over and the rain fierce. I decided the goats had gone up to the church ruins for shelter as they sometimes do and that Claudia had followed them, and when I arrived there I saw her with them in the lightning, crowded against the church wall. When the goats saw me running toward them they spooked to the front of the church and gathered inside the entry. Claudia followed them, and I ran to get hold of her. I saw she was not frightened. A roof beam jutting from the high wall had loosened in the wind, and I tried to scare the goats from beneath it, but before I could do so a twist of wind came rushing in and tore the beam away from the wall, spinning it up and dropping it down on the goats. After the beam was on the ground a bolt of lightning struck the ground beside us. Claudia was in my arms and we were both thrown down. The beam had fallen on one of goats and she could not get out from under it. Her kid was beside her—the other goats were bunched against the wall—and the kid came stepping toward us, but then a bolt of lightning came and struck it down. I felt the impact through the ground and saw a blaze of fire—the kid was on fire and bleating, though we could barely hear because of the thunder. I smelled the burning flesh and thought the current had also gone through us, and dragged Claudia to the wall and lay on top of her. After a while I took her and ran to the kiva. It was black inside, except for the flashes of lightning. Thunder shook the room. Claudia got out of my arms and began looking around as if she had never seen the place before. She did not respond when I spoke to her and I thought the lightning bolt had shaken her, as she seemed to be listening to something besides my voice, and turned her head about as if someone else were talking to her. When I tried to make her answer me, she said that she was listening to other people, that there were many other people with us in the kiva. The place was strange in its silence after the deafening noise. I asked her what the people were saying, but she refused to tell me. I asked her what they looked like and she said she didn't know. But do you see them? I said. No, she said—"I hear them." One of them—she said—is old. "What are they saying?" I asked her. "Maybe it's a secret," she replied, serious in her manner, but without apparent fear. Her hair was wet and hanging in her eyes, I saw her only by the lightning from the entry overhead. We stayed in the kiva until the lightning stopped, and then were left in darkness. Finally the rain let up and light broke through and we came out. Cleo came looking for us. The air was fresh. We went to the church ruins. The goats had gone back down the hill, but the nanny was still trapped under the beam. Her back was broken. Later I had to go back up and shoot her.

July 8. Milton went out in the yard with Claudia early this morning and came back without her. I found her in the kiva. She saw me coming down the ladder and ordered me to go away, and said she was talking with her "friends." I had to go to get the tourists from the train and made her come back to the house. Cleo says the kiva is a world between worlds, where boundaries can be crossed.

July 21. Vicente is gone two months now, and I have heard nothing. I watch the road as if he might appear. It is awfully quiet here these summer days. The purple color of the asters deepens the morning shadows that are not yet lost to the sun, the stalks of yellow mullein rise tall in noon heat and the asters are a darkish purple again at sunset with the insects droning among them when the cool of evening starts to settle in. Claudia's little voice echoes from the hills.

July 30, 1898.

My dear friend, Hannah Bass. I am writing to you from Cuba. It is three months since I left you. The thought of you has been my comfort through more grief than I am willing to describe. I am recovering from malarial fever. We have lost thousands of men to disease and hundreds to battle. Half of the Las Vegas men are dead or disabled from wounds and disease. I wish I had not come to this island. I had hoped to fight injustice and prejudice but instead have been a propagator and victim of those stains on our humanity. We have all come here for our own purposes, wanting the strength of our beliefs to translate into physical omnipotence. There is no correlation between the two. The greatest armies often create the greatest injustice. Everyone here believes that God is on his side, and yet I see no evidence of God's hand anywhere in sight. We have at times been days on end, without sleep, watching our friends suffer and die in the mud without so much as a bandage for their wounds. I have found myself in jungles blanketed with dead, the smoke not yet lifted from the fighting, and my view seemingly no less omniscient or powerful than God's, for all that he did about it. We have been short of medicine and food. We have lacked ammunition and supplies.

I will be coming home. In spite of everything we have won the war, though I have lost my skirmishes of thought in the grander scale of reality. I have had a disagreement with Roosevelt himself, which discredits me among the officers. It is hardly a legacy my father will take pride in. I believe I was born to shame my father. And yet I would not change a word of any truth I spoke to Colonel Roosevelt. He is a hero here among the Harvard patrician gringos and Indians and cowboys alike, and I have found myself shooting down Spaniards with the best of them. It has sharpened my anger toward the yellow press and the Imperialists who goaded us into this fight. This is not my war. It is not even our war. But I have fought on the side I came to fight on, and killed my share of Spaniards. I suppose I will be remembered for this if not for the grief it has caused me. I am sorry to have brought you to this hell even in my thoughts. Better that no thought of you had walked among the dead. There is rejoicing here over our victory. They are singing praises to Roosevelt. A shipment of shoes has just arrived for the men. But we have been sleeping in the mud, pitiful and hot with fever, and in spite of our bravery, our souls are in jeopardy of being damned. The flag of the United States is flying over the Palace at Santiago.

My friend, I hope to see you before I write to you again. We will be taken to the Jersey coast instead of Florida, and from there I will come home. It is my intention then to discredit the propaganda that has led us to conquer a country by pretending to liberate it. I pray that you and Elliott will stand by me.

Sincerely your friend, Vicente Morales

So there, Meg thought—there was Vicente's voice. It was not the voice of a man who could be guilty of killing a friend.

Someone was passing in the hallway; she heard the floor creaking, and the rustle of clothing.

Quiet settled again.

October 5 . . . he will write his editorials at the cost of everything, he has not been home long enough to recover from the fever and is putting all his strength into writing. It is all about Imperialism—Cuba and Puerto Rico and the Philippines. We are not freeing the people, he says, we are taking their countries. We are acquisitionists. We are sure to get Hawaii also. He has heard from our governor and other prominent people who disagree with his opinions. They dislike that he is not afraid of them, that he will speak his mind at any cost to anyone. Don Pedro has ceased trying to control him, he seldom talks to him. Even his colleagues at the paper have about had enough. No matter what the U.S. motives were in Cuba, New Mexicans are proud to have been in Cuba and would rather not listen to Vicente on the subject of morality. He is always fighting the status quo. I wonder if he isn't fighting Don Pedro in all these other battles. He was here at the house to-day, nearly a wreck, Elliott and I both failed to quiet him.

Dec. 1, 1898, Mexico City

Dear Heart, I found six letters from you waiting when I got to the city. I hope you will give me credit for the last packet of letters I mailed to you and count them as several, so you don't feel cheated.

About the Pecos land grant. Tell Señor Ruiz that the lawyer hired to incorporate the village is known to deal in land sales and is out for his own good. Ask Vicente to find out if the man who has the tax and legal titles to the grant is planning to use the land for timber operations. If he is, then we may have a problem, and so will everyone in the village, as the village is part of the grant. I will get into the fray as soon as I am back, but if there is no talk yet of evictions in the village then there is probably no danger at the moment. But we should think ahead. I'm sorry to have to place this on Vicente. I know he has got his own battles if the *Atlantic Monthly* is using the term "greasers."

So, our little girl is now a professional domino stacker? Every night I think about our tea party on the table she made from the cheese box and the pickle keg. I hope her diet is getting more varied than just the mustard pickles. She is such a grand little tyrant. Give her kisses from her papa. But do stop her from bringing the bone fragments and pottery into the house. I was sorry to hear that Argus tried to bite her again. No matter if it was her fault. I would presume that you are keeping him out of the house. We may have to consider getting rid of him. I can find you another watchdog.

Love to both my girls. Your devoted Elliott.

June 1899. Topeka

Dear Little Wife—We have finally put the pieces back together since the market fell out from under us, and have closed on the San Francisco and San Joaquin Valley Railroads. This is excellent news. The valley is open to us. There is nothing to stand between us and San Francisco. The Southern Pacific is on its knees and has lost the monopoly while we are back in the business of building and buying and will keep things going in Mexico. The Orange growers in the valley still think we're in collusion with the Southern Pacific but otherwise our reputation is intact.

Sweet girl, I hope my work does not give you too many doubts about our marriage. I would stay in one place for your sake if I had to, but you know how much I would dislike a sedentary life. I can barely even imagine a sedentary death! Do not ever shut me in a casket, that would be a terrible faux pas, my dear.

I will be home within two weeks. I can't have Colonel Roosevelt in Las Vegas and not be there to listen to him speak. As I assume he will. You can tell Vicente I said so if you dare to. I would like for you to come along with me and bring Claudia, so she can see him too, and not to be a slave to Vicente's opinions. He has too many opinions. Roosevelt is a hero to most of the country. We are not always the wisest country, but we are not deluded enough to worship a madman. As Vicente would have us think of Roosevelt. It's good the citizens have got themselves up for the events, but they are going to have to finish numbering the houses if they plan to put up mailboxes. I think they started twenty years ago.

So Illfield is selling toilet papers in his stores? That is very fancy. If you were bold enough to buy some, you were not bold enough to say so in your letter.

I am glad the city council did not throw the stonecutters out of business by endorsing cement sidewalks, even if they did evict the hogpens.

Take care of yourself, please, dear, and look after my sweet little pumpkin. She is a hard-headed little scamp and will rule the roost if you let her. Are she and Argus any friendlier? I imagine Cleofita is encouraging the conversations with the ghosts. I heard Cleo telling her about El Ojo last time I was home.

I will see you soon, though I can't name a date. Look for me when I am there. You are on my mind as always day and night. I hope I am not a disappointment to you in any way, and that you will forgive my absence.

Your faithful and devoted husband, Elliott Bass.

But Hannah was finding forgiveness difficult, spilling her frustration into a journal entry two days after his return.

She had merely wanted—she explained in the entry—to oil the leather satchel in which he carried his papers. But while removing items from the satchel she had discovered, tucked away in a buttoned pocket, a newspaper clipping that Elliott, it seemed, had carried with him for two decades, about the execution of the only Mormon ever convicted for the murders at Mountain Meadows—a man by the name of Major John D. Lee. The story explained that Lee had been an officer in the Utah territorial militia under Brigham Young, and was believed to be the leader of the massacre. It displayed two photographs of John Lee taken at Mountain Meadows at the site of the massacre twenty years after it happened, and just before he was executed at that place. In one of the photographs, he was seated on the edge of his own coffin, rocky hills rising in the background, in front of him the odd construction of a makeshift curtain behind which stood the firing squad. In the other, he was lying dead inside the coffin. A chronicle of the execution followed, describing the stoicism and resignation in John Lee's demeanor, his final speech in which he said he had done nothing intentionally wrong, that his conscience was clear before God and man, and he was ready to meet his Redeemer. He felt, he said, "as calm as a summer morn." He accused Brigham Young of sacrificing him as a scapegoat. None of his wives or children were at the scene of the execution, but he requested that copies of the photographs of him seated on the coffin be sent to the few of his many wives who had remained loyal to him. He was blindfolded, but asked for his arms to remain free, raised his hands over his head, and told the firing squad, "Center my heart, boys!"

"The old man never flinched," the paper said. "It made death seem easy, the way he went off."

But what most captured Hannah's attention as she read was the list of people who witnessed the execution. "Elliott Bass, railroad employee" was named.

He was, Hannah realized, twenty-six years old at the time.

She found him at his desk. He had not yet lighted the lamps, so the room, with its wooden floor and the shelves of books, gave a transitory feeling, with the summer light rapidly fading.

She wanted to know why he carried the clipping with him, and what comfort it gave him, and how he had learned of the execution and why he had gone to witness it. Faced with her questions, Elliott became mute and unreachable. He rose from his desk. At last he was defensive, and asked her why she had felt the need to "pry" into his things. The accusation stunned her. For years she had quietly acquiesced to his privacy and his secrets, believing that some day he would come to trust her enough to reveal himself. And now he had chosen to assign her the role of adversary instead. She was hurt, and hardened by the indictment, and accused him of fleeing his emotions and cutting himself off from her, and from Claudia. "Talk to me," she told him angrily. "Stop running away from me." She could not, she acknowledged, be part of his past. But she wanted to understand what he was suffering in the present that would cause him to carry this newspaper clipping around with him and never mention to his own wife that he had attended the execution of John Lee at Mountain Meadows. Was it the only time that he had returned to Mountain Meadows after the killings?

"No," he said. He gave her that.

"Was it the first time?"

"Not the first time, no." He stared at her in defiance. "I was seven, the first time." He stopped at that, and turned away, the movement in his body ceasing all at once, as if he suddenly were rooted to the one spot in the world that could possibly hold him—a patch of wooden floor close to the window, and in the line of Hannah's gaze. He turned back to her, and looked at her with a quizzical expression. "I went back there and buried my mother," he said, his voice drifting away.

"Oh, Elliott—alone?" she cried.

"A Mormon boy went with me."

"A Mormon boy?"

"With whom I lived. Don't ask me, please, my dear, any more."

"Elliott?"

"My mother's hair was still tied back with a shoelace."

And by this statement and the look of grief in his eyes, Hannah suddenly came to see that no matter what he revealed to her, he would never be open to her. He had sealed a part of himself away. Only by doing so had he survived.

THIRTY-TWO

The journal entries following were written in a frenetic run of words that hardly had spaces between them. Elliott seemed for a while like a stranger to Hannah, his past too horrible to fathom. He made no further reference to their conversation about Mountain Meadows, and she did her best to comply with his need for denial, behaving as if the conversation had not taken place. But compliance only intensified the emotional distance she felt from her husband. She sensed his urgency to head south into the mountains of Mexico again.

And privately, she longed for Vicente. She had intended, in support of Vicente's opinions about the Cuban war, to stay away from Las Vegas during the first annual reunion of Rough Riders, which was to be held there. But Elliott pressed her to go. Roosevelt would be attending a dinner at the Morales Mansion and Elliott wanted to meet him.

They took Claudia with them, and stayed at the mansion. At the dinner, Elliott talked with Roosevelt about finances and future plans for the railroads, and Roosevelt later sought him out and questioned him closely for nearly an hour about Mexico and its future. He was presently mayor of New York City, but was known to have higher ambitions, and Elliott, while not an ideologue for the Republican Party, was, like Roosevelt, an expansionist, and agreed with most of his philosophies.

Vicente refused to come to the dinner, and occupied himself that night by printing a single-page special-edition broadside that he produced in both English and Spanish. Early the next morning he and his employees began distributing the broadside among veterans camped at Lincoln Park.

Roosevelt was there, camping with his men. He led the morning parade on a mount borrowed from Don Pedro Morales, wearing a tan-colored uniform, leather gloves, and a hat with the brim pinned up on one side. The parade came to a halt in the Old Town plaza, in front of the Plaza Hotel, where a grandstand stood erected for the speeches. The mayor of Las Vegas extended a formal welcome, and Don Pedro introduced Roosevelt to a cheering crowd of thousands under a heavy sky. But when Roosevelt himself rose to speak a restlessness had begun to simmer among the audience.

Hannah was standing with Elliott, holding Claudia. She saw Vicente moving among the crowd and distributing the broadsides; he handed one to her, and one to Elliott. Elliott said to him, "I can't believe you are going to do this," and Vicente answered, "I am obligated, my friend."

Roosevelt began his speech, but was not deaf to the murmuring. He paused after only a moment, and called on a man at the front of the crowd to bring him the sheet of paper he was reading. Holding the broadside before his face, he squinted through his spectacles. The copy was in Spanish, so he turned to Don Pedro and handed it to him, asking Don Pedro to translate. Don Pedro looked at it. He looked at his son still moving among the people, then turned to Roosevelt and tried to dismiss the paper. But Roosevelt took it from him, and continued to scrutinize it through his spectacles, apparently comprehending enough Spanish to try to discern the gist of it. A man in a bowler hat came forward and offered a copy printed in English, and when Roosevelt had got it in his hands he held it up, reading silently for a moment. Then he called in his high-pitched, nasal voice, "Where is Vicente Morales?" Vicente came forward and stood at the foot of the bandstand. Roosevelt addressed him.

"Your name is on this broadside. You wrote this, I presume?" he asked pleasantly.

"I did," Vicente replied.

"I know that voice—I know you, Vicente Morales," Roosevelt called out. "I recognize you also. We had this argument in Cuba, did we not? I had hoped that if my words did not convince you which side you should be fighting on, then a number of Spanish bullets might." A ripple of laughter came from the audience. "You are not a quick study, are you,

Mr. Morales? I remember your fighting skills. I recognize them as courageous. But, sir, I deplore your manners." Here he turned to Don Pedro. "Is he any relation to you, sir? And would you claim him if he were?"

Don Pedro did not answer at once. People began to laugh. "It is his son! That is his son!" they began to call out, and Roosevelt turned and squinted, eyeing Don Pedro, and then smiled ferociously at him. Roosevelt opened his mouth to speak, but Don Pedro said in a humorless shout, turning to the assemblage, "He is not my son! He has been my son, but he is not my son." Then he walked down the steps of the bandstand, past Vicente, Elliott, Hannah, Claudia in her mother's arms, and across the street, into the Plaza Hotel.

Roosevelt seemed pensive. He removed his spectacles and cleaned them on his shirt and put them on again. A misty rain was beginning to fall. The crowd started to murmur. Vicente did not move at first from where he stood at the base of the grandstand, but then turned and made his way past Elliott and Hannah, without so much as a glance at them. Claudia reached out for him as he went past, calling him "Uncle," but he did not look at her. He did not follow his father into the Plaza Hotel, but walked away from the crowd, still carrying some of the broadsides under his arm, and walked down the street toward the building where his office and the press were housed.

"Family squabbles," Roosevelt said, maintaining his good humor. "Well, enough of that." He continued with his speech.

But he had lost the attention of most of the people. There was no one in the gathering who did not know the Morales family. There was no one who thought Don Pedro did not mean what he had said. Don Pedro was a man of his word, and he had just disowned his son.

Elliott lifted Claudia from Hannah's arms. They started down the street after Vicente. They saw him go into his office, and followed him there and found him seated at his desk with the lamp turned off and the office quiet but for the distant sound of the crowd in occasional bursts of applause.

"That was a mistake," Elliott said to him.

"I disagree," Vicente answered coldly. "I did what I meant to do."

“To insult your father,” Elliott replied.

“To say what was on my mind.”

“You might have done it less publicly.”

“I might have. And I might have said nothing.”

“Not a bad idea,” Elliott remarked.

Claudia then spoke from her perch in Elliott’s arms, her voice shrill and petulant. “Don’t you be mean to my uncle!” she cried, struggling to get down.

Hannah took her from Elliott, but Claudia reached for Vicente. “I want my *tío*!” she cried. “Put me *down*.”

Vicente looked at her, but blankly, and then at Elliott again. “So you agree with Roosevelt?” he asked Elliott.

“On some things. Yes, I do.”

“Then why are you here? Why did you follow me here?” He did not look at Hannah, who struggled to keep Claudia in her arms.

“Because I’m your friend, and one of the last you’ve got,” Elliott said. “Are you going to drive us away, too?” Elliott waited, but when Vicente didn’t answer, he said. “All right, you win. My wife and I are going.” He took Hannah by the arm and turned her away.

Vicente struck his palm against the leather top of the desk. “Am I supposed to ask you to stay—at the cost of my convictions? Is that the option?”

“At the cost of keeping your mouth shut now and then,” Elliott said, turning back to him. “I’m not asking you to change your beliefs.”

“You’re asking me to overlook yours,” Vicente answered. “You’re just as greedy as Roosevelt. You call it progress, but it’s ambition. And greed. You don’t care what the Mexicans think about what you’re doing down there. Or what they want. You don’t even care how Hannah feels about it.”

“Do not dare to bring my wife into this.”

“Don’t either of you bring me into it,” Hannah said.

Claudia ceased her struggling, and clung to her mother. Vicente leaned forward and said in a whisper to Elliott, “While I was in Cuba shooting Spaniards for your country, you were in Mexico laying railroad track for profit. Does that make any sense to you?”

Elliott took Hannah by the arm. Claudia made a whimpering noise and reached for Vicente. Vicente made no movement toward her. He remained at his desk.

August 24.

Sweet dear, you are caught between two stubborn men. I could make things a little easier by being softer on the subject but I won't do that my dear. Don't write me any more about Vicente. I'm not the kind to hold a grudge, but the fact is, I have nothing to say. A man can't very well insult another man in the presence of his wife and expect the incident will be forgotten. I won't ask for a retraction because he's right in some of what he said, but I am put off by the whole thing. I suppose it is all right for him to come and see you. I know how much his friendship means to you. Pity him, if you want to, but leave me out of it. You are not going to win me over by writing about how much danger he is in, though I am sure it's more danger than he has ever been in before. His father has always protected him from the surlier Republicans as well as from the lawless bunch of liberals with whom he has pitched his tent. Why he pitched it with them I will never know. They will turn on him eventually. He will give them provocation. But he did choose that path.

November 15, Sweet heart,

I will be home for Christmas. I have been dreaming about you. The rheumatism is worse, and a minor case of influenza has settled in my head, but otherwise I am chipper enough.

Send me more of those newspaper predictions if you see them. I have shared them with everyone here though I don't believe them. What a shame that we can't know if they come true. It would take the globe at least several centuries to get cool enough that everyone would have to move to the equator, and it will be at least two hundred years before we know if people's hands and feet become smaller in industrialized countries.

Also send me news. I haven't been in the city for a while. I hear Roosevelt has said the U.S. might as well give Arizona back to the Apaches as give the Philippines back to Filipinos. I bet Vicente has got his presses rolling on that one. I have to say it touched a nerve down here among the Mexicans, as you might imagine.

Is there any recent news on the train wrecks in Pennsylvania—on how many were killed there at Exeter and the fate of the young scoundrel guilty of the prank in Schuylkill County? Let me know if you hear anything,

Give my love to the little one. Be firmer with her, dear.

Your devoted husband, Elliott.

By the beginning of 1900 the journal had mutated from a record of Hannah's life to a chronicle of Claudia's. Hannah was deeply in love with Claudia. They awakened in the mornings entangled, stretching their arms like flowers to the sunlight to make hand-shadows on the wall. Claudia talked in seamless conversation from dawn to night and refused to take naps and dictated lists of planned projects. While Elliott was away in Mexico, Vicente came to visit almost weekly, Jewell arrived for another visit, the tourist business escalated: Hannah often escorted groups of eight or nine individuals around the ruins and down into the kiva. Cleofita was living in the spare bedroom by now, and Señor Ruiz spent his days on the back porch swing and the parlor sofa. But Claudia was the presence around which all activities at Pecos now revolved. She was rude or charming to tourists, depending on her mood and if she liked them, and doled out small gifts—flowers and pieces of rock—as well as her improbable, unsettling and disdainful stare. She cracked pine nuts by stomping on them, leaving small grease spots on the floors and the rugs, to Cleofita's annoyance. She marched about in the valley, swinging a stick, carving pathways through the grass.

July 15, 1900

Dear heart—you mentioned headaches. Please go and visit Dr. Middleton, do not rely on Cleofita's herbs. I am concerned about you. Write and let me know. I have been missing you. I spent July 4th a hundred miles out in the Mexican desert, a lonely place for a U.S. citizen to spend the independence holiday. I had to celebrate by reading all of your recent letters over again.

What in the world is going on in China? We have only rudimentary news down here. The last I heard the Boxers had killed thousands and the Europeans and Americans that had not yet been murdered were under siege in Peking. I know some people working for the railroad in Peking. Send me any news you can. I am cut off here. I am cut off from you. Forgive my being gone so long, the time has not got away from me, I know it is nearly a year, but I would have to leave the situation in someone else's hands and there is no-one I trust. All our labors could be wasted if the balance of diplomacy is disrupted. I intend to break from here in two months time but I am the only one to deal successfully with the government and can't be spared at the moment.

I received the copy of *The Man That Corrupted Hadleyburg*, and have read it twice but the other book has not found me. Do not send anything else expensive as it will not find me. Things are at risk of kidnapping on both sides of the border.

I am glad you are happy my dear. But do go to the doctor.

Your loving husband, Elliott

October 15— My dear sweet girl. I will be home in the next few weeks. I might arrive from any point on the compass. They want me out in San Francisco for a few days but I won't go unless it is critical for me to do so, I am too anxious to get home to wife and child. I may stop in El Paso to see the opening of the Electric railroad if the date correlates with my schedule. As I hope it will. I am very excited about all of the progress. That news about the wireless telegraphy making it across the Atlantic excited me so much that I began to think that I could leap across the ocean myself. Everything good involves projection. It is all about getting past and getting over.

Speaking of that, I have decided to shove my pride under the rug and talk with Vicente when I get home. I suppose he is better at holding a grudge than I am, as he is lasting longer at it. He is a slave to his beliefs. He ought to get married and put his passions somewhere besides his newspaper. What about the book that he was writing? That seemed like a good endeavor. Has he left off? I had thought he might, as writing a long history does not involve much immediate conflict, and he has got to be stirring things up, he has got to have his finger in the pie.

Dear heart, can you locate several packages of a medicinal powder made by a German Company called Bayer? Send them to me in the city. I will be coming back to the city before I start home.

You may not recognize me when you see me. I have grown a beard, which I will certainly shave if you don't like it. And don't lecture me about my health. I would prefer you not do so.

Kiss the wee one for her papa. Keep writing the stories about her. I often read them several times over at night while the wolves are howling and I am thinking of you.

Your devoted husband, Elliott

November 3. Sweet wife, I will be home as promised, though there are problems with the trackage south of Juarez that I will have to see to on the way.

The copies of *Outdoor Life* arrived before I left the city, also the novel, but not the *Field and Stream.*

Yester-day I lost my favorite pocket compass and can hardly find my way around without it. It was stolen from my tent. I have been awfully nostalgic about it, wandering about and cursing my carelessness. I am badly morose about it. I am like a hound without a nose when I have no compass.

Sweet wife. Arthritis in my joints has become very bad indeed.

My dear. I lie awake at night wondering why I am here.

Look for me soon. Forgive this scrap of cheap paper.

Your loving husband, Elliott.

November 6. Claudia awoke before daylight calling very strangely for her papa. She was in bed with me and sat up suddenly calling for him as if she had heard him enter the house. She drifted back to sleep after awhile but I could not sleep myself after that and got up and made my coffee, and sat alone in the kitchen until daylight listening to the wind chimes. It must have been a dream that frightened her.

And that was the last entry of the final journal.

Bassie had written an afterword: her father had not returned. Hannah had shortly afterward been diagnosed with tuberculosis. Determined to cure herself, she made arrangements with her brother for Claudia to come live with him in Chicago temporarily while she moved into a hospital restricted to the care of patients with tuberculosis, called Saint Anthony's Sanitorium, in Las Vegas.

Jewell Cartwright delivered Claudia to Chicago, and Hannah never saw her daughter again.

Hannah was dead within a year. Her body was sent by train to Chicago.

Meg closed the book, and closed her eyes. She thought of the child, Claudia, four years old, seated beside Jewell Cartwright on the rattling train to Chicago, ascending through the hills and descending into the arroyo where the train on which her mother had traveled nine years before had derailed into flood waters, and climbing again through the mountains, passing through the long, dark tunnel at Raton that her father had conceived, coming out on the far side into the rush of air and sunlight. She must have felt a powerful sense of passage as the train clattered down through Trinidad and screeched along the serpentine windings across the continent to a city she had never seen, where she would live with an uncle whom she did not know.

At the age of seventeen, she had read her mother's journals, and four years later had boarded a train for New Mexico, crossing again the continent and the mountains and ravines, traveling past Las Vegas and on to Pecos, where she stood in the valley where the house had been, looking up at Dog Hill and the mesa and listening to the winds howl over the roofless old church ruins.

She had put the pieces together—all the pieces she could find. She had traveled down to Mexico to try to find her father's grave and learn about his death, and to search for any hint of a trail Vicente had left behind when he abandoned Las Vegas at Hannah's death, and went to Mexico and never returned. She hoped, above all, to find him.

She had found neither her father's grave nor Vicente, and had moved on with her life. She had become involved in the women's suffrage movement and earned her doctorate at Columbia with a specialty in Southwest cultures. She had married, and given birth to a daughter, and lost her husband in the war. And then she had turned to the past again and devoted herself to the journals. Time eventually had led her in a circle, back to the foothills of the Rockies. She was like an old dog trailing her own scent to find her way back home.

Meg thought of how Bassie had stood on Dog Hill only days ago, in her old fur coat, leaning on her cane beside the tent over her father's grave. But the image had begun to lose its immediate focus. Bassie seemed like a ghost already, blurred, and hollow at the core.

Meg lay on her bed at thc Plaza trying to bring a clear picture of Bassie back into her mind. The quiet of the room was oppressive. At two in the morning she got out of bed and straightened the room and began packing her suitcase for tomorrow's departure. She continued to try to conjure a solid image of Bassie. But the more she tried to remember, the less complete the picture became—all of the young years from the age of four on. The relationship with Hannah's brother—her uncle. The love affairs. The men. There must have been those. There were gaps in the story that Meg would now never be able to know. In her defensiveness toward Bassie, she had left too many questions unasked.

By the time daylight finally began to illuminate the curtains, Meg realized that whatever pathways had been opened to her out here in New Mexico, with the reading of the journals and discovery of the grave, the path most essential to her life up to this uncertain moment had, with Bassie's death, come to a close.

THIRTY-THREE

She left the Plaza Hotel for Jake Montoya's laboratory and the airport at eight o'clock that morning in a morose frame of mind, finding it difficult to say good-bye to Martin Estes. In addition to his other kind gestures, he refused to let her pay for the rooms. She was touched by his generosity and unable to express her gratitude adequately, and so her departure involved nothing more notable than an awkward half hour of dragging suitcases about and searching for room keys and car keys. Only after the bellman had placed the suitcases in the car and Meg had started for the highway did she feel some sense of relief to be leaving Las Vegas behind.

She stopped at the cemetery for half an hour and stood under the elm trees beside the soggy mound of black soil that was Bassie's grave. The tent had been removed and she was alone in the cemetery and felt an overwhelming strangeness at the thought of abandoning Bassie here. Bassie's suitcase was in the trunk of the car, and Meg pictured herself, alone, dragging it into the old house on Bouldin Street this evening.

Two hours later Meg was waiting for Jim in her car in the parking lot of the Maxwell Museum when he swung his pickup truck into the place next to hers and got out, scooping some books off the seat beside him. She emerged from her car hugging her coat around herself and noting that the books tucked under Jim's arm like schoolbooks were three volumes of Hannah's journals.

"It's a bigger campus than I thought," she remarked.

Jim answered with a few comments about how the campus had expanded, and together they started toward the building that housed the museum and anthropology department, a two-story structure surrounded by large cottonwoods. The trees had only a few leaves still clinging to their branches; fallen leaves lay thick on the ground, soggy and pungent from yesterday's rain.

"Bassie would have liked your eulogy," Meg offered.

But Jim seemed embarrassed by the subject. "I thought it went all right," he said dismissively.

"Why do you have the journals with you?"

"Montey wanted to see the passages about the dental work, for his report."

"I finished reading them," she said, shrugging her coat more tightly closed.

They passed through the entry to the anthropology department, and made their way along a corridor through a set of double doors into a room labeled the Laboratory of Human Osteology. It was a large room with no windows. Desks and workbenches lined the walls. No one was in sight, but nevertheless there was the impression of industry. Computers sat on almost every desk and tabletop. Above the desks were rows of cabinetry, and in the center of the room a partially assembled skeleton lay on a long table. Meg thought at first that this was Elliott's skeleton, but Jim, at a glance, told her it was not.

When Jake Montoya stepped out from behind a metal partition, he seemed smaller and less bearlike to Meg without his down jacket. "Come on back," he said.

They followed him around the partition to where Elliott's skeleton had been reassembled and laid out on a table. The vacant eye sockets stared blindly up at the ceiling, but the gap-toothed mouth seemed oddly expressive and lifelike now that the bottom jaw was reattached. The arms were not crossed as they had been in the grave, but extended down the sides of the torso with the forearms rotated and the palms facing up. Each of the bones, including the smallest, was labeled in ink with the same several-digit number. "Sorry about the ink," Montey said to Meg. "It's the case number. We have to do that."

She was glad that Montey didn't offer his condolences about Bassie. The usual obligatory offerings probably seemed unnecessary to a man who spent so much of his time with the dead, she decided, and would have been perfunctory in this setting.

Jim handed Montey the volumes. "I marked the references," he said. "The dental work is mentioned in a couple of places. He had two amalgam fillings and at least two gold ones. And the vulcanite device." His eyes settled on a brown, plastic-looking piece that lay on the table beside the skull, two stained molars protruding from it.

"Yep, that's the vulcanite," Montey told him.

Jim bent over and studied it, then turned to Montey again. "In that volume on top," he told him, "I marked where Hannah mentioned buying the mechanical pencils from the Ward catalog."

Montey flipped the journal open to the page where Jim had placed a torn piece of paper for a marker, read the passage to himself, and then set that volume aside and looked in the next one. He read aloud Bassie's footnote about vulcanite and how Charles Goodyear and his attorney, Daniel Webster, spent a fortune defending the patents. "She was thorough," he said, shaking his head in admiration. "Here she's got the history of the regulation of dentistry." He looked at Meg. "What you have to remember," he said, "is that everything you're looking at here on the table depicts a life experience. The fillings don't just help identify the person, they tell us what he went through. Fillings were done with a pedal-operated drill that turned a thousand times more slowly than what we've got today. And there were no deadening injections. After the cavity was drilled it would have been filled with hot melted metal. That's why a lot of people let their teeth rot out instead of going to the dentist. But your great-grandfather was meticulous. He had all of his cavities taken care of."

Jim was looking at the burial artifacts laid out on the shelf beside the table, and Meg stepped over beside him. The artifacts had been cleaned, but most of them were tarnished or corroded. The abraded bones belonging to the dog Milton and the smaller ones of Paco the Chihuahua were still in boxes, except for Paco's skull, the shattered pieces of which had been fastidiously reassembled, revealing the hole where the bullet had entered at the back of the left side, and the place where it had exited the jaw.

"The dog was shot at close range by someone standing behind him and firing with his left hand," Montey said. "Like this." He positioned his trigger finger against the side of the dog's skull, aiming downward and forward. Then he took from the shelf the jewelry charm shaped like a dog and turned it over in his fingers. "We found it in the 1898 Ward's catalog," he said. "Also in a few contiguous years. If your grandmother was born in '96 then it could very well have belonged to her, just like she remembered." He put the charm back on the shelf and tapped his finger beside the corroded shaving razor. "Also in the '98 Ward catalog. And the same with the comb. So far, your grandmother is batting a thousand on her memory. We found the camera in the 1900 catalog but without the hinge. It's a Kodak Brownie. The hinges were put on in June of 1900, so Elliott could have bought this anytime after that. I understand he was in Mexico all of that year but he could have got it there secondhand. The point is, these cameras were around early enough for Elliott to have owned this one."

"What about the film?" Jim asked.

"Prentis is doing some voodoo on it, trying to get some images. We'll see." He pointed to a pile of six brass buttons. "Manufactured trouser buttons, Jordan Marsh catalog, 1894," he said.

"Fly buttons?" Jim asked.

"That's right. And these are suspender buckles. And jacket buttons here—not dress jacket but coat jacket. Which suggests he was buried in the winter, without a lot of ceremony. He wasn't laid out in his Sunday best."

Meg looked at the square jaw of the skull and the large front teeth with the distinctive gap between them.

"Shirt buttons, same period," Montey was saying. "And the coins all predate 1900—the peso is the latest date, 1897. Now these boot remnants"—he indicated a stack of irregularly shaped pieces of what appeared to Meg to be tattered leather and some nails and eyeholes—"don't tell us much, except that from the number of eyeholes we can figure they were high-tops and laced up to the calves. They weren't dress shoes, weren't cowboy boots, and they certainly weren't slippers. And then of course there are the tools. But no compass. He'd lost his compass—isn't that what you told me, Jim?"

"That's what he wrote to Hannah."

"And then here's the leather cover to some kind of a receipt book, or notebook. The pages, as you know, are gone except for these adhered to the leather." He flipped the cover open. "I had a specialist look at the writing. He transcribed this legible entry, which is basically a record of some fruit—a lot of fruit—purchased in Mexico. Apples and canned peaches. But he couldn't make anything out of the other entries. If you want to see his transcript, I've got it, but I don't think there's anything in it you weren't able to read yourself."

He turned back to the skeleton. "He was about fifty years old," he said. "Five foot six, probably five-seven when he was younger and in better health. Definitely left-handed. The joint disfigurement is rheumatoid arthritis but there's osteoarthritis too. You can see the osteo here, mostly in the peripheral joints. And if you look here, there's even some sign of it progressing to the vertebrae—these cervical vertebrae here. Which means he was in a lot of pain. I mean *a lot* of pain." He turned to Meg. "Have you ever been around anybody with advanced rheumatoid arthritis?"

"No," she said.

"It doesn't affect just the joints," he told her. "It's systemic. It can get in the lymph system and cause heart arrhythmias, also arthralgias, myalgias, you name it. It can get in the lungs. It can stop the kidneys, in which case the person can't urinate and the toxins kill him. By everything I'm seeing here, your great-grandfather was in pretty bad shape. Rheumatoid tends to be bilateral and symmetrical, as you can see it is here." He indicated the wrists, knees, ankles, and elbows on both sides. "Osteo is random. See these knots here"—he pointed to the knuckles—"that's rheumatoid. All this damage is from friction. Bone against bone. What rheumatoid does not do is fuse the bones together. They lock, and they're stiff, but they're not fused like they are in osteoarthritis." He paused, then said, "He was a tough hombre, I'll tell you that, if he was still on his feet before he died."

"He was on his feet," Jim said. "He was working."

"Pretty damn excruciating," Montey said.

"He referred to the pain, in his letters," Meg said. "But I wouldn't have thought it was at that level."

"It might not have been when he mentioned it," Montey said. "These things can flare up pretty rapidly. All I can tell you is that he was suffering." He shifted his eyes to Meg; his voice lowered a notch. "Now we get to the hard part." He turned back to the skeleton. "The bullet isn't in the brain case," he said. "I didn't expect it would be, judging from this here." He pointed to the decimated area of bone in the upper left front part of the skull. "This is where it exited," he said. "Anyway, I did a radiograph just to be sure there was no bullet in there, and I didn't turn up anything but some lead fragments. The caliber was about a .44, judging from the size of the hole. Generally speaking, the bullet can't be larger than the hole it makes, unless there's some kind of intermedial target and it gets fragmented in transit. Which wasn't the case here. You can tell by the range. This is pretty much a point-blank shot from a .44 pistol. There were .44 rifles, but this was a pistol shot." He pointed at the bullet hole in the temple on the right-hand side of the skull. "The bullet went in here, with a slightly upward, slightly forward slant," he said. "And then passed through to here. The skull here at the exit is shattered into exactly fourteen pieces. I've seen this trajectory at OMI, more times than I like to remember. It's a classic suicide trajectory."

Meg stood looking at Montey.

She heard Jim say in a flat voice, "It would be, for a right-handed person. Which Elliott wasn't."

"Yes, but look here," Montey answered, and beckoned the two of them to come around the table. He pointed out a grooved, rough area of bone on the left shoulder. "He didn't have much use of this arm," he said. "Because of the arthritis. So he used his right arm."

Jim studied the bone.

"It would be unlikely for anybody other than himself to have pulled the trigger from this range, at this angle," Montey was saying. "The trajectory is too precise. It's textbook." He looked at Jim. "You don't believe it," he said. "I can tell by the look on your face."

"No, I don't," Jim said.

"I think you've been holding this guy up to the light for too long," Montey told him. "He's started to take on a supernatural glow." He shook his head. "He was human, Jim."

"He wasn't the type to kill himself."

"I don't know about type," Montey said. "I just know about bones."

"He wouldn't do this," Jim insisted. "What is the explanation for why he would do this? What would have driven him to it?" He stared at the bullet wounds, and then said, "What about the gun used on the dog?"

"Same caliber," Montey answered. "My assumption is that he shot the dog and then shot himself."

"You said the dog was shot from the left. From behind. Why would he kill the dog with his left hand and then kill himself with his right?"

"Because he couldn't lift his left arm. It's one thing to hold a gun down this way"—he extended his trigger finger toward the floor—"and another to raise it to your head. He couldn't have done that with that shoulder. This is cut-and-dried to me, Jim. I know you feel like you knew the man. But things happen, and people do the unexpected, and what we've got in front of us is evidence of that. My finding to the OMI has to be that these are Elliott Bass's bones, and the cause of death is self-inflicted gunshot wound."

Meg was attempting to arrive at some genuine emotion in response to what was being said. But her feelings were transitory. Scenes from the journals passed through her mind. Jim, she could see, was suffering the same charged puzzlement.

He said, "I'd like to see that transcript from the notebook cover."

"Okay," Montey said, "but I don't know what you expect to find. I think you're looking harder for something than you should be."

"And I think you're being fairly goddamn condescending," Jim said.

Montey only half repressed a smile. "The transcript is in my office. I'll go get it. You realize that only one of the notations made on that page was legible, and it was in a different handwriting from the others."

"I realize."

When Montey was gone, Meg said, "Would you rather think Hannah and Vicente had something to do with killing Elliott?"

"I'd rather not know any of this," Jim replied.

"You can't bring yourself to believe he killed himself."

"Not unless there's something we don't know."

"Clearly, Jim, there's a lot we don't know."

"But something had to push him over the edge."

"Maybe he figured out about Hannah and Vicente. Or it could have been the arthritis—if the pain was as bad as Montey said."

"Elliott could take the pain. You've read his letters."

"When I was reading last night I figured out how he got home without anybody recognizing him," Meg said. "He'd grown a beard. He said so in one of the letters. So he might have come through the station in Las Vegas without anybody knowing who he was. And I also think I know why he wasn't buried in a casket. He asked Hannah not to in one of the letters."

"I don't remember that," Jim said.

"He wrote it like a joke, but I don't think it was. He was talking about how much he would hate a sedentary life, and said he would also hate a sedentary death. That it would be a terrible faux pas for her to bury him in a casket. If it was Hannah and Vicente that buried him, I think she took him at his word. Otherwise, it seems like they would at least have put him in something."

Montey returned to the room with a piece of paper that he gave to Jim. Meg stepped over and they studied it together. It documented the purchase of apples and canned peaches on November 10th of 1900 from Smith and Everts Fruit Company in C. Juárez. Meg said, "I wonder if the company is still in business."

"Well, there's a thought," Jim said.

"Though I don't know what it would tell us, if they were," Meg added.

Jim stood looking at the typed transcript. "It wouldn't hurt just to call and find out if they're still there," he said. "We know it's in Juárez." He looked at Montey. "Do you have a phone in here?"

"Right over there," Montey said, indicating a desk near the door. "Just dial nine to get a line out."

Jim went over to the phone, and when he was connected with Mexican information he requested a number for Smith and Everts Fruit Company in Juárez. He repeated the request a second time, this time in Spanish, and then, after an exchange in Spanish, hung up. "No listing," he said.

"They were checking in Ciudad Juárez?" Montey asked.

Jim nodded.

"There may be another Juárez," Montey said. "My aunt used to live down there and I think I remember her mentioning à Juárez that was some kind of a Mormon settlement. The Mormon Capital of Chihuahua, I think is what she called it." He chuckled, repeating the phrase, "Mormon Capital of Chihuahua. That's pretty funny."

But Jim didn't bother to pretend he was amused. "Is it near Ciudad Juárez?" he asked.

"I believe so," Montey said.

Jim picked up the phone again and eventually was connected to an operator in Mexico with whom he conversed in clumsy Spanish. At one point he placed his hand over the receiver and said to Montey, "Do you speak this any better than I do?" But Montey shook his head.

"*Un otra Juárez,*" Jim said into the phone. "*No, no es Ciudad Juárez. Creo que hay un otro pueblo se llama Juárez también. Es más pequeño de Ciudad Juárez. Pero creo que es en la misma area.*" At last he said, "*Colonia Juárez?*" He looked at Montey, who nodded. "*Sí,*" Jim said into the phone. "*Es bien. Necesito un número para Smith y Everts Fruit Company. Es una empresa que se venden frutas.*" In a moment he began searching the desktop, and located a pencil and a scrap of paper. He wrote a number down, and then hung up the phone. "It's still there," he said. "Smith and Everts is still in business." Before Meg could respond, he was dialing another number. "Hey, Phil," he said when he got an answer. "I need you to check on something for me, if you would. Look on those shelves beside my desk; you'll find a set of Hannah's journals. Get out volume four and look in the index under 'Smith.' I'm pretty sure that's the name of the Mormon guy Elliott lived with after the massacre. What I need are his initials." He paused, listening. "Yeah, the last name's 'Smith,' but there were also some initials." He waited, looking at Meg and Montey, and then his attention was drawn back to Phil's voice on the phone. "That's it. E. H. Smith. Thanks." He hung up, and then dialed the number for Smith and Everts Fruit Company. "*Hola,*" he said. "*Habla Usted ingles?*" The answer was affirmative, as Jim proceeded to introduce himself in English as the archaeologist at Pecos Pueblo in New Mexico. "We've run across a situation," he said, "where I need to talk to somebody who might know something about the history of your company." He waited, and then took up the pencil again. When he had finished writing, he said, "Yes. Thank you, I'll call him. That's very helpful. In the meantime, I'm wondering if you could tell me when the company was founded, and who the original owners were." His eyes settled on Meg's. "Yes. That's what I needed to know. Thank you very much." He hung up the telephone. "Founded in 1887," he said. "By two partners. William Everts, and Edmund Hoyle Smith. That would be E. H. Smith."

"You're thinking it's the E. H. Smith that Elliott was forced to live with after the massacre?" Meg asked.

"It's possible."

"And what would that mean?"

"I don't know exactly, but I want to go down there and see if I can find out."

"To Mexico?"

He nodded.

"Because Elliott bought some fruit from a guy there?"

"Because he came home to Pecos afterwards and shot himself, according to Montey."

Montey had not commented until now. "I don't know what you're trying to get at, Jim, but I think you're grasping at straws," he said. "Still, it's getting interesting."

"They told me to talk with Andrew Smith, who's part of the Smith family that still owns the company," Jim said. "He teaches history at a school there. Juárez Stake Academy."

"What if I go with you?" Meg asked. "How far is it?"

He considered her. "Let's look at a map."

Montey went to his office and returned with a map, which they spread across the desk. Jim calculated the mileage. "I'd say we could drive it in eight hours," he concluded. "Depending on traffic at the border. We could probably get there by dark." He looked at her. "We can turn right around if we want to, or if we have to stop, we can." He paused. "So, what do you think? Do we call the guy, or just go?"

"We should make sure he's there, at least," Meg said.

Jim placed a call to the Juárez Stake Academy at the phone number given him by the employee of the fruit company, requesting to talk with

Andrew Smith. He was told that Mr. Smith was, at the moment, teaching a class, but could return the call shortly. "I'll call him later," Jim said.

When he was off the phone, he said to Meg, "We'll call him from the road."

She thought about it. "I need to cancel my flight," she said at last. "And call the car rental place. Are we taking the truck?"

He nodded.

Dragging her airplane ticket out of her purse, she called the airline and postponed her reservation, while Jim went into Montey's office to call Judith.

By the time Jim returned, Meg had left Montey in the laboratory and was already outside, leaning far into the trunk of the rental car for protection from the drizzling rain and searching her suitcase for a cosmetic bag and other overnight necessities.

THIRTY-FOUR

When they had pulled onto the highway, Jim reached over and opened the glove compartment and removed a packet of chewing gum, offering a piece to Meg and taking one himself. They drove for a while, chewing the gum in silence except for the sound of the windshield wipers and the exchange of a few remarks about the route and the need for gasoline. At last Meg ventured to ask, "Did you get hold of Judith?"

"I did," Jim replied. He made no other comment for a moment, and then said, "She wasn't thrilled about the idea. But you shouldn't think that has anything to do with you." He paused. "Or with me, for that matter. The main problem seems to be that I was supposed to drive carpool in the morning." He glanced in the rearview mirror, changing lanes. "Judith had an affair with one of her clients a couple of years ago on a rafting trip. We haven't gotten past it yet."

Uncertain how to respond to this revelation, Meg watched the road in front of her, the cars maneuvering between lanes.

At last Jim said, "When I tried to call you a couple of days ago, several times, and you didn't call me back—I'm wondering why that was."

"I guess I was preoccupied with Mother."

"I think it's more than that," he said. "But you're inscrutable at the moment."

"I just usually handle things better on my own," she answered.

He accelerated to pass a U-Haul that was holding up traffic.

After a moment, Meg said, "Have you tried to get past the affair?"

"I'm not sure I want to," he answered. He adjusted the heat control and took the chewing gum out of his mouth, wrapping it in a dirty napkin from a Burger King and stuffing the napkin into a plastic cup. He turned his blinker on and exited the highway, pulling into the parking lot of a strip mall and parking outside a small used-book store. "I need a guidebook on Mexico that has something about Colonia Juárez," he said.

Inside the store they located the travel section and scanned the indexes of guidebooks to northern Mexico for a listing. Meg finally found one in a travel guide for Chihuahua, and read it aloud to Jim. The colony, it said, had been settled in 1887 by Mormons attempting to escape U.S. polygamy laws. Most of the one thousand current inhabitants of the town were descended from the original settlers and relied on fruit farming and ranching for a livelihood. The town was best known for its school, Juárez Stake Academy, which held classes for kindergartners through twelfth graders using a bilingual curriculum that fulfilled requirements for both U.S. and Mexican high schools and diplomas. Students typically boarded with Mormon families in the town.

After they had looked through several more guidebooks and found no further information, they moved briefly to the history section in search of general background on Mormon settlements in Mexico, but discovered only one reference, listing the several colonies that had been founded at the turn of the century and stating that most of them had been abandoned during the Mexican Revolution and were never resettled.

Jim purchased the book while Meg used the pay phone near the restrooms to call Paul at his office. "I'm not going to get home today," she told Paul. "It's a long story, but I have to drive down to Mexico. I can probably get a flight out tomorrow but I'm not sure when. Or it might be the next day. So I'm just wondering—do you still have that appointment in Austin tomorrow?"

"Tomorrow afternoon," he said.

"Would you mind going by Bassie's house to water some plants? I can tell you where the key is hidden. I think they were almost dry when we left, and they're probably just barely hanging in there."

"I guess I could do that."

"I know it's out of your way."

"But you're possibly going to be home tomorrow?" he said, and she briefly took this to mean that he was looking forward to seeing her.

Then he added, "I mean, I'm not sure that a day is going to make much difference."

"You mean for the plants?"

"Yes."

"Forget it, then," she said.

"No. I'll do it. I don't have a problem with doing it. It's just that I didn't think Bassie cared that much about those plants. Weren't you the one who always took care of them? And now—" He stopped himself, having apparently realized, even later than Meg did, where this thought was going.

"And now—what?" Meg pressed. "Now that Bassie's dead, who cares about her fucking plants?"

"That's not what I meant. It's just that," he paused, "it's the difference between my getting home in time to work out, and not. If I go by her house, I'm going to be stuck in traffic. And if it's just the difference of one or two days for the plants, then—"

She hung up the phone before he finished, and turned to see Jim looking at her.

"That was Paul," she said, by way of explanation.

Leaving the city limits of Albuquerque they passed a stretch of desert and several villages and the ruins of an old pueblo. The sky began to clear as the afternoon wore on, and the sun broke through. They stopped at a taco joint and purchased chicken tacos, and ate them as they drove, and then stopped at a convenience store for gasoline and bottled water. Meg put gasoline in the truck while Jim used the pay phone to try to reach Andrew Smith at Juárez Stake Academy. She watched him talking on the phone. He fished a pen out of his shirt pocket and a wrinkled receipt out of his khaki pants and wrote against the wall. Returning to the truck, he said, "All right. He's expecting us."

"What did you tell him?" Meg asked.

"I told him we had found a receipt book from 1900 with his company's name in it, and were trying to solve an old mystery. Here's the kicker. He wasn't surprised."

"What do you mean?"

"He asked if this had anything to do with Elliott Bass's grave. I said it did, and he told me he would meet us at the school. He doesn't think we'll be there until eight or nine o'clock tonight. He gave me directions of how to get there."

"So, what do you think is going on?" she asked when they were back in the truck and pulling onto the highway again.

"I think he's read about the grave, and he figures there's a link."

"Did he sound defensive?"

"Not in the least."

They drove on toward Socorro. Jim talked of how the landscape had changed over the years, and about a camping trip he had once taken with Billy in the Manzano Mountains to the east. Billy had been five years old at the time, and Jim had bought him a new sleeping bag. They had read a Dr. Seuss book and the story of Icarus from a children's mythology book beside the firelight. Meg asked him if his own father had ever had the chance to take him camping when he was a boy, before the accident.

"If he did, I don't remember," Jim said, and in a moment he added, "I used to envy Bassie because she had the journals. I didn't have anything like that from my parents. Just some photographs." He hesitated. "I started keeping a journal, with that in mind, after Billy was born. Just so the kids would have some way to know me if anything should happen to me when they were young. But you can imagine how circumspect it was. With all the self-censorship, when I was writing with the kids in mind. I ended up tossing it out."

"Because it wasn't interesting?"

"Because it wasn't really my life. It was a record of my days. You know—'got up at six, took the dog out, went for a run, went to work . . .' I couldn't put my real life in there. My conflicts with Judith. I guess I decided I'd rather the kids not have any image of me, than to think I was that dull." He paused. "It matters to me, what they think. Raising kids wasn't the thing I expected to do with my life, but it's what I've been most successful at. When Billy was six, every time I looked at him I saw myself and what I went through at that age. All I wanted to do was protect him and Meredith. And I've managed to do that."

"You know what I think?" Meg said. "I think you're a terrific father."

"Driven by fear of not being," he answered. "It's why I've tried so hard to make the marriage work."

He talked about growing up on the horse farm in Kentucky where his grandfather had been the foreman. They spoke of Elliott and Hannah. Meg tried to explain the nature of her relationship with Bassie, and the tenuous nature of her relationship with her mother. She tried to explain her mother, but found herself talking mostly about her father, and then about Bassie again. "I remember when things used to feel like they were falling apart, and I would look at Bassie, and she always seemed steady. I always thought it was everything else that was going to fall apart."

They shared a gallon jug of water and watched the mountains close around the road and then withdraw and become more distant again. Jim spoke of the geography and wildlife and of Cabeza de Vaca journeying westward from Florida for nine years on foot and learning six Indian languages along the way, and about Coronado and the discovery of the pass through the mountains of northern Chihuahua, which eventually became a trade route and resulted in the settlement of Cuidad Juárez and El Paso. He talked of the U.S. invasions and purchases of land from Mexico, and pulled over at a deserted roadside tourist lookout, where he and Meg got out of the truck and stood at the rail watching a hawk glide over the canyon.

They were following the basic railroad route that Elliott had surveyed when he was young, long before he knew Hannah, and in places they caught glimpses of the tracks, mostly to the left of them, winding along the Rio Grande. Jim exited the highway and looped through a dilapidated commercial area in a small town in order to show Meg a discovery he had made long ago of a street named Bass Street. Elliott Bass, the famous survey engineer—the marker on the street informed them—had camped here with his survey team, and a town eventually had grown up around the campsite.

Jim said he had not returned to this street since he had first discovered it twenty years before. It was not as he remembered it, but marred with potholes and lined with rusting warehouses, and he made no attempt to hide his disappointment.

When they were back on the highway, Meg rolled her coat into a ball and used it as a pillow against the window, closing her eyes against the afternoon sunlight that had spread itself glaringly over the landscape and the pavement. Later, she awakened to the monotonous reverberations of the motor.

They passed the U.S. inspections stop at Elephant Butte and a series of small desert towns, the Franklin Mountains looming on the horizon to the east, and then ascended through the mountain passes into El Paso, a metropolis of half a million people and the northern gateway to Ciudad Juárez. It was a gritty, large, unnerving city, nestled at the south end of a barren mountain range. Meg had seen it from the air and from the airport when she and Bassie had changed planes here on their way to Albuquerque.

Jim stopped to change some money, and then they maneuvered their way through the traffic toward the border crossing. Juárez was spread across the valley below them in a haze of pollution, with old steel mills and slums lining the river. The river was brown and shallow. They descended, approaching the bridge in a cloud of car exhaust and factory fumes. The railroad trestle spanned the river upstream from the bridge, cut off from the land by large gates. A crowd had gathered on the Mexican side, waiting for the gates to open and admit a train, so they could run the tracks across the river. No one seemed to be there to stop them from doing so. Meg watched them waiting at the gates, and wondered what Elliott would think of the end results of his labors. He had brought the Santa Fe Railroad down through here. He had dragged the Mexican Central thousands of miles farther across the Mexican deserts. It was easy, with the advantage of time, to condemn the effect as conquest motivated by American greed.

The bridge across the river was noisy, with several lanes of traffic moving in both directions and pedestrian lanes on either side. Jim rolled down the window of the truck and presented his vehicle registration and driver's license to the customs officer. The officer examined the documents, looked in through the window at Meg, and then asked Jim how long they would be staying in Mexico and how far into the interior they intended to go. After Jim had made it clear that he and Meg were only day tourists and would stay no more than a day and a night at most, the man asked for a credit card imprint to guarantee that the truck would be returned across the border. After he had made the imprint, he waved them through.

They crossed the bridge and entered the old part of Juárez on a busy street lined for the first few blocks primarily with bridal shops, their windows crowded with mannequins in wedding gowns, and then with entire blocks of pharmacies and dental offices.

By the time they had made their way through the traffic in a congested part of the city and were beyond the city limits, entering more barren areas, the afternoon shadows had lengthened. The roads narrowed, bordered by farms and occasional fruit orchards. Hills became rolling; livestock grazed in pastures fenced by barbed wire, and flat-topped mountains rose in the distance against the darkening sky. At last the truck rounded a curve and Meg and Jim could see, in the dusky light, the valley with Colonia Juárez and its fruit orchards, the fruit trees growing in rows out of the rocky soil.

It was a small community, surrounded by ranches. The houses were an odd assortment of architecture, everything from frame to stucco structures and red brick bungalows. There was not much of a commercial district. Following the directions that Andrew Smith had given, they wound their way down to a two-story stone building with pillars out front. A chain-link fence surrounded the property and a wide cement walkway led up to the entrance. This was the Juárez Stake Academy.

The gate was open, and most of the building was dark, though some of the rooms on the ground floor and two on the top were lit. Meg and Jim could see, as they approached the arched front doors, that the lighted rooms on the ground floor were classrooms. Someone was cleaning in one of the rooms, and in another a teacher and a student who appeared to be high school age were working at a chalkboard.

They found the front doors locked, but the sidelights revealed a man seated on a bench in the entry hall with a stack of papers he was leafing through. He rose when he heard Jim attempt to open the door, and admitted them into the building, introducing himself as Andrew Smith. He was younger than Meg had expected; she assessed him as about thirty. His hair was blond, his torso plump, and his face boyish and likable, if too pale. He was wearing a white button-down shirt with a striped tie, and pleated navy-blue trousers.

The entry hall into which he admitted them was broad and had the cold, expansive feel particular to old stone buildings that have seen a lot of use. It generated a hollow sound when they spoke. Andrew Smith led them up the stairs to the second floor, inquiring if their drive had been pleasant, and if they had had any difficulty finding the town. Halfway down the hall on the second floor he escorted them into an office that was not large, but had the smell of opulence, with polished wood and an oversized desk lamp with a large shade that outshone the vague overhead lighting. After motioning for them to sit in the chairs opposite his desk, he took a seat behind the desk, and only then did an awkward silence descend. For a moment, he seemed to stall. He fumbled at some papers, shuffling them from the center of the desk to the far side, and then placing his elbows heavily on the space that he had cleared. "So how can I help you?" he asked.

Jim pulled from his coat pocket the transcript of the entry from the ledger book. "I understood from our phone conversation that you know about Elliott Bass's grave being found at Pecos," he said.

"I read about it in the papers," Andrew Smith replied.

"And you know who Elliott Bass was?"

"I do."

"We found a notebook in the grave," Jim said, "with the pages missing, except that there was a record on the end page of a purchase apparently made from your company in November of 1900."

Andrew Smith took the transcript and read it. He settled back into his chair and looked at Jim, and then at Meg. "You're his . . . what—great?—granddaughter?" he asked.

"That's right," Meg said. "How did you know?"

"I did some research on your family a few years ago," he explained. He sighed deeply, placing his hands behind his head and looking up at the ceiling, and then placing them in his lap and looking at Meg. "I read Hannah Bass's journals." He hesitated. "This is complicated," he said.

They let him wrestle a moment in silence. At last he said, "My father lived here in Colonia Juárez, as did his father and grandfather and great-grandfather, who was the one who started the fruit orchard and built the cannery. My brothers run the company now."

He paused, moving the papers on his desk again from one side to the other but leaving the space in the middle cleared, and then took from the pocket of his pants a ring of keys, one of which he inserted into a drawer of the desk, withdrawing a lengthy document of a number of pages paperclipped together. Meg could see that the pages were old. The paper appeared to have been handled a great deal. "My brothers and sisters have thought I was doing the wrong thing to hold on to this," he said. "But my father left it for me, specifically, and I always thought that if he wanted it to be destroyed, he would have done that himself." He paused. "The truth is, I haven't known what to do with it. And now . . . this comes up. I guess God intends me to show it to you." With a smile that seemed forced, he added, "I can't imagine He brought you all this way so I could lie to you about it." He seemed to continue to weigh the decision, and finally said, "It concerns an incident very sensitive to Mormon history. And to my family. You might guess that I'm talking about the massacre at Mountain Meadows. There are a lot of Mormons who don't believe in calling it a massacre, but I think we ought to call it what it was."

He had begun, Meg noticed, to perspire. He drew a handkerchief out of his pants pocket and wiped his forehead. "There are a lot of Mormons today who still deny that our church is responsible for what happened," he said. "Or they try to justify it. But it's my belief that the only way we're ever going to get past it is to admit that we did it, and that it was a crime, and never the will of God." He was looking only at Meg now. "The main reason I feel this so strongly," he said, "is this document."

He picked it up and handed it across the desk to Meg. "I think it will speak for itself," he said, and then added, "which is actually a relief to me, since I don't want to have to speak for it. I should tell you that my family would be opposed to my showing it to you. It would be a favor to me if you would simply look at it and give it back." He stood up. "I'll leave you alone to read. Come and find me when you're finished. It was written by my great-great-grandfather the week before he died, in 1934."

. . . . .

When Meg and Jim were alone, they sat looking at the door through which Andrew Smith had departed. It was a moment before they brought themselves to look at the document. The room was cold, the windows dark; Jim pulled his chair in close to Meg's, and both of them read silently to themselves, remarking on nothing until they were finished, the air disturbingly quiet and smelling of pastewax, the desklight shining fiercely on the words.

February 16, 1934.

I, George Parley Smith, having lived according to the mandate of the Lord, as a righteous and devout believer, a member of the Church of Jesus Christ of Latter-day Saints, now face my death with a clean conscience, knowing I have served God faithfully in all that He has called me to do. I have no regrets in my life but one—the subject of this confession—and that is the fate of the orphans whose parents were sacrificed at Mountain Meadows in 1857. I participated in that event as a sixteen year old boy, and under my father's orders, having convinced myself, though with a heavy conscience, that I was doing the work of the Lord and that my reluctance in the work was due only to my being yet unworthy as a true soldier of His will.

I will not here provide a specific account of the massacre and how it came to happen, as I am not in the business of confession for anyone other than myself. It is sufficient to say that it happened. It is sufficient to say that my father was among those who believed that events that day, and on the days previous, unfolded according to the will of the Lord. When the killing began, I was stationed between the wagon that was bearing the wounded and the smallest children, and the women and older children who were following on foot. My orders were to kill every emigrant who fell within my reach, but for the smallest children, too young to atone for their parents' sins and too young to tell tales. These children were to be spared. I was to fire my gun and make use of a knife given me that day solely for that purpose. These orders I fulfilled in part, discharging my gun several times before withdrawing from the bloodshed. On one occasion at least my aim was accurate. One of the emigrant women was running in the direction of the wagon that carried the youngest children, rather than away toward the hills, and I shot her as she came near. I also discharged into the backs of a number of fleeing women who were attempting to escape with their children. There was a man of our party who spent his ammunition rapidly and when I saw him set to work with his knife on two children no more than nine or ten years of age, who clung to him for mercy, even as he cut their throats, I then took my gun and withdrew. It was at this point that I encountered Elliott Bass. He was at the side of a woman who without question was dead, having several arrows lodged in her back, either by the Indians who assisted us, or by one of our party, many of whom were dressed in the guise of Indians. In the midst of the carnage the boy did not leave the woman's side, but attempted diligently and forcefully to extract the arrows from her back. As her body made no movement except by his exertion, I knew her to be dead. The exertion of the boy was so intense that I recall the sweat on his face and the way he grimaced and the sounds he made in his effort. He showed no sign of fear, and no awareness of danger, and when told at gunpoint to stand, refused even to glance in the direction of the speaker. I thought he would be shot without consideration, but he kept to his task, and when the killing was finished, he was seated by the woman, whom I presumed to be his mother, without any sign of awareness toward anyone but her. He refused to move when told to do so, and was at last captured with his hands bound. He was put in the wagon with the other children. This I observed.

An event then took place on which I will not elaborate, as there is nothing to be said to justify or explain it. A girl was brought to the wagon and was deemed too old to be spared. She was then removed a few feet distant and shot within sight of the other children by a man with whom I was well acquainted. This girl, I later learned, was a sister to Elliott Bass. I believe her to have been his only sibling. I know that he witnessed the killing, from the wagon, with his hands and feet bound, as I saw him do so, though to my knowledge he never spoke of it afterwards.

It is a known fact that the children who had not been sacrificed were driven to the house of Jacob Hamblin, and there separated and assigned to homes among the members of our faith. Elliott Bass was taken to live with us. We were instructed by church elders to change his name but were unsuccessful, as he was too mature to forget his given name, and refused to answer to another. Therefore we continued to call him Elliott. A small girl, well-spoken for her size, by my estimate about three years of age, was also assigned to us, though it was decided that either she or Elliott Bass would later be removed to another household so that they might more easily adjust to their homes and to the Church. However, the small girl, whom my parents referred to as Nancy, though she was previously known by another name, was dependent on the influence and care of Elliott Bass, as if he were her brother, and for this reason my mother pled that the two should remain together. On occasions when Elliott was hired out to work, Nancy was despondent to the point she would not eat. I tried to befriend her, as did my siblings, but it was only Elliott Bass whom she wanted, and always when he was not in her presence she was subdued and watchful for his return. I also befriended Elliott, attempting in this way to pacify my conscience and atone for my part in the killings, believing, as my father had told me, that if we were to save the souls of these children we would further justify our cause. After several weeks in our home he was partially won over by my mother's kindness but did not, I believe, ever lose suspicion toward us. He was primarily mute and withdrawn, reticent toward my father, though after some time he became cooperative and a hard worker. My father at times was forced to discipline him, as he was hostile to religion. On more than one occasion he refused to pray, and once spat on the Bible during his first days in our home. But after several months with us he was more compliant. I believe that his emotions were shut off. Several times he was heard reminding the girl, Nancy, of her true given name and the names of those in her family, so that she would not forget them. My father reprimanded him severely, convincing him that the effort would only harm the child, and eventually Elliott ceased to do it. He once, when I was with him, accosted a Mormon woman on the street in Cedar City whom he recognized to be wearing one of his mother's dresses. This woman he approached, and in a voice devoid of emotion said, "That is my mother's dress." The woman denied it, claiming to have bartered the dress from an Indian, but this I know not to be true. After having resided with us for several weeks Elliott came to me one day and requested me to go with him to Mountain Meadows so that he might bury his mother and his sister, whom he supposed would still be lying on the open ground. My father being away on business, I took it on my own advisement to comply with the request, against my mother's wishes, and Elliott and I took the wagon and went to the place, half a day's journey away. This event is among the most disturbing of my memories. The bodies of the dead had remained on the ground since the day of the event, and Elliott was able to recognize his mother only by the shoestring that secured her hair. I will not attempt to describe his feelings as he wandered among the dead in search of her, as I cannot know them, but I will say it was a hellish thing to watch him do so. In spite of his usual abilities to every situation at hand, he was a pitiful sight on that day, with the tremors of an old man, though he was but seven or eight years of age. We buried his mother, though not his sister, as we could not identify her. The bodies had been stripped of clothing and were decomposed, the wolves having haunted the field. The little girl—Nancy—the way she clung to him when we returned—was pitiful. She had thought he had abandoned her. They were a pair that made my heart heavy day and night, and I could not reconcile what we had done to their parents. Even my mother, who had no part in the killing, was grateful when the children were finally taken from us, as they were a constant burden on her heart. The girl, at the time, had an eye disease as did many of the other orphans when the army came and took them off in a wagon. I learned later that she became blind and died after being taken from us. I heard that Elliott was brought before Congress to testify about the massacre, as was one other of the boys. I did not, for many years, know what became of him after this. I made my peace with the event at Mountain Meadows, but never with the tragic plight of the children. Elliott's silent and withdrawn demeanor, his pitiful attempt never to show his grief, plagued me for the year that he was with us, and haunted me for many years after that, and unto this day. I wished him to find peace in his life, but know for a fact that he did not.

I know this from an event that took place in November of 1900. At that time I was fifty-nine years of age and my father was an old man. We resided in Mexico, in Colonia Juárez, in the very home where tonight I am writing these words, having come here with the passage of laws in the United States opposed to our religious beliefs on marriage and also to escape those, even among our own people, who were seeking to make a few of us into scapegoats for the killings at Mountain Meadows. We had built our business from barren land to extensive fruit orchards and a fruit cannery, and it was at the cannery that Elliott Bass appeared.

I did not at first know his identity, nor he mine, as he followed on the heels of a man in his employ, a Mexican, who had come to my office to negotiate a purchase of apples and canned fruit for a maintenance team employed on trackage alongside our orchards. I was conducting this transaction when Elliott Bass appeared at the door and made a humorous comment about discovering a worm at the core of one of our apples, and I replied in similar fashion, warning him how apple thieves were dealt with in Mexico—as he had not yet paid for the apple. He offered, then, to get a string and "string the little devil up," referring to the worm, and we had a laugh about that, Elliott translating our discourse for the Mexican. We exchanged further pleasantries but at this point I began to experience a prickly and pestering recognition, and to feel that perhaps I knew the man before me. And yet he appeared a stranger. He was younger than I by a decade at least, of muscular and powerful composition, though thin, and ill-used by the weather, with a full beard, and it was evident by his labored movements and the inflamed state of his hands that he was greatly affected by rheumatism. He moved stiffly, and only by necessity, and turned his head with evident difficulty. I could not, though I attempted, place him, and intended to introduce myself and inquire of his name when Father came into the office, this being the appointed time for his daily tour of the warehouse. As I have stated, he was old, and in poor health; he used a cane and spoke in a slurred fashion. He was not lucid in the mind.

It was the sight of my father that first moved Elliott Bass to recognition. His eyes moved rapidly from my father to me. It was at this moment that his identity occurred to me. I attempted to close the transaction swiftly by presenting a bill of sale, which Elliott Bass received and signed, though I noted that his hands had begun to shake as he did so. He withdrew from his coat a ledger book which he opened as if to record the sale, but his hands were incapable, and so he gave this book to his assistant, instructing the man in Spanish to note the purchase. The assistant inquired of his welfare, having seen the tremor in his hands, but Elliott Bass only repeated the instruction that the purchase be recorded. The assistant then complied. It was now that Elliott Bass inquired of my father if he knew the time. My father withdrew a pocket watch and consulted it, speaking the time in his slurred fashion.

"I was wondering," Elliott Bass said in a voice so filled with quiet wrath that it shook my soul and I felt as if the hatred of God Almighty had descended upon us, "if that watch was still in your possession. It is my father's watch."

I knew this to be true. The watch had been among the emigrants' possessions taken at the time of the massacre. I had known that act of my father's to be one of common thievery. The emigrants were killed in the name of our Lord and according to the doctrine of blood atonement, but the theft of their belongings could not be sufficiently justified. My father then made some answer, unintelligible; I do not know if he understood who Elliott Bass was. Mr. Bass then turned and left us, and the assistant followed him. Within ten seconds, however, he returned with two pistols drawn. "Get on your knees, old man," he said to my father, his face terrible to look upon. He was not now, as he had been, in control of himself. He looked like the very devil, his eyes flaming, his fingers, disfigured, drawn tight around the triggers of both pistols. He was a small man, but fiercely powerful. His voice was loud. "On your knees, you savage old bastard!" he began shouting, and when at first my father did not comply, he took the cane away from him and pushed him to the ground. I attempted at this time to aid my father, but one of the pistols was then aimed at my head, the other being directed at my father, and I believed that we would both be killed if I should try to help my father. Elliott Bass squatted over my father and placed the barrel between his eyes. I do not recall all that he did or said at this point. He recounted many of the deeds at Mountain Meadows, staring my father in the eyes and accusing him of having murdered women and children in cold blood, of having slit their throats like pigs. He recalled a beating that my father had once given him when he refused to pray, this in a whisper at first but then in a voice increasingly like that of a madman, which made the blood throb in my own ears because of my part in the killing at Mountain Meadows, of which Elliott Bass was unaware, even to this moment, as he had not been witness to it. He demanded of my father to know if he still believed in the doctrine of blood atonement and should like for him to pull the trigger. My father did not appear to understand what was asked of him. I believe, that had he understood, he would have said that in the eyes of the Lord he had done no wrong. But this could not negate the fact that in the eyes of Elliott Bass, an innocent at the time, a small boy, he had committed sins too horrible even for me to recall. My father cried pitiably on the ground, with Elliott Bass crouched over him, and I recalled how the victims at Mountain Meadows had clung to him and begged him to show mercy. When Elliott Bass began to demand a confession from him, he made only unintelligible sounds, scratching his hands against the floor to try to free himself. I thought that Elliott Bass would shoot him, but then he drew himself off of my father and lay on the ground beside him, crying and sobbing as I had never seen him do when he was young—as a boy would. "I let you take me over," he cried, repeating this, several times. "I ate your food, I lived in your home, you made me betray my parents—you took everything from me." He said these things, and many more, all in a state of such terrible agony and folded over on the ground as a child would, as if he had just at the moment learned, for the first time, that his parents had been taken from him, rather than having lived with this fact all of his life. I cannot describe the torturous nature of his affliction. Finally he got to his knees and took the watch from my father, who was on the floor, incoherent and frightened, and then hurled the watch to the floor and departed, leaving the crates of fruit which had been paid for.

From this event, I have lived the rest of my days with the image before me of a man destroyed, not saved, by the grace of God Almighty. While I have made my peace with my own deeds, I have kept it with great difficulty, and suffering, and with a most agonizing doubt as to the justification of the fate of those children orphaned at Mountain Meadows, always facing the fact of Elliott Bass. There have been moments when I wished I myself had offered the confession he attempted to extract from my father, for there was not another opportunity, and it is my belief that he deserved to know my own guilt in the affair.

To that end, I now confess.

May God grant me forgiveness, if I have strayed from His will, either in deed or confession.

George Parley Smith

Jim stood and walked to the window, having finished reading before Meg did. Meg reached the end, and leaned back in the chair, then straightened the pages and placed them back on the desk, feeling a painful sadness and longing for Bassie. She felt as if she had seen Elliott for the first time—as if the person she had come to know through the letters in the journals was only a fictional character, and here, finally, was the man himself, with his deep, endless reservoir of suffering. She felt the injustice of how Hannah, who had loved him, had longed, without effect, to know him, while now, after so much time had passed, this document simply revealed him to Meg as if he were slit open. All of Elliott's life he had kept his terrible memories private, holding on to them as if containing them was the only way to keep his sanity, and now after his death they had all come spilling out. Meg felt she was not entitled to know them.

Jim had turned from the window and was looking at her. He looked tired, spent. She realized that the revelation of Elliott's tragedy could only remind him of his own, raising his own insurmountable suffering and loss to the surface.

But he did not seem inclined to say so.

She put her hands on her knees, and stood up.

They found Andrew Smith in the hallway, his back against the wall, his arms crossed over his chest, rumpling his tie. He looked like a man awaiting a verdict; his eyes settled on Meg's.

"You've read it?" he asked.

She nodded.

"I don't know what to say about it," he said. "An apology is hardly enough."

"You aren't the one to blame," she said.

"But I might have been," he answered. "I have to tell you, that document has tested my faith more than anything I've ever come across. And I'm not talking about my faith in God. I'm talking about faith in myself. I don't know what I would have done at sixteen if my father had told me to murder people in the name of Almighty God. I might have done it. I don't know." He uncrossed his arms, and straightened himself. "But that's my burden, not yours. You've driven all the way down here, and I don't know if I've answered what you wanted to know."

They had wanted to know why Elliott Bass might have killed himself. And they had found, if not the only reason, then enough reason: he had lost not only his bearings; he had lost his momentum. In spite of setting himself always toward the future, he had somehow, unexpectedly and unprepared, found himself facing the past again.

"You've told us enough," Jim said. "I would ask for a copy of the document, but I think you'd be uncomfortable with that."

"I would be uncomfortable," he said. "My family would oppose it. But there is one thing. If you're looking for information, there's a man in Ciudad Juárez who supposedly has some connection to Vicente Morales, and he has a photograph of Hannah."

The statement seemed, to Meg, too casually blunt to be true. She assumed that Andrew was mistaken.

"Who is he?" Jim asked.

"His name is Hector Romero. He writes for the newspaper, *El Sol*. I've never met him, but a member of our church who used to work at *El Sol* came and told me about him when she found out I was interested in Elliott Bass. She got to know Mr. Romero because he helped her son out of a problem with the Juárez police while she was working at the paper. He's in charge of crime reports, so he has a lot of contact with the gangs and the police."

"And he had a photograph of Hannah?" Meg pressed, still dubious. "Did your friend see it?"

"That's what she told me. I don't have any reason not to believe her. Apparently she was in his home a couple of times, and he had a set of the journals, and she was looking at them, and three or four loose photographs fell out. One of them was of Hannah. He said he got them from his father, who was a friend of Vicente Morales."

"Could we get in touch with him?" Jim asked.

"I've got his phone number in my desk if he still works for the paper," Andrew said. "I tried to get a hold of him a couple of years ago, and he never returned my phone calls."

THIRTY-FIVE

The drive back to Ciudad Juárez took three hours in the dark. They stopped and had dinner in a roadside café, and reached the outskirts of the city at ten o'clock at night, passing several motels until they found one that appeared to be decent. Together they trudged into the lobby, Meg with a canvas bag of overnight accoutrements which she had dug out of her suitcase in the parking lot at the UNM campus, Jim with only the clothes he was wearing and a plastic sack containing a toothbrush, a disposable razor, and a cheap pair of men's underwear which he had picked up at an all-night pharmacy.

After waiting a while for someone to appear at the reception desk, they rented two rooms, climbed a flight of outdoor stairs, and said goodnight to each other outside their doors overlooking a dreary parking lot, Meg fishing a tube of toothpaste out of her bag and squeezing some onto Jim's toothbrush as he stood holding it out. He gave her a brief and awkward parting embrace, and after he had gone she noticed that the toothpaste on his brush had smeared onto the sleeve of her jacket in the process. She wiped it off in the bathroom, wondering if Jim would return for more toothpaste when he saw there was none on the brush. But he didn't return. She considered knocking on his door, but decided against it, and showered and got in bed. For her usual period of wakefulness, she lay staring up at the ceiling, listening to the traffic going by. When eventually she fell asleep, she was thinking not of Hannah or Elliott, or even of Jim in the next room, but of the little girl called Nancy whom she had read of in the confession. She wondered how long Nancy had lived after being separated from Elliott, and what kind of eye infection had made her blind.

In the morning, Meg was awakened by Jim knocking on her door. She got up and threw her clothes on and let him in, and he sat on the edge of the bed watching a morning news show in Spanish while she washed her face and brushed her teeth. At eight o'clock, Jim called the newspaper, *El Sol*, where the man, Hector Romero, was last known to have worked, and was told he was still employed there, though he had not yet come into the office that morning, and was not expected until ten o'clock.

They checked out of the motel and found a McDonald's on the corner, where they purchased coffee and Egg McMuffins and sat for half an hour sharing an El Paso newspaper.

At ten o'clock Jim used the pay phone to call Hector Romero, and this time, after being placed on hold for nearly five minutes, finally got him on the line. Meg stood listening to Jim's end of the conversation, which was in English, and from which she was able to glean that Hector Romero was impatient and almost hostile but admitted at last to having a photograph of Hannah and one of her daughter, Claudia, as a child. He had inherited the photographs from his father, who had received them from Vicente. With pressure from Jim, he finally agreed that Meg was entitled to see them.

"He'll meet us in a café, at eleven-thirty," Jim explained when he hung up. "He has to go back to his apartment to get the photographs, and that apparently involves a bus ride. I give him a fifty-fifty chance of showing up."

They spent the next half hour wandering the streets and alleys in a shopping area nearby, but were targets for the numerous street vendors, and returned to the truck after Meg had purchased a half dozen plastic beaded bracelets that she had no use for, from a woman toting an infant in a sling, and Jim had bought a wooden chess set for Billy from a young boy whom he had watched carving it.

They arrived early at the appointed meeting place, a café on a street called the Strip that was lined with nightclubs and liquor stores, many of which were closed during these daylight hours. The café was wedged between two bars that were shut down for the day, their storefronts secured by garage doors. Meg was relieved to find the place quiet and dimly lit inside, jarred as she was by the bright noon sunlight and the chaotic noise of the city. She and Jim took refuge in a booth under a colorful painting of a rooster and sat listening to the background music of a male vocalist singing a love song. The waiter came, and they each ordered a beer and sat drinking it and looking at each other across the tabletop.

"How will we know who he is?" she asked.

"I assume he'll know us," Jim answered.

She looked around the room. Not only were they the only Anglos in the place, they were the only customers. It was a narrow room with booths down either side. The single door to the street was glass and admitted a stream of sunlight.

Meg went to the back of the building in search of a restroom and found one near the kitchen. Surveying herself in the smudged mirror over the sink, she examined the dark circles under her eyes, and decided her skin looked ruddy. She went back out and sat in the booth opposite Jim. He had his back to the wall and his legs stretched out along the seat so he could see the door. They nursed their beers, and watched the door.

In a moment a man carrying a manila envelope under his arm came in, and when he saw them, started toward them. He was elderly, with gray hair and a mustache, and was wearing eyeglasses that were patched with masking tape. One side of his face, Meg noticed, was scarred from what appeared to have been a burn. The cheek was pale and tightly drawn, slick in contrast to the craggy complexion of the other side of his face.

Jim slid out of the booth and got to his feet, and Meg stood halfway up, but the man dismissed the courtesy with an impatient gesture, pulling a chair to the end of the booth and sitting down. He laid the envelope on the table; it was soiled and the clasp was missing.

The waiter appeared. "*Quiero una Coca-Cola,*" Hector Romero said without looking at him. "So, here are your pictures," he said to Meg in a heavy accent, pushing the envelope across the table to her.

His mustache, she noticed, drooped over most of his lip but was sparse where the scar reached the corner of his mouth. Behind the glasses, the skin was unaffected by scarring, and hung in loose folds around his eyes.

"Your father knew Vicente Morales?" she asked him.

"Yes. He knew him."

"And did you know him?"

He considered her. "I did. You Americans. You have a fascination with the past. And in the present, the children are starving. The women of Juárez are murdered and left in the desert. Ask me to show you pictures of that, and I will like you better."

"How did your father know him?" Jim asked, ignoring the statement.

"Politics. Always politics. Vicente was a good man."

"Did Vicente live in Ciudad Juárez?"

"He did. He died in Juárez. In a house not far from where we are sitting."

"My grandmother tried to find out what happened to him after he came to Mexico," Meg said. "But she couldn't find any trace of him. She assumed he might have been killed in the revolution, because he was political."

The man laughed. "In the revolution? No. He lived for thirty years after the revolution. I was born in 1920, and I saw him many times."

"In Juárez?" Jim asked.

"Yes. I saw him here. I have lived in this city all my life, and he was living here all the time until he died."

"What did he do here?" Jim asked.

"You are interested, only because Vicente knew Hannah and Elliott Bass? Is that what makes him of interest? Well. I will tell you what he did. When the revolution started, he was living in Durango. He supported Madero and was put in jail in San Luís Potosí for letters he wrote to the papers. When he got out of jail, he began to dislike Madero. He also disliked Villa and the rebels, but was a great defender of the poor. He supported Zapata. In the end he disliked power, and powerful men, though he believed in Zapata's efforts for the poor, and wrote his opinions in the newspapers, up to the time Zapata was murdered."

The waiter appeared, setting a bottled Coke on the table.

"He couldn't have written under his own name," Jim said. "Claudia Bass would have known it. She was very thorough with her research. She would have found him."

"I believe that is true," the man said. "I often knew him to use a different name."

"What name would that be?" Jim pressed. He had become more pointed in his questions, and now was fiercely holding the gaze of Hector Romero.

"I was young," Hector Romero said dismissively. "I do not recall."

"What newspaper did he write for?" Jim asked.

"For different ones. There have been different papers."

"Was it *El Sol*?"

"I cannot know."

A silence settled. At last Jim said, "What about your father—how did he know Vicente?"

"My father was devoted to helping the poor retain their rights to land. He fought for the communal land. He knew Vicente through this effort and their connection with Zapata."

"Did Vicente ever marry?" Meg asked.

"I know very little about his personal life."

"But your father ended up with the photographs that belonged to Vicente," Jim said.

Hector Romero shrugged. "Yes. He did. With the photograph of Hannah Bass, and of"—he looked at Meg—"it was your grandmother, yes? Claudia Bass? When she was a child."

"And why did Vicente give those photographs to your father?" Jim pressed.

The man was growing more impatient. "You have asked me questions. I have answered to the best of my ability. I know very little more."

"Vicente was writing a history of New Mexico," Jim persisted. "Was it ever published?"

"He had nothing to do with New Mexico when I knew him."

A fly had landed on the rim of his Coke bottle, and Meg brushed it away.

"Ah," Hector Romero said. "You frightened the fly. Americans are wonderful. We Mexicans—we owe you so much. You come here, and you frighten our flies for us. Our children are picking through the garbage in search of their dinner, but, ah, now there are fewer flies to pester them. And, you have given us business. When I was born, Mexico's wealth had been stolen by foreign empires, and the good people of the

United States amended your constitution to prohibit alcohol in your country, so that the Americans living on the borders of our country could come to Ciudad Juárez and buy our alcohol, and use our prostitutes, and gamble, and give us business. It has made us rich. You see how rich we are."

Meg saw that Jim was about to react to the insults, and she touched his leg with her foot under the table to stop him. His eyes shot over to hers.

"You write about crime here, is that right?" she asked.

"Yes," he said, almost pleasantly, as if willing to shrug away his inclination to challenge them if neither she nor Jim was going to argue with him. "Drug traffickers and the police. Often they are one and the same in this city, you know. But, it makes unpleasant conversation."

When they did not respond at once, Hector Romero added, "Last week a friend of mine, Alicia Mendoza, was killed. She was coming out of a supermarket holding her child in her arms. His name is Jorge. He is two. The *federales* shot her in cold blood. In the middle of the day—at this time. They said she was a *narcotraficante*. But it was not true. They knew who she was. She was a journalist. She was writing a story about how the *federales* are in bed with a certain gang." He shrugged. "But when you are my age, and you have been doing this as long as I have, neither the gangs nor the *federales* are as likely to kill you. They have already tried. There is intimacy in that. And after a while, there is safety. And after that, who cares what happens to an old man."

Meg found that in spite of Hector Romero's self-righteous condescension, and for reasons she could not define, she did not dislike him. Here he sat, drinking a Coke and divulging more information than either she or Jim had asked for. She had the distinct impression that he was terribly lonely.

"I see that you are looking at my scar," he said suddenly, and Meg realized that while she had been analyzing Hector Romero, her eyes had settled unintentionally on the damaged side of his face.

"Is it a burn?" she asked, having dealt with similar accusations from Bassie long enough to know that there was often less conflict stirred up by admitting to things than by defending herself.

The room darkened noticeably as the light from the door was blocked by a group of people stopping outside on the sidewalk to converse.

"There was a fire in Colonia Tarahumara," Hector Romero said. "I went there to report. And discovered there were children."

She waited. "Did you get them out?" she finally asked.

"Two of them," he said. He sighed. "There are always fires in the *colonias*. In this case a mother had built a fire in the center of the floor. She was trying to heat the home."

He talked for a moment more, about the *colonias*, and crime and poverty in the city. There was not a day that passed, he said, when he was not called to the scene of a dead body lying in its own blood: he had seen more people in this position, he said, than had passed the door of the café since they had begun their conversation. His wife had died of a blood disease a decade before; a daughter whom he had not seen in almost three years was a single mother working as a housekeeper in a large hotel in San Francisco; a son in Mexico City worked with police to combat the gang problem and was in love with a girl but would not marry her, claiming that his life must be his own to sacrifice. The son had worked for a year in the office of the attorney general, for the human rights officer, but had resigned to take his work into the streets, "where"—Hector Romero said—"he will not live five years."

He paused after saying this. Then he gestured toward the envelope lying on the table near Meg's beer. "But, there are your photographs," he said. "You may keep them. Why not? Now, there are people waiting for me." He stood, and putting the Coke bottle to his lips again, tipped his head back, emptied the bottle and set it down. He looked at Jim, and then at Meg. Jim got to his feet. "It has been a pleasure," Hector Romero said, and added, "I am not lying about that."

When he had left, however, Jim turned to Meg and said, "But he's lying about something."

"What do you mean?"

"There's something he's not telling us. What he knows and doesn't know just seems a little too convenient. What's that business about how Vicente wrote letters to the paper under a different name? Why a different name? And why doesn't Romero remember the name? He's too quick to praise Vicente, and too invested in him, to know so little about him." He paused, reflecting. "I want to find out more about this guy."

"How?" Meg asked. She was slipping the photographs out of the envelope. There were two of them; they were small, brown from age, and spotted with silvering.

Jim moved from his side of the booth to sit beside her and view them, his arm stretched out on the tabletop, the shirt-sleeve rolled up. His proximity to Meg, the closeness of his arm, presented a startling contrast to the distant world that she shifted her eyes and peered into.

There was Bassie, aged four or five, posed in a studio, looking at the camera. She was wearing a white pinafore and sitting in a child's chair, her knees propped up, her elbows planted on them. Her chin was resting in her hands. She was not smiling, but there was a tilt to her face and a shine in her eyes. Her skin was pale under the dark curls that framed her face and fell in ringlets down below the squareness of her jaw. In the bottom right-hand corner, embossed in faded gold lettering, were the words "Talbot Photography, Chicago."

"This was after she moved to Chicago," Meg said. "How do you think Vicente had it?"

They discussed the possibilities. Nothing was written on the back of the photograph to give them any clue. "The most likely thing would be that Hannah's brother had it taken and sent it to Hannah in Las Vegas while she was at Saint Anthony's," Meg finally concluded.

"And she must have given it to Vicente, or left it for him when she died," Jim said.

Meg glanced at the second photograph. On the margin at the bottom was penned in faded ink, "Saint Anthony's Sanatorium, 1901." Peering more closely, Meg was suddenly transported from the restaurant in which she was sitting to the room shown in the photograph. It was a large lobby, sunlight cutting brightly through the slats of window shutters, and rugs strewn across a hardwood floor. Potted plants stood around the edges of the rugs. Fewer than a dozen people were standing at the windows or seated in the chairs. Meg's eyes passed over them and returned to a certain face: a woman's face. The woman was looking directly into the camera lens; she was sitting in the center of a formal sofa near a palm tree in the farthest corner of the room. The familiar peacock shawl was draped around her shoulders, the edges of embroidered feathers encircling her arms.

Hannah, on the sofa, was thin. Her face was drawn and pale. And yet there was a settled, eternal look in her face, almost an expression of affection. She seemed to be seeing Meg from across the lobby of Saint Anthony's and the distances imposed by time. For a moment, instead of watching from the outside in, Meg felt herself to be within the frame.

When she became aware again of her surroundings, Jim was speaking to her. "I want to figure out where the archives are in this city," he was saying, "and find out more about Romero."

THIRTY-SIX

By two o'clock that afternoon Jim finally located the relevant archive, having spent a frustrating half hour at a pay phone assembling information in English and Spanish from a reference librarian at the main city library and a friend in Santa Fe whom he knew to be familiar with Mexican papers.

The archives were housed in an old stone library near some municipal buildings. Jim engaged in a conversation in Spanish at the front desk with a young male reference assistant, some of which Meg understood, as Jim was forced by his limited Spanish to use a number of English words like "microfilm" and "card file." The man was eager to help, and when he excused himself and vanished into a back office, Jim explained the situation to Meg. "The newspapers are all kept on the second floor," he said, "but someone has to go over to a government building near here for the key. He's sending somebody over. They'll bring us the key and then wait with us while we look at the papers. The papers haven't been put on microfilm; they're just bound and filed by date. This man says they weigh so much they're cracking the walls down here."

Meg looked at the walls. Everywhere, the plaster was warped and crazed. In places, it was falling off in chunks.

"How long will it take to get the key?" she asked.

"He said about half an hour."

While waiting for the messenger to return with the key, they searched the card file and discovered, under the name Vicente Morales, cards for three individuals who were not the Vicente Morales for whom they were looking. They closed the drawer, and moved down to the *R*'s, flipping to the name Romero, and discovered there a card for Hector Romero. "Let's see," Jim said slowly, attempting to translate the Spanish for Meg. "It directs us to *El Sol* from the years 1959 through the present, where Hector Romero has been a staff reporter . . . first in general news, this says, and then for the last ten years specifically for the crime section. And then there's also a notation to see the obituary for . . ." he stopped. He was leaning over the card, but turned his face to look at Meg. Then he looked at the card again, "for Vicente Romero in *El Sol* of August 11, 1939."

"Vicente Romero?" Meg asked. "Who's that?"

He straightened. "From the date, I assume it could be his father," he said thoughtfully.

"That's weird," Meg responded reflectively, "that Hector's father would be named Vicente." She thought of how Hector Romero had talked about his father's friendship with Vicente Morales. He certainly had not mentioned that they shared the same first name. "Do you think it's just a coincidence? Is the name that common?"

"Fairly common, I think," Jim said thoughtfully. "But I'm not convinced it's a coincidence." He was looking at the card. "Apparently he died in 1939."

Meg found herself reluctant to state her thoughts, as the implications, if the thoughts proved to be accurate, could be so numerous as to explode in her face. She found herself to be whispering. "Hector said something about how long Vicente Morales had lived after the revolution."

"Thirty years," Jim responded quietly. "Which would place his death around 1940."

"Which is pretty close to 1939," Meg said.

They stood looking at each other. Then Jim leaned suddenly down and flipped rapidly through the remaining cards on Romeros, stopping when he came to the card for Vicente Romero. He looked at it, then marked it with his finger; Meg leaned down to read it. "Romero, Vicente. 1861 to 1939."

"That would have made him thirty in 1891," Jim said. "When Hannah went to New Mexico. That's about right. That fits."

The card listed three items: newspaper commentaries by Vicente Romero in *El Sol* spanning a period from 1913 to 1938, the obituary in the August 11, 1939, *El Sol* and a vertical file of miscellany.

They decided to look through the vertical file first, but when they returned to the desk and asked the man who had assisted them where they would find the vertical files, he said it would be necessary for someone to be with them while they looked at the files, and the only person available to do such things was the woman whom he had sent to the Presidencia Municipal for the key to unlock the *hemeroteca,* where the newspapers were filed. He apologized, saying they would have to wait.

At last an exquisite-looking young woman dressed beautifully in stockings and high heels and wearing heavy eye makeup appeared before them and spoke to them in Spanish, showing them a key. Leading them up the stairway and into a hallway she admitted them to a dark room that had the distinct odor of old newsprint. She turned the light switch on, illuminating long rows of expansive, bound material. "*Cuál es el que quieren ver?*" she asked.

"*Queremos ver copias de* El Sol," Jim said, explaining in Spanish that they were particularly interested in the issue of August 11, 1939, and also in the issues for the years 1913 through 1938.

"*Están escritos de acuerdo con las fechas,*" the woman said. "El Sol *comiensa en esta area.*" She indicated an area of shelving just in front of them, and explained a few more things to Jim in Spanish, at last taking a seat in a chair near the door. Meg and Jim walked along the rows in the area that she had pointed out until they found the shelf containing the copies of *El Sol* for the period 1930 to 1939. At the end of this row, Jim pulled from the top shelf a large binder marked *Julio–Agosto,* and carried it to a table near a window shuttered by a venetian blind.

They opened the volume and Jim turned the large pages of newsprint until he came to August 11. The woman was watching them, her slender legs crossed and a high-heeled shoe dangling from one foot.

Jim was scanning the headlines.

"What's the Spanish word for 'obituary'?" Meg asked.

"Necrología," he said.

He turned a few more pages. Meg sat down beside him, reading headlines to herself but comprehending almost nothing. "I can't believe I grew up in Texas and can't speak any Spanish," she said, apologetically.

"Another one of those rebellions against Bassie, probably," he commented, turning a page. "Here it is. *Necrología*. Now," he moved his finger down the columns of print, leaning in close, and then settled it on the name Romero. "It's him," he said after only a second. "It's him. He changed his name."

Though she had been tossing the idea around in her mind for the last half hour, it still registered as a shock. "It's Vicente?"

"It is. He dumped his name completely, from the looks of this," Jim said. "I don't see 'Morales' anywhere in here."

"What does it say?" Meg asked, looking at the print but able only to pick out dates and a few phrases.

"It says he was born in Las Vegas, New Mexico, in 1861, and moved to Mexico in 1902."

"The year Hannah died," Meg said.

"Yes. He taught English at the University of Durango from 1902 to 1910, when he married Elena Gálvez, and two months later was jailed in San Luís Potosí—" he glanced at Meg, "like Hector said—for supporting the revolutionary Francisco Madero. After that—" Jim scanned down a bit, muttering phrases, "a period of controversial politics . . . proponent of the poor . . . support of Zapata . . . vocal advocate for rights to communal lands . . . moved to Ciudad Juárez . . . had a daughter in 1912, a son, Hector" he paused—"in 1920. He was a devout Catholic . . . formed an organization of renowned journalists to ensure freedom of the press . . . was seventy-eight years old at the time of death . . . funeral to be held at his parish church, the Mission of Guadalupe—I've been there," he said. "And then it tells where he's buried. And that's it."

They sat looking at the newsprint. "How could Bassie not have found him?" Meg said at last.

"We wouldn't have found him either, if Andrew Smith hadn't told us about Hector Romero," Jim said.

"And I guess we wouldn't have known about Andrew Smith if we hadn't found the grave, which we wouldn't have looked for without Bassie," Meg added. "But it still seems like she just missed it somehow, if he was writing for the newspaper for that many years. He's bound to have had the same writing style and apparently he was writing about the same causes. The same politics he had cared about in Las Vegas."

"That's true," Jim said. "But she didn't have any reason to be looking for him in Juárez. There were probably any number of impassioned editorialists writing in cities all over Mexico. It isn't like the politics were exclusive to Vicente. The liberals in Mexico were fighting for those causes; that's what the revolution and then all the political instability was about. Madero and Zapata, Pancho Villa, all those guys were in favor of rights for the poor." He paused briefly, seeming to think things over, and then said, "I don't think Bassie missed anything. She might have even seen the editorials he wrote. There probably wasn't much difference between them and a lot of others like them. And she didn't have any reason to think he'd changed his name. She was looking for Vicente Morales. Not Vicente Romero."

"This is so strange," Meg said. "The idea that he had a life we didn't even know about. That Bassie didn't know about. I can't help wondering what she would think."

She was wishing—she realized—that Bassie could have made this discovery. It seemed unfair to her that having never given the slightest attention to the journals until a week ago, she would be the one here.

They left the volume open on the table and revisited the shelves, pulling down two volumes of *El Sol* from 1913, Vicente's first year of employment there.

After half an hour of poring over several passionate political commentaries written by Vicente that year, including a condemnation of a brutal general by the name of Huerta and of the United States for supporting him, Jim sat back, rubbing at his eyes, and Meg said, "Let's call it quits on these. We could be reading these for weeks."

He nodded. "Let's look at the vertical file."

They returned the copies to the shelves, and the woman led them back into the hall and several doors down, unlocking a door to a room similar to the one they had just come from, equally large and well lit, but filled instead with rows of file cabinets and smelling heavily of cement. The odor, Meg realized, was from the plaster in the fireproof cabinets.

While the woman made herself busy sorting through a stack of papers on a table near the door, Jim and Meg located the cabinet containing the file on Vicente Romero. Withdrawing it, they took it to a table where Meg sat down and Jim remained standing, as she opened it, exposing the first item. It was a folded program printed on thick paper and dated 1929. Jim read the Spanish silently to himself and then explained to Meg that Vicente Romero was listed as making the introductory remarks for a speech by the Mexican aviator Captain Emilio Carranza. The page was decorated with a drawing of Charles Lindbergh's airplane, the *Spirit of St. Louis*, and commemorated a meeting between Carranza and Lindbergh.

Setting the program aside, they encountered a stack of loose clippings from Vicente's newspaper commentaries with op-ed responses paperclipped to them. They did not bother to read these, but turned past them and past several single-page programs for meetings, dated 1921 to 1926, of the press organization that Vicente had founded. At last they came to a packet of small photographs. Meg withdrew the photographs and placed them on the desk.

The first was of two men standing in an alleyway of low adobe houses, the alley stretching off behind them, divided down the center by a slant of sunlight that illuminated half and left the other half in shade. A donkey, loaded with canvas sacks, stood at the end of the alley; dogs lay in the doorways on the shaded side. The men were also in the shade, standing at an open doorway, engaged in conversation. They were seen in profile. The older of the two was wearing a dark suit with a vest, a short tie, and a derby hat; the younger was wearing wire spectacles, a white shirt, and loose trousers, though a crease down the length of the photograph obliterated most of his features. Otherwise the image was crisp and the lighting remarkably good, showing folds and wrinkles in the clothing and cracks in the adobe walls.

She turned it over. "Las Vegas, New Mexico," it said.

They speculated for a moment on whether the man in wire spectacles might be Vicente, but found themselves too impatient to study the photograph for long, and moved on to the next.

In this one, a man—the same man, wearing the same wire spectacles, a duster coat to his knees and loosely fitted trousers—was seated in a parked buggy with the reins in his lap. The wind had lifted his hat from his head, and the camera had caught the image as the man reached to retrieve the hat, which hung suspended in the air, beyond his reach. Certainly, Meg thought, this was Vicente. He looked amused. His face was to the sky. The sunlight lay across his jaw and glimmered on his glasses, but the rest of his face was shadowed by his arm. Meg recognized the background as a row of buildings on the plaza in Las Vegas, across from the Plaza Hotel. She passed this photograph to Jim, but even as she handed it to him, she saw that his gaze was fixed on the next one, which she had picked up and was holding.

She looked at the photograph in her hand. It was a winter scene: the man was pictured alone, standing before a shed and holding a hunting rifle, the butt of the rifle resting on the ground and the barrel in his hands. He looked about fifty years old, possibly younger, and was dressed in trousers, a heavy corduroy jacket, a fur cap with flaps down over his ears. His beard was silver stubble though his mustache was black. His eyes behind the wire glasses were looking toward a string of birds dangling from a rafter to the left of him. To his right was a primitive grill on which something—presumably one of the birds—was cooking, emitting a haze of smoke that obscured a portion of the photograph but gave depth to the scene, making it appear surprisingly real.

Yet there was something here that cast an eerie feeling over Meg's emotions. It was Vicente's face. The image was oddly present, the face and the eyes disturbingly familiar.

She gave the photograph to Jim, and looked at the next. And there within the frame was Bassie. It was Bassie's face. Not Bassie as a child, but Bassie as an old woman. In the guise of an old man. He was holding a felt hat, facing the camera, leaning his weight on a cane on what appeared to be a Mexican city street, in front of a newspaper office. The color of his skin, the shape of his face, the downward turn of his eyes—all of them were Bassie's.

Meg felt herself stop breathing. "Jim?" she said.

He took the picture from her and set it on the table, staring at it.

"He looks like Bassie," Meg whispered.

"Yes. He does," Jim said slowly.

"Exactly like her," Meg said. "Look at his face." When Jim didn't respond, she stated the obvious question. "Could he have been her father?"

"I'd say he could have," Jim replied quietly. "Was there anything unusual about the dates in the journal? Like when she was conceived?"

"I remember thinking it was a little sketchy, how it fit together," Meg answered. "Hannah found out she was pregnant while Vicente was there. It was when he came out to Pecos because of the threats—when the hens and the goat were killed. But she was thinking she was pregnant before he came there; I'm sure about that. And Bassie would have studied those dates, and known if there was something about them that wasn't right."

"A week or two in one direction or another wouldn't tell her anything decisive," Jim observed.

"Hannah never seemed to question who the father was," Meg said.

"Would she, in the journal?" Jim asked. "While Elliott was alive?"

"But Bassie would have thought about this. She would have looked into the possibility."

"Maybe she tried to. She tried to find Vicente."

Meg attempted to think the idea through. "If she had some suspicion, for a long time, that was never put to rest, then that might explain why she would be so quick to believe that Hannah and Vicente had something to do with Elliott's death," she finally said. "It wasn't like her, to jump to that conclusion so fast. But if she had always been harboring some doubts, then I can see how that piece of evidence—Argus in the picture—would put her over the edge and make her assume that maybe Hannah had lied about a lot of things." She stood up, and then sat down again, looking again at each of the photographs, and then at Jim. "I can't believe that I can't ask her," she said.

"I don't think she knew the answer to this one, Meg," Jim answered. "She might have asked the question at some point, but I don't think she had the answer. I think she just chose to believe what her mother wrote." He paused. "There's someone who does have the answer, though. Hector Romero."

But Meg's thoughts had moved to another path now. "If Vicente was her father, he was my great-grandfather," she said, trying to settle on such a confounding possibility. "And Elliott," she added after a moment, "was not."

They called Hector Romero from the lobby of the building. When Meg informed him they were calling from the library archives, he became silent.

"Mr. Romero?"

"Yes. I am here."

"We've found some things that suggest Vicente Morales was your father. That he changed his name to Vicente Romero. We're wondering if he might also have been Bassie's father." She waited. "You can see why it's important to me."

"Yes, I can see," he said in a low, disquieted tone.

"I can't think of any reason why I shouldn't know," she said.

He was silent a moment more, and then said, "There is something I should give you. You are still in the library?"

"Yes."

"And where are you going from there?"

"We were thinking of going over to the cemetery where he's buried."

"Ah."

"But we could meet you somewhere else."

"No. I will meet you at the cemetery in one hour. Five o'clock," he said.

THIRTY-SEVEN

They found it, with some difficulty, sequestered from a busy street by a stone wall and a row of trees. Parking proved to be a problem, and by the time Meg and Jim had circled the block and veered off down a side street in search of a place to park, Meg was becoming nervous about the time.

"I'll let you off at the gate," Jim said, "and park and come find you."

She agreed to this. The intense afternoon sunlight was casting long shadows when she passed through the iron gates. The temperature was colder within the walls. The gravestones were old, and covered in lichen of various kinds—yellow and black, mossy and flowerlike. The leaves overhead on the massive trees were a golden autumn color, the graves decorated with plastic flowers and replicas of saints.

Hector was waiting for her, just inside the gates. He was carrying a brown, folded sack under his arm, which appeared, by its size and shape, to contain a book. He said nothing by way of a greeting.

"Jim's parking his truck," Meg explained.

Hector had no intention of waiting for Jim, but took Meg down a narrow pathway between the stones, to the far end of the cemetery where the traffic sounds were distant. A flock of noisy crows was roosting in the trees. "*Vayanse! Vayanse!*" Hector shouted at the crows, waving his arms. They rose from the trees and flew out over the wall. "They make a mess of the stones," he said to Meg, leaning to straighten a small ceramic statue of the Virgin that had toppled on a grave.

They came to Vicente's stone. It was gray and porous, the engraving worn and intruded upon by lichen, but deeply cut and easily discernible: the birth and death dates and the name.

"He used the name Romero," Meg observed.

"He did," Hector Romero replied.

"Even on his stone," she said.

"To my shame, yes. You see, he wanted the name Morales on the stone. But I was unhappy about this. I was young. 'A son should have his father's name,' I told him. 'A father should have his son's name.' Bah. It was all theory. It was not life." Hector looked at the stone. "Now that I am old, I understand why he should want to use the name Morales. He was born Morales. For half of his life he was Morales. More than half. I should not have asked him to give up everything. He had lost too much. I believe he hoped that Claudia might someday come to look for his grave. I believe he wanted to leave something for her to find. But, there I was. Young. Brash. Hector Romero—standing in his way. And he did not trouble me with his desires. And Claudia did not find him. But here you are. You have found him."

He turned from Vicente's stone to the stone beside it. "My mother's grave," he said. "My sister and her husband are buried over there. My wife is buried here"—he pointed out the next stone in succession—"and here is where I will be buried, after the *federales* shoot me for a *narcotraficante*. Or after *los traficantes* separate my ears from me and let me bleed to death."

Meg was thinking of Vicente. "Why did he come to Mexico?" she said.

"He was a romantic, with a broken heart," Hector Romero answered. "His sense of destiny was inflated. Hannah was the woman he could not have. Claudia was the daughter he could not acknowledge. He had lost them both."

"But Claudia was living in Chicago. He could have gone there."

"To watch her from a distance?"

"He could have brought her to Mexico."

Hector dismissed the idea with a wave of his hand. "There were people who wanted to kill him. He lived a dangerous life. No one knew he was her father. He could not have proved it."

"Hannah could have proved it before she died."

He looked at her, and she thought she saw in his expression something close to disgust. "Claudia had two fathers," he said. "The father

Hannah did not choose, and the father she did." He leaned forward, close to Meg, looking her in the eye, the smooth side of his face waxy in the dappled sunlight. "The child's name was Claudia Bass," he said, and then drew back. "Why make her into a bastard? I am not saying it would have been impossible for my father to take her. I am not saying it would have been wrong. But my father was a lost man after Hannah died. He was consumed by grief and shame. He despised himself for Elliott's death, and held himself responsible. And not unrightly so. He turned to God. He came to Mexico, and left everything, even his name, behind. The book he was writing about New Mexico—he burned it; he wanted nothing to remind him of that place. And even so he lived with great regret. You see, he was a man of passion. Passion was his weakness. All of his life, he tried to make it his strength, but it was always his weakness."

A breeze passed overhead. "So you have always known that Elliott was buried at Pecos," Meg said at last.

"Of course," Hector Romero replied. "My father was not by nature a secretive man. He kept plenty of secrets. But this was never an easy task for him."

"He kept the secret from my grandmother that he was her father."

"He kept it from her. For her own sake. But not from me." He paused. "And I tried to keep it from you. He swore me to secrecy. But you have found out. So. Here. This should belong to you." He took the package from under his arm and offered it to Meg. "Hannah gave this to my father when she died," he said. "He took Hannah's body to Chicago to be buried. And then brought this with him to Mexico."

She received the package from him. "It was Vicente who took her body to Chicago?" she asked.

"Of course. What did you think?"

"I thought her brother had made the arrangements."

"My father made the arrangements. He attended the funeral. He saw Claudia there for the last time. She did not see him. She did not know of his presence. He left the journals for her, as Hannah had asked him to. And then he got on the train and did not get off until he was in Durango. He came dragging his grief into Mexico like a stone. He carried it forever. Hannah haunted our house. She haunted my mother. I have known her ghost all of my life. I have known of her daughter, Claudia, and I have wanted nothing to do with her. When my father died, he was at peace with Mexico. Lázaro Cárdenas was president, and my father felt that Mexico was saved. But he himself was lost. He carried in his mind always the death of Elliott Bass, and the loss of Hannah. Sorrow was in his nature."

"But his daughter tried to find him," Meg said. "He was still living when she came to Mexico to find him."

"Yes. He knew that she was looking for him. And he believed in his heart she was better off not to find him. What was he to tell her? Lies? To find the grave—that would be different. To find the man—no." He paused, looking at Meg with an expression in which she saw, for a fleeting instant, Bassie. "Don't mistake me," he said. "My father was a good man. He deeply loved my mother. She was young when he married her, she was beautiful; he was very kind to her. But he did not love her as he loved Hannah. I said this to him once, and he did not deny it."

Hector fell silent, turning his eyes to his father's stone. "When he was old, he thought of returning to the United States and telling Claudia the truth. 'Yet what would it be worth to her,' he asked me, 'suddenly to have an old man for a father?' Too much time had passed. Too much life had passed. 'Why make it all a lie to her, simply to gratify an old man?' "

He paused, and then said, "Claudia was conceived in the kiva, at the pueblo."

"He told you that?"

"As much. 'How is it,' I said to him once when I was young and arrogant, 'that you make love with another man's wife?' "

" 'I will tell you,' he said—and he was not angry with me for my impudence—'how it is. You go into a very deep hole in the earth. A sacred place. And you never come out again.' "

She stood for a moment, looking at Hector Romero, at his jacket with a tear in the pocket and his gray hair slicked with oil. He was a dissatisfied man, bitter and disappointed. He was not unlike Bassie. He had the same intrusive honesty, the same grudge against injustice. He was an uncomfortable companion, too bluntly critical to be at ease with. And yet Meg couldn't help but like him, and admire him: neither he nor Bassie had lived their lives in fear of the truth.

She unfolded the paper sack that he had given her, and removed a slender red notebook with a faded illustration on the cover—rolling hills and a barn in the distance, sheep grazing in a pasture. The edges of the book were frayed, the lettering scratched and rubbed. "Writing Paper Tablet," the lettering said.

She opened to the first page. "Hannah Bass" was written in ink in Hannah's peculiar, slanted handwriting. On the line below appeared the word "Noctuary."

"Noctuary?"

"I will have to teach English to an American?" Hector Romero asked. "It is a journal. But different from a diary. A 'diary' is an account of the day. 'Noctuary' is an account of the night. My father said he didn't know why Hannah called this book a 'noctuary'; it is a diary, like the others. Except that it reveals the nighttime of her soul."

Meg looked again at the strange word, "Noctuary," then turned a few pages, searching through the script. The glue of the binding was crumbling; some of the pages were loose. The paper was thin and ruled, a deep, yellowed color, darkened with age. There were smears of ink and stains of what appeared to be tea or coffee. The words were cramped. Some of the entries were written in pencil and some in ink; they covered the front and back of every page without consideration for the margins. Tucked between some pages in the back of the book, Meg discovered and withdrew three separate, folded letters, each beginning with "My dear Mrs. Bass."

"From her doctor, when she was dying," Hector Romero explained.

The noisy crows were lighting in the trees again. Hector Romero squatted beside the headstone and scratched at the growth of lichen that had begun to intrude on the name VICENTE ROMERO. After a while, he ceased to scratch at the stone, and tilted his face toward the crows in the trees and the blue sky spreading over the haze of pollution. He touched his fingers to his chest, forming the cross, and said in a tone as if he addressed the sky, "Everything we ever do in this life comes back to us in the end."

Jim was coming down the pathway. He was walking, hurriedly, toward Meg and Hector Romero, through the speckled sunlight, between the stones. Meg was aware of the noise of wings in the air. The birds were taking flight again. Hector was speaking to her; she could see that his lips were moving. But his voice was lost to the rising sound of the birds.

THIRTY-EIGHT

The old hotel where Meg and Jim had dinner together was just off the main plaza, its darkened restaurant decorated with potted trees, candlelight glittering on the varnish of the terra-cotta floors. They had decided to take rooms and stay the night and have an early start in the morning rather than drive all night to Santa Fe. This way they could sift through Hannah's journal together.

Meg settled into her room at eight o'clock in the evening and waited for Jim to meet her there. It was a plain, pleasant room, with a reading light on the bedside table and a print of a bullfight hanging on the wall beside the bathroom. Traffic noise was loud, and she stood by the window, looking down three floors to a congested street corner. Then she sat down in a chair with the journal, and removed the letters, written by Hannah's doctor, that were folded inside.

There were three of them. None of them had envelopes. The ink had paled to ghostly gray. Meg read some random lines; the script was large and excellent, the punctuation flawless. "I received your letter of the fourth. . . . You may be able to prevail in present circumstances if you follow my instructions precisely. . . . Headaches and the rapid pulse are to be expected. . . . Secure a bit of oily iodine. It is sold as Europhen. . . . Do not, under any circumstances, kiss your daughter."

Meg refolded the letters and placed them back in the journal, the last line lingering in her thoughts. "Do not, under any circumstances, kiss your daughter." She recalled passages that Hannah had written about how she and Bassie would wake in the mornings next to each other. How they would lie in bed and make shadows with their hands in the sunlight on the wall.

She got up and retrieved from her purse the envelope with the photographs that Hector Romero had given her in the café: Hannah seated on the sofa in the corner of the lobby of Saint Anthony's, and Bassie as a small child in a Chicago studio. The photograph of Bassie seemed unnervingly alive, the gaze intense for a child, the black eyes hard and inquisitive. Meg propped the photographs against the base of the lamp on the bedside table and sat looking at them, growing impatient waiting for Jim. She felt a need to be rid of the past, unwillingly captured by it.

At last she attempted to turn her attention to the stack of notes and articles that she had tossed into her bag, pertaining to the presentation for the FDA seminar she was to attend the following week. But she could not bring herself to read them. She spread them on the bed, but only looked at them. The subject involved a debate on the use of high-flux as opposed to high-efficiency dialysis, which at the moment seemed like a concept from a different world.

She imagined the FDA meeting. For years she had attended these seminars, and she knew how it would be: there would be a cocktail party where employees of the CDC—the Centers for Disease Control—would talk with the medical directors of hospitals. People from the FDA would keep to themselves. Everyone else would stand about, discussing transplant rejections and developments in medical instrumentation. Plastic tubing would be a topic of conversation; there would be talk about recently built manufacturing plants in Scotland and Mexico. The following morning the vendors would showcase new equipment in the exposition hall, and there would be panel discussions on the proper treatment protocol of Epogen, and on cultures versus lipopolysaccharides in the application of dialysis. Listening to traffic in the Juárez street below the window and waiting for Jim, Meg could not fathom herself sitting in an auditorium in Los Angeles taking notes on the mutation capabilities of pseudomonas, with its five thousand genetic codes. The exponential rates of replication in colony-forming units seemed like a strange piece of knowledge to have at the moment.

Jim finally arrived, freshly showered, his hair wet. He was wearing the same khaki pants he had worn for the past two days, and a navy blue T-shirt from the gift shop with "Ciudad Juárez" on the front in multicolored lettering.

Meg sat cross-legged on the bed with the journal open in her lap, and Jim pulled a chair up beside her. As she began reading aloud, she thought of Hannah composing the flow of words, and let her fingers follow the slant of the letters, looking at the smudges in the ink and wondering about the various stains. There were childish scribbles on some of the early pages, presumably done by Bassie. Eventually Meg grew accustomed to the writing, and read easily and swiftly, and Jim leaned back in his chair and watched her read.

Elliott had returned from Mexico. He appeared with his bags on the doorstep of the house at Pecos on the night of November 15 with Paco at his heels, having been gone for over a year this time—longer than ever before. Hannah was stunned by the disintegration of his looks and his affect. He seemed not only old and sick; he seemed despondent, and crippled. Claudia declined at first to relate to him or even to speak to him, having all but forgotten him, due to his long absence.

He had brought toys for Claudia—small wooden chickens that pecked at the ground when a string was pulled, marbles and puppets, an iron car to attach to her miniature train.

He could not lift the child. His arm was useless. "Carry me like Vicente!" she cried to him, and when he explained his debility, she did not understand, and answered, "Let me try to move it! I can do it! I can do it!"

He seemed at a terrible loss. His mood was inexplicable to Hannah, and did not resemble that of the man who had been writing to her enthusiastically from Mexico. His usual momentum had vanished and was replaced by a dull, slow, methodical manner of movement, even of his eyes, which turned in their sockets deliberately and settled on Hannah as if with a forced, willed focus that frightened her.

Cleofita roasted peanuts and spread a feast on the table. But the mood was not festive. The night was cold, the ground frozen under a blanket of snow from the week before, the sky clear and the moon full—all a glittering whiteness. Cleo went to her room. Hannah put Claudia in bed and lay beside her until she fell asleep. Elliott looked through a stack of papers and magazines: *Scientific American* and the *London Journals of Engineering*. He nursed his knees with a bag of heated salt. He went to the kitchen and drank Bayer powder mixed with wine. "He has built a fortress of bravado," Hannah wrote in her journal that night. "He would rather suffer pain than immobility . . . There is something terribly wrong, beyond the pain . . . He will not talk to me. . . ."

In the next entry, the words looked different on the page. The date was a month later. Meg could see from the first sentences that Elliott was dead. Hannah, in a frame of mind unimaginable to Meg, was attempting to recount the facts of what had happened. Her words had lost fluidity; they padded across the page, back and forth, flat-footedly, not in search of meaning but from habit and a routine sense of duty.

Hannah was numb with grief.

She began by assuming blame. Claudia, she said, was her only reason to live. Claudia was the result of her wrongdoing, the source of her greatest and most unbearable loss. And her only reason to live.

She described how Vicente had come to Pecos on the morning after Elliott's return. It was a Sunday, and he was accustomed to coming on Sundays. He and Elliott sat in the parlor and talked. Hannah heard part of the conversation as she passed in the hallway, and found it troubling and awkward. Elliott seemed empty of any emotion. He forgave Vicente too easily for the accusations Vicente had made in Las Vegas on the occasion of Roosevelt's visit. Vicente perceived the lack of feeling from Elliott, remarking that the reconciliation seemed half-hearted. He was disturbed to find his energetic friend turned cold and withdrawn. "I know you, my friend, and what you are giving is not forgiveness," Hannah heard Vicente say. "You are not forgiving me. You are excusing me. I have withdrawn everything I said about you, if not about Roosevelt and his war. But from you, I feel nothing. Your heart is not in what you are saying."

Later in the day the four of them, at Claudia's urging, put on their coats and went outside and walked in the snow—Hannah, Claudia, Elliott, and Vicente. Elliott moved clumsily with a cane, his left arm stiff at his side.

Night fell early, under the rise of a full moon. Cleo returned to the village. Elliott prepared the horse and buggy, intending to take Vicente down to the station at Rowe. Claudia was put to bed, and when she had fallen asleep Elliott took a candle and went to the bedroom to kiss her.

He did not return for a while. Hannah and Vicente sat in the parlor, waiting. When Elliott returned, the fire was down to coals. There was no light in the room but moonlight from the windows, and Elliott stood in the doorway from the hall, wax from a candle he held dripping onto his hand. He seemed—as Hannah wrote—not actually there. "Should I ask?" he said.

He said this only to Hannah. She knew his meaning at once. What she had most feared, had happened: he had seen Claudia's resemblance to Vicente. It had become too plain. Hannah felt herself a hostage to the truth, and looked at Elliott's face in the candlelight and was mute.

"She is not my daughter, is she?" Elliott said. He did not look at Vicente. When Hannah did not answer, Elliott turned back to the hallway. Hannah watched him go. She heard the back door close, the sound of his boots on the porch. She and Vicente did not look at each other, but sat listening to the tick of the mantel clock. Hannah stood up and went to the bedroom alone, where Claudia was sleeping. She did not look at her child, but sat in a chair, and in a moment heard the gunshots, one and then another. She could not tell their direction. She said to herself that a poacher had fired them, and went into the hall.

Vicente was there. He went out through the back door, following Elliott's footsteps. Argus followed behind him. Hannah remained inside. She went in search of Elliott's dog, but did not find him, and returned to the bedroom. From the window she looked at the barn and the valley covered in patches of snow. She heard Vicente calling for Elliott, his voice carrying downward, from Dog Hill, in the crystal air. He called for Elliott twice, but there was no answer. Hannah went to look for him herself. She went to the barn and the pens, and then to the ruins. She looked in the kiva and the church. She returned to the house, and as she entered the bedroom to see if Claudia was still asleep, she heard Vicente in the hallway. He came to the door of the bedroom, and when she turned, and saw his face, she knew that Elliott was dead.

His dog, Paco, was dead also. They were lying close to each other, on a flat area of soil within a circle of large boulders on Dog Hill. Hannah did not, on writing this, remember her feelings upon seeing him there. She remembered lying in the snow beside his body. She remembered that the place where he had fallen was in a ring of stones. The moon was overhead. Vicente wanted to go to the village and find the sheriff, but Hannah asked him not to. Even if neither of them—Hannah nor Vicente—should be implicated in the death—and Vicente, she feared, would be—the truth itself was enough to condemn them both. She was thinking of Claudia.

Better for all—better by far for Claudia—that Elliott had never returned.

They dug the grave to bedrock.

They burned the travel trunk and all the belongings that Elliott had brought back with him from Mexico—save those they put in the grave.

By morning, Vicente was gone, and Argus with him. Cleofita came, and Hannah, weeping, told her the truth of what had happened, and begged for her compliance. The grave, she said, must be accounted for, and for this reason, Vicente had taken Argus.

When Claudia awoke, Hannah told her that her father had returned to Mexico. And Argus, Hannah said, blinded by tears, had been shot in the night by poachers, and was buried on the hill.

It was a fabrication the little girl refused at first to believe. She denied that the dog was dead.

Meg became aware of music in the street below as she ceased to read. Jim rose from his chair. "I need a few minutes to think," he said. "I'm going down for a cup of coffee."

"Do you want me to come with you?" She closed the journal and put it aside.

"No," he told her over his shoulder, moving toward the door. "I just need a minute on my own."

She leaned back, and lay still, and closed her eyes, and listened to him close the door. She wondered if she should follow. But he had wanted to be alone. Her mind began to drift. She imagined herself in the house in the valley at Pecos, a witness to what she had read. The shots were fired, the sky swallowed the sound. Claudia remained in bed. But she did not remain asleep, as Hannah believed. She awakened at the sound. Her eyes opened to see her mother leaving the room.

Hannah went into the hall. Vicente met her there, they spoke in whispers, trying to keep their fears at bay. They denied the truth at first. They believed that Elliott could pass alive through flames. He could suspend himself from mountains to make his measurements without risk of falling, and live on the bark of trees.

Hannah waited, pushing down her fears. Then she went out looking for her husband. Snow was on the ground, air filled her lungs with biting sharpness. She ran rapidly across the snow in the valley, to the goat pens and the barn. She heard the bleating of the goats, saw them in the moonlight. She called to Elliott in the barn, but did not expect him to answer. She saw Dog Hill and the mesa rising above it, the roofless church standing in ruins. Time evaporated in the stillness. Hannah turned, and running, took the pathway to the ruins, gathering her skirts about her legs, climbing the ascent. She peered into the darkness of the kiva, speaking to Elliott in whispers that echoed around the empty walls, her tone threaded with fear that he would not hear her. And fear that he would. How, she asked herself, could she face him again?

She went to the church then, but did not find him. Panic was spilling out of her now. She sought the trail, the bottom of the hill, the house, the room where Claudia, curled under the blankets, appeared to be sleeping. And then Vicente came.

Hannah cried against him with desperate, pitiful tears. Claudia lay in the bed. Afraid. Mesmerized to stillness. Pretending not to hear. The memory searing itself into her brain so vividly it would remain there as the only vestige of her childhood for nearly ninety years.

They climbed the hill together in the moonlight, Hannah ahead of Vicente. Up the hill she ran, between the jagged boulders, tripping on her skirts, conquering the rocky incline with a flitting movement like a bird's. The bodies lay together on the ground, Elliott and his dog, bright blood melting garish pockets in the moonlit snow. Hannah dropped to her knees. She lifted her face to the old ruined church on the mesa, a wail ascending from her throat and trailing into the cold—freezing on the silent air, as if her soul were hanging there.

And what had happened then? What words had passed between them? Had Hannah and Vicente gone together to the barn, for the shovel and the pickax? At what point, as Vicente swung the pickax at the frozen ground and Hannah shoveled the dirt away, had they thought of how to account for the grave? A hole in the earth the size of a man's body—or that of a large dog—would be in need of an explanation.

And when, in the meantime, did Claudia, too frightened to sleep, steal out of her bed and go to the porch and stand in the cold, watching their strange labor in the moonlight? She was unsettled by the scene that she had witnessed in the bedroom—her mother crying, utterly forlorn, choking incomprehensible words of guilt, turning the world that Claudia had formerly known—twisting it askew.

She crept back to her bed, and did not see the fire when Elliott's traveling trunk was set ablaze and Vicente stood tending the charred remnants, watching the sparks ascend in the air and shoveling snow on the ashes. She listened, in the morning, to what her mother told her—Argus had been shot by poachers, and was buried on the hill. Her father had returned to Mexico.

But her mother seemed like a stranger telling her this. Her mother and Vicente were not the people whom she knew. Their eyes were glazed, their movements unnatural, their voices hollow in the vastness of the world. And the dog, Argus. Had she seen him, while they dug his grave? Had he stood beside the grave while they were digging? Had he—perhaps—stood beside Claudia, on the cold porch?

Claudia knew the dog was not dead.

And yet he was gone this morning. And her father had left again. Vicente was gone. She was strangely alone in a world that was changed forever.

So this, Meg thought, was the way it happened. Elliott chose the hardest punishment conceivable for Hannah. He had not allowed her even the chance to ask for his forgiveness. Since the age of six—when he had sat beside his mother attempting to extract the arrows from her flesh while women and children were slaughtered around him—since that day he had managed to avoid having anyone else taken from him. Only Vicente and Hannah, and then Claudia, had finally compelled him to risk himself in the name of love. And now the betrayal of these three people—their complicity—only one of them in innocence—had stripped away all that was left of his desire to live. It was too clear to him, and to them all, that the man who conquered mountains was fragile at the marrow.

Meg opened her eyes, and sat up, stretching her legs to the floor. She took up the journal again.

Christmas came and passed. Hannah turned away from Vicente. He was more of a ghost than Elliott, his presence seldom mentioned, hardly noticed, his absences unremarked on. He came to Pecos to see his daughter. But Hannah, lost to herself, could not bring herself to notice him. She wrote of Elliott instead—"I am unspeakably guilty. . . . All my dreams are of Elliott. . . . I think of nothing but Elliott. . . ."

Claudia was Hannah's link to sanity. But Claudia was drifting away. She talked to the goats in the barn. She talked with the dead in the kiva. Vicente tried to coax her to eat, pretending that his fingers were pecking chickens scrambling for the crumbs of her bread. He led her around on the dirt roads on a small gray spotted pony; he was immune to the bitter winds. It was a dreary and macabre existence for a child—a cold and heartless season.

Hannah developed a strange fatigue and lassitude, which she attributed to sorrow. A continuous cough kept her in bed. Then headaches and night sweats began to consume her. Cleofita soaked garlic cloves in brandy; Vicente brought medicines from town. Hannah was on the mesa one day, showing a tourist a view of the snowcapped mountain peaks; the wind was blowing; she stood where the path to the mesa entered the pueblo walls. She recounted the tale of a Pecos slave who lured the Spaniards away from the pueblo with the promise of gold on the horizon. And as she turned her head to cough, she tasted blood.

"What will ever become of my little girl?" she wrote in anguish that night. "For myself, I care nothing."

She boarded the morning train to Las Vegas, to the office of Dr. Middleton, who examined her with a stethoscope, a laryngoscope, a bronchoscope. He asked her to place a drop of saliva onto a small glass slide, and this he studied under the microscope and found the tubercle bacillus.

"What will become," she wrote again that night, her pulse rapid, her breath short, her cough disjointing even her thoughts, "of Claudia?"

On the following day she wrote to Fred Harvey, asking permission to discontinue the tours of the ruins.

Meg set the journal aside and went out in the hall and knocked on Jim's door, but there was no answer. She went back to her room and put her shoes on, and took the elevator downstairs to the restaurant, and found him at a table in the corner, nursing a cup of coffee.

"Do you think Bassie knew, before we started digging, that it wasn't Argus in the grave?" she asked.

"She knew it the night he was buried, and the next morning," he said. "I don't think she knew it last week." He looked tired, and older. "I wonder when she managed to forget it. Do you want some coffee?"

"No." After a moment, Meg said, "There were secrets all around her. And she knew that. No wonder she needed to have control over other things in her life."

Jim didn't seem to have heard her. "I've studied Elliott's life," he said. " 'Here's a guy who knows how to put the past behind him'—that's what I always thought. I admired that about him. It's what I admired most. And now it's pretty clear that actually he failed at that. What happened at Mountain Meadows was bigger than he was. It destroyed him. It's not a happy thought for me." He reached in his pocket and extracted some Mexican coins and dropped them on the table. "Do you want to take a walk?" he asked.

"All right."

"Do you want to get your coat?"

"I'll get yours too," she said. "Give me your key."

Leaving the hotel, they were greeted by exhaust fumes and stalled traffic. The sidewalks were crowded; doorways shuttered earlier were open now. They made their way through the people, past disco bars with neon signs. At last the street opened into a large plaza surrounded by storefronts and movie theaters, with an area of trees in the center. At the far end was a towering cathedral, its intricate spires ablaze with light, and beside it an old mission.

They turned toward the mission and walked in silence again. A woman seated on a blanket, on the sidewalk, with a small child sleeping beside her, held her hand out to them, and each of them rummaged through their coat pockets for coins and dropped them into her palm, then kept on walking. A barefooted child who witnessed this came running up behind, demanding something, but Jim waved him off.

"If you'd rather be alone—" Meg offered, as he had hardly spoken.

"I wouldn't," he answered abruptly.

"Jim?" she said. "Elliott spent his life running away from the past. And you have not done that."

"I'm not so sure I haven't," he answered. In a moment, he said, "I know there's no escape from it. If I haven't proved that, Elliott did."

A group of teenagers with spiked hair, wearing black leather and silver chains, passed from behind on the sidewalk.

"People are always saying you have to 'deal' with tragedies," Jim said. "That I haven't 'dealt' with my past. But I've been 'dealing' with it all my life. I think about it every day."

"You remember it that well?"

"Of course I remember it," he said bitterly. "What do you want, the gory details? What it's like to spend the night in a car with your father when he's been decapitated? What it's like when you can't recognize your mother's face? When she won't speak to you anymore?" His voice broke; he kept on walking and didn't look at Meg. She kept her pace beside him. At last he said, "But that's not what I remember the most. I remember the abject loneliness. I remember telling myself over and over again that it would be all right."

They had arrived, now, in front of the small old mission beside the larger cathedral. The structure was made of adobe and painted white, the exterior glowing a ghostly shade against the black night sky. An iron fence surrounded the two buildings; the gate was standing open. "I went to see a psychologist once, and he said I would need to confront the past. What does that mean?" Jim asked. Pausing, he gazed toward the lighted spires of the tall cathedral next to the mission. " 'Deal with it.' 'Confront it.' I don't know what any of that means. Do I want to think about things I can't change?" he asked. "Do I want to think about what happened? Do I want to think about the fact that I can't make love with you, because I have to think about my kids?" His eyes swung around to meet hers, and she saw he was crying. “God,” he whispered, “I am so . . . goddamn unhinged.”

She wanted to put her arms around him but resisted. They stood looking at one another. He shook his head. “Meg.”

“I know,” she whispered.

He waited a moment, looking at her, and then turned back to the mission. “I wanted to show you this place,” he said. “It’s the Mission of Guadalupe, the oldest building in Juárez. It was Vicente’s church that was mentioned in the obituary.”

They walked through the gate, and entered the mission through the heavy wooden doors. A cold silence greeted them. The place was lit with candles. An old woman wrapped in a blanket slept on a bench against the back wall. To the right of the door was a life-size Christ carved from wood, lying in a glass casket, wearing a crown of thorns. Candles burned on the steps leading up to the altar. The beams across the width of the nave were heavily carved with flowers. Meg took a few steps forward, the sound of her shoes echoing off the walls. Looking at the paintings on the walls, the statues of Jesus and the Virgin Mary displayed on pedestals beside the altar, she felt Vicente’s presence. There was a soundless quality, a cold, airless feeling that defied the limits of time. She turned around to look at Jim. He had crossed his arms at his chest. He was looking at the heavy beams spanning the nave, the intricate carvings of lilies and roses.

THIRTY-NINE

In Meg's room at the hotel, she sat with her legs folded, the journal nestled in her thighs, and read two passages aloud to Jim as he sat in the chair by the bed. They were undated, and scribbled without form.

The creosote and eggs have made me sick I believe the medicine has opium, I cannot think clearly. The snow is deep enough now to cover the ground. and I am glad to have detail erased as it does nothing but confuse me. . . .

The sun is blindingly white. I cannot focus, Claudia has gone out in the snow. Vicente believes I will not die. He is more convinced than I, I cannot eat the eggs. . . .

She gave the book to Jim, not having the heart to read. "You read for a while," she said.

He took the journal, and withdrew the three letters from Hannah's doctor that Meg had tucked inside. Unfolding them and looking at the dates inscribed he turned through pages in the journal and placed the letters into the proper places chronologically. When he began to read, Meg stretched onto her side, resting her cheek in her palm and watching his face in the light of the bedside lamp, listening to his voice moving over the pages.

For an hour they passed the book between them.

March 9, 1901

My dear Mrs. Bass,

I received your letter of the fourth. Please excuse my delay in responding. We are overwhelmed. The trains bring new arrivals daily, they come here for the altitude, but without funds, and the camps are overcrowded.

Let me begin by reminding you not to seal your letters with saliva. It is not a risk to me—I am immune—but to others. You must keep precaution foremost in your mind. Do not allow your child to be too close to you.

You may be able to prevail in present circumstances if you follow my instructions precisely. You must, in answer to your question, and with all discipline, consume the raw eggs, drink eight glasses of milk a day if you can, and try to keep the weight on. Eat as much red meat and butter as you can possibly tolerate. If you add some chocolate or vanilla to the milk and egg it will render the drink more palatable. Chocolate will not hurt you. As for creosote, it cannot be rendered tasty; you must force it down. Think only of recovery. Think only optimistically. I know you are reluctant to move your daughter to a separate bedroom, but this must be done. Explain to her the danger. You owe this to the memory of your husband: to preserve your daughter's life at all cost to yourself. It is difficult, but you must do it. Now, pertaining to the cough syrup you received from the catalog supplier, if it is said not to contain opium derivatives, then I believe the company reliable. However, I do not believe the syrup will be of benefit. You may use it if you like. But do not use patent medicines sold here in town; they contain opium and will do you no good.

The night perspirations and pains you are having in your shoulder are predictable effects of the disease. As I informed you in my office, your life will be compromised for some time before you can achieve recovery. But recovery is not, with the blessings of God, beyond your reach. I achieved it myself at your age and have had no relapse since. I will be your guide. My respect for your deceased husband, and my deep admiration of you, make your welfare of supreme concern to me.

Headaches and the rapid pulse are to be expected. You inquired about X-rays. There is no machine in town. It would be of little benefit, at any rate, as we have achieved a clear diagnosis by the microscope. Knowing the extent of the disease would not help us at this point: you must defeat it, large or small. Assessing the size of the giant would not have aided David in the battle.

I advise you to take light exercise if you are able. Keep the windows open day and night. This is beneficial to your lungs and safer for the child. Spend several hours of each day outdoors; the lungs are purged by air. Some of this we spoke of in my office, but I remind you how important every item is. Secure a bit of oily iodine. It is sold as Europhen. Massage it underneath your arms and in your inner thighs for half an hour every morning. I am not a great believer in the iodine, but many of my colleagues say it is beneficial. The odor is extremely foul. If you are suffering from nausea I suggest that you delay the applications. Keep me informed of your progress. Write to me with any questions. The fate of your body depends to a great extent on the state of your mind, and while God is the ultimate ruler, and His decrees cannot be known to us, there is a great deal we can do to save ourselves.

Please refer to Knopf's pamphlet that I gave you. It contains the information you will need about contagion. Adhere to it strictly. Do not, under any circumstances, kiss your daughter. Place strict limits on any contact with her; she must wash her hands hourly. Be sure to boil linens and bedclothes, and use separate utensils.

Remain as cheerful as possible. Dedicate yourself to gaining weight.

Yours, and Ever Sincerely,
Joshua Middleton

March 13. It is impossible for me to be easy in my mind as I am aware of every breath that leaves my lungs, for fear a shift of air will carry it to Claudia—I leave the house to go outdoors when the coughing is strong but I am uncertain if this is enough to protect her. The fever is up, I feel lightheaded—the sputum rags are stained and I wonder if it is possible for the germs to survive the boiling? I cannot allow Cleo to wash the rags, but feel so tired all the time and barely have the strength to wash them myself, and feel careless if I am not thorough. . . .

. . . It is the second monthly periodical that I have missed I am so thin, I suppose that it is for the better, I should not be losing blood from both ends or I will have none left. However, I was out of bed, the snow is gone, I sat an hour on the porch while Vicente was with Claudia. He is pressing me about the sanatorium, and says he can secure a room for me, wants to care for Claudia, is willing to pay Cleo to stay on, the insurance was lost as Elliott remained in Mexico too long and failed to pay, at any rate he is not deceased according to their books and I cannot collect a penny, Vicente will have to support us—

March 24. Claudia has fever and a cough—my fear is unbearable, my love too painful to endure, she is everything to me, I want nothing on this earth but to hold her in my arms

March 27, 1901

My dear Mrs. Bass,

Be calm now, for the child's sake. No doubt her fever will dissipate before this letter reaches you. A minor spell of coughing and a sore throat are to be expected at this time of year. I know your apprehension, it is not unreasonable, but you cannot live every moment plagued by fear. Be optimistic if you can. Concern is detrimental to your health and to your daughter's happiness. You must retain whatever aspect of control you can. If Claudia has not recovered fully in two weeks, bring her to my office. If you cannot put your mind at rest, bring her to me earlier.

Yours Ever,
Joshua Middleton

. . . it happened as I was taking the dishes from the table to boil them, Cleo was outside, Claudia stacking dominoes under the table. A bird distracted me by fluttering at the window and I left my milk glass on the table when I went to look. Claudia climbed up and got hold of the glass, she says she did not drink but when I turned she was setting the glass on the table and wiping her mouth with her hand—I vomited blood I was so seized with fear, and begged her for the truth but she would only say she had remembered not to drink and had not done so. I pled with her to wash her mouth but she refused, insisting that she did not drink the milk. I was unable to touch her until I washed, the blood caused me to choke, I called for Cleofita but she did not hear me, I was able to scrub my hands and get Claudia to the washroom though she fought me, I tried to wash her mouth with soda and stripped my clothes off as they were covered with blood, and stripped her and ran water in the tub—Cleo came—but Claudia would not get in, the water was ice cold. She was screaming and we had to force her in, Cleo put her finger down Claudia's throat to make her vomit so the germs would come up. I went to sterilize the kitchen floor but suffered more clots in my throat and had to go outside to vomit them without my clothes on. could I have killed my child because of the harmless flutter of a bird, could I have murdered her?

April 7, 1901

My dear Mrs. Bass,

I received your letter. While I wish I could advise you in good conscience to remain in your home where you prefer, my medical opinion mandates otherwise. Quarantine is always the safest measure in these cases, and while I oppose the recent proposals of some of my colleagues concerning mandatory quarantine for patients like yourself, I must in honesty advise you that your greatest chance of recovery, and of prevention of contagion to your daughter, is to place yourself in the care of professionals in a reliable institute. If you decide to heed this difficult advice, the institute I recommend most highly among a number of adequately operated sanatoriums in this area is Saint Anthony's hospital here in town. I am sure you know of it. Your friends in the Morales family are great benefactors. It is run by the Sisters of Charity of Leavenworth, Kansas. Two reliable doctors are affiliated with the place, one of whom is a friend of mine, Dr. Herman Steinfield, a German Jew and a recovered consumptive himself. He is a specialist in pleurisy and pulmonary cavities, and has studied the science of bacteriology in Germany and at the Pasteur Institute in Paris. He taught at the Medical College of South Carolina before coming to Las Vegas. I have the highest respect for his medical assessments, and would recommend you to his care if you should place yourself at Saint Anthony's. The sole objective of the Sisters is to cure their patients. The rules of hygiene are appropriately strict. Patients discovered spitting on the grounds are expelled. Otherwise the mandates are not overwhelming. Patients are not deprived of liberties, and the rooms are private. There are twenty four rooms. I have looked into the matter and your friend Vicente Morales could easily secure one. He informs me he has spoken with you already on this matter but that you are reluctant to leave your home. I recommend you pay a visit to the place. Your chances of recovery would be better at Saint Anthony's than in your home. Your progress would be monitored, sputum measured daily, weight and temperature recorded.

This is my recommendation. Yet should you choose to remain at home, you will find me, as always, at your service.

Yours Ever,

Joshua Middleton.

. . . she ran close to me on the porch as I was coughing and Vicente saw her do so, he is pressing me to go, I cannot endure the thought of leaving her, yet here I must study every move she makes, and constantly measure the space, every draft of the air, she defies the boundaries and only wants to be near. Brother wrote again last week urging me to send her to Chicago. If I should do this, I can dedicate myself to getting well. I could move to Chicago also but my chances of recovery are better in Las Vegas. I need her safe. I want her not too far away from me, but should not have her near. She does not know Brother, she does not know anyplace but here. If only I had someone other than Vicente to advise me. He is set against her going to Chicago. Says she will not be happy. Believes she will be too much for Brother—it may be true. He wants her here with him. He thinks only with his heart. I will stay at Pecos a little while longer.

Claudia has had a septic fever two days now, I cannot care for her when I cannot be near her, it is unbearable, she calls for me all night, she suffers so, Cleo had been nursing her, I cannot stop coughing cannot stop crying—

She was better today but got hold of a rag with sputum and put it on her head to taunt me, would not take it off, Cleofita stripped her clothes—we scrubbed her hair

In the past I loved the solitude out here, but now it gives me too much time to think, my thoughts expand beyond their normal realm and from the murky areas of my deliberations reality keeps surfacing to haunt me—exposure leads to infection—and Claudia by accidents and increments is constantly exposed—Everything I touch, I clean, but everything I clean, I have to touch, I cannot eradicate myself no matter that I try—It is spring and I feel nothing but despair. The expanse of sky only gives my fears more room to grow. I cannot protect my child. Cleofita is in the kitchen now forcing her to drink sage tea, it is supposed to prevent infection. But she will not drink it. She spits it out. Cleo wants her to eat raw garlic but she will not swallow it down. We have had to force it down. I feel unfocused. My palms are hot and dry. My pulse is rapid as a rabbit's, I perspire in the night and must sponge myself off. I must find, in my heart, resolve.

May 3. A letter from Jewell to-day that she is transferred to the Castañeda Hotel in Las Vegas and will come to see us when she is settled. Mr. Harvey's death has brought about changes; employees are shifted about. I am going to be forced finally to tell her my situation, but cannot stand the thought of theatrics, and do not want her tracking drama into my home

. . . it is as if my flesh is falling off of me—the fever is steadily high, my cheeks are burning red, when I try to read aloud to Claudia my voice will not project. . . .

The cough was worse last night, Vicente would not leave me. He is not afraid of contagion. He does not care. There is still the wall between us—everything that once united us divides us now. Even Claudia. We cannot agree on what to do. He rubbed europhen on my arms while I was coughing up clots, boiled resinous balsamic substances and emollient herbs and carried me to the kitchen to inhale the vapors. They did no good. I am not sensually passionate and have not been. I need Vicente with me, yet cannot bring myself to look at him, he is the only one who knows me for what I am.

Claudia thinks I am unreasonable and perverse. She defies the rules. To-day I was standing at the base of the steps to the porch and looking toward the hill and she leapt from the porch onto my back as she used to do, wanting me to carry her about. Instead my balance was knocked off and I was forced to my knees and began coughing up the clots and shoving her away—I am breaking her heart. She turns to Cleo and Señor Ruiz. She cries when Vicente leaves. She is always in the kiva talking to the dead. I wonder if someday she will go there and talk to me.

Señor Ruiz has died. The funeral was on Sunday. I was not well enough to go, Claudia went with Cleo. Vicente stayed with me. Claudia came home and would not talk to anyone. I found her in the barn digging with a stick in the offal of a pig. She dragged the paunch aside and squatted down to look at it, I asked what she was looking at, she said it was the soul. Bless her, bless her—we are all disappearing.

My suffering is seamless—an attempt was made on Vicente's life—the bullet passed between his body and his arm and tore the flesh of both—he came this morning early—I lay in his arms all morning, his tears fell on my face—the walls are broken down—nothing separates us now—we are past sorrow— We are resolved, as to what we must do. We will send her to Chicago. At any cost to us, she will be safe. The farther she goes from here, the safer she will be. I have got my path laid out. I am determined to be well. I will do everything to recover and have her back soon.

How can I bear this any longer. I walked on the ruins with her to-day. fever hot as the sun. We sat on the church wall and removed our shoes, and looked down at the house in the valley. Cleofita was out, hanging up the wash, and Claudia asked why she looked so small from where we sat. We talked of distances and how they can distort and rob us of detail, when in reality it is still the same—it is Cleo, hanging up the wash.

Vicente has put his rosary beads in Claudia's traveling trunk. Cleo wanted to wrap some Juniper berries so Claudia could keep the smell of them and be reminded of our home, but I have asked her not to. There is something too powerful in the smell of Junipers, they would evoke this place too vividly. I have given her the photograph of Elliott, and one of me, and have told her everything of where she is going, and why, and that I will have her back with me soon. She is putting up a brave face. She perceives my terrible sadness, but I have been so strange to her, for so long now, that I think she hardly knows what to expect from me. Vicente is staying tonight. He is now with me in the parlor as I write. Claudia is sleeping in Cleo's room. I have looked to see that she is comfortable a thousand times. Vicente paces the floor. The house is utterly quiet but for his footsteps.

I am writing only for something to do with my hands. Vicente has taken Claudia to the train. Jewell will meet them and take Claudia from there. I cannot stop weeping. She tried to be brave. She looked very small in the buggy. Turning back to wave. I cannot write it. cannot see the page. I feel cut in half.

July 29. Nearly a month I have been here, and not inclined to write. Have fever even on cool nights. Melancholy for Claudia. To-day the heat was harsh. To-night there is a breeze. We have electric lights, the curfew is not kept. I want my child. I want my child. I imagine her. I hear her voice. It is the perfect punishment for me. But for Claudia? What is this for Claudia? I cannot believe in God or a conducting providence. Nor can I believe in happenstance. It all goes unanswered.

About this place. Saint Anthony's. I am lonely at night. I have my thoughts but they are hideous company. Let me see what I can write. About the rules. They have mostly to do with hygiene. We cannot shake hands, we wash our hands before we handle public books or money. The men are required to shave. We spit in spitcups. We don't send our linens and clothes to the public laundries.

My consumption is the galloping kind. It progresses rapidly. Everything is monitored. Sputum measured daily in the spitcups. Temperature and weight recorded. The rooms have got electric call bells. I have a bed, a rocking chair, two tables, a chest, a Turkey rug. A fireplace. The window has an arch and looks down at the lawn. The building is two and a half stories of brick and stone. Steam heat. A library. A chapel. Sun parlors with chairs and make-shift beds, one of them enclosed in glass. An elevator operated by hydraulics. Meals are served in the dining room for anyone able to go. The dining room is narrow, with a fireplace and two long rows of tables.

All day we chase the cure. We sit in the parlors or out on the lawn. There is a balcony on the roof where we go to fill our lungs with balsamy air from the mountains. The days are not much different from each other. I am awakened at six-thirty. I take a sponge bath with cold water and apply the oily iodine and pull the bell. Sister Mary comes to rub me with a towel. This stimulates the blood. Once a week I am allowed a cold tub in the morning. At seven-thirty we have breakfast in the dining room. It consists of milk and raw eggs from the poultry yard. We are supposed to eat six eggs a day and drink two quarts of milk and one of cream. We mix vinegar in the eggs to hide the mawkish taste.

We stay outside in the chairs throughout the morning. In the middle of the morning we are served a raw egg in a glass of milk. At noon we go to the dining room and are given meat, bread, butter, milk and eggs. We go to the chairs again. Visitors come in the afternoon. Vicente comes. Jewell comes. Diana Morales came last week. It is not too dreary. We walk in the garden. Some of the patients play croquet. We take twelve hours in the chairs each day. To be reduced to eight in winter. Some of us attend church on Sundays. I am not among these. Sister Rebecca and Sister Agnes have tried to bring me into the fold. But I am not going.

Dr. Middleton comes once a week and Dr. Steinfield every day. Dr. Steinfield has a German accent. He says I have an excavation in the lower portions of the left lung, also disintegration in the front portion at the top. My right lung is emitting breath sounds of vesicular nature and dry crepitations but there is no evidence of cavitation (these are the clinical words by which I live my days now) some of which is hopeful. Dr. Middleton insists the outcome of our efforts will depend on how devoutly I will follow the regimens. Dr. Steinfield—though he will not say so—is not so optimistic.

I am doing everything exactly to the letter, but the flesh is drawing off of my fingers all the same, and my nails are curling at the ends. The flesh around my eyes is nearly black, the pupils are large, my skin smells like stale beer. My breath is offensive. I suppose that I am only vaguely human. But I am supposed to keep my spirits up, and must do the best I can. No one here is better off, and no one is complaining.

I keep the journals under the bed. I never look at them. I don't know why I continue to write. I have nothing to say. It is all input and output, the measure of sputum. My thoughts are only about Claudia and she is not here. I should read what I have written in the journals long ago and black the pieces Claudia should not see. But I don't have the heart to do it. To relive it. I don't have the strength.

August 3. Very hot today, and with a fever. All morning throwing up the sponge. Took castor oil to stop the vomiting. Stools watery from castor oil and purgative powders, also from Epsom salts yesterday. A flyblister on my breast for more than an hour, followed by hot towels. Nearly burned a hole in me. Breast resembles a porterhouse. Sputum doubled today from yesterday—five ounces. Half blood with clots of pulmonary matter, very foul. Yet it signifies we might have broken down a nodule. Temperature is septic. My life is down to this. I think only of my beautiful Claudia and write only of this ugly body that I am somewhere lost in.

We were awakened earlier than usual for fumigation of the rooms. Breakfast at five-thirty. That is too early for raw eggs. Got them down but threw them up. The problem is the strychnine tonic and the sulfate of magnesia prescribed to ease pressure on my circulation. Relieved me from the wrong end I suppose. This after-noon a cupping followed by a blister. left me very weak. Blister had half an inch of water. Gave me a headache and a blue mood. Jewell came. Then Vicente. Also a young woman named Betty who came to apply the laudanum. She suffered from consumption at the age of five, recovered at age ten, is therefore immune. She is half Negro, younger than I, the daughter of Mr. Bell's cousin who operates a cafe in Old Town. She does not believe in optimism, but in prayer.

August 25. Very hot in the chairs to-day. Perspired from heat all day, from fever all night, pulse at 122, was given injections of nitroglycerine. Was given ice to eat. Apparently I am good and rotten inside. Iodine toxicity is back, so I am off the oil. Dr. S. and Dr. M. in disagreement about calomel and ergot. I am off those also. Have been for a week. Penelope died last night. I knew when I heard crying in the hall. Dr. M. all night working in the camp in town—has got lice in his hair, says the consumptives all come with a one-way ticket, there is nowhere to house them, they are treated as pariahs by the citizens. The Sisters are worn down. Sister Mary at the camp all day, and with Penelope last night

Dr. S. here earlier on a soapbox about the drinking dippers at train station—has done some good with his reforms—but not for me, I appear to be a gone case actually. Cannot walk 100 yards without assistance. Remember climbing to the ruins with Claudia. That was when I still had lungs. I write to her. Lies, sometimes. That I am becoming well. Coughed up blood today, thick but without matter, eight ounces, by the mouthful. I suppose I have no pulmonary matter left. Lay two hours with a rubber bag of icy water on my chest. Better than a fly blister, I must say. Vicente was here with me. He cares nothing for the rules of quarantine, will not stay out. I wrote again to Claudia—a story—

Mrs. Rhodes refused a flyblister but agreed to a plaster of croton oil and now is sick with a vesicle—has a queasy appetite from creosote and not the stamina to bear it quietly—all of us are suffering constipation from the iron, or diarrhea from the salts, but go about it quietly, except for Mrs. Rhodes. . . .

A letter from Brother—and pencil sketch from Claudia—of mountains. They remain all right, for this I need to be grateful. He promises to send a photograph. There is some affection between them but slow in coming, he is not patient, and she is demanding and prone to a test of wills, I know this about her. And he is capable of being selfish. However, he desires to be helpful in this situation. If he will be patient he will win her over. I have tried to communicate all this to him in a letter. Bless him, he is doing the best he can.

Weather smells of junipers and autumn—Mrs. Morales came—we sat in the garden—sky threatened rain, wind tossed leaves about and sent them skittering— We spoke of Vicente. She wants me to come to the mansion. Yet I will not go dragging illness into her home.

Sarah Connally has got it in the right lung now. Has had it in the left. Could live a while on one lung. But I cannot think she will do well on no lungs at all.

Polly vomited her morning lunch, was given whites of eggs which she retained, would not drink any milk. Her temperature high, her throat sore—they suspect diphtheria.

Liquid stools all day and vomiting. Morphia gave me an hour of sleep continuous, no coughing. Gave me visions of Claudia. Had no desire to go out. I could possibly sleep to-night if not for ice on my chest—am chilled—writing upside down—the reason for the pencil, so not to spill the ink—arms as heavy as lead. Could not drink the eggs. Drank beef tea. Vicente came, talked about McKinley being shot. Talked about Roosevelt—still angry about him. Room smells like iodine and blood, even with the windows open. Must lie here till the fever drops—ice numbs my chest. teeth rattling. Something disagreeable happening in the hall but cannot see from here.

More codeine today—hours in the chairs but the weather good. However my mood black. No need to use a stethoscope, or auscultation and percussion and compare the sounds to wool or silk, new or old leather. They are like a crackling fire. Loud enough to hear without the instruments. I suppose I have not been here long enough to turn myself around. Another letter from Brother last week. Claudia suffered from cough. I wish he would not tell me. To-day a card, to say she is all right. If I die then I will never get my mind at ease about her. Brother says she doesn't ask for me so often anymore. She anticipates the letters however. She liked the story I wrote her about the goats. The housekeeper reads to her.

October 20. I am better to-day and off the codeine but the weather is cold. Mr. Talbot who arrived last month has been sitting all day shivering with his head down nearly on his chest. His rales are bad, he cannot breathe, he pulls at his shirt. He used to greet me when I passed him, now cannot. He has six children still in Cincinnati, no one to support them. Hallie down the hall is also doing poorly but has set her mind to getting well, she requested wet rubs rather than the dry, with alcohol or cold douche, and kept down eighteen glasses of milk to-day. Yesterday I kept down seventeen. Mr. Gillis has pleurisy, is wearing a plaster on his chest yet shows nothing but good spirits, Mr. Butte is worse, cannot walk, his spine is nearly gone. He hailed me from his room. Nelda T. has made it out of here. She left three days ago and was improved. Sue B. is incoherent on the codeine but her cough is less persistent.

October 31. I am not well, may never be, but to-day I am not coughing up the matter. The weather is cold. Vicente's visit was a feast of reason, a flow of soul. Letters arrived from Brother and from Claudia; Brother took dictation. They had gone to see the buildings left from the World's Fair. He told her that her papa and I had been there, but she denied that I had been alive before I knew her.

If only I could be alive now that I do.

November 12—I have gained two pounds. Yester-day half a loaf of bread and slab of butter thick as a book stayed down—

November 16. I have gained another pound and have got my breasts back now, there is some improvement in the cough. Dr. Middleton gave me a manual by a doctor associated with the Phipps Institute and having success with the cure, and I will keep his rules to the letter—

—remain improving, Am staying in the chairs longer than required. though afraid to hope. If I continue to do well I can use the strength to look at the journals with an eye to editing. Perhaps there are passages worthy of readership, though I will need to make deletions, too much is revealed.

November 30. A blister to my chest to-day failed to raise a vesicle of decent size so we blistered my back, am now lying on my side, will do everything I must so not to lose ground.

December 5. Remission for three weeks has made me hopeful forever. But the cough has returned.

December 11. Cough was harsh again to-day—sore throat—have lost all of the weight. Am trying not to be discouraged. Was in the chairs longer than required, on the balcony until midnight. Very cold. The others fold their blankets twice— They may do so, I will not. Vicente is arguing with Dr. S in the hallway—thinks the treatment too harsh, that I am blue from freezing.

Rather I am blue from dying. That is what I am blue from.

It is all bad news. Tubercles in the larynx now also. Dr. Steinfield saw them yester-day. Dr. M. confirmed to-day. I have been weeping all this terrible afternoon. It is cold here. I want my girl. I wonder what she is doing. Brother said she has a friend next door. Betty built a fire but it only made me melancholy. Vicente stayed all day. I want my little girl here. My weight has not come back. Breath is bitter. Vomited the cream and butter from this morning. Have not written Claudia in several days—can think of nothing to say.

December 15. Claudia has convinced herself that I will visit her for Christmas. She will not hear otherwise. Insists to brother I am coming though he tells her I am not. I will break what is left of her heart.

A difficult day. Jewell and Vicente here to show me the gifts for Claudia. Ribbons and dresses. A turquoise bracelet. A silver ring. Jewell is going to send them.

Dec 19. Lay about all day looking at Claudia's picture.

Cleo here to-day. We talked of Claudia. Remembered everything. Cleo is too kind to me. She loves my child. It is a long way for her to come and see me.

Dec. 21. I cannot find a balance between optimism and despair. I do not know which is better. My hope has drifted off as irretrievable as air. Maybe there is still some reason to try to hold on— I have discipline, have care, have the chance of living long enough for someone to find a cure. Mr. Phipps has given a million dollars to that end. We have vaccines for rabies, antitoxins for diphtheria—Why no cure for me? I would pray for it, had I not long ago forfeited my right to prayer.

I got the journals out to-day and looked at them but will not do it again. I should get rid of them but they are all that is left of me, that I can leave for Claudia. I have no strength to read them and strike things out.

Too much time spent staring up at heaven after dark on the balcony alone. Life seems just outside my focus, beating its wings—

Fell asleep in the chairs on the roof and dreamed of Elliott. Dreamed that he was with me. It was only Betty leaning over me and blocking the stars. Asking me to come in. "Are you trying to freeze yourself to death?" she wanted to know.

No, no, I'm freezing myself to life.

My room is no warmer than the roof—the ink is frozen—therefore the pencil—ice in the pitcher—urine frozen in the bowl—spit frozen in the cup—Since the dream I think of Elliott at every waking moment. I see him on the hill. Paco beside him in the snow. The absolute whiteness of moonlight, the eternal quiet. What cannot be remedied must be endured.

I may live to see spring. I will fight a little longer.

January 15. My throat is infected with lesions. Voice is nearly extinct. Sputum is half blood. Fever down to 102 by bedtime. Cannot cease from coughing long enough to write.

Too much pulmonary detritus, took hydraulic acid for my stomach, pepsin for my liver—

The house at Pecos has burned. There is nothing left. Vicente and Jewell did not tell me but the sheriff came from Pecos, Vicente blames the White Caps but the sheriff disagrees—it is all gone—I had hoped to go home to the house. To have Claudia there. It is probably for the better. Not to have a ghost without a soul inhabiting the valley. The slate is clean, the valley empty. The grass will grow

Cannot keep the milk down—have more matter coming up than going down, pulse rapid and weak.

Dislodged a six ounce clot in coughing, was given sulfate of magnesia for purging—tonic of strychnine and phosphorus did no good.

All day staring at a seam of light between the curtains.

Pulse up to 134 so was given digitalis. A cold sponging. Bismuth and magnesia for nausea. I have no memory of ever being warm

Jewell came but not permitted to the room. Nitroglycerine. Claudia watches from the frame.

Vicente here all day, my voice ruined, hard to swallow, I am going to have a grave beside my parents, Vicente will take me, he will tell Claudia, he will bury Claudia's letters with me I want everything of Claudia with me. Have written to Brother. There is nothing to be done about it. Where is my courage.

coughing all day. pancreatin for digestion. Sulfuric acid on my chest. Hemorrhage of thirteen ounces sanguino purulent matter. I miss my child

There is blood on the bedcovers and on the flowered wall. I am coughing my lungs up ounce by ounce. The matter will wash away. The stains will stay.

Feb 8. Nausea and fever. Difficulty breathing. Cannot talk. It is raining. I remember the fortune teller said all sorrow and repentance

Jewell was not admitted to the room. Rain continues. I want to go home. Temperature 104. Vicente with me.

I am on my back—ice on my chest—writing upside down. Vicente is here and will not leave. Bless him he has built a fire. I gave him Claudia's picture. To take away. She ought not have to watch.

More quinine, which I did not want. I do not feel bothered about my condition Or want help. I do not care.

I am becoming tired of the taste of blood.

That was the final sentence. The last entry. It was Meg who read it aloud. She sat looking at the words when she had finished. Hannah, to the last, had clung to the only thing left to her: it was not hope, but an understanding of the vagaries and vulgarities of life and human effort.

Wanting to hide the depth to which the journal had affected her, Meg did not look at Jim, but turned through a number of blank pages to the end of the journal. There she found the last page littered with notations. "There are notes back here," she said, studying them.

Jim moved to the edge of the bed to see them. They were disorderly; the ink had not flowed evenly. The words were turned in various directions, the letters slanted. Some of the pencil markings were so pale that they were difficult to read.

"She was writing to Vicente," Jim observed.

They sat silently discerning the words, Meg turning the book now and then to follow sentences down the length of the page. "FOR WHEN SHE IS OLDER" one notation said. ". . . WHAT IS THE DATE? . . . WILL YOU FIND BETTY PLEASE . . . I CAN'T EAT IT . . . GET DR. M. INSTEAD OF DR. S. . . . WHAT IS THE NOISE IN THE HALL? . . . TELL THEM NO MORE CODEINE PLEASE. . . HAVEN'T YOU SOME SHEEP TO TEND TO DEAR HEART? . . . IT WAS A DREAM ABOUT CLAUDIA . . . IT IS TOO LATE FOR THE BLISTER, IT WILL NOT HELP. . . NOT SO CLOSE, WOULD YOU HAVE ME TAKE YOU WITH ME? . . . WILL YOU GO ACROSS THE HALL AND SEE IF SARAH IS BETTER . . . I DO NOT WANT ANY MORE . . . I WILL NOT BE BOTHERED IF YOU CRY." There was also a Scripture copied in Hannah's handwriting in splotched ink:

Make us glad according to the days wherein thou hast afflicted us and the years wherein we have seen evil. The days of our years are threescore years and ten; and if by reason of strength they be fourscore years, yet is their strength labour and sorrow; for it is soon cut off, and we fly away.

Hannah had not rejected God as devotedly as she had claimed.

Jim, at last, stood up. Meg closed the journal. She was trying to fathom what it held. The words, somehow, seemed almost to be the least of it. The regrets and shame, the physical discomfort and the pain, were in many ways more visible in splotches in the margins and faded smears of what appeared to be blood on the page before the end, than in the succession of words that was so stalled and tortured that the punctuation had fallen away and the dates were omitted.

Bassie, Meg realized, must have lived her life from the age of three in apprehension of the truth of Elliott's death—or of some notion of it—that eventually was obscured by time, though intensified rather than diminished by that obscurity, like the fears of a child in the dark. She remembered the gunshots, the whisperings, the grave. Lodged somewhere in her memory was the knowledge that Elliott had been with her that day—that he had come home, and sometime in the night simply disappeared, his disappearance strangely confused with that of the dog, Argus, and with the digging of the grave.

Meg got up and walked to the window, listening to the street noises from below—voices, occasional shouts, the thud of distant music.

"I should go to bed," she heard Jim say behind her.

She turned, and looked at him. She looked at the clock, and saw that the time was nearly two in the morning.

"But I don't want to," he said.

She did not want to be alone. "I think you should," she said.

When he was gone, she changed into a T-shirt and turned the lights out and got into bed. A yellow sheen from the streetlights glowed through a gap in the curtains. From somewhere down the street came the rhythmic and repetitive thumping of drums.

She was utterly saddened. She wanted to knock on Jim's door. Short of that, she wished she could bring back the dead. She found herself longing for Hannah and Elliott and Vicente, as well as for Bassie. She felt that she had spent her life facing into a strong wind and had managed only to stand against it; she had not made any forward progress. She was thirty-seven years old with no family of her own. She could not help but wonder how different she might have been, had the past been different. Had Hannah lived. And Bassie continued to be loved. The pages of the noctuary had revealed to her how violently the family had been torn apart. And now here she was, likely to be the last of Hannah's descendants, lying sleepless in a dark hotel room alone, unsettled by the past, dreading the future, and wanting to take refuge with a married man. She felt weak and vulnerable.

An hour later, at three o'clock in the morning, she was still awake when Jim knocked. "It's me," he said through the door.

She pushed the bolt and unfastened the chain to let him in, then closed the door behind him, shutting out the light in the hall. The soft light from the streets below remained. He put his arms around her. He was barefoot, his shirt hanging open. He kissed her. She reached her arms around him. They moved together to the bed and lay down on it; he dragged himself away from her only long enough to peel his clothes away. He pulled her T-shirt off and dropped it on the floor. She moved against him, and felt his chest against her skin. She opened her eyes, and saw on the bedside table the photographs that she had propped against the lamp, the images illuminated by the yellow thread of street-lights shining through the curtains: Bassie as a child—the stare, the black curls—in a lacy pinafore. And Hannah seated on the sofa beside the palm tree in the corner of the lobby of Saint Anthony's, her shawl around her shoulders, her eyes looking directly into Meg's.

Meg closed her eyes again and lay for a moment nestled, naked, against Jim. She saw clearly the pattern of all their lives—Hannah's and Vicente's, Elliott's, Bassie's, Nina's, her own. The wrongs had filtered down through generations. And now Meg was left in the ruins.

But she was still here. With a life that seemed inconsequential when compared to these others, without the texture and fame, without the force of tragedy—without any of these things—Meg was still the one with time stretched out before her. The pathways to the past had been opened and she had been drawn in. But they would not, even if she pursued them, lead her very far. Darkness would eventually descend. She needed to turn around and get on with her life again.

"I can't," she whispered to Jim.

He moved his lips against her breasts.

"Don't," she whispered. "Please."

She felt his movements slow. He lifted himself onto his elbow.

"I'm sorry—we can't do this; we can't, Jim."

"We can."

"I won't," she said.

He studied her eyes in the dim light for a moment, and then rolled off her, and sat on the edge of the bed. At last he leaned and lifted her shirt from the floor, turned and handed it to her. He pulled his own shirt on, stood up, and put his pants on.

She put her T-shirt on, and he turned around and looked at her, then sat on the bed again. She moved to the edge of the bed, and put her feet on the floor, and sat beside him. They sat side by side saying nothing for a while, staring down at their feet.

"Let's go back," he finally said.

Half an hour later they crossed the border into El Paso and began the long drive north. They made their way through the mountain passes, the air around them sharp and clear, the lights twinkling from the dark hills along the highway, distant and otherworldly. Meg felt as strangely isolated from the outside world as if she were traveling across the face of the moon. They drove mostly in silence, connected to one another by every emotion that seemed to matter, and yet separated by the circumstances of their lives.

They stared ahead through the windshield, the lights of the dashboard glowing green on their faces.

FORTY

It was just before one o'clock in the afternoon when they arrived at the parking lot of the Maxwell Museum on the university campus, Jim pulling the truck to a stop beside where Meg had left the rental car. He turned the motor off, and looked at Meg.

"Don't say anything," she said.

For a moment he complied. Then he said, "Will you call me before you leave?"

She agreed to do so, and got out and unlocked the rental car and tossed her bags in. Jim came around to where she was standing.

"I'm just going to leave," she said.

"I'll talk to you later, then," he answered, understanding her aversion to a display of emotion, and went back around to the truck.

When he had driven off and she was pulling out of the parking lot, Meg let the tears flow. She stopped the car to get hold of herself, but for at least five minutes did not attempt to do so. She sat in the car, parked crookedly at an open curb in broad view of anyone passing by, and put her head back and allowed the tears to roll down her face shamelessly. The afternoon sun shone through the car window and warmed her face, but she felt cold, and almost sick with exhaustion.

After she had stopped crying, she drove to a filling station to fill the car and use the pay phone. She called the airlines to see what flights were available for the afternoon or the evening, and found they were booked full. Disappointment almost overwhelmed her. The thought of being trapped in New Mexico overnight, without Jim's company, was horrible to her.

A Motel 6 stood across the street from the filling station, so she drove over and got a room and fell on the bed without even removing her shoes. She found the energy to pick up the phone and dial Paul's office number. "Glad to know you're still alive," Paul said. "I didn't appreciate being hung up on. I didn't deserve that."

She could barely remember the incident now. "You did, Paul," she answered tiredly. "I'm sorry, but you did."

"Well, I would have watered your grandmother's plants, but you didn't stay on the phone long enough to tell me where to find the key."

"Paul? I think we need out of this relationship," she said.

"Why? If I might ask" was his response.

"Because we don't care about each other. We just don't. And I'm not talking about the plants."

He afforded her a moment's silence. "I know," he answered at last. She heard him sigh. "But if I'm not in love with you, I don't know who I'll ever be in love with."

Leave it to Paul, she thought, to attempt to turn the conversation into a discussion about himself. He was even worse than her mother in that proclivity. She almost corrected his grammar, as Bassie would have done. "*Whom*," she almost said. "*Whom* I'll ever be in love with. And don't end on a preposition." But she didn't care enough about his grammatical inaccuracies, or his inability to love, to comment on either of these at the moment. She didn't have any emotion left to spend. He could find someone else to counsel him.

"You'll work it out," she said.

"You think we shouldn't see each other at all?" he inquired.

She wouldn't care if she never saw him again. She wondered briefly how she could have given nearly a year to a relationship that offered her so little. And it wasn't the first time she had done so. She had suffered through too many similar skirmishes with self-absorbed men. "I don't know," she said carelessly, in answer to his question. "Can we talk about it later?"

"All right," he said, "but I want to go on record saying I was going to water Bassie's plants, and if there's anything else you need in the meantime, I'll do that too."

He did not, she knew, expect to hear from her again. She felt suddenly lost, at how easily he could release her. "I would ask you to help me pack up Bassie's books and things," she said, "but you should probably stay away from the molds."

"You're still mad about my headache?" he asked resentfully.

She wasn't, actually. She was disgruntled about a few things, but his headache had only been a symptom of his deeper flaws. She said, "I didn't intend for that to sound so mean."

After she had hung up, she fell asleep and awakened several hours later, disoriented and depressed. She lay on the bed for a while and thought about Jim. She considered taking a shower and getting something to eat, but realized she had nothing clean to wear. Finally she dragged herself up and called the front desk and inquired if there was a laundry on the premises. There was a Laundromat down the street, they said, so she dug some clothes out of her suitcase and stuffed them in her canvas bag and walked the distance. It was late in the day by now; the sunlight was faded, and disappeared utterly while she walked.

She found the Laundromat deserted when she entered, though a woman with four children came in as she was putting coins in the washing machine. She was relieved when the woman only retrieved a mound of clothing from a dryer and then departed again.

She watched her clothing tumbling around in the soapy water. The circular motion had a numbing effect on her nerves, and she found herself sedated by the sleep, though her thoughts were too clear. She thought of everything awaiting her on her arrival in Austin. Bassie's house. The Pontiac parked in the drive. The cracked walkway, paint peeling off the porch rails. She imagined herself entering: how she would flip the light on. A musty illumination would reveal the rolltop desk encumbered with its oversized computer and the fax machine, the electrical wires festooned over the back. The orange plastic couch would be squatting in front of her, combative on its short chrome legs, like an obstinate old bulldog. The lacquered bass would stare down from the mantel with its glassy eye. Everything—the books, upholstery, the curtains—would emit a rank smell. Meg thought of moments from her childhood spent in this room with Bassie, a fire in the fireplace and Bassie clicking away on her typewriter, rising occasionally to make her way to the fire and take the old puffer down from where it hung on the mantel and try to bring life back to the ashes.

What—Meg wondered—would she do with the rotting old puffer now? It was still hanging from the mantel. What would she do with the books? Most of the books contained Bassie's markings in the margins. Bassie had critiqued even fiction as she read it, unable to resist the deletion of commas, the substitution of words. Meg could not imagine giving the books away and scattering these random notes among strangers.

There were also all the numerous files and papers. The hallway to the bedroom was lined with stacks of pages. Meg could still see Bassie moving down the narrow path between the stacks with her black cane, disrupting not a page. She recalled this and allowed herself a moment of self-pity. Why should she have to deal with all of this alone, her bereavement so grotesquely complicated by this pile of detritus? Bassie, of course, would have wanted her to keep it all, to move into the house and live there burdened with the superficial trappings of a famous grandmother who was also a pack rat.

But Bassie was no longer here to tell her what to do. Meg would be forced to do everything in her own way. She would have to discover how to deal with Bassie's history, as Bassie had been too involved in dealing with Hannah's to worry much about her own. She had been too busy shoving back the edges of her world, tromping through her front yard, whacking weeds with her black cane.

The mementos she had left had all been odd ones: her collection of artifacts, old drafts of manuscripts, file cabinets filled with every piece of correspondence she had written or received in the last half century of her life. There was the drawer in the bathroom filled with her hair.

And Hannah's journals tucked in a file cabinet, in the dusty old file room.

Meg sat watching the clothes revolving, and wondering what she would do with all of these items in Bassie's house, and wondering, most of all, what she would do with the final journal—the noctuary—that was now in her room at the Motel 6. It was, after all, the ending of a story, but not of the story told in the previous journals. The story that Bassie had built her life and her career on was a fabrication. If not a lie.

And here the truth had made its way to the surface.

The question that Meg now found herself to be facing was whether or not to bury it again.

FORTY-ONE

Meg arrived at the Pecos visitors' center early in the morning, and saw that Jim's truck was not in the parking lot. She entered the center and found the park ranger, David Valdez, at the desk.

"Will Jim be coming in this morning?" she asked.

"Oh, yes," David replied. "Jim comes in every morning. They tell me that he comes on Christmas day."

"When he gets here," Meg said, "would you tell him I'm up at the ruins and ask him to come find me?"

She climbed the path to the ruins, and descended the ladder into the kiva, leaving the morning sunlight washed across the surface of the ground. She allowed her eyes to adjust to the dark. The scent of the cold earth encircled her, and she thought of Bassie in the grave. She thought of Bassie here in the kiva as a small child conversing with the dead.

Bassie, it now seemed to Meg, had always listened better to the dead than to the living.

And now it was Meg's turn. She crossed the subterranean room and seated herself with her back against the circular wall, folding her legs in front of her and setting the envelope she was carrying on the ground beside her. She sat a moment, quietly, listening attentively. And heard no voices at all. Nothing from Bassie.

For a moment she almost resented this. She still resented, she realized, a number of things about Bassie.

She thought of Hannah and Vicente making love here in the kiva. The place had been one of connection for Hannah and Vicente and then Bassie, through nearly a century, down to Meg. The Pecos Indians had believed it was a world between the worlds, the entryway to life. It had been the entryway for Bassie, if it was here she was conceived. The kiva, with its earthy smell and dirt walls, was a kind of wormhole, a portal joining one world with another. Through it flowed the barriers of time. The slump in the dirt on the far side, where the morning shaft of sunlight did not reach, was to the Pecos Indians the *sipapu*—the navel connecting the world above with the world below, an entry to the mysteries of the underground.

Meg wished that she could find a way to unite Bassie with Hannah again here, and dispel the disillusionment and misconceptions that Bassie had suffered about her mother in the end. For so many years in her childhood, exiled in Chicago, Bassie must have longed for Hannah, only later finding a semblance of resolution: she had made her mother's journals into a labor of love to which she sacrificed all other people in her life. And then, in the last hours, it had come crashing down.

Meg, at least, knew the end of both of their stories—Hannah's and Bassie's—while they had lived their lives not knowing the end of each other's. She was the one with the chance to make sense of it all.

Yet here she was at the end of the family line. And she did not know how to talk with the dead.

She sat with her back to the wall, a beetle moving slowly near her boot, leaving a trail in the dirt.

There was a sound above, and the light darkened. Jim was coming down the ladder. He was wearing his park uniform but had left the Smokey the Bear hat dangling from the tip of the ladder; Meg could see it when the square of light appeared again. He reached the ground and turned to her. "I didn't expect to see your car in the parking lot," he said. "I thought you had left without calling."

"The earliest flight I could get was eleven this morning," she said. She saw him look at his watch. "There's time," she said. "I had something to give you."

"There's something I want to say," he told her, "about what happened in Juárez. I don't want you to think there was any kind of moral cluelessness on my part." He paused. "I thought I was in control of myself. I thought that right up until the moment I wasn't. And then I just allowed myself to believe that you could be my way out."

"It was the other way around, for me," she said. "Resisting you was my way out." She managed to smile. "Jim?" she said, trying to think of a way to express how she felt about him, and knowing even as she spoke that her words would fall much too short. "It would have been so nice."

"Sadly near perfect, in my opinion," he answered.

He sat down beside her against the wall, pulling his knees up and resting his arms on them. After a moment, she said, "I've been thinking about what to do with the journal. I was wondering if you might want to take it, and edit it."

He looked at her. "To publish it?"

"It seems like the right thing. Bassie might not like it. But she can't determine everything forever. And this seems like the right ending. It's the true ending, anyway."

He pushed his fingers through his hair, and settled his elbows back on his knees, looking at her.

"Also, it makes things between you and me feel like less of a loss," she said.

"I don't agree with that part," he said. And then he added, "Have you considered doing it yourself?"

"You're the historian," she answered, handing him the envelope.

He half smiled as he took it. "And I'm the one who needs a purpose?"

"Unless you want to clean out Bassie's house."

He withdrew the journal from the envelope, opened it, and turned a few pages. "I don't know, Meg. It seems like too big of a gift."

"Actually, it would be a favor to me," she said. "You're the only person I trust to do it. I trust you with these people. I talked it over with Mom, and she agrees we wouldn't want anyone else to handle it. There could be a lot of money involved, but we would want you to have most of it, if you do the work. Not that that would be the reason you would do it. But we would work that part out. We could give a portion of it to Hector Romero, if you wanted. He'd use it for a good cause." She was quiet, awaiting his answer.

He slid the journal back into the envelope. "Can I think about it for a day or two?" he asked.

But she could see that the idea had taken hold.

"It would need an extensive foreword, which you could write," she said.

"Or you could write it," he said, and added, "Maybe we could write it together."

"Maybe," she answered.

He sat for a moment, then got to his feet, and turned and offered his hand to pull her up. "I'm worried you'll miss your flight," he said.

But she felt, now, strangely unhurried. She felt at peace here in the kiva with Jim. She could not remember many moments in her life when she had actually felt peaceful, and found it strange that she would feel so now, at this moment, when she was returning home to nothing she wanted to return to, and leaving so much behind.

"I have some good news," Jim said. "I talked to Phil last night. They've scrapped the plans for the addition, because of Elliott's grave. Everyone seems to think the publicity about the whole thing would be too unsavory."

"So Elliott gets his grave back?" she asked.

"That seems to be the end result," he said. "The hill would remain as it is. Just as Bassie wanted." He smiled. "And you said she couldn't determine everything forever."

"Like a hand from the grave," Meg answered. She moved to the ladder and began to climb to the top, and Jim followed her up.

"I want to show you something," he said when they were standing in the sunlight. He pulled from his shirt pocket a stack of photographs, small and slightly rectangular, and handed them to her. "Prentis sent over the photos from Elliott's camera. David Valdez just gave them to me."

Meg took the prints and held them in the sunlight, flipping from one to the next. "Have you looked at them yet?" she asked.

"On my way up here," he said.

They were only just discernible; the first five were of landscapes and revealed the irregular shapes of hills and mountains, a wash of light for the sky, nothing notable in the foregrounds. She studied them, with their indefinite grays and milky areas and delineated darker places corrupted by splotches of damage.

Then she came to the sixth one in the stack. It was murky, like the others, but the content seemed to radiate from the background: three figures standing on the rocky, snow-covered slope of what Meg recognized to be Dog Hill. She could see who the figures were. They were facing the camera lens. Elliott stood on one side, wearing his coat and his hat, his stance the same as that in the familiar photograph taken beside the train. Vicente was on the other side. He was tall, his hair blown back from his forehead. Bassie, a child, stood in the center, bundled in a coat. She was holding Vicente's hand. She stood between the two men, only slightly higher than their knees, the sunlight slanting on her jaw, the jagged, frozen boulders looming up behind her.

So this was how it was, Meg thought: Elliott returned from Mexico a lost man, and the next day walked on the ruins with Hannah, Vicente, and Bassie. Hannah made this photograph, using his camera and the last of the film. And Elliott shot himself that night. They buried him. They buried the camera with him. In doing so, they buried the truth of his death, and also, in more ways than were obvious to them at the time, buried all of them—Hannah and Elliott, Vicente and Bassie—in the grave together.

"It doesn't add much to the puzzle," Jim observed, as Meg studied the photograph.

But for Meg, it completed the puzzle. She saw the vision through Hannah's eyes, uncorrupted by the camera lens—the two men whom she loved, the child between them. Bassie holding on to Vicente's hand. It seemed that the image had been sealed on more than celluloid. It had been sealed on time. She stared at the likeness of Bassie, the black curls tossed in the wind. There she stood, the day her world collapsed, not knowing she would spend her life in search of these two men. How strange that it was Meg, after all of Bassie's searching, who had, in the ways that mattered, found them.

She looked at Jim. He was looking out over the valley. She thought of Bassie in the valley, swinging her cane, telling them where the house had stood, sniffing the air to smell the sage. She realized she would miss the brightness of the light here, the lightness of the air. New Mexico had worked its way into the places in her mind where perceptions were oddly lucid, connected more to light and sound and a deep reservoir of feeling than to anything that might be taken hold of.

A train whistle blew in the distance. The sound trailed over the mountains. Meg turned to look out over the valley. She wondered if she would ever see it again, and under what circumstances that might be. It was covered in dry grass now, and barren, but she imagined it as Hannah had described it once in the journals, abundant with yellow mullein and purple asters.

Acknowledgments

Several people dramatically influenced the development of this story, among them Judy Reed, who currently holds the positon of my character Jim Layton as the archaeologist at Pecos Pueblo. Judy patiently suffered through years of my questions, proofreading for mistakes and correcting me more times than should have been necessary on miscalculations of the feet and inches involved in the meters that comprise an archaeological grid.

Charles Meeks spent hours, even days, explaining to me the vagaries and complications associated with water purification and escorting me through mechanical rooms of dialysis clinics so that I might learn enough to write accurately about the machinery.

Jim Landis suggested that I submit the manuscript of *The Night Journal* to his friend Gail Hochman, who is unsurpassed as a literary agent. This was a great gift to me. The manuscript could not have found its way into more capable hands. Certainly it could not have found a finer publishing team than Clare Ferraro and Molly Stern at Viking. Molly's editorial comments miraculously included only perfect suggestions, not a single one I could take issue with.

Stephen Harrigan read every word of this book many times over, including a number of words that he convinced me to strike from the pages of numerous drafts. I will always be thankful to him, more than anyone else, for helping to guide this book into existence.

Other friends and family members read early drafts or portions of the book while it was still in progress and supplied helpful criticism. My gratitude, for this, to Louis Black, Michelle Bonilla, Caryn Carlson, Eleanor Crook, Jeff Long, Noel Crook Moore, Judy and Paul Reed, Rafe Sagalyn,

Marco Uribe, and Eileen Vance. My husband, Marc, was my greatest support in this regard and, as always, in every other.

A number of professionals and friends provided crucial information on subjects ranging from train wrecks to forensics. For their generous gifts of time, I am deeply indebted to the following people: Charles J. Adams III, George Adelo Jr., Beau Barton, Roberto Bayardo, Dave Bennett, Barbara Brown, Eric Brunnemann, Keith L. Bryant Jr., Gilbert Duran, Brian Ford, Sister Helen Forge, Philip O. Geier, Tom Giles, H. Gill-King, Alden C. Hayes, Ronnie Horn, Kurt Huffman, Philip Jonsson, Kathleen Kroll, John Loleit, Lillian MacDonald, Jan McInroy, Adair Margo, J. Sam Moore Jr., Carter John Morris, Rick Pappas, Bill Pennington, Turk Pipkin, Tom Potthast, Jody Potts, Joseph Powell, Ann Rasor, Stanley Rhine, Lori Roybal, Dick Rudisill, Roger Sanchez, Phyllis Sawyers, Carl D. Sheppard, Bobbi Simpson, Wid Slick, Phillip K. Smith, Elena Stoupignan, Dominique Turner, Lupe Uvillo, Kermit Welch, Melanie West, John White, and Carmen Zacarias.

I would be negligent not to acknowledge a few individuals, long deceased, whose journals and correspondence helped me to understand life on the western frontier in the 1890s, most notably a remarkable survey engineer, employed by the Santa Fe and other railroads in the second half of the nineteenth century, by the name of William Raymond Morley. A portion of his character and one or two turns of phrase from his memorable letters home to his wife have found their way into my portrayal of Elliott Bass. Likewise the writings of Ethel Waxham and letters of John G. Love and the correspondence of tuberculous patients such as George E. Macklin and physicians such as Lawrence F. Flick helped me to hear the voices of my characters. The Romero family in Las Vegas may notice similarities in their history and that of the fictitious Morales family.

I should note here also that the Montezuma hotel has, in the years it has taken me to write this book, undergone a reincarnation from the dilapidated ruin that I encountered in the hills outside Las Vegas to the stately, newly remodeled administrative headquarters of the Armand Hammer United World College of the American West.

And last I apologize for razing, in the story, the building that was Saint Anthony's sanatorium in Las Vegas. It is currently owned by the state of New Mexico and is still in use.